PASSIONATE YEARNING

She strained toward him, wanting him to know that, yes, she would marry him, and he slowly trailed his hand down across her neck and cupped one of her full breasts, rubbing his thumb in small, slow circles over the peak. Her chest seemed full to bursting, and she had difficulty breathing, but still he caressed her. His lips left hers and followed the trail left by his hand, down the slim column of her neck and on to the hardness his hand had produced. He lifted the breast out of the water and, when his lips made contact, she thought she'd faint . . .

Gentle Thunder

Rebecca Craig

JOVE BOOKS, NEW YORK

GENTLE THUNDER

A Jove Book / published by arrangement with
the author

PRINTING HISTORY
Jove edition / April 1995

ISBN: 0-515-11586-X

A JOVE BOOK®
Jove Books are published by The Berkley Publishing Group,
200 Madison Avenue, New York, New York 10016.
JOVE and the "J" design are trademarks
belonging to Jove Publications, Inc.

PRINTED IN THE UNITED STATES OF AMERICA

10 9 8 7 6 5 4 3 2 1

To Craig, who believed in me enough
to allow me to believe in myself.

Acknowledgments

I would like to thank my family for their support and encouragement. I have learned through the years that having someone say "you can do it" means the difference between success and failure.

Also, a big thank you to my editor, Judith Stern, who made my dream come true and made it all seem so easy.

❦ 1 ❦

Maggie Longyear's stomach was tied in knots as she strained to see the approaching town through the private railcar's window without actually opening it and sticking her head out as she would have liked to do. Snow covered the landscape and shrouded the mountains in white, making her shiver inside her traveling suit and cloak which had been made for the much milder climate of South Carolina. Even though her uncle, Simon Longyear, had told her all about his home and the people she would be meeting there, she felt totally lost. She had never traveled this far from home before, and she already missed her parents and friends. This trip had seemed a good idea five days earlier when her life seemed to have collapsed on her, and while they were on the train, she felt as though she were on some grand adventure, like something out of the books she used to read. But now she was here in Wyoming, and she wasn't sure she was ready.

In this year of 1892, thanks to the advent of the transcontinental railroad, she and her uncle had been able to make the trip in less than a week by rail. Less than a week since she had been jilted at the altar by Charles Eversley. Less than a week since she had gone from being a bride, anticipating her new life with a husband at her side, to being the same plain Maggie Longyear, twenty-three years old and an old maid. It wouldn't have been so bad to be an old maid, she thought, if she hadn't been so humiliated at the wedding.

She could still hear the man's voice, slurred with drink, as he had shouted, "I know a reason they can't be married, Reverin! He's got my Cathey with child, the filthy bastard!" Her mother had fainted, and Maggie, stunned beyond belief, had looked to Charles to tell her it wasn't so, to tell her it was all a mistake. But one look at her bridegroom's face told her all she needed to know. When all the wedding guests had left the house and her parents explained to her that Charles had been ordered to marry her by his father or lose his inheritance, she understood the black fury evident on his face at the wedding. And she had no doubt that his father would follow through on his threat to disinherit his son. Now she was not only an old maid, but also whispers were already circulating hours after the scandalous scene that Charles had been forced to ask for her hand in marriage.

Simon had come to her rescue, suggesting to his brother, Lawrence, and sister-in-law, Elizabeth, that Maggie come back to Jackson Hole with him and spend a few months until the gossipmongers found something new to talk about. He couldn't bear to see her an object of ridicule, or worse yet, pity.

She was their only child, and they had been reluctant to let her go, but in the end Simon convinced them it was the best thing for her. They planned to come out themselves in the fall and bring her back. Fall hadn't seemed so far away in South Carolina, where flowers were blooming and the swamps were already green, but here it seemed a long way off, with winter still cloaking the earth.

A shrill whistle split the air, and she could feel the train slowing down. The knots in her stomach tightened, and she wondered what was keeping her uncle. Simon had gone to see to the unloading of the mares he'd brought back with him and had said he would be back to get her in plenty of time. She put her hat on her head because she thought she should arrive looking proper, but her hands felt awkward. She hadn't worn a hat since she was fifteen, and her mother had given up trying to make a lady out of her. Maggie had dressed how she pleased as she went her way working around the stables and learning the bookkeeping for Longacres, the plantation where she had been born and raised and which would one day be hers. More often than not, she pulled her dark red hair back in a knot to keep it out of her face, and if she wore a headcovering at all, it was a scarf. Her hands shook now as she tried to tie the hat ribbons, and Simon, coming in just then, seemed to know what she was feeling.

"Here," he said, smiling at her, "let me help. I told you there's nothing to worry about. These are all good people, and they won't know anything about you that you don't tell them."

"But what if I forget their names? I remember Will is your foreman. Will Sutten, is it? And Pete and Bertha somebody cook for you, and then there's Dave, and . . ."

Simon laughed. "You don't have to remember everything. Give it some time, and it'll come to you. Just be yourself, and they can't help but love you."

The brakes caught then, and the train slowed with a great hissing, throwing them off balance. Simon caught his niece and hugged her, then said, "Well, we're here! Come on and see Wyoming!"

They stepped off the train, and she looked around eagerly, excited in spite of her jitters, while Simon checked on the unloading of her enormous amount of baggage. There were four large trunks, three small ones, a rocking chair, two small tables, and her overnight luggage which consisted of four bags and two small cases. He looked at his one bag and was struck with amazement at how much a woman thought she couldn't do without. He left her under the watchful eye of the stationmaster while, shaking his head, he went to the livery to get his horse and hire a wagon.

Will Sutten caught sight of Simon bending down to say something to a tall woman in a dark green suit. He was about to call out his name, but just then Simon headed toward the livery, and the woman turned around.

Will felt as if someone had hit him a good wallop in the chest. She was the most beautiful woman he had ever seen. She held herself tall and proud and looked around her with a lovely smile as though Rock Springs was the most interesting place she'd ever been. Hell, it probably was. She looked as though she'd come from one of those suffocating cities back east. Then she reached up and, taking out a pin, removed the hat from her head, and his legs suddenly went weak. Her hair was the color of one of his horses, a deep chestnut, and the sunlight sprinkled it with shiny copper. She lifted her face to the sun, closed her eyes, and took a deep breath. He figured she probably did that pretty often because her face was as freckled as a little kid's. Tendrils of hair had come loose from the pile on her head, but she didn't seem to notice, and he thought the more of her because of it. She reminded him of one of his fillies, long-legged and eager. God! and she was married to Simon!

Maggie breathed deeply of the clear, crisp mountain air and drank in the bustle and commotion of the town. It was so different from back home, where everyone seemed to move in slow motion because of the heat. She had turned to get a better view of the mountains when she became aware of a man standing some distance away from her, staring as if he'd seen a ghost. She didn't want to acknowledge that she'd caught him at it, but his boldness made her decidedly uncomfortable.

He was tall and had dark hair which she could just glimpse under the big hat he wore. There was something about him that twisted her insides in a funny way and made her breath catch. His face was rugged, with a thick mustache over a full mouth and more than a day's growth of beard darkening his jawline. His booted feet were planted apart, and the snug denim pants he wore accentuated the muscles in his legs. Altogether, he was devastatingly good-looking.

Knowing she herself was not, she wondered what he found so interesting about her, and then had her answer as Simon came up and exclaimed, "Will! What are you doing here?" The man grinned, showing beautiful white teeth and deep dimples in his tanned cheeks, and she felt her heart constrict, knowing he'd never even notice her as a woman.

"When I got your telegram that said 'we' would be arriving, I figured you'd gone and got yourself married, so I came with a couple of the men to get the horses and luggage back to the ranch so the two of you could ride the stage."

"Married!" Simon and Maggie said it at the same time, then looked at each other and laughed.

Will looked bewildered and then heard the best news he'd heard in a long time.

"Will Sutten, meet my niece, Maggie Longyear. She's going to stay with us for a few months, maybe more. Maggie, this is my partner and foreman Will."

She smiled at Will, and he got lost in her eyes. They were like blackstrap molasses, dark and smooth, the brows above them straight and fine.

"Pleased to meet you, Miss Longyear." His voice was deep and resonant and made her feel as though he'd stroked it across her back. She felt goose bumps along the imaginary trail.

"Well, that explains why our wagon and horses are in the livery. Where are the men?" Simon asked, and Will tore his eyes away from Maggie, while trying to digest the thought that she wasn't Simon's wife, and would be traveling with them back to the ranch.

"They're over to the Red Rock eatin' an early dinner. I told them as soon as they heard the whistle to hustle over here." Then he looked at the immense amount of baggage stacked on the platform and asked, "Which of this is yours?"

"All of it." Simon looked at it as if he couldn't believe it was really all going to the ranch.

"All of it?" Will looked at the trunks and bags and what appeared to be a chair wrapped in something. "How long did you say she was staying?" He grinned at Maggie.

"My mother was concerned that Uncle Simon wouldn't have everything I needed, since he lives so far from, well, from her, I guess." She giggled. It really was an enormous amount of baggage for one person. Maggie was rather embarrassed but didn't want to let on to Uncle Simon that her mother thought she was going out into the wilds and wouldn't even be able to buy a decent handkerchief.

Will pushed back his hat, letting a few locks of unruly hair tumble onto his forehead, and with his hands on his hips and his feet planted wide, he grinned at her. His eyes were beautiful, deep-set and crinkled at the corners as though he'd spent a lot of his life laughing. Maggie hoped he would be very busy on the ranch. She didn't think she could very often bear the things he did to her emotions. Fortunately, he would likely be out on the range most of the time, and she would see him only briefly. She'd wilt from embarrassment if he discovered she found him attractive. He probably had dozens of homely women throwing themselves at him and didn't need another. She tried to quiet her frantic heartbeat and get control of her breathing so she could defend herself.

"There really isn't all that much. You have no idea how much room a gown takes up in a trunk. And one of the big ones is full of things mother sent for the cabin."

"For the cabin? Like what?"

"Don't ask," Simon answered dryly, then rolled his eyes and shook his head at Will.

Will laughed, and the two men he'd brought with him chose that moment to make their appearance.

"Simon! You worthless piece o' possum hide, you! We thought maybe you got yerself killed, you was gone so long!" A short, wiry-looking little man came up and slapped Simon on the back and pumped his hand vigorously. "Whoeee! And is this the new missus?" he asked, catching sight of Maggie.

"This is my niece, Maggie," Simon said to introduce them, "and this one whose mouth is bigger than he is is my cook Pete. The shy one is Dave. He's one of our best wranglers." He indicated the other one, a tall young man holding his hat in his hands. He gave a quick nod to acknowledge the introduction. Maggie smiled at them both. "I'm so pleased to meet you. Uncle Simon has told me so much about you."

"Well, knowin' Simon, I'm sure it was all lies," assured Pete. "Now where is the missus? You got her hid somewheres so we can't tell her the truth about you?"

"I didn't get married!" Simon exclaimed, exasperated. "There is no missus."

"Well, why in tarnation did you go and wire Will that you did, if you didn't? Now we got Bertha all in a tizzy 'bout yer wife acomin', and there ain't even one! I don't mind tellin' you I don't wanna be the one to tell her you was foolin' all of us." Pete spit off the edge of the station platform and wiped his mouth and gray, bushy mustache with so much disgust in his actions, it was all Maggie could do to keep from laughing out loud.

"I never said I got married!"

"Are you atellin' me it was Will done dreamed all this up?" Pete looked from Simon to Will with one eye squinted, the bushy white eyebrow above it almost covering it, as though he could peer into their heads and see who was telling the truth.

"Will did a little reading between the lines, as far as I can tell. I guess I should have said the woman I was bringing back was my niece. It just never occurred to me that any of you fellows would think I'd up and marry a woman I'd only just met. Why, Kate would've killed me if I'd dared!"

"You ain't kiddin' on that one!" Pete shook his head, remembering. "When she got the news she stomped outta her place and clear across the square to the telegraph office to check that we wasn't just pullin' her leg."

"And she hasn't quit stomping since!" added Will.

"Thanks, fellows. It's always good to know a man can count on his friends," Simon said, looking disgusted.

"Yeah, and you're gonna have one heck of a time mollifying the lady this time!" They all laughed then.

Maggie thought they were delightful, and she could see why Simon had spoken of them in such warm tones. She liked them already and could hardly wait to meet the others.

The men hitched the horses to the buckboard and loaded all her belongings into it. It was a tight squeeze, and several bags had to be carried aboard the stage, but she'd need some items for the overnights on the journey to Jackson.

Simon had explained that his ranch was north and east of Jackson and consisted of some of the best grazing land in the whole state. The valley didn't get much rainfall, although it rained briefly almost every day. The water from melting snow fed the many lakes and streams that crisscrossed the valley floor and caused the grass to grow lush and deep. He and Will had been lucky, he'd told her, to have bought their spread from one of the early settlers, and so had a prime location.

Simon had been talking with Will and now turned to Maggie. "Would you mind terribly riding the stage with Will as your escort? He already stocked up on supplies, but I need to take care of some business before I leave here, and there's no need to hold up everyone. I'll catch up with you sometime tomorrow."

There wasn't much of anything Maggie wanted to do less than ride in the close confines of a stagecoach with Will Sutten, but she couldn't think of any logical reason why she shouldn't. It was only one day. Not even that, really, because it was now late in the morning. She didn't dare look at Will. "Of course I wouldn't mind, Uncle Simon, but Will needn't ride with me. I'm sure I'll be quite all right alone for one day."

"No, you can't ride alone. Wyoming is a bit wilder than you're used to, and an unescorted lady is considered fair game." Simon frowned. "If you don't want to ride with Will, you can wait with me until tomorrow. They can tie my horse on with the others."

Seeing that Simon was disappointed, she hurried to assure him. "I have no reservations about riding with Mr. Sutten. I just didn't want to cause him to be cramped inside a stage when he'd rather be riding out in the open. I know I would prefer to ride a horse than be closed in a stage."

Simon and Will looked at each other. "She rides as

well as any man I know. She's not used to the snow, but I think she can handle it." Maggie was inordinately pleased at the compliment her uncle had given her.

In the end, they tied her remaining luggage to the sides of the buckboard and set out with Pete driving the team, and Dave, Will, and Maggie riding the horses she and Simon had brought from home. Maggie had helped raise and break these horses and was more at home on their backs than in a drawing room, and she showed it. She had changed into a riding habit in the hotel while the men had finished packing the buckboard. She was glad she had packed this one in her overnight bag, because even though it wasn't quite warm enough for the cooler climate, it suited her. She tried to tell herself that Mr. Sutten wouldn't look at her, so it didn't matter what she wore, but she was glad, anyway. The dusty green jacket was short and fitted snug across her bosom, with a froth of cream lace that buttoned inside and spilled across the front. The split skirt fell over her hips like a glove, and stopped about mid calf. Her riding boots came up to her knees and were made of the finest kid leather. She rode as straight in the saddle as her weary body would allow and tried not to think of his eyes on her. She'd freeze to death before admitting she was cold; otherwise he would think her a silly woman who should have ridden in the stage.

Will brought up the rear, mostly so he could watch her ride. She sat the horse as if she'd been born in the saddle. Simon hadn't exaggerated. Damn, she was beautiful, he thought, and it felt good to feel desire for a woman again. But it scared him. Will realized with a start that she was the first woman he'd looked at this way in years. Since Charity.

Charity seemed like a dull ache now. Sometimes he had trouble remembering what she looked like, and then he felt guilty all over again. He felt guilty now for looking at Maggie Longyear as he was. He grinned lopsidedly. He was a fool. Maggie had made it pretty clear she didn't want to have anything to do with him. And, anyway, what did he have to offer her? He couldn't tell her to wait while he found and killed the man who killed his wife. It sounded foolish, even to him. Besides, she was Simon's niece. She was probably betrothed to some rich fop back in South Carolina, and the family wouldn't even consider him a suitable match for her. No, Simon's niece wasn't for the likes of him. He rode along and told himself he wasn't looking at her, but he never took his eyes off her.

Every pore in Maggie's body was aware of Will Sutten behind her. Her heart thumped, and she hardly heard Pete as he chatted on about the scenery and the ranch, Jackson and the Tetons, the trail they were on, the birds and other wildlife they saw. She struggled to pay attention to the old man and even managed to ask him a few questions, but all the while she was conscious of where Will was. She knew when he fell behind and when he guided his horse to the other side of the road. She felt his eyes boring into her back, and then chided herself for her foolishness. She was not so ignorant to think Mr. Sutten would admire her, so she could get that out of her head. He probably had a girl somewhere, or maybe even a wife and six children. Uncle Simon hadn't said whether he was married or not, and he very well could be. She'd have to grow up and face reality.

Pete had lived long enough and seen enough to know what was going on with the "two young'uns," as he told Dave later. "The lady hardly paid any attention at all to what I was tellin' her. Why I coulda told her a jackrabbit was a griz, and she'd have said 'how interesting.' And it waren't like Will to hang back and have nothin' to say, neither. Nope, this little lady is gonna cause old Will to get his spurs tangled up, and it's about time, too. Whoeee! Just wait 'til they get back to the ranch and the two of 'em is closed up in that little bitty cabin together. Just wait and see the sparks fly! Yep, this is gonna be some show!" Pete spit a brown stream out to the side of the road and grinned like a weasel peeking into a henhouse door. The rest of the winter was lookin' pretty interesting, he thought. Maybe even more interesting than if Simon had brought back a wife.

The cold shadows from the mountains had long since covered them when they rounded a bend in the road and saw the stage stop ahead. Maggie wasn't tired—it had been wonderful to get a horse beneath her again and be out in the crisp mountain air and sunshine—but she felt drained by the strain of ignoring Will all day. The sun had come out, and she'd been passably warm most of the day. They'd stopped several times as they had climbed to higher altitudes, and each time she had stayed as far from him as she could get. It would be good to close herself away in a room tonight and finally let her guard down.

The way-station manager and his wife were old friends of the ranch hands, and they were introduced to Maggie as Billy and Edna Watson. Billy was huge, his hands as big as two of Maggie's, and his arms resembled hams. He was red-faced and quick to grin, and he joked with the men as they helped him unhitch the horses and bed them down for the night. His wife was plain and strong, with graying hair pulled back into a neat bun. She wore a man's flannel shirt over a split skirt. Edna took Maggie inside while the men were tending to the horses.

"Here's some nice warm water to clean up with, Miss Longyear, and you holler if you need anything else. I'll just see to getting supper on the table. You all must be starved, riding all day like that."

She left Maggie alone in a toasty warm, clean little room with a big soft feather bed and a stand with a pitcher of warm water and a bowl, towel, and fresh bar of homemade lye soap. Nothing had ever looked so good. Maggie unbuttoned her jacket and took out the lace so it wouldn't get wet as she washed. Then she decided to wash her neck and upper body along with her face, so she pulled the jacket off and stood in her lace chemise. The water was heavenly warm, and the soap smelled clean. She smiled. It smelled like Wyoming, raw and strong and good.

She pulled the pins out of her hair to brush it and tidy it up before supper, because the bun she'd started the day with had worked itself loose, and she'd have to start all over again. The small bag she'd brought in held her night things, and she was rummaging in it to find her brush when someone knocked.

"Oh, come in, Edna. Is it time for supper already?" She turned, and Will was framed in the doorway, holding her larger bags, one in each hand.

Only a few seconds passed, but they seemed like hours as Maggie and Will stood there, their eyes devouring each other.

Will knew he should turn around and leave, but he couldn't move. Maggie had let her hair down, and it curled around her shoulders and down her back in thick, luxurious waves. A man could get lost in that hair, he thought. He looked her straight in the eyes, as though asking permission and, finding it, slowly moved his gaze down her long, graceful neck and to the thin lace which was all she wore from the waist up. Her skin was beautiful, peachy and smooth, and the thin material of her chemise barely covered the full breasts hinted at there.

He wanted her. He wanted to cross to her and slowly pull the rest of her clothing off, and then slide the chemise down her arms and push it to the floor. Then he would kiss her, and his hands would touch that silken skin, and he would lift her to the bed and gently make love to her. It had been a long time since he'd had a woman, and he would make it last.

But he didn't.

Maggie felt his eyes burn a path from her eyes to her breasts, and she felt something deep inside her that made her want him to come to her, to touch her and quiet the furor that raged in the depths of her. She closed her eyes, waiting for him, and then she heard a sound, and when she opened her eyes, he was gone. The door was shut. Had she dreamed it? But, no, there were her bags on the floor.

She felt her whole body blush crimson. He'd come upon her half dressed, and she hadn't even tried to cover herself. There was no way she could face him again. What must he think of her? What kind of woman was she that she had stood there, bare to the waist, and let a man who was a stranger and not her husband see her? What would Uncle Simon think? He would send her packing back to her parents before she even got to see his ranch.

By the time Edna knocked on the door, Maggie was drowning in mortification. She thought about pretending to be asleep, but couldn't do that to the good woman, and besides, she was starving. Of course, it would serve her right to miss supper, but she thought of what she would face when Uncle Simon heard, and she knew she needed her strength.

"Edna, I hate to be a bother, but could I possibly have a tray here in my room? I don't feel up to eating at the table."

Edna looked at the young girl and saw that she was plumb tuckered out, and no wonder, her having ridden here on horseback all the way from Rock Springs. Most ladies rode the stage and spent the whole evening complaining about the rough ride. Not this one, though. She was a real lady. "You just get your nightgown on and settle into that big bed. You'll be nice and cozy soon, and I'll be happy to bring you a tray."

Maggie did as she was told and had no sooner pulled the thick coverlets up under her arms when Edna returned with a bowl of steaming stew, buttered bread, cold milk, and a slice of deep-dish apple pie with cream on top. Maggie didn't think she'd ever had a meal that tasted so good. The plain food filled up the emptiness in her, and she finished it to the last crumb.

When Edna returned for the dishes, she exclaimed, "Why, honey, you really were hungry! Can I get you some more?"

"Edna, that was absolutely the best food I have ever eaten," Maggie praised, "but I am quite full and couldn't eat another bite."

Edna beamed, pleased that the young lady had liked her cooking. "You get to sleep now, Miss Longyear. You have a long ride ahead of you yet." She blew out the lamp and shut Maggie into the cool darkness where she lay staring at the ceiling, thinking of Charles, and of Will Sutten as she drifted into a deep, dreamless sleep.

*   *   *

Will didn't sleep. He hadn't known how he was going to face her at supper, because he wouldn't have betrayed her for the world, and the others wouldn't have missed that something was going on. But he thought it would have been more obvious to skip the meal, so he'd gone in bracing himself for the ordeal and was tremendously relived when Edna had said that Maggie was tired and was having a tray in her room. As it was, Pete kept giving him smirky looks, so as soon as he finished he left to go check on the horses. He needed the night air to cool his senses.

He sat out in the frigid darkness a long time, smoking a cigar and watching her window. The cold air bathed his body, but the heat inside him made him plenty warm. He kept seeing her standing in her room, a heady mixture of pure innocence and sultry seduction. She hadn't even tried to cover herself. And when she'd closed her eyes and parted her lips, he knew he had to get out of there. If he hadn't left, he'd not have been able to stop himself from taking her. This was totally unlike him, and he tried to sort through his feelings.

She was beautiful, but there had been many beautiful women who'd tried to seduce him in the past few years. He hadn't even looked at them. What was it about her that was different? Was it the fact that she didn't act helpless, hadn't flirted with him like the others? But he hadn't know that when he'd seen her standing on the railroad platform. She'd just hit him between the eyes.

He wondered about her past. She wasn't so very young any more. Had she had suitors? Was she a virgin? He couldn't figure her out. Any of the women he'd ever known would have screamed and covered themselves if a man had intruded upon them like that.

He wondered if Charity had stood there undressed and let Jake Greeley look at her. She had always been so prudish with him, undressing in the dark even after a year of marriage. He couldn't imagine her doing that, but there must have been things about her he didn't know or understand, because he'd have bet all he had that she would never have entered a whorehouse, much less worked in one.

All these years his days and nights had been haunted by the vision of Charity going into that place. He could see her as clearly as though he'd been there himself. She had been dressed in a red satin dress in his mind. If he closed his eyes now, he'd be able to see her in that fancy room, and her face and eyes would have lost the vacant look she'd had for a while. Will clenched his teeth against the pain as he chastised himself for the thousandth time. If he hadn't been so proud, he could have had money, and then Charity wouldn't have had to go to town seeking whatever it was she'd been looking for, and she'd not have met up with Jake Greeley.

Jake Greeley. After Will buried Charity and set fire to their Kansas homestead, he'd ridden all over the country chasing rumors that the man with one blue eye and one brown eye had been seen here, and then there, always a few days before Will got there. He'd been tired and felt beaten enough to give up, when he'd met Simon Longyear. Simon knew horses and had commented on Will's fine stallion, and the two had struck up a friendship, traveling together some. Then Simon had asked Will to go into partnership with him, because he was going to add cattle to his spread and needed a good man he could trust. Will said he couldn't, that he had some unfinished business to attend to. He didn't tell Simon all of it, but enough so that Simon had said if this fellow he was hunting was from Wyoming, wouldn't it make sense to stay put and wait for him instead of always being two days behind him?

It had made a lot of sense at the time, and so Will had agreed to be Simon's foreman. Not a partner, because he had to be free to leave if he needed to. They had started out with about a hundred head of cattle and now ran over a thousand. They raised fine beef and horses and sold most of them to the army, but since the railroad had come through Wyoming, the markets on the coasts were opening up, too, and business was better than ever. Even though Will hadn't wanted to be a partner, Simon insisted, depositing half of their income in Will's name. Will didn't even know how much was there, had never cared. Now that Charity was gone, what did it matter?

Will had been content to stay on the spread, even though Simon had bought them a house in town. Will didn't like being in town and he didn't like Simon's relationship with Kate, but it was none of his affair, so he stayed out of it. When Will did go to town, it was to listen. He had never asked right out about Greeley, but found that the man made an impression wherever he went. Will had only to keep his ears open, and he could usually discover the man's whereabouts.

Greeley had been down Texas way for a long while now, and Will had just about decided to follow him down there when he'd overheard Millie, one of the waitresses in the hotel, say the man was coming up with the spring herds. Millie was always his best source of information about Jake Greeley. Greeley had promised to marry her years before, and she still thought he would come back for her when he'd made his stake. She was past her prime and had gotten soft and lumpy, but she told anyone who'd listen about her man. This time she'd seemed more excited than usual and had been telling one of the other women who worked in the hotel that he'd written and was coming back to Wyoming in a few weeks, supposedly to marry her. She was to get some things ready for him, and he'd come for her.

Will's stomach had tightened, his hands had started shaking, and he'd broken out in a sweat. He'd felt like a boy facing his first gunfighter. He wondered what he'd be like when he actually faced the man who'd driven him for the past six years. The man who'd taken his life away.

Will sighed. Now here was Simon's niece coming upon him unaware like that and complicating things. He hadn't thought what he'd do after killing Greeley. He might be hanged for murder. He'd never thought of that before, because he hadn't cared. But now he had the ranch, and it was worth something to him, and he was smart enough to realize that it was Maggie who'd made him think of it, to think of the future at all.

He didn't often think of Charity—he didn't allow himself to. But now he thought of her delicate little body, her white hands and thin arms, and he knew she hadn't been cut out for a life on the frontier. She'd been bred for fancy drawing rooms and a life of leisure. Still, he hadn't made her come. And he found he was still angry with her, even after all this time. Angry because he hadn't been enough to keep her happy. Angry that she'd run off, the first time he'd left her alone.

He closed his eyes, and the image of Maggie as he'd last seen her came to him. Now there was a woman who'd embrace this rough life and conquer it joyfully. She was strong and seemed made for the outdoors, and he wondered what she'd be like in bed.

But he couldn't think of Maggie. Until he did what he had to do, she was not for him, and he didn't know if she'd even have him, especially after he'd killed a man—and if he remained a *free* man. He was too old for her, anyway, he thought, and that made him feel better. And worse. It was just best to keep the girl out of his mind.

He dropped his cigar in the snow and slowly ground it out with his boot, then slipped silently in the door of the dark depot, took off his hat and coat, and found his way to the back of the room where there was a row of narrow cots for single men. The depot wasn't large, and there was only one private room, occupied now by Maggie. He chose a cot as far from Pete and Dave as he could get in the small room, and it creaked in protest as he settled into it. He stared up at the ceiling and kept seeing Maggie. He turned on his side and curled up, but she was still there. He was so aware of her in her bed not twenty feet from him that she might just as well have been stretched out beside him. Was she, too, unable to sleep? Or did she think of him at all? Surely she must feel the current between them, even as he felt it. Something that strong, it couldn't be all on his side. He tried to shake her image, but it stayed.

He imagined that he could pick out her breathing from among all the inhabitants of the depot. Pete and Dave were wheezing and snoring, respectively, and he could hear Billy's heavy snoring through the wall, wondering how poor Edna slept through it night after night. The logs in the stove fell with a soft hiss and gentle tumble, and he could see the sudden bright flare through the crack around the door. The wood of the building popped with the cold, and he wondered if she heard it and knew what it was so that she wasn't frightened. He turned over again and pulled his feather pillow over his head to shut out the sounds, but he still heard her soft breathing in his head and felt her skin under his hands. It would be cool and smooth, he knew, and she would still the awakening fire within him. He turned again, the cot groaning in protest to the silent building. *Get yourself under control,* he told himself, *or you're going to make a fool of yourself with that girl.*

As soon as it was decently morning, Will awakened Pete and told him he was riding ahead to check the river crossing and scout for trouble.

"What you wanna do that for?" Pete squinted at him. Was he hallucinatin'?

"Well, because," Will had answered irritably, "you just never know what might come up. We've got to answer to Simon if anything happens to that girl, and I just want to check things out." *Yes, I have to answer to Simon, and I don't know how he'd take it if I ravished his niece.*

Pete scratched his head and stood up to pull on his pants. "Yeah, you're prob'ly right. You go on and do that. I'll tell Simon where you went off to." And, he thought, what was he gonna tell the lady? That Will had done run off 'cause he was plumb scared of 'er and what she was doing to him?

❧ 2 ❧

Maggie woke up the next morning feeling wonderful. She was rested and warm, and the aches she'd expected weren't there. She stretched, threw back the covers, and swung out of the bed. When her feet hit the floor, the cold jolted her out of her euphoria, and she jerked them quickly back under the blankets. Mercy! Were all the rooms in Wyoming this cold, or just hers? Then she realized there was no fireplace or stove, and her door had been shut to the only heat source.

She laughed to herself. *Maggie, my girl, you're in the Wild West now, and things are different. Men come into your bedroom when you're half dressed, and the looks they give you make you tremble.*

Will. How would she ever face him? Just remembering the night before made her blush. And there was Uncle Simon to reckon with, too. She wished she could just stay in this bed forever and not have to face any of them. But if there was one lesson her mother got through to her, it was how to face difficult situations like a lady; and so she got up and dressed carefully, paying special attention to her hair, which always seemed to be coming loose from the pins. Satisfied, she gathered her things together and, taking a deep breath, opened her door.

No one was there except Edna. "Oh, you're awake! Did you sleep well? The men have already had breakfast and are out hitching up. You come right on over here and sit down and fill up on some good, hot food. You have a long day ahead of you, although it looks to be some

19

warmer than yesterday. O' course, warm weather brings
its own problems, what with mud and the river ice
breaking up and such. But Will rode on ahead to check
on that. And don't you worry none, 'cause your uncle
will be along soon, and he knows what's safe and what
isn't. Not that the others don't, mind you, it's just that Mr.
Longyear'd be taking special care of you, you being his
niece and all."

Edna chattered on, but Maggie hardly heard her,
except for the fact that Will had already left. Relief
flooded over her. She wouldn't have to face him just yet.
It would be good to get some distance from this place
with its memory of Will Sutten's eyes burning a path
across her skin.

"Now, I packed some sandwiches for you. You won't
see another stop until tonight, and being out in the cold
sure makes a person hungry." Edna didn't quit talking the
whole time Maggie was eating, which didn't bother her,
because then she didn't have to think. And if she thought,
she'd think of Will and wonder what *he'd* been thinking
as he'd stood there watching her.

Pete came in then and said they were ready to move
out if she was, so she went to get her bags and put on her
outer garments. Today she put vanity aside and wore a
long woolen cloak Simon had insisted on buying for her
at one of the stops along the way. She thanked Edna for
all she'd done for her, and then they were on the trail.

It seemed empty without Will along. She wondered if
he'd be coming back to report on the conditions ahead,
and what he'd tell Uncle Simon when he did. Pete
jabbered along as usual, and they seemed to have been
traveling for days when Simon caught up with them just
a few hours later.

They had stopped for dinner in a protected place with
a southern exposure. It felt like spring, and all around
was the sound of dripping and running water, and the
smell of dark earth thawing. She wondered as they ate
what Will was eating, and then chided herself for not
being able to keep her thoughts from him. Heavens, at
this time yesterday, she'd not even known he existed, and

that, finally, was what made her see the foolishness of her thoughts. One day, and she was mooning over him as if they were star-crossed lovers! She laughed then, and when Pete looked askance, she just smiled at him.

When she was sixteen and had gone to her first dance, the girls had all gone up to a bedroom to freshen up, and some of them had positively swooned over this boy and that. She had thought it silly and childish then, and here she was, a full twenty-three years old, behaving the very same way. Now she knew what Will thought of her. He thought she was a silly, naive little girl from back east who didn't know anything about real life and went all giddy over the first man she met. No wonder he'd ridden off ahead. Well, maybe he'd for sure stay out of her way now, and she'd have time to consider what had made her act that way before she saw him again. She vowed that she would be all grown up and totally ladylike when that time came, and he'd never know what her secret thoughts were. She idly wondered if all spinsters had a man they dreamed of during the long, lonely nights of their lives.

"Is there any food left for a hungry traveler?" Simon interrupted her reverie, and she hadn't even heard him ride up.

"Of course. I think Edna packed enough for four times this many people." She handed him the packet of food. "I didn't think you'd catch up with us until tonight."

Simon dug through the bag and picked out a sandwich and some huge sugar cookies. "I left before dawn and rode straight through. It doesn't take nearly as long on horseback as with a buckboard."

While Simon ate, Pete told him about Will riding ahead, and Maggie told him what good care Pete was taking of her and said she was mightily curious about Dave's voice, because thus far she hadn't heard him utter a sound. They all laughed, and the object of their attention turned bright red and dropped his head.

"Oh, Dave, I didn't mean to make fun of you. Sometimes silence is a virtue."

"When it comes to Pete, it sure would be," Dave said dryly. "It isn't that I don't have anything to say, it's just that he don't even come up for air so's a fellow could break in." They laughed again, and the smaller man turned to Dave, disgusted.

"He don't hardly say a word for a week, and then he has to go and complain, the first words outta his mouth. I swear, but it's hard when a man's friends turn on 'im."

Simon, Dave, and Maggie exchanged a look and grinned at one another. Pete kept right on talking, and finally Dave said, "You could use him to keep the windmill going." They all laughed again, not only at what Dave had said, but because, incredibly, Pete just kept right on.

"All's I was tryin' to do was keep the lady comp'ny and tell her about the country we's goin' through, but, no, these idiots don't know what polite conversation is. You'd think a feller would get a little respect, what with him being around longer than all of 'em put together, but, no, they treat him like a pole cat at a picnic. Seems they'd treat their cook a little better, seein' as how they got to depend on him to keep their bellies full. It can be mighty miserable to have poor vittles, you know."

Simon smiled fondly at the old man, then whispered to Maggie, "He's full of vinegar, but his heart's as big as the whole country."

They started out again, with Pete in a huff and Simon acting as tour guide. Sometime after dark, they reached the next stop. Will had not come back, but Simon didn't seem to be worried about him, and Maggie didn't want to ask, so they passed another pleasant night without incident. The following three days of the trip went easily, with no trouble either at the river crossings or with mud on the steep road.

It snowed lightly on them a couple of times, but not enough to delay their progress. One morning the clouds lifted, and there were the most beautiful mountains Maggie had ever seen. They were so powerful, she could feel them, one in particular as it rose the highest, its jagged peak outlined against the deep blue sky. They were coming into a valley, and these mountains seemed to rise straight up from the very floor. She was used to the gentle foothills of the Appalachians, their peaks softened with trees. But there was no softening here. She thought of a phrase from the Bible, "I will lift mine eyes up unto the hills, from whence cometh my help. My help cometh from the Lord." As her eyes searched the forbidding face of these mountains, she felt that God himself could easily be up there. Goose bumps rose on her arms and back.

Simon saw her face and said, "I felt the same way the first time I saw them. I knew I'd never be the same again. They get into your soul, and when you're away you still think of them. That's why I live here. I can't leave them."

"You live here? This is where your ranch is?" Maggie could hardly believe they'd finally made it.

"Well, not right here. We'll be getting into Jackson today, and we'll stay in our house in town. Tomorrow or the next day we'll head out to the ranch."

"But why do we have to wait? Why can't we go there today?"

Simon laughed. "It's a goodly distance from Jackson to the ranch. We couldn't make it before dark today, anyway, but I want you to meet Kate and see the town."

Maggie remembered that Kate thought Simon was coming back with a wife. "Are you so sure Kate will see you? After all, she thinks you got married. I can't imagine her being anxious to meet your new bride."

He made a face. "I'll probably have to do some fancy talking to get in the door, but once I explain, she'll think it's funny. Kate doesn't let things bother her."

"Do you love her very much, then?"

He sighed and looked up to the mountains. "Yes, I do."

"Do you think she'll marry you?"

"I don't know. I hope so, but if she says 'no,' I'll just have to be more persistent." He looked at his niece. "I'm tired of being alone. It was enough to have the ranch when I was younger, but now it's thriving, and there's no more challenge. Now I want to settle down, and even if we don't have children, at least we'll have each other."

Children, Maggie thought. Would she ever have children of her own? Would she be alone all her life, or

would someone like Simon come along to save her
before she was an old lady? She wondered how old Kate
was, and then her thoughts turned to Will. She hadn't
thought of her looks much as she was growing up. It was
only after all her friends got married and no one spoke
for her hand that she'd even noticed that perhaps she was
different. She wished she could be like the other women
she knew.

The traffic on the road had picked up, and they passed
many other wagons, horses, carriages, and freight haul-
ers. Soon the town came into view, and to Maggie it
looked exactly the way she thought a town in Wyoming
should look. It nestled against a steep mountain on the
south and looked out across the valley. As they came
down into the town, however, she could see that the view
was blocked by some lower hills and that the main part
was lower than she'd at first thought.

Jackson had been built around a square and was
bustling with people on the wide boardwalks. Everyone
seemed to know Simon, and he was greeted on all hands,
many of the people congratulating him on his marriage
and complimenting him on his choice of a wife. Some of
the men said he was brave to bring the new missus right
into town, what with Kate being like she was, and all. At
first Simon tried explaining, but then decided the best
thing for him to do was to take Maggie right to Kate's
and explain the whole thing. How the facts had all gotten
so blown out of proportion he couldn't imagine, but he
dearly wished people would just mind their own business. He'd have to have a talk with Will about it, because
the misunderstanding obviously originated with his reading between the lines of the telegram.

"Pete, you and Dave go on to the house. I need to get
something straightened out." Pete and Dave grinned,
following right along behind Simon and Maggie. They
knew Kate very well and weren't going to miss this
confrontation for the world. Simon threw them a disgusted look when he realized what they were up to and
spurred his horse ahead of the wagon.

Maggie rode after him to a hitch where they tied their

horses. She dismounted and stretched her back, then followed him up the steps to the porch. She couldn't imagine where they were going. She had thought they might be going to Kate's house, but this looked more like a tavern. She looked up at the sign over the doorway and read Seven Squaw Saloon, and then Simon was at the door. He didn't see the beer mug coming at him, but the aim was off, and it hit the post behind him, shattering and raining glass all over the boardwalk. He was ready for the next one and ducked as it came flying out and hit the street. "Maggie, you stay back," he ordered as he pushed her away from the open door.

"Kate?" A bottle came flying out next and hit him on the shoulder as he opened the wing door. "Kate, listen to me!" A spittoon clanged against the door, brown slime running down it and dripping onto the bare boards beneath.

The last missile had come to rest under the horses and had caused them to rear up and try pulling free from the hitch. Maggie hurried down to soothe them. She had no idea what was going on and couldn't imagine what this Kate was like that she'd behave in such a way. And what was she doing in a saloon? This was supposed to be the woman Uncle Simon wanted to marry?

By this time, quite a crowd had gathered. They'd been waiting for this for days, watching Kate getting madder and madder, and knowing that when Simon Longyear finally showed up there were going to be some fireworks. A woman near Maggie said she thought it was disgraceful that Simon would bring his new wife to meet his mistress, and Maggie turned to her and explained as though to a child, "I am not his wife. I am his niece. He did not get married. Someone made a big mistake." The people around her had quickly passed this latest bit around, and then the show promised to be even better.

"Kate, damn you anyway! Will you listen to me? I didn't get married, Kate." A chair came out next, but apparently she couldn't throw something heavy as easily, so it fell far short of its intended target.

Finally Simon had had enough. He slammed the doors

apart and stomped into the building. Maggie couldn't see what was going on, but heard a very angry woman's voice, and Simon's, just as angry. Then she heard a slap. Then nothing. Simon came out the door holding in his arms a woman with flaming red hair, who was holding onto his neck and looking at him as though the sun rose and set with him.

The crowd laughed, slapped each other on the back, and paid off bets. Simon brought the woman down to where Maggie was standing with the horses and said, "Maggie, meet Kate."

Kate was beautiful. There was no other word for her. Her eyes were sparkling green, and her cheeks were flushed with her recent exertion. Maggie had never seen a prostitute before, but figured this woman must be one, since she'd come out of a saloon, and the men had talked about Kate's "place." Somehow, though, Kate didn't fit Maggie's idea of what a loose woman looked like. She hadn't really given it much thought before, never having had a reason to, but this woman, in her elegant dress and with her flaming red hair piled regally on top of her head, did not fit Maggie's image of a lady of the evening.

Now she understood Uncle Simon's oblique references to the woman. She had somehow thought Kate owned a ranch and ran it singlehandedly, or perhaps that she ran a restaurant or store. But never had it occurred to her that the object of her uncle's infatuation was a prostitute.

"So you're Simon's niece. Maggie, I have never been more glad to make anyone's acquaintance in my life." Simon had put her down, and she smiled into the younger woman's eyes. They were about the same height, and Maggie immediately liked her. Simon had his arm around Kate's shoulder, and said, "I can't believe you thought I'd even look at another woman when I have you."

"But, darling, you were halfway across the country. I know how fickle men's hearts can be when the one they're supposed to love isn't available. And how was I to know that you didn't meet up with a long-lost lover?"

"It's nice to know you can be jealous. I was beginning to think you took me for granted."

"Never." The look she gave him let Simon and Maggie both know she meant it.

Simon grinned. Maybe this mix-up had been a good thing. If Kate had gotten so mad at the thought of losing him, she just might consider marrying him. He decided it might be in his best interest to stay in town for a few days instead of going out to the ranch tomorrow.

"Simon, get this poor girl over to your house and let her get cleaned up. I know she must be dying for a hot bath." She took Maggie's hand. "You must both come back when you've had some rest, and we'll have supper together. You're probably tired of trail food, too, so we can celebrate with a special meal. And then we can talk." She squeezed the girl's hand. "I just know we're going to get along famously."

Kate's face was glowing as she looked up at the tall man beside her. He reached out an arm and brought her close to him in an affectionate hug, then dropped a kiss on her forehead. He had missed her more than he knew. "See you, love," he said with an easy familiarity.

As they rode to Simon's house, Maggie thought about her uncle and Kate. They were quite a striking couple, both tall and good-looking. Simon's darkness was the perfect foil for Kate's shining brightness. Maggie had never been near two people who showed so obviously that they wanted each other. She'd always known her parents were very much in love, but they seldom touched in front of her, and if they did, it was only to take the other's hand. She didn't know what they did behind closed doors, but she couldn't picture them acting like the two she'd just witnessed. It must be nice to have someone you could be so close to and trust not to refuse your caress. She thought again of Will.

"Well, what do you think of her?" Simon looked straight ahead, trying to act casual, but Maggie knew the answer was important to him.

"I think," she said, smiling at him, "that your Kate is wonderful."

He did look at her then, and beamed. "Oh, she is, and you'll find out just how much so. Does it shock you that she runs a saloon?"

"I don't know. It was entirely unexpected. You could have warned me, you know."

"But then you'd have formed an opinion before you'd even met her. I wanted you to judge her on her own merits. She's not a prostitute, you know."

Maggie had the good grace to blush, but they had reached his house by then, and he didn't seem to notice as he dismounted and tied his horse. Maggie slid down before he could help her, and Dave was there to take the horses to the stable and care for them.

"Thank you, Dave. Would you please bring in Maggie's trunks and other bags? We plan to stay in town for a few days. You can just leave the buckboard here, and you and Pete can go on out to the ranch. You're probably anxious to get home, and those new horses need to get where they're going. The sooner we get them settled, the sooner they'll be back in top form."

"A few days! I thought we were going to the ranch tomorrow," Maggie wailed. She'd waited so long and traveled so far. To be so close now and have to wait seemed unjust.

Simon smiled at the girl. She'd been such a good traveling companion, never complaining. "I'd like to stay in town. A certain lady needs my attention. But there's no reason you can't go on out to the ranch tomorrow. Will can show it to you just as well as I can, and Bertha's out there to act as chaperone. Pete and Dave could stay here one night. We're all tired, and they'd probably rather sleep at the hotel tonight than make the ride out to the ranch this late."

Will was at the ranch. Maybe she would be just as well off staying here in town. After all, she was in Wyoming, she could see the beautiful scenery, and she did want to get to know Kate. It seemed totally selfish to keep Dave and Pete in town when they no doubt wanted to get home.

"I'm sorry, Uncle Simon. I guess you would want to

spend time with Kate. It was my fault you weren't back here two months ago, so the least I can do is wait until you're ready to go."

"Thanks, Maggie. You're a very special woman, did you know that?"

She smiled at him but felt a bit guilty. She hadn't changed her mind because of him and Kate, but because she didn't trust herself not to act like a fool around Will Sutten. She needed time, she thought, to put her feelings for him in perspective. As she soaked in the big copper tub later, she decided she'd made the right decision. The time and distance between them would be good.

Will had seen the group ride into town from his vantage point in front of the telegraph office. He had thought that when he saw Maggie again after the space of almost a week, she would be just an ordinary woman, like any of the others around, and would affect him as little as the girls who had been making passes at him over the past years. But the sight of her had set his heart thumping, and after she and Simon had ridden out of sight, he found that his hands were shaking.

Damn! He didn't know what about her made him feel like this, but he didn't have the time or emotional energy to spend thinking about it. He'd been in town long enough to hear that Jake Greeley was back in Wyoming, and he knew he'd need all his faculties to plan his actions.

One thing he knew for sure. When Simon went back out to the ranch, he wouldn't be going with him. He needed to stay in town where he heard what bits of information came through. So far he had managed to keep his interest in his nemesis a secret, and he planned to keep it that way. As for now he needed a bath and some clean clothes, and then he'd come back tonight and listen to the talk around town.

The house that Simon and Will owned was a two-story wooden structure, with a porch running around two sides. The porch afforded protection from the heavy snows, but at this time of year, the piles had melted down considerably. The bottom of the valley of Jackson Hole, where the town was located, was much lower in altitude than the ranch, so it didn't get as much snow as they saw up there, but it was still plenty, and the porch roof kept most of it away from the doors.

The house was large, more than the two men needed, especially since it was used only infrequently and usually by only one of them at a time. Simon used it the most, for entertaining Kate while he was in town. The front door opened into the parlor, and a dining room lay to the right through the French doors. The parlor was decorated with fancy furniture—too dainty by far for Will's taste. A small settee and two chairs without arms left him feeling that if he sat in any of them, they'd break under his weight. The dining table and chairs were solid oak, however, and he had always thought he'd like a set like this one in his own home. A kitchen opened off the back of the dining room, and a bedroom was behind the parlor. The four rooms shared a chimney in the center wall, with a fireplace in the parlor and a cookstove in the kitchen. Off the kitchen was another porch, with a half wall and cotton cording stretched above where they could dry clothes in the summertime, it not being proper in town, according to Bertha, to lay clothing out on the grass to dry as they did on the ranch. A door in the kitchen opened into a large pantry, where the shelves were mostly bare because there had been no one here in the summer to put up food. It contrasted sharply with the ranch cabin's pantry, which was a huge room, lined on all four sides with cabinets bulging with the winter's store of supplies.

Beyond the bedroom, which Simon used, was a small room that the previous owner had used for a sewing room, but which was now empty. Four doors opened off the small room, into the bedroom, the parlor, a bathroom, and the steps leading to the upstairs, where there were three more bedrooms.

Will had come in by way of the kitchen and had taken a look in the ground-floor bedroom to see Simon stretched out on his bed, sleeping. There wasn't any sound he could detect, so he figured Maggie was sleeping upstairs. Apparently Pete and Dave had gone out to the ranch already, because their horses, as well as the new stock from South Carolina, were gone. The buckboard was still in the stable, and he had known from the way the tarp looked that some of the trunks had been removed. He figured they were staying the night at least.

He was determined not to think of the woman upstairs. He would be out of the house before she awoke and would come in long after she was sleeping again. She would be behind a closed door, and he'd be damned if he'd knock on it. They should be able to get through this short time without running into each other at all.

There were large pans on the cookstove full of hot water, and the buckets they used to carry it to the bath on the floor beside it. Several more pans were empty, but not dry, so someone must have taken a bath already. Maggie. He didn't allow himself to think of her in the bath.

Methodically he poured the steaming water into two of the buckets, and then went by way of the dining room and parlor to the bath. The door was closed, to keep the heat from the little stove in, and he set the buckets down to open it. It swung to the inside, and he picked up the buckets again and carried them in, then set them down to close the door. He didn't get that far.

She was sleeping in the tub, her arms up on the sides and her head resting against the tall back. Her hair was hidden beneath a towel wrapped turban-style around her head. The sight of her snatched his breath away and filled him with a desire so strong it was painful.

He didn't stop to consider what he was doing. He seemed destined to come upon her in various states of dishabille. He moved to the side of the tub and felt the water. It was still very warm—the room was almost hot. She must have sunk down into that water, and the strain of the long journey had taken hold. He couldn't see all of her. The water was cloudy from the soap. But her breasts were barely covered, showing that what he'd imagined with what little he'd seen before was true. He watched in fascination as her rhythmic breathing lifted them out of the water, then lowered them again. He didn't seem to be able to stay his hand as it reached over and traced a line from one side, across the top of one full breast, and down into the deep valley between. The rosy crests hardened in the molten fire left by his touch, and he looked up at her face to see her dark eyes looking into his own, as full of desire as he knew his were.

He reached up then and, cupping her chin in his hand, he lowered his mouth to hers and drank full and deep of the promise waiting there.

Maggie had never been kissed before, but she had been dreaming of Will there in the bath. He had told her he loved her and wanted to marry her, and she had looked at his face, that man's face with the strong jawline softened by deep dimples, and the distant look in his eyes replaced by a boyish charm she found impossible to resist. When she opened her eyes to see him there, the dream seemed so real. She strained toward him, wanting him to know that, yes, she would marry him, and he slowly trailed his hand down across her neck and cupped one of her full breasts, rubbing his thumb in small, slow circles over the peak. Her chest seemed full to bursting, and she had difficulty breathing, but still he caressed her. His lips left hers and followed the trail left by his hand, down the slim column of her neck, and on to the hardness his hand had produced. He lifted the breast out of the water and, when his lips made contact, she thought she'd faint.

She wanted more, but she didn't know what. There was a fire deep in the pit of her that needed quenching, and she knew he had the means to do it. She didn't care that she wasn't married to him, didn't care that she hardly even knew him. She only knew she wanted him.

And then he was gone.

He left her so abruptly that she looked up just in time to see the door closing behind him. Her heart was pounding in her chest, and her body still needed his touch. She should have been shamed to the core, given her ladylike upbringing, but she only felt cheated that he'd left before fulfilling the promise he'd seemed to make.

Shaken, she stood and rinsed herself with the clear water in the buckets standing by the tub, then toweled herself dry. Covering her body from head to foot in a woolen wrapper, she gathered her things together and opened the door cautiously. The house was still silent, and she crossed the cold floor on silent bare feet and scurried up the stairs to the room Simon had said would be hers.

At the top of the stairs she hesitated. The door to one of the other rooms was closed, and there were sounds of drawers being slammed shut, and then something being thrown against the wall. Will. Will would be in the room next to hers. She slipped inside her own room and silently shut the door and bolted it.

Will. Why wasn't he at the ranch?

Will. In the very next room, with one thin wall between them. And two doors.

Will. What would he do if she opened his door without knocking as he seemed to have a penchant for doing to her?

Will. Did he want her? Did he think she was pretty?

Will. She didn't know enough about him to even guess what he might be thinking.

What did she know of him? He very likely wasn't married. Surely he would have gone straight home to his wife if he had been. He must be a good and trustworthy man, or Uncle Simon wouldn't have trusted his niece's well-being to him. And he must be a good character, or he wouldn't be Uncle Simon's foreman, for she knew he wouldn't have chosen a man for such a position unless he trusted him implicitly. She was probably lucky that he was of strong moral character, because twice he could have taken advantage of her, and he hadn't. Well, not as much as she knew he could have, anyway.

What had stopped him? Did he respect her? Then a horrible thought came to her. What if he thought she was throwing herself at him, and he couldn't make himself do anymore because he found her unattractive?

No, she told herself sternly. She hadn't had anything to do with either time. He had been the one to intrude upon her solitude. And both times he had looked at her with desire. She couldn't mistake that look, for she had never seen such a look before on any man's face. He had seemed to devour her with that look, and she shivered now as she remembered his blue eyes turning dark with desire.

She had to find out. She had to know if what she had read in his face was true, and wasn't just something she was imagining. She hadn't particularly tried to attract Charles, and she had lost him to a serving girl. So she took extra special care with her clothing and the way she fixed her hair. When she next saw Mr. Will Sutten, she wouldn't be travel-worn and disheveled. She would dress with as much care as she had for her wedding, scarcely two weeks before.

❈ 3 ❈

Will heard Maggie come up the stairs and pictured her again in the bath. He slammed a drawer shut. He again felt her smooth skin under his hand and slammed another drawer. Then he remembered her response to his kiss, a response such as no woman had ever given him before, and he kicked a chair against the wall.

Damn! He remembered the nights of his marriage and knew this was more even than he'd ever felt with his wife.

He had been older when he married, twenty-eight, and had had his share of women. His had been a wealthy family, and he was the second son. He hadn't been pressed to marry and beget an heir as his older brother had, but many girls and their mothers had set their sights on him. There had been money and land to go around, but Will hadn't wanted something handed to him. He'd been restless all his life, and when he began hearing about the vast reaches of land in the West, he knew that was where he was headed.

His parents had arranged his marriage to Charity in an effort to keep him home. They had not forced him but had informed him the girl was agreeable to the union and would bring even more land into the family, as she had been an only child. He wondered how her aging parents had taken her leaving. Regret was a long time coming, but he should never have taken her away.

He had met with Charity, a timid little thing, but pretty and good-tempered. He'd thought her mostly a bore until

35

he'd mentioned going West, and then her eyes lit up with
a fire, and she told him endless tales of the things she'd
read and heard of places far away. He'd been pleasantly
surprised, and when he asked her to marry him and go to
those places with him, she'd readily agreed. But now she
was gone, and he had a man to kill.

Maggie had no place in his life now. Not until he had
settled his past could he see a future, and the only thing
he could do now was stay out of her way. He waited until
she left the house with Simon some time later, and then
he washed up and headed to the hotel restaurant as he
usually did when in town. She would be gone tomorrow,
and he could get on with his unfinished business. When
Millie served him, she seemed in a talkative mood
tonight, and he was ready to listen.

Maggie had never been in a saloon before. She had
only been in a restaurant once before beginning this
journey, and that was a very elegant tearoom with her
mother in attendance. The dining car on the train had not
been much different from the tearoom, except for the
menu. The patrons had been elegantly dressed and had
behaved with the utmost decorum. The Seven Squaw
Saloon was full of bawdy talk and laughter. She found it
all fascinating, and she vowed to spend as much time
here as Uncle Simon would allow.

Maggie had read adventure books and had dreamed of
going places and experiencing life as it was lived in other
cultures. She had always thought, though, that she would
have to settle for the vicarious pleasure of reading about
it. But now, thanks to Charles, really (she giggled at
that), she had broken out of that placid life—and she
intended to take full advantage of her freedom.

She didn't have much time to study the interior of the
saloon as Simon hurried her through it and into another
part of the building. They crossed a dark hall and entered
an elegant sitting room much like the ones Maggie had
seen as she grew up. She was immediately disappointed.
It was quiet and elegant and just like home.

Kate appeared and held her arms out to the two of them. "You're just in time! Did you get all rested up?"

"I hate to admit it, but I even slept a bit," Simon answered as he pulled her to him and placed a light kiss on her lips.

"Ummm, your age is catching up with you. You can't do everything all at once anymore."

He laughed. "Yes, and I want to talk to you about that later."

"I can't do anything about your age, dear."

"Yes, well, we'll see about that." He patted her behind, much to Maggie's amusement.

"Maggie," Kate said as she took her hand and led her into the dining room, "I hope you're pleasantly surprised at the meal we're going to have. It should rival any you've had back home."

If the decor was any indication, it certainly would. The room was tastefully decorated with paneled wainscoting with gilt paper above. A glistening chandelier hung over the handsome table flanked by eight high-backed chairs. Highly polished silver, fine china, and delicate crystal set the places on a beautiful embroidered linen tablecloth.

"Oh, it's wonderful!" exclaimed Maggie, and she went around the perimeter of the room to study the fine prints hanging there, all the time wishing she could have stayed in the saloon and studied the people coming and going.

Simon and Kate exchanged a loving look not lost to the younger woman. She imagined that before the night was over, they would be engaged, and the thought pleased her immensely. She'd never seen her uncle looking so happy and content. Her parents would no doubt be shocked at his choice of a woman, but Maggie sensed that out here, who your family was didn't matter as much as what you were yourself. Kate had a strength about her that Maggie liked and no doubt Uncle Simon would admire. Kate also filled Maggie with hope, because the two of them seemed to be so much alike.

A sweet older woman whom Kate introduced as Della helped Kate carry in the platters of steaming food. Della was plump and jolly-looking, and kept smiling at Maggie, showing deep dimples. Her gray hair was braided and wrapped around her head, and she looked like someone's grandmother. She wore a plain dark blue dress with a snowy white apron covering it, and the dark dress made her bright blue eyes seem to twinkle in her lined face. She looked as though nothing but good had ever happened to her, and Maggie took to her immediately.

"Della does most of the cooking around here, and Kate helps her out," Simon explained.

"You do your own cooking?" Maggie couldn't picture the elegant Kate working in a kitchen, and why would she, when she had a servant to do it for her?

"Of course I do, when I have the time. I'm a very good cook, although not as good as Della, and it's something I love to do."

"I can't imagine anyone loving to cook," said Maggie, making a face.

"You mean you don't like to?"

"I don't like to, and I don't know how."

"You don't know how to cook anything?" Kate was incredulous.

"I'm afraid Maggie's education has been neglected when it comes to domestic abilities," Simon explained.

Maggie looked chagrined. "I thought it all a bore, I'm afraid."

"What on earth did you do?" queried Kate.

"Oh, I rode horses, helped with the bookkeeping, worked in the stables. My mother is quite active in charity work, and I helped her with that. And I read a lot." It seemed pathetic when she said it like that.

"Why, you poor child." Kate looked at her with sympathy. "Was your mother not able to teach you anything?"

Simon threw back his head and laughed, and that got Maggie tickled as some of her worst disasters on the domestic side came to mind, and she started laughing, too.

Kate looked from one to the other with disgust. "I don't see what's so funny about that. Is her mother mad about horses or something?"

The two laughed even harder as they tried to imagine the dainty, elegant Elizabeth in the stables caring for horses, or even astride one, for that matter. Her tastes ran to well-sprung carriages, and she had probably never stepped within a hundred feet of the stables.

Finally Maggie was able to bring herself under control and explain to the increasingly irritated Kate. "My mother is elegant and tiny, and the very essence of good breeding and polite manners. She loves me dearly, but I'm afraid I have been somewhat of a cross for her to bear. My father wanted sons, and all he had was me, so he allowed me freedoms most gently reared young ladies never enjoy. I did learn proper manners, however, and how to be a lady, so I do realize my behavior here has not been exemplary, and I apologize."

At that, Kate laughed. "You needn't apologize to me, Maggie. Heaven knows I've not had much chance to learn good manners in my life, although I do try to pick up as much as I can."

"Nonsense, Kate," Simon protested, "your manners are above reproach, and I dare anyone to say otherwise."

"Dear Simon. You are blind when it comes to me, aren't you? You know I've learned most of what I know from you, and I'm not ashamed of it, so you needn't try to hide it from Maggie." She looked at the girl. "I'm afraid I didn't have the advantageous upbringing you did."

"And I didn't take advantage of my upbringing, so that should make us about even, shouldn't it?"

Kate grinned. "We're going to have some good times together, Maggie. I can feel it already."

It was some time later, and they were just finishing brandied peach crepes, when Maggie got the feeling the older couple wanted to be alone. Simon had placed his hand on Kate's and was looking deep into her eyes, and she was gazing back with unabashed love. The candle-light was growing dim, making golden highlights on the silver and crystal, and bathing the two of them in its warm glow. Maggie felt an unaccountable yearning deep inside and saw Will's eyes once again.

She slipped from her chair, thinking to leave them alone, but Simon said, "Maggie, I'll take you home."

"Oh, I just thought I'd go help Della with the cleaning up. You two probably want to be alone."

"You needn't do that, Maggie." Kate stood and started gathering up the dishes.

"I know, I just feel the need to do something. If I were still at home, I'd go for a long walk. I feel kind of restless." She shrugged her shoulders. "You two go on into the other room. I think I can figure out how to carry these into the kitchen without breaking them."

Kate smiled at her and said, "All right, then. Thank you, Maggie, you're a very sweet girl."

Maggie stacked the dishes together and carried a large pile to the door, then pushed it open with her backside and turned into the kitchen. Della was up to her elbows in dishwater, but quickly pulled her hands out and, drying them on her apron, came over to get the stack from Maggie. "Land sakes, girl, what are you doing, bringing me the dirty dishes!"

"Kate and Uncle Simon wanted to be alone." She grinned and raised her eyebrows.

"Oh, that." Della nodded her head. "If the two of them aren't stuck on each other! Kate deserves something nice in her life. I'm real glad your uncle was the one she found."

"Have you known Kate long?" Maggie was curious about the relationship because they seemed more like friends than servant and mistress. She had never heard a cook call her mistress by her first name.

Della was back to washing, and she kept on scrubbing a plate as she answered. "We've known each other for about eight years. She was just a new bride, and I'd been married for ten years. Had five children." She said this last softly, as if talking to herself.

"Where are they now?" Maggie asked the question gently because Della seemed so sad.

"Oh, they're dead. All of them are dead. My man and all my children. Kate's man, too, he's dead."

"I'm very sorry." So Kate had had a man before Simon.

"Oh, it was long time ago."

Maggie took up a towel and started drying the dishes after Della rinsed them in the hot water pan. She didn't know what to say to the woman. She'd never had anyone close to her die, and to lose a husband and children must have been very painful. She wondered if they had been sick, but didn't want to ask. It didn't seem quite right to ask about Kate's past either. She didn't want to pry so she kept her curiosity to herself.

Della asked her about her family, and Maggie told her about her father, who was so much like Simon, and her mother, and then described the grand house, with the huge expanses of dark green lawns, the flowers in full bloom when she'd left two weeks before, and then the stables and the horses, which were her father's passion.

"Flowers," Della said softly. "It seems like years since I've seen flowers. It's so cold here, you know."

"No flowers grow here?" Maggie was shocked. What kind of place was this that no flowers grew? Was it always this cold?

"Oh, flowers grow here, just not the kind you were talking about. Yes, in the summer there are thousands and thousands of wildflowers of every color you can imagine. One day there's snow on the ground, and the next, the meadows are blazing with color. It's like they know they don't have much time, so they have to hurry up and bloom before it's too late. I lived in Savannah when I was a girl, is all, and I was remembering the gardens there."

"Bougainvillea, jasmine, azaleas—I don't imagine they grow here."

"That's right. All that heat and humidity. We took it for granted when we lived there, even cursed it at times, but it was a forgiving climate. This isn't."

"You don't like it here?" Maggie wondered why Della didn't leave if she was unhappy.

"Like it?" Della turned amazed eyes to Maggie. "Honey, I love it here! Don't get me wrong, it's a rough place, but it's alive! Down south it seemed like everyone was asleep most of the time. Here, we're just like those wildflowers. We got to make the most of every day. And there's things up there in those mountains, wonderful things, that you just can't believe until you see them. You'll have to get Simon to take you to the hot springs, and to the mountain lakes and waterfalls. Once, a man came through here and climbed to the top of that biggest mountain up there, and he made tintypes with a big black camera he carried all the way up. It was like being on the top of the world just to see them, the clouds below you, and mountain peaks as far as the eye could see. I want to go up there some day."

"How do you get up there? Is there a road?"

Della laughed. "No road up there! You have to climb, with ropes and picks. But there's some talk about an easier way than the photographer took. They say most anyone can do it."

"Well, then, we'll go together!"

They passed the time pleasantly, and soon everything was clean and in its place again. Della had rooms behind the kitchen, and after assuring herself that Maggie didn't mind being left alone, she retired for the night. Maggie was left wondering what to do. She really didn't want to bother Simon and Kate, so she found a pen and some paper in a small desk and wrote a note to tell them she'd decided to walk home after all. By the time they found the note, she'd be home.

When Della had opened the other door in the kitchen to go to her rooms, Maggie had seen it opened onto the same hallway she and Simon had passed through, and immediately a plan formed in her mind. Her cloak was on the back of a chair in the front room. She would have to pass Simon and Kate to get to it and go out the door of the front room, where they'd come in, but if she slipped through the kitchen door into the hallway, she could open the front room door, and get it without them ever seeing her.

She was able to do what she'd planned, and she thanked her lucky stars that they'd been so wrapped up in each other they hadn't heard the door creak as she opened it. She wrapped her cloak tightly around her and searched the hallway for a way out. She knew better than to go through the saloon alone, and she soon found a door that opened to the outside.

The night was frigid and utterly still. She looked up and was astounded by the stars. There seemed to be millions of them, and they were so close she could almost reach out and touch them. The cold air felt good after the steamy heat of the kitchen. She took a deep breath and decided to explore just a bit on the way home. No one seemed to be around, and she surely couldn't get into any trouble.

She peeked around the end of the building and saw that the main street and square were straight ahead, so she strode through the alleyway and stepped up onto the boardwalk. The saloon was to her left, and she didn't want anyone there to see her, so she headed right. Simon's house was left, so she could go all the way around the square and then head down that way.

Most of the business places were dark and closed up, but there was another saloon and a hotel with lights in the windows. She figured she could go around the backs of both places, and no one would even see her passing. She had sorely missed her walks and needed one now to clear her mind—or to leave it free to dream of Will Sutten. There hadn't been much opportunity in her life in the way of romantic dreaming, so she allowed herself to pretend he was escorting her and telling her about the places they passed.

Will had been watching Kate's place to see when Simon and Maggie came out. He figured he'd given them time to get home and safely in their rooms before he headed that way. It had occurred to him to take a room at the hotel for the night but didn't want to imagine the speculation that would cause. Then he'd thought that was a cowardly way out. Surely he could stand one night in the same house with the girl.

When she'd first come out from between the saloon and hardware store, he'd not thought much about it. But then something about the cloaked figure caught his attention, and he watched her intently. She didn't want to be seen, whoever she was, and he became more sure by the minute that it was Maggie. Surely Simon wouldn't have let her out alone on these streets. She wouldn't stand a chance if a drunken cowboy got his hands on her.

She was keeping close to the buildings, and he almost didn't see her duck into the alleyway behind the Pink Garter. Two men were weaving their way out the door, and Will thought she must have seen them and tried to hide. He'd better get over there and keep an eye on her. Blast Simon anyway. What had he been thinking to let her go out alone? Probably so caught up in Kate's charms he'd forgotten all about his niece. It was a good thing Will happened to see her, or she'd be in big trouble over there.

He left the dining room of the hotel and, grabbing up his coat and hat, slammed out the door and traveled at a trot across the square. He had no sooner reached the other boardwalk in front of the Pink Garter when he caught her out of the corner of his eye coming out from between the hat shop and grocery farther down the street.

What on earth was she doing? he wondered. Had she lost her way in the dark? He decided to stay back aways and follow her, and if she got in trouble, he'd be there.

Her passing was making no sound that he could hear, and sound carried in the cold like this. His boots were another story. He tried to stay back far enough that she wouldn't notice him, but twice she stopped and looked behind her. Both times he nonchalantly leaned against a building and pointedly looked the other way. He didn't want her to know he was following her, and he didn't want to meet up with her again until some time had passed and he could distance his emotions from her.

She was going around the square, he figured, as she crossed the street again and headed down the boardwalk in front of the hotel. She hesitated there and then ducked into the alleyway again. Where was she going? What was she trying to hide? She hadn't been in town long enough to meet anyone, so he ruled out a clandestine encounter. Unless some man had followed her on the train and then up here. But no, that was too far-fetched and unfair to Maggie, when it was Charity who would have done something like that. Besides, surely she couldn't have reacted to him in the way she had if she'd had a lover following her.

He cut across the corner of the square and peered into the darkness between the hotel and gunsmith. There was a stable back there where some of the hotel patrons kept their horses if they were only going to eat in the dining room or might need to leave in a hurry. He would just as soon she didn't run into one of those people back there and so he hurried down the empty space. He hadn't seen which way she'd turned, but if his theory was right, she'd have turned left again. Then an idea hit him. She was going behind the open establishments to avoid being seen, and Simon probably didn't even know she was out here. In order to go home the shortest way, she'd have had to cut right in front of the Seven Squaw and would surely have been accosted by some of the men milling around the entrance. The alleyway behind there was blocked except for the way she'd come out. He grinned. She was using her head. He turned around the corner, and there she was.

"Maggie," he started, but he didn't finish what he was going to say because something very hard came down on his head, and the last thing he remembered was trying to reach for her before he hit the ground.

❦ 4 ❦

Maggie had been aware of the man following her since he'd crossed the square. She'd seen him as she was coming out from between two buildings, and then he had slipped along behind her, staying in the shadows. She hadn't been frightened because she knew if she screamed, any number of people would have come running, but the man's presence bothered her enough to make her heart beat a little faster. Who was he, and why was he following her? She wished she could get a look at him, but every time she turned around, he looked the other way and lowered his head. It was so hard to tell people apart because they all wore the same kind of hat, coat, pants, and boots.

When she got to the hotel she contemplated simply heading straight across the square and back into the saloon she'd just left. The last alleyway had been muddy and wet, both from the unseasonably warm air and from the slop water that was habitually thrown out the back doors, and her feet were soaked. She was reluctant to brave the back of the hotel, where there must be even more mud. Simon probably hadn't noticed she was gone yet, and she could slip back in and destroy the note before he or Kate ever found out. But she was reluctant to go back in there. They were so much in love, and watching them made her feel left out. A couple of people came out of the hotel then, and she decided quickly to go behind. She threw a quick glance back and saw the man cut across the square and quicken his pace.

47

What should she do? She knew she could probably outrun him, but the snow and mud would make her path slippery, and she'd be at his mercy if she fell. There were stables back there she could hide in, but she didn't know where she was going, and he might know the place very well. Then she spied a log pile and quickly took up a long piece of wood from the top, pressing herself against the back of the building, the log raised above her head.

It all happened so quickly she didn't have time to comprehend that he had said "Maggie" before she hit him and he slumped to the ground with her cloak in his hands.

"Will! Oh, Will, what have I done to you?" She knelt beside him and felt for the rise and fall of his chest, terrified that she'd killed him. She was greatly relieved when she felt his warm breath on her cold hands. But now what should she do? He was too heavy for her to move alone, and she didn't want to leave him alone back here in the dark while she went for help.

Then she remembered seeing a man back home who had been knocked out in a fight—they'd thrown a bucket of water in his face. She looked around. She of course didn't have a bucket, but maybe if she threw snow in his face it would do the same thing. What a horrible thing to do to him, she thought, especially since it was her fault he was lying there, but she gathered up as much as she could hold and stood up, then let it fall right onto his face.

It worked! He sputtered and spit, wiped the icy wetness off his face, and then tried to sit up.

"No, don't try to get up." She dropped to her knees beside him. "Oh, Will, I'm so very sorry. I didn't know it was you." She wiped away as much of the wetness as she could with her cloak, but he was still wet and cold, since the snow had gotten down into his coat.

"Do you think you can walk if I help you? You need to get home and into some dry clothes."

"Yeah," he said, and his voice was so full of pain she was filled again with chagrin.

Will slowly sat up. Then, with her support, he stood shakily.

"Good." She put his arm around her neck, and he leaned heavily on her. Thank goodness she was tall and strong for a woman. He was a big man. Thank goodness for that, too, for he had been so tall she'd not hit him full force with the log. She'd have had to stand on a barrel to bring it down on top of him. She thought of the predicament she'd gotten them into, and then giggled at the sight they must be making. She looked like a wife getting her drunken husband home.

"What's so goddamn funny?" Will growled. The idiot girl could have killed him, and as it was, he was bound to have one whopping headache come morning.

"Oh, Will, I'm sorry. Look, we're almost there." She helped him up the steps to the porch and then around the side to the back door. He leaned his forearm on the side of the door while she opened it, then slowly moved inside and slumped into a chair by the stove.

Maggie lifted a lid off the cookstove and dropped in several pieces of the split wood from the woodbox. Then she moved the kettle to the front and dropped her cloak to the back of a chair.

"Will you be all right while I go get you some dry clothes?"

He had his elbows on his knees and was resting his head in his hands, covering his eyes and forehead. He nodded, so she clutched the lantern and ran through Simon's bedroom and up the stairs to Will's room.

There were no clothes in evidence, so she pulled open the top drawer and found a soft flannel shirt and, in another drawer, a pair of pants. She hesitated when she spied a pair of long johns. Knowing from the feel of him that he must be soaked through to the skin, so she grabbed them up, too, and hurried back down to the warm kitchen.

He was in the same position she'd left him, and the sight of him in pain brought a lump to her throat. Her eyes watered, and she blinked the tears away at the thought that she could have killed him.

"Here, Will, let's get you out of those wet things and into these."

He lifted his head, moving his hands down his face with his eyes closed. Then he let out a huff of air and pushed himself up into a more upright position with his hands on his knees. He pushed back his shoulders and stretched his back slowly, then started unbuttoning the sheepskin-lined coat.

She helped him shrug it off his shoulders, and after it his shirt and the soaked top of his flannel underwear. Her hands brushed against his bare skin, and shivers ran up her back. She was thankful to be behind him so he didn't see the blush she could feel. His hair was dripping, so she gently dried the back of his head, then pulled the dry shirt up over one arm and across his back to the other one. His back was beautiful, smooth and muscular, and she tried not to think of it, tried to think of anything but his bare skin, and missed something he said to her.

"What did you say?" she asked in confusion.

He had dropped his head back down to his hands. "My head. It's bleeding." He lifted the bloody fingers of one hand to show her.

She was suddenly blinded by tears, but she didn't have time to cry. She wiped the back of her hand across her eyes, then snatched up another towel and the wash pan, and poured the hot water from the kettle into the pan. She knelt in front of him and gently began to clean the wound. She must have caught him with the edge of the log, for the split was about two inches wide. The hair around it was matted with blood, which had run down onto his forehead. She gently bathed the cut until the blood stopped flowing, then folded a clean cloth to cover the wound. She studied every inch of his face as she carefully bathed it. He had a scar above his eyebrow, and she wondered how he'd gotten it. His hands were still bloody, so she put the basin in front of him and, taking one hand at a time, she lowered it into the warm water and massaged his skin with her fingers until each hand was clean. She dried each finger slowly, trying to study his hands to keep her mind off the rest of him.

She was acutely aware of his masculinity, so close to her. His shirt was still unbuttoned, and his chest, with its dark curling hair, was fully visible to her. She caught herself staring, wanting to run her hands over that, too, and was glad he wasn't very perceptive at the moment.

There was still the matter of his soaked pants. The back side was muddy, and the pants clung to him. He was holding the cloth to the wound, his elbows on his knees again.

"Will." She paused, then plunged ahead. "We've got to get you out of those wet pants."

He uncovered one eye and looked at her. "There's no 'we' to it. I can change my own pants."

"Don't be ridiculous! You can't even stand up on your own, and we need to get this done quickly so you can get into your bed."

"Miss Longyear," he said with a sigh and a shake of his head, sitting up again and locking his eyes into hers. "You just help me up the stairs and into my room, and I can handle the rest, I assure you."

She started to argue, then bit her lower lip and nodded. He put a hand on her shoulder and pulled himself up. She took his dry clothes with her other hand, and they made their way across Simon's bedroom and to the stairs.

"Maybe you should just sleep in Uncle Simon's bed," she suggested.

"I'll sleep in my own," he said in a tone that let her know he meant it.

The stairway was somewhat narrow, so she had to press even closer against him as they ascended. Her emotions were running riot, and she had a burning desire to press her face into his chest. The stairway was dark, for they'd come without the lantern, and she was thankful he couldn't see her face. She didn't need light to see his; she had memorized every detail about his looks. He seemed even bigger when she was this close to him, his massive arms across her shoulders. His black hair, as curly and unruly as hers, topped a wide forehead with a few wrinkles across it and a furrow between straight, dark brows that became more evident when he was concentrating on something or someone. His eyes were deep-set and dark blue, with crinkles at the outer corners. A mustache kept her from seeing all of his lips, but his jaw was strong and covered with the shadow of a beard. His hands, when she'd washed them downstairs, had fascinated her. They were strong and brown and callused from hard work. She compared them to Charles' hands and found the thin, white ones of the latter sadly lacking. How naive she had been, she thought, to think a weak fop like Charles could have made her happy.

When they reached the top of the stairs, she tried to get as far as possible from him while still supporting his weight as they went into his room. She had to keep her thoughts to herself. The room was bathed in a silvery light from the full moon, and it made their situation seem all the more intimate.

He headed for the bed, but she stopped him. "You cannot sit on the bed with clothes that wet and muddy. You'll get the bedding wet and you'll never get dry. Now, let me help you change."

He allowed her to lead him to a chair instead, and then said, "You can leave now."

"I'll turn around but I won't leave you alone. What if you fall?" She turned her back and tried not to think she was alone in his bedroom with him, and no one else was in the house.

Will was amused by her behavior. His head hurt damnably, but he'd had much worse wounds and had managed on his own with no help for a hundred miles. The warm, soft curves of her body were causing him trouble this time.

"You can make yourself useful. Help me off with my boots."

She turned, not trusting her voice to make a saucy reply, and knelt down to pull them off. At least his feet were dry, but they were icy cold, and he was shivering. She placed both his feet on her lap, then reached for the buttons at his waist. His hand stopped her. "I said I'll do it myself."

"I don't know what you're so shy about. You've seen a lot more of me than this!"

He grinned at her. "So I have. You trying to get even?"

"No. I'm trying to get you dry and warm and in bed so I don't feel so bad about almost killing you."

"You're trying to get me in bed?" His feet on her thighs quickly warmed from the heat through her thick skirts, and in spite of being somewhat dizzy, his body was reacting to her. He'd be damned if she'd get his pants off him in that state.

"All right. Do it yourself." She stood up, dumping his feet back on the cold floor.

She didn't turn around this time, but crossed her arms under her breasts and looked right at him, so he decided to call her bluff. He opened the waist of his pants and began sliding them down. Her eyes didn't leave his. He hadn't undressed in front of a woman for a long time. Infuriatingly, dizziness came over him, and he had to clutch the footboard of the bed to steady himself. She was at his side instantly but refrained from saying "I told you so." She pushed him back down onto the chair and, taking hold of the bottoms of the pants legs, she pulled the soaked things off him.

The longjohns were wet, if not too muddy, and she knew they should be changed, too. The top, where she'd pulled it down before, was hanging cold and wet from his waist. The bedroom was not even close to being warm, and he mustn't get chilled.

"Will, I'm going to help you to the bed, and then it will be easier for you to do the rest."

He nodded, cursing his weakness in front of her. What must she think of him that a little knock on the head had rendered him helpless? She had pulled back the sheets and blankets, and she lowered him down to the mattress, then pulled the sheet over him and handed him the dry undergarment.

"Miss Longyear, I would appreciate it if you—" He had been about to ask her to leave again, but didn't finish the sentence because darkness overtook him.

*   *   *

Maggie didn't at first realize what had happened and waited for him to finish the sentence. When he didn't, she panicked and put her ear to his chest to listen for his heartbeat. Relief flooded her because it was beating strongly, but then she knew she had to get help. Cursing his modesty, she threw back the sheet and peeled the wet underwear from him and replaced it so quickly with the dry pair that she didn't have time to think of his bare flesh. Then she pulled all the quilts and blankets back over him and tucked them around him. Feeling on the nightstand for the matches, she lit the lamp and then turned to see how he looked.

His face was so pale that she was scared to leave him alone. She didn't know how badly he was hurt but knew he needed a doctor. She flew down the stairs again and across the space to the kitchen to throw on her cloak and run back to Kate's to get Uncle Simon, but he came in the door just as she turned around.

"Maggie! You're all right! What were you thinking to be wandering about this town after dark?"

"Oh, Uncle Simon, I'm so glad you're here! Will has been hurt, and he needs a doctor quickly!"

"Where is he?"

"Up in his bed. He has a head wound and he passed out."

"Go back to him. I'll get the doctor here as fast as I can." Then he was gone. Maggie finally let the tears come. "Please, God, let him live."

She was sitting in the chair by his bed, holding his hand, when Simon returned with the doctor, and she moved out of the way so he could work. Simon went into another room and brought back another lantern, lit it, and then placed it next to the other one so the doctor could see better.

The doctor was a young man, medium height and stocky. He had light brown hair that fell onto his forehead, but the face beneath it was serious as he looked at the wound, and the hands were sure as they worked over the injured man. He stitched up the gash, then bandaged the wound expertly and checked Will's ears, then looked into his eyes. After several minutes he turned to them.

"What happened?"

"He was struck on the head with a log," Maggie answered quickly.

"A log? How long ago?"

"Maybe an hour. I don't know for sure."

"Were you there when it happened?"

"Yes." She squirmed. Uncle Simon was looking at her, bemused.

"How hard was he hit?"

"As hard as I could." She might as well admit it. They were going to find out anyway.

"You did this?"

"I didn't mean to. Oh, what does it matter how it happened? How is he? Is he going to be all right?"

Dr. Chase Wolcott had seen many things in his practice, but this was a first. His gaze moved from her own mud-stained gown to the pile of wet clothing Will must have been wearing. He would really like to hear what had gone on between the two of them. He'd known Will Sutten long enough and well enough to know he wouldn't have made improper advances to a lady. And who was this woman anyway? Why was she in Will's bedroom? Simon didn't look worried. Chase knew about Will's wife, and also that the man hadn't even shown an interest in any woman for as long as he'd known him. Satisfying his curiosity would have to wait, however.

"Tell me what happened. Did he black out?"

"Yes. Then I threw snow in his face to bring him to. He was dizzy, and I had to help him back here. I bathed his wound, and when he lay down on the bed, he started to say something, then passed out."

Chase appreciated her succinct account. She had a level head on her shoulders and she hadn't panicked in an emergency. He still wondered why she'd hit Will in the first place. Her concern for him was obvious, and Simon had stood back and let her have the lead. Was she a relative of his? He'd been out on ranch calls all day and had only just gotten home when Simon caught him. He considered what to tell her, then decided to give her the truth.

"I don't think he has a fractured skull. His ears and nose are clear, and his eyes seem okay. But he probably does have a severe concussion. That means his brain is bruised, and he needs to be kept in bed and as still as possible. Knowing Will, he's going to think he can get on a horse tomorrow and go riding off somewhere, but he needs to stay in bed for a few days at least. I'll be back tomorrow to see how he's doing."

"But is he okay? Why did he pass out?"

"Sometimes concussion does that. He'll be just fine if he stays put, but he could cause all kinds of problems if he doesn't." He turned to Simon, who had been leaning against the wall with his legs and arms crossed. "I need to get back, but don't hesitate to get me if his condition changes."

"Thanks, Doc." He smiled at the younger man, who was eyeing his niece. He hadn't thought of the doctor where Maggie was concerned, but she could do a lot worse. It was gratifying to Simon to see the attention she was getting, not only from the doctor, but also from Dave and possibly Will as well. Exactly why had she hit him over the head? he wondered.

"This is my niece, Maggie." He nodded to the doctor. "Dr. Chase Wolcott. He's a trifle young, but we think he's a pretty good sawbones."

"I'm very pleased to meet you, Dr. Wolcott. And thank you for coming so quickly."

"I'd stay, but I have a baby that's going to be born before morning if I don't miss my guess, and it's a first, so the father is a little nervous." He smiled at Maggie. "I think Willa wants me there mostly to keep Jim occupied so he doesn't drive her crazy."

Maggie smiled in return, and Chase didn't miss how lovely that smile was.

"I'll see you out, Doc," Simon offered, and, nodding to Maggie, Chase followed him down the stairs.

Maggie felt suddenly exhausted, and she dropped into

the chair by Will's bed. How could she have done this to him? He would never forgive her, she was sure of that. Now all that remained was to nurse him back to health, and she would give that job all her energy. She blew out one of the lanterns and turned the other down low, then settled into a rocking chair for the night. These few days might be all she had of him, and as the men's footsteps faded away down the stairs, and the lamp cast a cozy glow over them, she thought, *If this is all I get, I'll make the most of it.* Simon followed Chase out the door and across the yard, pausing at the end of the stone walk.

"Thanks, Doc."

"Sure." He hesitated, then commented. "That was quite a blow she gave him."

Simon grinned. "It sure as hell was."

"Do you know what happened?"

"No, and I don't know if I want to, either. Sometimes it's best just to leave things unsaid."

"She seems very nice. Your brother's child?"

"Yes, but she has my temperament, I'm afraid."

"Well, that explains some things." The doctor grinned. "She has some of your looks, too. That hair of hers is something."

"Would you like to come calling, Doc?" Simon's mouth twitched, but his eyes couldn't conceal the humor there.

"She isn't spoken for?"

"Whatever gave you that idea?"

"Well, I thought maybe she and Will . . ."

"Not that I know of. But then, I don't know what happened tonight, either. I guess you'll just have to take it up with her."

Chase grinned. "I'll do that. Maybe tomorrow, if this baby decides to get here soon." He started to leave, then turned back. "Seriously, Simon, keep him in bed. A blow like that can kill a man."

▩ 5 ▩

A sign creaked as gusts of wind rocked it, and somewhere a shutter banged back and forth. Will rode into town slowly, his horse kicking up the powdered dust on the street, making the air thick and hard to breathe. He felt eyes on his back, and it sent a curious chill up his spine. The town looked deserted, but a curtain dropping back into place made his skin crawl. He tried to shake the feeling, but it persisted. Something was wrong here—he knew it as well as he knew his name—and he got a sick feeling in his gut.

There was something at the end of the street, but he couldn't quite make it out through the air that shimmered in the heat. There was black, a lot of black, and he rode toward it, knowing that what was there waited for him. As he got closer, he could see the black shapes were people, and they were looking at him, watching, but no one would meet his eyes. He rode through them slowly, floating almost, and then he saw the coffin, crude and handmade, and in the coffin was Charity.

Awareness came to him slowly.

He opened his eyes, squinting them against the light, and saw Maggie curled up in a big rocking chair next to the bed, sleeping. The sun was shining in the window, turning her hair to fire, and he thought for an instant he'd died and gone to heaven, but then she stirred, and her eyes opened, and she smiled at him.

"Good morning, sleepyhead," she said softly. "That was quite a nap."

59

"How long have I been out?" His voice was harsh and rasping, surprising him.

"Two days," she answered as she stood up and came to smooth the hair back from his face. Her hand was cool and soothing, making his headache seem better. Two days? "Where's Simon?" he asked and tried to sit up.

"I'll get him. You just take it easy. The doctor said you were to stay flat on your back until he had a chance to look at you."

"Chase? He's been here?"

She blushed, and he noticed. "I'll be right back," she said.

He heard her go down the stairs, and then Simon came up. Had she gone to get Chase?

"Well, welcome back!" Simon grinned at his friend. "We were beginning to wonder if you'd ever wake up."

"What happened?" Will asked and slowly shook his head, trying to remember.

"That's what we'd like to know." Simon laughed. "Maggie said something about hitting you over the head and getting you back to the house. You blacked out."

Will nodded. It was coming back now. He had been about to change out of his wet longjohns . . . he moved his hand down his side. Well, at least she hadn't gotten him out of them. He tried to sit up again, and this time Simon helped him, putting several plump feather pillows behind his back. He felt slightly dizzy, but all right otherwise.

"I've got things I need to do, business to attend to. If you'll help me—" Will began, but Simon cut him off.

"You're not going anywhere, and there isn't anything you need to do that can't wait a few more days. Doc needs to check you out before you move out of that bed."

Will sighed and closed his eyes. He needed to get away from Maggie before he did something stupid. He needed to finish with Greeley and be done with his past. He wondered again about Maggie's blush when Chase's name was mentioned. What was going on there?

He opened his eyes again as he heard footsteps coming up the stairs. Maggie came back into the room, her cheeks rosy with the cold and her recent exertion, Chase on her heels.

"Well, how do you feel?" the doctor asked as he took off his coat and bent over his patient, checking his eyes and stitches.

"Okay, I guess. My head hurts a bit, but I've been worse. I need to get out of here, Chase."

"Now, why would you want to leave when you have a nurse as pretty as Maggie?" he asked and threw a grin in her direction, causing her to blush again. That irritated Will, and then it irritated him more because it bothered him. "She's been sitting here in that chair the whole time taking care of you. She even ate her meals here. Why, I'd even stay in bed for that," Chase teased.

Will looked at Maggie and saw that her face was red from more than the cold.

"Who took care of my . . . personal needs?"

Simon grinned. Maggie turned even redder.

Will closed his eyes. Maybe she had gotten him out of his pants. He'd been out cold. He wondered what else had gone on.

"We'd best be getting out of here, Maggie," Simon said, still grinning, "so the Doc can check him out."

Maggie felt as if she were floating on air, she was so filled with relief that the man she loved was alive. She'd been afraid the first day when he didn't awaken, but the fear had turned to terror the second day. She had left Will in Simon's care long enough to seek out the doctor and demand that he tell her the truth. Chase had tried to reassure her that Will's recovery would take time, but she was so burdened with guilt she wouldn't listen. She knew she'd killed him.

As she'd bathed and taken care of him, fearing he'd die from not eating, fearing he'd never wake up, it had hit her with a stunning blow that she loved him. She told herself she couldn't possibly be in love with a man she'd only just met, but her heart told her otherwise.

She had shaved his face and run her fingers over every plane. She had bathed his body, reveling in the hard strength of it. She hadn't known a man's body could look like that. Simon had stretched the truth when he'd let Will think she'd taken care of his personal needs, because Simon himself had done that, but she had done everything else, staying in his room until her uncle had come and forced her to leave to take care of her own needs.

"He suffered a tremendous injury to his skull," Chase explained to Simon and Maggie later, "but he was totally lucid today, and that's a very good sign. A couple of days in bed, and he should be good as new."

Quick, hot tears filled Maggie's eyes, and she turned away to get the coffee and two cups for the men. She was relieved that Will was going to be well again, but she suddenly felt the effects of two days with no sleep and lots of worry. She stumbled a bit, and Chase was at her side immediately.

"I'm fine," she said, pushing him away from her.

"No, you're not. You're exhausted, and you need to get some rest. I don't need another patient, even one as lovely as you."

"Doctor, I'm fine. I've just been worried about him."

"He means so much to you, then?" he asked gently.

"Of course not!" she snapped back. "I simply feel responsible for his condition. After all, I hit him." She turned to pour Simon's coffee to hide the blush she felt rising maddeningly to her cheeks.

"In that case, perhaps you'd consent to accompany me to a dance next Saturday night. They have them every week when the roads are passable, and this will be the first of the season."

She appealed desperately to Simon, but he buried his face in his cup. She didn't want to go with the doctor, but if she turned him down, she'd have come up with a legitimate excuse, and she hadn't one. She turned to him with what she hoped was a delighted smile and answered, "I'd be happy to go with you, if it's all right with my uncle."

Simon gave a sort of choking sound, then shook his head, amusement barely concealed in his eyes. "I've no objections whatsoever."

"Fine!" Chase exclaimed. "I'll be here by seven to pick you up."

Three days later, Maggie and Will were in his room, and she had been reading to him from the newspaper. An article on the coming election had spurred a political debate between them.

"But Cleveland has proven that he's honest, and his actions follow his beliefs. I think he deserves another chance at the White House."

"He's a Democrat, Maggie, and he's stepping on a lot of toes with his so-called reforms. He'll never get reelected," Will declared.

Will was much recovered, although Chase had told him it would do him good to spend a few more days in bed; having Maggie there every day had made it seem a good idea. They had had several lively discussions during the hours they'd spent together, and he had been delighted to discover that she wasn't an empty-headed female with nothing on her mind but gowns and balls.

"Harrison has been trying for four years to settle the issue of the tariff, and spending the surplus created by the high rates doesn't make economic sense. His 'billion-dollar Congress' has gone a long way toward economic ruin for this country." Maggie jumped up from her chair beside the bed and paced the floor. "Cleveland is cautious about spending."

"Cleveland spent ten thousand dollars to give grain seed to farmers in Texas, where it wouldn't grow because of the drought. You don't call that throwing money away? And he's the one who wanted to reduce the high protection tariffs in the first place. How much worse off would the country be if Harrison hadn't kept the tariffs high and made the surplus possible?"

"Do you think General Weaver would be better?" Maggie spoke of the People's Party candidate, who denounced money power.

"No!" Will answered, thoroughly enjoying the discussion. "Why, he'd ruin us all with his talk of government ownership of the telegraph and railroad!"

Maggie, too, was enjoying the discussion as she had

the ones around her own dinner table. "Oh, how I wish I could vote!" she exclaimed.

"You can here in Wyoming. You know that," he told her.

"I'm not a resident. And besides, I won't be here then. I'll be going home in a few months," she said a little wistfully. There was so much yet she wanted to do and see, and already she felt her time was running out. This was her first taste of freedom, of venturing beyond the confines of her home and the pages of a newspaper or book, and she didn't want it to end.

Her words brought a chill to Will's heart. During the past few days, he had felt himself come alive, beginning to care again about the world around him. For too long his world had been defined by the whereabouts of Jake Greeley and the confrontation that would come when he finally caught up with him. He had thrown himself into the building of the ranch because he was so full of frustration and anger that he had to vent his feelings somehow. It was no good to live that way, though, and he was going to have to settle the matter. If Greeley was coming back to Wyoming, to Millie, then Will had to be ready for him.

"Why do you have to go home?" he asked her. He wondered if she was, indeed, engaged to be married.

She smiled at him. "I can hardly stay here forever. My parents will be coming in the fall, and I'll be going back to South Carolina with them."

He wanted to ask her why she'd come, but it wasn't right to dig into someone's past. Maybe she just wanted to see some of the world. There didn't have to be a reason, he figured.

"Are you hungry?" she asked him and, at his affirmative reply, she went downstairs to get his meal ready. Thoughts of going home had saddened her, and she didn't want to talk about it, especially to Will. Simon was at the stove, stirring yet another pot of stew. He turned to her when she came in and smiled.

"I think our patient can take some biscuits today with

his meal. His stomach seems to have recovered completely."

She laughed. "His appetite has, too. It seems like he never gets filled up." She got the tray and began placing dishes on it.

Simon studied his niece and noted how tired she looked. The past few days had been trying for her. "Kate has been begging me to send you over there for a visit. Why don't you run over there now, and I'll take care of Will."

She started to protest, but he cut her off. "You've been in Wyoming for almost a week and you haven't seen anything or anybody yet. We'll be going out to the ranch soon, but you need to get out of the house. It's a nice day, too, warm and sunny. It will do you good."

Later, as Maggie walked the short distance along the boardwalks to Kate's, she did feel better, although her idea of warm differed greatly from Simon's. She could fill her lungs with the fresh, cool air, however, and it was warm enough that she didn't need to cover her head. Simon had cautioned her to go through the side door and avoid the saloon, so she made her way around the building, then stepped inside the hallway and knocked on Kate's door.

"Maggie! I was beginning to think you'd never come!" Kate hugged her as she pulled her inside and took her cloak. "I told Simon you had to get out of there. Being in a sick room is so depressing."

"Believe me, it wasn't depressing at all. Far from it, in fact," Maggie replied, following Kate into the kitchen.

"Ooooh, do I detect a certain attraction to your patient?" Kate raised her eyebrows and looked at Maggie.

Maggie blushed. "Of course not. It's just that I enjoyed it. I've never nursed anyone before."

Kate laughed. "I can clearly see we should have gotten you out of there sooner. Falling in love with the patient is a common pitfall of nursing, you know."

"It isn't like that." Maggie blushed an even deeper red.

Kate got out two cups, put a spoonful of tea in each,

then poured hot water from the kettle on the stove into them. "Why don't you sit down and tell me about it?"

Maggie sat down and stirred her tea. "There isn't anything to tell. Will is a very nice man." She grinned. "And he argues politics like my father."

"Like your father. Hmmmm. And yet there isn't anything to tell."

Maggie stirred her tea and watched the grounds swirl before they settled to the bottom. "Kate, how do you know when you're in love?"

"I don't know. You just wake up one day and you know." Kate kept her eyes on her own cup, not wanting Maggie to see her smile. "Why, do you think you might be in love with Will?"

"I don't know. It seems silly—I've only known him a few days really—but there's something about him. I can't describe it. I only know that I was going to marry a man back home and I didn't feel any of this with him."

"Are you planning to marry him when you go back?" Kate wondered why Maggie had come west with Simon, but he hadn't explained, and she hadn't asked.

"No." Maggie said the single word, then quickly took a sip of her tea to help her swallow the lump in her throat.

"Do you want to talk about it? I'm a pretty good listener," Kate said gently.

Maggie's eyes filled, and she couldn't keep the tears from spilling over as she told Kate about Charles. She told her what she hadn't been able to tell her parents about the overheard conversation so many years before, in which she'd been described as "horsey," and certainly didn't have her mother's looks. After that, she explained, she had always felt big and awkward, and had quit going to the dances and parties because she didn't know how to act. Kate got up and hugged the girl to her side, handing her a handkerchief.

"I'm sorry," Maggie said, "I'm not usually a crybaby."

"Oh, honey, don't apologize. You've had a rough time of it. Heaven knows you deserve a good cry." She held Maggie a bit longer, then brought her another handkerchief and a cool, damp cloth to put on her eyes. "My husband said he chose me because I was tall and looked regal to him. He was going to be rich some day, said nothing was going to stop him."

"What happened to him?" Maggie asked.

Kate came back to the present and gave a short laugh. "Oh, he never made it to rich. Things got in his way after all. But the point is, you are a beautiful woman, Maggie. You just need to take another look at yourself and realize what's there. Come with me." She led the way to her dressing room where she sat Maggie down in a small chair before a dressing table with a mirror.

Two hours later, Maggie looked at her reflection in the mirror and slowly lifted her hand to touch her cheek. She had to see if this vision that gazed back at her was real. Her hair was piled high on her head, with saucy ringlets tumbling down the back and wisps of curls framing her face. Kate had insisted on a tiny hint of color on her lips and cheekbones to accentuate them, and the effect was dramatic.

"Well? What do you think?" Kate stood back and surveyed her handiwork.

"I don't know," Maggie answered honestly. "It's amazing. My mother tried for years to get me to take an interest in my appearance, but I didn't think it would do any good, so I just went along my own way." Her voice held a touch of wonder.

"Try this," Kate said as she held a dress up for Maggie to see. It was a deep claret in color, more daring than anything Maggie had ever worn before. She looked at it, and her heartbeat quickened a bit.

"Oh, Kate, I can't."

"But why ever not? It suits you perfectly. It's the wrong color for me—my hair's more orange than yours, I'm afraid—and I only wore it once."

"But it's so beautiful. What if I ruin it?" But already in her mind, she wanted it. She knew she shouldn't, but oh, to feel desirable just once in her life, not to feel clumsy and out of place.

"You won't ruin it," Kate said with a laugh, "but it

doesn't matter, anyway. I'm not loaning it to you, I'm giving it to you."

When Maggie left sometime later, she felt like Cinderella, transformed for the ball, her feet encased in glass slippers.

Will was missing Maggie. She'd been gone for several hours, and he'd had only Simon for company. It wasn't that Simon was bad company, but Maggie was better. The past days had offered a haven in his troubled mind. Maggie was so good, so natural. She didn't have the wiles and coquettishness of other women he'd known, and he knew as sure as he knew his name that she'd be true to the man she loved. It had almost seemed as if they'd been married, as she'd cared for him here in his room, and he had been hard-pressed not to pull her down on the bed with him and make proper love to her.

Would she marry him? he wondered. She was so much younger than he was. Maybe she just thought of him as a nice friend of her Uncle Simon. Or maybe she saw him as one of the hired hands and wouldn't consider him suitable. He couldn't believe he was even having these thoughts, but Maggie was someone special. She was a woman a man could be friends with, as well as love, and she was a rarity. He fought with himself, trying to forget the man he'd vowed to kill, trying to put it in the past and convince himself he had a right to a good life with another woman.

Thoughts tumbled around in his head, and he made disjointed plans to build his own cabin on the ranch, back closer to the mountain in a clearing in the aspens that he liked. Maggie would like it there, he knew, from the first tentative green in the spring to the solemn stillness of deep winter, when the whole world seemed shrouded in white. He'd show her the meadows around Emma Matilda Lake, and they'd ride their horses up Pilgrim Creek. He'd show her the summer grazing grounds of the elk and take her out some starlit night to hear the bull elks' bugles floating across the darkness.

They'd have children, too, maybe four or five. He

wanted some sturdy little boys, but he'd like a little girl just like Maggie, with that hair that glowed like new copper, and her smile. They'd all learn to ride and rope, and they'd build a wonderful future together.

He'd take her up into the mountains, to a small glacial pool he liked, and they'd have a picnic there. Then he'd make love to her in a field of wildflowers and pick her a bouquet of them to remember it by.

But surely she wasn't going to want to marry a man who did nothing but lie around in bed all day. He threw back the covers, deciding his doctor's time limit had just run out, and went down the stairs to take a bath. He felt aches and pains he'd never known before as he lifted the kettles of water on and off the stove and decided the bed rest hadn't done him any good at all.

Half an hour later, he was at his mirror combing his hair when he heard the back door open. He swallowed hard and tried to slow his racing pulse, but it only got worse. His stomach felt as if something hot and heavy had settled there, but he took a deep breath and slowly went down the stairs.

She had just come into the front room and was placing her cloak across the back of a chair when he turned the corner and saw her. His breath stopped.

The firelight was playing across her, setting his senses on fire, and making her glow like a torch in the darkness. She was in some kind of clingy red gown, and as he moved slowly toward her, he could see that it was a Maggie he'd never seen before. What had she done to herself? he wondered. She was beautiful, but there was something . . .

And then he saw it. She had painted her face, painted it like a whore. She had just come from Kate's, and he knew what had happened. Dark fury swept through him, and he shook with it as he stopped in front of her. She had lowered her eyes, then slowly lifted her long eyelashes and raised her head to look him straight in the eye.

"What have you done to yourself?" he demanded angrily, afraid to touch her, afraid of losing control.

She looked startled, then stepped back from him. "I . . . Kate . . ." she stammered, suddenly unsure of herself and unable to understand his meaning.

"What have you let that woman do to you?" He took her by the arm and pulled her closer.

"Will, what's wrong with you?" she cried as she jerked her arm out of his grip. "I haven't done anything except fix my hair and get a new gown!"

"You've painted your face. Why did you do that?"

A crimson blush crept up her neck and darkened her cheeks even more. "What I do with my face is none of your business!"

"None of my—damn you, Maggie!" He pulled her to him roughly, not knowing what he meant to do, but finding himself drawn to her mouth by a current of fire.

"Will, Maggie." Simon's voice threw them apart as if they'd been doused with ice water.

Simon shut the door behind him and crossed to the fireplace, where he picked up two logs to add to the flames. "It's good to see you out of bed, Will. I was just coming to ask if you were up to supper at the hotel." He straightened and had to hide the twitch in his mouth as he turned to his niece. "Maggie, I must say you look more beautiful than I've ever seen you. No wonder Kate suggested we take you out tonight. Don't you agree, Will?"

Will had turned away from them, fighting to get his emotions under control, but now he turned back, not daring to look at Maggie. "I'm not sure it's such a good idea to go out on my first day out of bed."

"Oh, well, then, if you don't feel up to it, perhaps you can join us another time. Do you need anything before we go? There's some stew on the stove and biscuits left in the pie safe."

Will wasn't sure he could handle being close to Maggie right now, but on the other hand, he didn't want her going out without him looking the way she did, so he answered, "Actually, it would be real nice to taste some cooking other than yours for once. I'll just go change."

Simon couldn't contain his grin as he watched Will

leave. He wasn't sure what had been going on when he'd come upon them, but it was, after all, his duty to protect the innocence of his niece.

"You haven't said a word, Maggie. Are you feeling all right?"

Maggie was wishing the floor would open up and swallow her. She was mortified that she and Will had been found in a very compromising situation, and she was sure every inch of her was beet red.

"I'm . . . fine, Uncle Simon, but we really don't have to go out for my sake. Why don't you and Kate just go?"

"Oh, no, the whole point of the thing is to give you an evening out and give me a chance to show you off. I'm sure the town is anxious to get a look at you, and Kate reminded me that I'd been remiss in my duties by keeping you inside the whole time you've been here. Now, I'll just get ready, and then we can go."

Simon closed the door to his bedroom, and Maggie sank down into a chair. How on earth was she to get through a dinner party with Will at the same table with her? And what had happened between them? He hadn't, as Kate had declared he would, fallen at her feet. He had seemed angry, and she didn't know what she'd done to cause it, except try to look beautiful for him. Now she felt like a fool with the color on her face. She didn't understand men at all, and tears started in her eyes. She furiously wiped them away, then realized she'd have to go up to her room to repair the damage.

Maggie's heart pounded as she climbed the steps and passed the room in which Will was changing his clothes, and she thought of him in bed, and what the sight of his bare chest had done to her insides. While she was shaving him one day she had looked down at him to see his eyes fastened on the open front of her dress. She had shamefully kept right on with her task, but she had been so conscious of his interest, she'd cut him. They had looked deep into each other's eyes while she had slowly dabbed the blood away and washed his face with a warm, wet cloth. Then she had washed his chest, massaging the

soap in small circles on his warm skin, then rinsing him
just as slowly. All the while their eyes never left one
another's, smoldering with the fires that were raging
elsewhere in their bodies. Or at least that was the way she
had felt.

Glory! And she had thought she could love Charles.
He seemed such a pale imitation of a man after Will. Will
would never let his father or anyone else tell him whom
he should or should not marry, or anything else for that
matter. Will was strong, strong enough for a headstrong
wife with ideas of her own. But had she been mistaken
about his feelings? Had she been carried away by her
own?

When she got her lamp lit and looked at her face in the
mirror, she could see that she'd have to wash it. The color
on her cheeks had smudged when she'd wiped her tears
away. She did it slowly, feeling let down. And she had
come home so excited about having Will see her like
that.

She heard his door open, then his steps fade away on
the stairs, and a bit later the front door close. She looked
at herself in the mirror and knew that she hadn't really
changed. She was still the same plain Margaret Longyear
who hadn't inherited any of her mother's looks. She
picked up a shawl to wear over her dress, not wanting to
anger him any further, then followed him downstairs.

The evening had a warm touch to it, as if a breeze from
somewhere down south had wandered out of bounds and
had settled in the valley for the night. People strolled on
the boardwalks and went in and out of various establishments. Kate's place was milling with a good-natured
crowd as they pulled up in front. Several people greeted
Simon as he made his way inside, and others told Will
how good it was to see him around again. Maggie was
introduced to three or four men, and by the time Simon
came back with Kate, Maggie had attracted a small
crowd, which Will was trying to disperse.

"I see you've been noticed," Kate commented, making
sure Will heard, "so expect some gentleman callers."

Will frowned. He couldn't very well declare himself

right now, but he sure as hell didn't want any cowboys sniffing around Maggie. He decided to make it quite obvious that she was claimed, without actually making the commitment, so he tucked her tight against his side, and with his arm around her back escorted her into the hotel.

Maggie was furious about his proprietary attitude, unasked for and unwanted after his actions at the house, but she could hardly make a scene on a public street, so she held herself stiffly and as far away from him as she could get.

The hotel dining room was quiet and elegant. There were many women in lovely dresses, and their partners wore evening clothes like Simon's. Will was dressed in simpler clothing, but he had on a white shirt and a string tie, with tight-fitting black pants and boots. The outfit was no different than those worn by the remaining men in the room, but in Maggie's opinion, he looked absolutely splendid. His long-sleeved white shirt seemed to make his shoulders even wider, and the black pants emphasized his narrow hips and strong thighs. He had combed his hair into place before leaving the house, and although she preferred his hair loose, it made him look very distinguished and almost aristocratic coupled with his height and chiseled features.

Maggie found herself admiring his thighs and, embarrassed, raised her head and met his smoldering gaze, which was so intense it almost took her breath away. What was he trying to do to her?

Simon and Kate stopped to talk to someone, and Will took the opportunity as he led Maggie to a table to bend down and whisper in her ear, "Simon was right."

She looked quickly down, and he knew she'd been hurt. He tried again. "You really do look beautiful," he said as he pushed her chair in.

She blushed, and his warm breath sent shivers down her back. "I'm not even pretty, but thank you." She pulled her shawl tighter around her sounders and stared out a window at the black night. But all she saw was her own reflection, mocking her.

He looked at her quizzically. Surely she must realize how beautiful she was, even without the fancy adornments, but she didn't seem to be the type to fish for compliments. He took the chair next to her and sat studying her.

Will watched her reflection in the glass, fascinated with her looks. She had a graceful bearing he'd never seen in a woman before. Her eyes were large and dark and wide set. Her nose was small and straight, her lips full and sensuous. And her hair, that glorious, shining, copper hair—what would it feel like to have her above him with it falling around his face? He remembered the feel of her smooth, warm skin beneath his hands and wished she'd take off the shawl so he could again see the peachy color of it. But he wouldn't likely have that chance now, because he had hurt her, and he knew he would somehow have to make it right again. But how could he explain it all to her?

"My, you two are certainly quiet!" Kate's voice was full of laughter as she and Simon reached the table. "Have you run out of things to talk about already?"

Will blamed Kate for the change in Maggie and found it hard to be polite to her. He looked at Maggie. Her eyes, as she turned to look at him, had a sadness in them that hadn't been there before.

"Well, I'm ready to order," Simon announced, breaking the awkward silence, "so let's get the waitress over here. How about the rest of you?"

They got their meal ordered and settled into small talk.

"Will, I went out to the ranch again today. The men are getting restless." Simon smiled. "It must be spring fever."

"It gets to the best of us. We need to take Maggie out there pretty soon, or she's going to think there isn't a ranch." He tried the light banter to see if he could bring her out of her sadness.

"Oh, when can we go?" Maggie asked eagerly. She felt the need to get of town where she could walk and ride again.

"How about tomorrow? That is, if Maggie can get packed that fast." Will looked askance at her.

"Of course I can."

Simon looked doubtful. "Remember, I was there when you packed before." He turned to the others. "It took her, her mother, and about a dozen servants the better part of a week to get her stuff packed to come out here."

"Oh, that isn't true, Uncle Simon!"

"I remember the size of the pile at the station in Rock Springs. I believe it," Will said with a perfectly straight face.

"And we don't even have any servants here." Simon rubbed the back of his neck, thinking. "I suppose I could have Dave and Pete come in to help. Of course, they saw the pile. I may have to pay them extra to do it."

"But most of it is still on the wagon! It won't take long at all for me to gather the few things I brought into the house."

"Few things?" Simon raised his eyebrows. "You call two huge trunks and three bags a few things? Not to mention the odd items you've dug out since we got here."

Their food came then, and Maggie was spared any further abuse. The sad look had left her eyes, and they glittered in anticipation. She asked questions about the ranch and the working of it, and they told her all she wanted to know and more. Will felt the need to get her out to the ranch, where he wouldn't have to share her with Kate or anyone else. He was beginning to wish he was still in his room in bed, in need of her nursing. He knew, even if she didn't, that things were going to happen that might lose them to each other forever, and these next few days might be all the time they had. He wanted to savor every minute spent with her before he had to go.

He did have to go, although he'd tried to convince himself otherwise. He just couldn't go on with his life until he'd buried the past; and until Jake Greeley was dead, the past would keep rearing its ugly head and taunting him. There was no peace until it was done. And so he joined in with the talk, even as he felt the presence of the man he had to kill closing in around him.

They were laughing at Simon's story of Pete's wife, Bertha, and how it was starting to drive her plumb crazy, being cooped up with him all winter as she was, when Maggie looked up and met Chase Wolcott's eyes across the room. She smiled at him, and he crossed to their table.

"Good evening to you all," he said as he came up, "and, Will, good to see you out of that room finally. I was beginning to fear you'd stay there forever."

"You're the one who told me to stay put for a few more days!" Will accused.

"Yes, and you didn't even put up a fight. I wonder why?"

"No doubt it was the wonderful food," Simon put in, and they all laughed as Chase pulled up a chair.

"You ladies are certainly looking lovely tonight. All eyes in the room seem to be on you." Maggie blushed as Kate thanked Chase prettily.

"Simon, I see you rode out to your ranch today. How's Bertha?"

"She said to thank you for the powders. They did wonders for her headaches. But she also said if she could just get Pete out of the cabin, her head wouldn't bother her anymore!" They all laughed, and then Will pointedly mentioned that they were all moving out to the ranch the following day.

"Tomorrow! I'll have to come out early to pick up Miss Longyear for the dance Saturday, then." He smiled at Maggie. "We are still on, aren't we?"

Maggie caught Kate's slight nod and remembered her resolution not to let Will know how she felt about him, so she sent a warm smile the young doctor's way. "Of course. What time shall I be ready? I don't know how far away the ranch is, I'm afraid."

"Oh, I'll be by around five. It takes a little over an hour to drive in, but I have a call to make out your way, and I'll just pick you up on the way back. I have room for two more, so maybe Pete and Bertha can ride in with us. You may even want to get ready at the house here in town, as there'll be plenty of time. The dance starts at eight, but everybody gets there early to socialize."

"That's very thoughtful, Dr. Wolcott. I'll be ready at five." She felt horrible leading him on when all she could think about was Will, and she didn't dare meet his eyes as the doctor stood up.

"See you Saturday, then. Please excuse me for now. I was just leaving to check on a patient when I saw you." He nodded to the others and told Will, "You take it easy now."

After he left, Simon said he would walk Kate back to her place, and Will and Maggie could come along whenever they were ready. Will stood up until Kate left and then sat back down in the chair Chase had vacated. Will had to talk to her without so many people within hearing and needed to get her outside. He wanted to find out what Chase meant to her, but if he got her alone, he was afraid he'd not be able to keep from kissing her again. Chase had been right about one thing. Every man in the room had stared at Maggie at some point during the evening, and he didn't like it. But she hadn't even seemed to notice it.

Maggie looked up at him then. She felt guilty for leading the doctor on, because she truly felt nothing for him. She started to say that Chase meant nothing to her, but then remembered that she wasn't going to let Will know how she felt, so she remained silent.

Will felt the eyes of curious onlookers, and decided they should leave. "Are you ready?" he asked her softly.

She nodded, and he pulled out her chair, then guided her to the cloak room and wrapped her woolen cape around her shoulders. His hand brushed her shoulder, and she jumped away as if she'd been burned.

Once out on the boardwalk, his irritation at the doctor reached the point where he had to ask, "You aren't really going to the dance with Chase, are you?"

Maggie looked up at him, her gaze level and cold. "Of course I am. Why would you think otherwise?"

"Well, when did this all come about?" He knew he sounded like a petulant child but couldn't help himself.

"He asked me one of the days he came to see you. Uncle Simon said it was acceptable for me to go with him."

Well, he certainly hadn't wasted any time. But why would Simon give his permission, anyway? Will wondered. He knew Chase was a womanizer. "And you said 'yes' just like that? You don't even know the man."

"I didn't know you a week ago, either, and I've certainly done a lot more than go to a dance with you," she shot back, then could have cut her tongue off. When, when would she learn to keep her mouth shut?

Will didn't stop to think of who might be watching. His emotions were stretched almost to the breaking point, and her reference to stolen intimacies fired his imagination and caused him to react physically. He wanted her and felt utterly frustrated that circumstances kept him from her. He pulled her roughly into his arms and poured all that frustration and desire into his kiss, trying, without knowing it, to make her understand that he had made his claim on her.

Maggie was at first stunned that he had grabbed her in such a manner, then found herself lost in the utter passion with which he possessed her lips. When he released her, she stood unsteadily for a moment, furious eyes locked with his, then she slapped him on the face, turned around and, taking long strides, walked back to the house. She didn't care that her shoes and Kate's dress were ruined. How dare he humiliate her on a public street like that? How dare he play with her emotions and treat her like some woman of easy virtue? Her own reactions to him came to mind, but she pushed those thoughts away as she walked out her anger at herself for being so foolish, and at him for being so . . . him.

Will knew he should stop her before she ruined her gown in the slushy mud, but he thought she probably deserved it. How could she remind him of those times and still go to the dance with Chase? Had he been wrong about her? Was she just another pretty girl who didn't care how many hearts she broke? She hadn't ever given any indication that she was, though. He gave a great sigh and followed her, getting madder with every step he took.

Maggie had no more than slammed the door when he yanked it open again.

"You've ruined your dress!" he thundered at her.

"I don't care!" she yelled back, and as if to prove it, she threw off her cloak and began tearing the dress off as she stomped through the house to the stairs. He followed her, still railing. "What's wrong with you?"

"Nothing's wrong with me," she cried, "nothing!" She had reached the bottom of the stairway and had to leave off trying to unhook the back to lift the sodden skirts as she ran up to the top. She turned, and he was following so close behind her that he almost collided with her.

"Then why are you acting like this?"

"Like what?"

"I tell you you're pretty, and you say you're not. I kiss you, and you slap my face. I thought we had something together, damn it, and you go to a dance with another man!"

"Had something? I was nursing you because it was my fault you got hurt, and that's all! You have no right to tell me how to dress or anything else!"

"Maggie . . ." he started, but she twisted away from him.

"Get away from me, Will Sutten!" She ran into her room, slamming the door shut and bolting it. Will stood there, angry enough to kick the door in, but he knew he'd be making a big mistake if he did. He heard Simon come in downstairs, and that calmed him down in a hurry. He met his partner in the kitchen.

"Damn it, Simon, it's all gone to hell! I have to get out of here!" he ground out as he came into the room and threw his coat down on a chair, then grabbed a cup and filled it with coffee.

"Do you mind filling me in? I seem to have missed something here," Simon answered calmly. Neither he nor Kate had missed the current flowing between Maggie and Will during the evening, but he wanted to hear it in Will's own words.

"You didn't miss anything, but apparently I did. When did all this with Chase and Maggie come about?"

"I didn't know there was 'all this.' I thought they were just going to a dance together."

"That's the point. I thought I knew her pretty well. I guess I was wrong."

"Had you given her reason to believe you might be in love with her?"

"No! Of course not!" Will answered, angry that Simon was putting him on the spot, but realizing that he and Maggie were both right. He had no right to interfere in her life.

Simon looked at his friend's anguished face. "Do you love her?"

Did he love her? He wanted her, but he couldn't very well tell Simon that every time he was around her she made his blood boil, and he could think of nothing but bedding her. Could he love her? Or were his emotions so bound up with his memories of Charity and hatred for the man who had killed her that he wasn't fit to love anyone? A vision of Maggie in the bath came to him, and he closed his eyes.

"No. I don't love her." *Liar*. He turned and stared out at the night, his hands shoved into his back pockets. "Hell, I've only known her two weeks."

Will's eyes took on the look Simon knew so well, the one that made him expect to wake up one morning and find Will gone. He was in another place, seeing things Simon couldn't even guess at.

"Are you leaving?"

"I don't know."

"There's still the man you have to kill, then."

"I thought I could forget it, but I realized tonight I can't."

"You might be killed yourself."

"I know that. That's why I can't tell her."

Simon sighed. He knew his friend needed a strong woman to make him forget his past, and he had hoped

Maggie would be that woman. He fixed Will with a piercing look. "I won't have her hurt. If you have to go kill this man, do it, and then come back to her. But don't you take her heart and then go get yourself killed."

🕸 6 🕸

Will was having a hard time pretending to be indifferent to Maggie. He'd saddled up and ridden far ahead of the buckboard on the way out to the ranch, although he'd wanted to point out his favorite spots along the way and tell her all he knew about the valley. When he reached the gate, he'd waited for them to pass through, then closed it behind them and rode ahead again, but he was itching to hear her comments on the ranch.

Even though he'd told Simon he wouldn't be a partner, he'd helped build the ranch into what it was and was extremely proud of it. The bloodlines he'd started with had built a herd of horses unequaled for a five-hundred-mile radius around Jackson Hole, and they were in demand by the army and private individuals alike.

The ranch itself spread out like a fan from within the folds of a mountain, most of it flat, lush grazing land, with several spring-fed streams running through it. The summer grazing land was higher, up where the elk migrated each spring, and there was plenty of timber, both pine and aspen, on the land.

He was constantly amazed at how it all looked different every day, depending on the weather. At this time of year, the snow covering camouflaged the rough terrain and brought a peaceful feel and sound to the ranch. He would rather Maggie had seen it for the first time in the fall of the year, when the aspens burned orange flames on the hillsides, and the wildflowers spent their last burst of energy in gaudy excess. But it looked good, he thought, as he rounded the last curve and the cabin came into view, sort of homey and solid. Yes, he thought, and I'm looking at it as though I were bringing home my bride, instead of setting out here in a few days to kill a man. His good mood vanished, replaced by frustration and anger that he couldn't let go of the past and couldn't declare his feelings because of it.

When he reached the barn he took his horse inside and unsaddled it, then picked up a brush and began working his frustration out. Pete had been in the barn, and after a bit he wandered over to where Will was vigorously brushing the stallion down.

"You got some bone to pick with that horse?" he asked, then spit into the straw.

Will didn't answer, but kept on brushing with the stiff-bristled brush.

"What'd he do, throw ya?"

"No, he didn't throw me, and what business is it of yours anyway?" he growled.

"Well, I was just wonderin', seein' as how you're takin' the hide right off 'im."

Will stood up and glared at the old man. "Don't you have something better to do?"

"Nope." Pete spit again.

"I'd think with Simon and his niece coming right behind me you'd have something to do to get ready for them," he said pointedly.

Pete spit again. "So that's it."

"What's it?"

"Why that poor dumb animal is gettin' all that abuse."

"What are you *talking* about?"

"Simon's niece. Miss Maggie."

"What in hell does she have to do with anything?"

"So things is still that way."

"What way?"

Pete just smiled at Will, spit again, then maddeningly turned around and sauntered out the door, heading for the house.

Will stood a few seconds staring after the old man, then threw the brush hard against the door after him, causing his horse to shy and rear. Quieting him, Will cursed Pete and Maggie and Simon and the whole blasted world.

Maggie's throat was tight with unshed tears all the way out to the ranch, as she watched Will ride ahead and tried to figure out why things had gone so wrong between them. Why had he gotten so mad at her, and why had she gotten mad back? She only wanted to be friends with him again and have him to talk to, to share her life with. Instead, it was just like back home, when she didn't know how to act around men. She was back to being awkward and out of place.

Well, she would just go to the dance with Chase Wolcott on Saturday night and have a good time. She felt comfortable around the young doctor—probably, she reflected, because she didn't feel the need to act like someone she was not in an effort to impress him. He was no doubt an intelligent man, too, to be a doctor, and she might be able to discuss issues with him without his recoiling in horror. All the time she was thinking these thoughts, she was watching the way Will sat his fine chestnut stallion as he cantered ahead of them.

"We're here!" Simon broke her reverie, and she realized she'd not even noticed the landscape after they'd left town. She'd been so caught up in her own thoughts, she'd passed the whole trip without seeing a thing.

Now she looked around her and was pleasantly surprised at the fine cabin and outbuildings on the place. "What are all these buildings?" she asked.

"The biggest one is the barn, of course." Simon pointed it out proudly. There wasn't another barn so fine in the whole valley. "There's a room, on the side there where the window is, where a boy sleeps in the warmer months, but it's too cold out there now. The long one, over there"—he indicated a low building with several windows and a porch running the length of the front of it—"that's the bunk house. Only four men are there now, but it will hold three times that many."

"Where are the men now?" The place seemed deserted

compared to her home, where there had always been people bustling about their daily work.

"Most of them go into town for the winter. There's not much to do up here when the snow's this deep. Some of them get odd jobs here and there. The other two sheds are the smokehouse and the corncrib, and the open place at the end of the bunkhouse is the woodshed.

"Pete and Bertha live in the little cabin over there by those trees, and this one is the main house." He indicated a large cabin that looked bigger than Maggie had expected, but otherwise was just as he'd described it. "Pete and Bertha move into the big cabin during the coldest months, too, but by this time they've probably moved back to their own place. It takes a lot less wood and coal to heat two places than four, and it gets extremely cold here."

"Colder than home?"

"The worst winter day back there is like springtime here. It gets to forty below pretty often."

"Forty below zero?" asked Maggie, astounded.

"That's right." He smiled at her. "Now maybe you can understand the somewhat unconventional living arrangements. Let's get inside. A good hot cup of coffee would go good about now."

He helped Maggie down from the high seat, then hefted some of her bags out of the back and led the way into the cabin. They crossed a long porch and Maggie stopped at a triangle of iron hanging from a chain, with another straight piece of iron dangling below. At her questioning look, Simon demonstrated by grasping the straight piece and running it gently around the inside of the triangle, producing a clanging sound. He explained that they used it not only to call the men to dinner, but also in an emergency, in which case everyone within hearing distance came running. Simon passed ahead of her and opened a sturdy wooden door, waiting for her to go into the cabin before him.

Maggie loved the house from the moment they entered the kitchen, which was warm and bright from the wood cookstove and the wall of glass windows through which the noonday sun was streaming. The sturdy ceiling beams had baskets and dried herbs and flowers hanging from them. Several pots of red geraniums lined a shelf below the windows, and their spicy scent mingled with those of the wood fire and freshly baked bread. A cast-iron kettle sat on the stove steaming merrily, and a pot of something that smelled like stew bubbled near the back.

A long table, glowing with polish, was set with five places. The blue tin plates and cups were sitting on blue-and-white-checked cloths to protect the table, and another pot of geraniums had been placed in the center. On the simple table there were two cut-glass bowls filled with sparkling jellies that would have graced a table in the finest home.

The room seemed to be a jumble of doorways, with the one through which they'd just come, and five others. She didn't have time to check them all out, for Simon had taken her bags into one of the open doorways, and she followed him into a small room with a bed and dresser. She spied a spot right away for her rocking chair, near the bedside table and close to the lamp for reading. In one corner a closet had been fashioned with pine boards, and a curtain hung from a rod across the opening. The floor was covered with an oval braided rug done in bright colors, and there was a lace-curtained window through which the mountains were visible.

"Well, what do you think?" Simon wanted her approval, and she wholeheartedly gave it.

"I love it! It's everything I ever dreamed a ranch out west would be. I love the setting, the view, the way you have the buildings laid out, but mostly I love this cabin. It's so warm and inviting. I'm going to love staying here." She threw her arms around her uncle. "I am just so grateful to you for bringing me here. I was beginning to think I'd live the rest of my life without seeing anything but Longacres. I mean, I love it there, but I've always dreamed of actually going to the places I've read about all my life. And now here I am." She spun around and out of her bedroom back into the large main room, almost colliding with a tiny woman who was just coming in from one of the other doors with a pie in each hand.

"Oh, my, gracious! I'm sorry!" Maggie apologized and snatched one pie just as it slipped from the woman's hand.

"Well, for heaven's sake! What kind of commotion is going on in here?" the woman scolded.

Laughing, Simon introduced the two women. Bertha was tiny, her white hair wound in a braid on top of her head, her blue eyes covered with wire-rimmed glasses. She was scowling at the moment, and Maggie hoped she wasn't that way always. "Bertha here lets me think I run this place, but actually she does," Simon said. "No one steps out of line when she's around."

"Hmmph," Bertha snorted, "If you'd just use the sense the good Lord gave you, I wouldn't have to keep you in line. And what I'm going to do with this girl around here when Pete says Will and her are sweet on each other, I don't know, but I think it's my duty to stay on here until she leaves or Will moves out, one or the other. I don't have time for all this foolishness, I'll tell you that!" Her speech finished, Bertha scooted back out the door through which she'd come, leaving a breeze with her passing.

Maggie looked at Simon, and they burst out laughing, but managed to snuff it when they heard the tiny woman's staccato steps returning.

"I'm very pleased to meet you, Bertha," Maggie said. "I hope we'll be friends."

Bertha looked Maggie up and down, then nodded abruptly. "Sit. The meal's ready."

As if on cue, Pete came in the back door, slipped out of his coat, and sat in one of the chairs. Bertha didn't spare him a glance but said as she dished up the plates, "Will's not coming, I take it."

"I don't believe so," Pete answered, more subdued than Maggie had ever seen him. She had to suck in her cheeks to keep from laughing at the garrulous man finally silenced, and by such a mere wisp of a woman.

Bertha placed each of their plates in front of them

before sitting down and bowing her head for grace. That finished, she nodded to them, and they began to eat. It was amazing that she had dished out the food without even asking what they might or might not like. Maggie hadn't seen a meal so completely dominated by one person since her own grandmother Margaret had died. But this woman was no more than a servant, really, and Maggie wondered at her authority.

"This is very good, Bertha," she complimented the older woman.

"Thank you," Bertha tersely replied, then returned to her eating.

Maggie tried again. "It's good to see you again, Pete. How have you been?"

Bertha answered for him. "He's been busy."

Pete looked at Maggie helplessly, and Simon wouldn't meet her eyes. He seemed to be having difficulty swallowing, and he took a long drink.

"Uncle Simon," she said as she smiled brightly at him, "tell me all about how you started this ranch. Was there anything here when you bought it, or did you build everything? Did you hire your servants after you built the place up?"

Simon knew the determination in Maggie's eyes; he'd known it years ago in her mother. And he knew what she was getting at. In her eyes, Bertha was a servant, and as such had overstepped the boundaries of propriety. Maggie had been raised in a household where the family's many servants had their place and kept to it. Simon didn't know how to explain about Bertha. He might employ Pete, but Bertha ran the place since the first day she'd stepped on the ranch and grimly set to work cleaning and making a home for two bachelors.

"Will and I had decided to pool our resources and knowledge and become partners. The ranch I had before wasn't suited to the kind of ranching we wanted to do, so we talked about a lot of different places. We kept coming back to this valley. Both of us had been here before, and, well, it kind of gets into your blood." He got up and walked to the stove to get the coffee pot and pour them all a cup of the steaming brew.

"This was a harsh land then and still is. Neighbors here help each other, and that first winter we needed lots of help. Neither Will nor I had ever seen snow or cold like that, and we just weren't prepared for it."

"They were as green as two grown men could be," Bertha interjected, "and they'd be dead if it hadn't been for Pete and me finding them."

"Oh, they prob'ly wouldn't be dead, but they sure woulda been mighty hungry and cold," Pete added.

"Oh, my stars, Pete! You never remember anything right!" Bertha turned to Maggie. "You see, Pete and I were going to town from our cabin on up the creek aways, and we noticed that the new people who lived here hadn't shoveled the snow off their roof, and no smoke was getting out of the chimney. We thought at first maybe they'd just gone to town, but there were no tracks, and we hadn't had new snow for a few days. That's why we were able to get to town. Anyway, we stopped just to see if everything was okay, you know, and Simon here, he opened the door looking like a dead man. I knew right away what was wrong with him, and pulled him outside and made him breathe plenty of clean air, while Pete went in and brought out the other one. They were lucky. I've seen many people die from asphyxia caused by snow blocking their chimney." She shook her head, remembering.

"They really did save our lives. We thought we were sick. We were about out of food and wood, which was probably a good thing, because we didn't have as big a fire as we would have. It was some cold."

"Yep, now that you say it, that's the way it was all right," Pete said.

"Pete, if you can't say anything intelligent, just don't open your mouth," Bertha scolded, and Maggie understood why Pete had fallen silent in her presence.

Simon chuckled. "Bertha took one look at this place, and without anyone even asking her, she dug in and cleaned up a winter's worth of filth and turned a cold, bare cabin into the home you see now. We owe her a lot," he said pointedly to Maggie.

"Well, I owe you, too. You gave Pete a job when he couldn't run his own place anymore. On account of his legs gave out, don't you know," she said to Maggie in an aside.

"So, we have a mutual agreement. Bertha takes care of us here in the winter, and in the spring, when we don't need so much heat, she goes back to her own cabin. We aren't home much then anyway, and she just occasionally gives the place a sweeping out. Pete takes it pretty easy in the winter, when his arthritis gives him fits, and in the warmer months he serves as range cook."

Maggie was deeply chagrined. Now that she thought of it, she hadn't seen any servants such as they'd had back home—just neighbors helping out. That was kind of a nice concept, she thought.

"I can't abide town life, so this way I get to keep on living out here, and doing my Christian duty, too." Bertha stood and started picking up dishes. Maggie rose also and began to help, but Bertha stopped her. "I been doing this for a good number of years. I don't need help. You just get your stuff unpacked and put away. From the looks of that wagon, though, I don't know how you're going to get it all in that one room. Maybe we'll have to store some of the stuff in the front room for the time being, and then when the men go back out on the range and we open our cabin again, you can store it in our room. Maybe it would be a good idea for Will to sleep in the bunkhouse for a while." This last was directly pointedly at Simon.

"Will is not going to be put out of his own house, Bertha. You're here to act as chaperon, and Pete and I will be around for a few weeks yet."

Maggie blushed, wondering what had been said about her and Will to make Bertha so suspicious. She must remember to act with the utmost discretion and not give her feelings away for anything. She had the feeling that Bertha was very intuitive.

"We'll get the rest of the things from outside and put the horses away." Simon and Pete rose to go out.

"We'll be needing help with all those trunks," Pete said.

"Where is Will, anyway?" Simon asked.

"He's in the bunkhouse. Hadn't seen the boys for a while, you know." Pete winked at Simon and made a not-too-subtle inclination of his head toward Maggie.

"Oh, I see. Well, maybe we can get Dave to come and help." They went out, and Maggie stood by the door to open it when they came with her trunks. Half an hour later, the wagon was finally emptied, and Maggie's room was full. She was beginning to have regrets about bringing all of these things, but it really hadn't seemed that much when they'd been packing. She pulled a trunk around and opened the lid.

Tears sprang to her eyes when she saw the paper-wrapped objects she had packed with her mother. It seemed like years ago, but it was just a little over three weeks. Did her parents miss her, too? she wondered. Maybe she was just tired, and her reception from Bertha had been anything but warm. Or maybe it was Will. How could she be in love with a man she'd only just met, but who was so fractious all the time? She never knew what to expect from him. One minute they'd be talking like old friends, and the next he'd be spitting mad at her for no reason she could discern. But the way he acted didn't seem to matter. She just knew, as Kate had said she would, that she loved Will Sutten. He filled her thoughts day and night. In the daytime she could control her thoughts, but in the darkness he came unbidden, and she blushed at where her dreams led her.

Was it because she'd never known a man's love before? She didn't think so, because she had certainly had the opportunity to fall in love with Charles Eversley and hadn't. She shuddered when she thought that, but for a quirk of fate, she could now be his wife, and she would never have met Will Sutten. What did the future hold for her here? Was she brought here for a purpose, to marry Will maybe? She closed her eyes and shook her head.

Foolish thoughts to have, she scolded herself, and began unwrapping the treasures in the trunk. She took several of them out, putting a music box Uncle Simon had sent for her tenth birthday on the table by her bed. Then she put a couple of figurines on the dresser and decided to leave the rest of the knickknacks packed. Simon's cabin didn't need any homey touches.

The late afternoon sun was slanting across her floor by the time she'd gotten the last of her clothes unpacked and put away and the empty trunks had been put inside one another and slid to an empty wall. She had made her room as cozy as the kitchen, with doilies on shining wood surfaces, cushions on the rocking chair, and her own coverlet and pillows from home on the feather bed. She had taken down two pictures of rather dubious taste and replaced them with good prints, and had added a large woven rug to the braided one to cover more of the bare floor. She was extremely thankful her mother had insisted on the rug, as all the floors she had encountered so far had been as cold as ice.

Sounds from the kitchen had long since subsided, and Maggie wasn't surprised to find the room empty when she came out of her bedroom. Uncle Simon didn't seem to be in evidence either, so she decided to explore the rest of the house.

The four bedroom doors were open, and Maggie knew which door they'd come in from outside, so she figured the closed door through which Bertha had first entered the kitchen had to lead to the rest of the house. She wanted to go see Will's room, the room where he had been living for the past few years, and see what she could learn of him there. One peek into the room next to hers revealed a woman's long nightgown on a wall hook, and showed that it was Pete and Bertha's, which meant the remaining two were Simon's and Will's. But which was which? she wondered. She felt slightly guilty as she reached the second door and looked in. The room was neat, austere almost, with nothing except a set of brushes on the dresser to give a clue about the occupant. The final room was much the same, and disappointment took the place of her earlier guilt. She sighed and turned back to the kitchen. The only door left was the one through which Bertha had first entered the room, so she opened that door, and when she felt the cold air, she almost decided to put off exploring until at least July, but then went and got a shawl instead.

The cold and utter stillness she felt when she shut the door must be what it felt like to be in a tomb, she thought. It seemed infinitely colder than outside, and there was a stuffiness as though no one had stepped in here for years. A door to her right opened into a huge pantry, lined on all four sides with shelves bursting with canned goods and boxes of all manner of dry rations. In the center of the room there was a large cabinet with a worktable on top. Maggie knew this must be the pantry the men had described to her. Having never paid much attention to the kitchen at Longacres, she was astounded by the sheer volume of food stored here. There were loaves of fresh-baked bread covered with a tea towel on one shelf, and the smell was heavenly. Under the counter huge bins held flour, sugar, and meal, and strings of onions hung from the beamed ceiling. Food would have rotted if stored like this in South Carolina, but, she realized, this room was as cold, if not colder, than an icebox filled with a fresh block of ice. Shuddering suddenly, she closed the door to the room and continued down the short passage-way to the large main room of the house.

Wooden shutters covered the windows, and even though it was still light outside, the room had a tenebrous atmosphere that made her shiver in spite of her shawl. The furniture, crude and heavy, was sparse, and no effort had been made to soften the lines with cushions. The floors were bare, the cold seeping through her thin-soled shoes.

She had decided to leave when a frame on a table caught her eye, and she picked it up. It was a tintype of two people, she realized. She took it to where a shaft of light cut in through a crack in a shutter to see it better. The man in the picture was a much younger Uncle Simon, with his arm around a beautiful, laughing girl, and he was looking down at her with an adoring look on his face. The photo was old and the light dim, but Maggie knew without a doubt that the girl was her mother.

Maybe that was why he had never married, she thought. It gave her a curious feeling inside to see her mother as a young woman with a man other than her father. Had she loved Simon? If so, why hadn't she married him? But Maggie knew her parents were deeply in love, so maybe Simon's love had been one-sided. Like Maggie's love for Will. Would she end up all alone for the rest of her life, with nothing more than a faded photograph—if that—to show she had once been young and in love?

Uncle Simon had said he was going to ask Kate to marry him. Had he? she wondered. Or had he decided to go on as he was? Maggie decided as she left the room that she'd ask him at the first opportunity, whether it was any of her business or not.

A welcome rush of warmth hit her as she opened the door to the kitchen, and she closed the door tightly behind her.

"There you are! You'd think a body could tell someone where they were going, just in case they were needed for something," Bertha scolded.

Maggie fought the urge to apologize. "What did you need me for?"

"You can set the table. The food is about ready, and it's time to call the men in."

This totally amazed Maggie, as there had been no evidence of supper cooking when she'd left and she surely hadn't been gone that long. But she set out the plates and cups, putting a knife, fork, and spoon at each place; from a drawer, she took linen napkins, which she folded and placed on the side of the settings.

"Hmmph," the old woman said from behind her, "seems kind of fancy for supper."

Maggie smiled. "I'll just call the men in if you're ready." She might not have grown up with knowledge of domestic duties, but she at least knew what a properly set table looked like.

Bertha nodded curtly and began spooning mashed potatoes out of a large pot into a bowl.

Maggie had no idea where the men were, or if they could even hear her if she called, but she spied the dinner bell on the porch, so she took the rod and ran it several times around the triangle, then waited to see if anyone would come. She was reluctant to go back into the house with just Bertha there, and she also wanted to see Will again while she was in the shadows and he couldn't see her face. If Pete, of all people, had noticed, what had Will noticed?

It seemed almost like a dream, or a story someone else had told her, when she thought of the intimate times they'd shared. They were so brief, and yet so burned into her soul. She closed her eyes and remembered when he'd come upon her in the bath, and goose bumps followed her mind's eye as she remembered the feel of his hand as it traced a path of molten fire across her breasts.

"Good evening, Maggie." The soft voice was almost part of her dream, but he was so close she could feel the heat of him. She slowly opened her eyes and saw that he stood so near he could have kissed her without even moving.

They stood there for what seemed an eternity, and they would probably have gone on so, if Simon and Pete hadn't come across the yard laughing. Maggie was in the door in a flash, followed by the two older men, and she scurried to the table and sat down before they got their coats off.

"Will not coming again?" Bertha asked as Pete went to the sink to wash up.

"He's comin'," he said as he dried his hands and moved to his chair. The door opened, and Will came in. Maggie couldn't resist the urge to look at him, and her heart swelled in her chest. He looked so good to her, so familiar, and so dear. And yet she hadn't a clue to what he was thinking. That distant look had come into his eyes again, the one that made her feel that his thoughts were far away, with someone else.

"Did you get settled, Maggie?" Simon asked.

She tore her thoughts away from Will. "Yes, I did. It feels good to have my own things around me again. My room is so nice and cozy." She looked straight at her uncle but was aware of Will's eyes on her as he helped himself to the food.

The meal progressed with sporadic conversation at best, and all the while Maggie and Will avoided each other's eyes and tried to pretend the other wasn't there. The sparks between them were felt by the others at the table, though, and they each reacted in a different way.

Pete enjoyed the meal tremendously and looked forward to the days ahead, as the weather signs showed a big snowstorm coming sometime tonight, or tomorrow at the latest. If these two were like this now, imagine what they'd be like after being in the same house for a couple of days straight, never mind that there were other people around.

Bertha was disgusted and figured she'd have to keep her eyes open so the girl wouldn't do anything foolish. Bertha wasn't so old that she didn't see the attraction her Will would be for a young girl. He was like a son to her, and she loved him, but she also knew he had a score to settle, and it just wouldn't do for Maggie to set her hopes on Will marrying her. Pete had been right about there being something going on between the two of them, though if she'd been a betting woman, she'd have bet the attraction was all on the girl's side. In the years she'd known Will, she'd never seen him go foolish over any woman. And yet, here he was, right in front of her, acting like a lovesick calf.

Simon wondered if Will knew yet that he was in love with Maggie. He certainly hadn't admitted it, and maybe he didn't want to, but it was there on his face plain as day. Simon knew it was no good to spend one's life alone, and he didn't want to see either his friend or his niece make the same mistake he had. He'd known twenty-four years ago that Elizabeth wouldn't marry him, and yet no other woman had ever measured up to her. He realized now that they didn't have to, that being themselves was enough.

He sighed. Kate had turned him down and, as usual, wouldn't explain why. He didn't know if it was something about him or about her past that kept her from him, but she was adamant. If he'd been years younger, he thought, he would have said to hell with her and gone to find someone else, but it was too late for that. Something had to be done, though. He wouldn't live the rest of his life alone.

Will thought he'd never seen Maggie look so desirable, and in his present state of mind that fact irritated him. He'd been about to kiss her on the porch when Pete and Simon had interrupted, and he'd let them go on in ahead of him while he allowed his senses to cool. He shouldn't have bothered, though, because as soon as he sat down at the table and looked at her, he heated up again.

Maybe it was her being in his house that made her look so good. Having her sit at his table with his bedroom only steps away created intimacy for which he was unprepared. She looked as though she'd spent the day cleaning and cooking for him, and he just wanted to take her in his arms and hold her. He wanted to wake up in the morning with her beside him. It had been a long time since he'd had feelings like these, and there wasn't a thing he could do about them. Not yet, at least. It was probably just as well, because Maggie Longyear wasn't for the likes of him. She needed someone her own age, someone like Chase, he had to admit. That thought made him angry all over again. Damn! Why had she come into his life now?

Maggie thought about people she knew who had met someone, fallen in love, and gotten married, just like that. It seemed so easy for other couples. But then, it wasn't so easy for a man to fall in love with a tall, plain redhead. Oh, why couldn't life be simple for her? She looked at her uncle, and he had such a sad look in his eyes that she sent up a silent prayer. *Please, please, don't let me spend my life alone.*

❀ 7 ❀

The snowstorm that Pete had predicted moved in late the next morning. When Maggie got up long before dawn, the men were already outside securing the shutters and moving the horses into the barn. The wind was swirling madly, blowing ominous-looking clouds and causing ground blizzards even before the new flakes began to fall. The sunshine of yesterday was forgotten as winter let loose its last burst of fury before giving way to spring.

Bertha was wrapped up to the eyes and ready to go out and, at Maggie's offer to help, waited for the girl to get dressed. Maggie put on her warmest cloak and wrapped a woolen scarf around her face and head. She really hadn't any clothing suitable for weather so cold, but she didn't want to seem like a sissy. Bertha took one look at her and declared, "You'll have to dress warmer than that or you'll be a burden instead of a help."

"This is the warmest I have," Maggie answered truthfully.

"Well, we'll just have to put you in some of Will's things, then." Much put out but trying to hide it, she took off her scarf. She went into Will's room and returned with longjohns, Levi's, and a flannel shirt and handed them to Maggie, who looked at them and then at Bertha.

"I can't wear these. They're . . . they're . . ."

"They're warm is what they are, and it isn't a breach of etiquette to wear them out here. Now, if you want to help, get dressed, and I'll get you a coat and boots. But

99

if you don't, stay inside and make some hot food. We'll be needing it."

She disappeared into Simon's room next, and Maggie did the only thing she could. She couldn't tell Bertha she didn't know how to cook, and have the woman think her totally useless, and she knew she could help outside, so she took the clothing into her room and put it on. Bertha was back with woolen stockings and a pair of boots by the time she had pulled the pants on. They were big around the waist, somewhat snug around the hips, and too long, but she didn't have time to think about any of that as she pulled on the stockings, big boots, and a long, heavy coat with a split up the back for riding.

Maggie had to admit that even in the house she was much warmer than she'd been before. The longjohns kept drafts out, and she tucked the soft flannel shirt deep into the pants before buttoning them up. She felt indecent as she did so, and because they were Will's she also felt that same feeling she got whenever he was near, that kind of jittery, shaky feeling deep inside.

Bertha showed her how to wrap the scarf so it covered the turned-up collar of the coat and kept her face under wraps, then gave her a hat to put on top. By the time they were ready to go out, Maggie was suffocatingly hot, and it had only taken a matter of minutes.

When she got outside, though, she was extremely thankful for Bertha's foresight. The wind seemed to curl up under the long coat and almost took her breath away.

"The weather's turned on us," Bertha shouted so Maggie could hear, "and here we were, thinking spring was just around the corner."

The woman sounded the way Maggie felt—exhilarated. There was something in the wind that filled her with excitement and made the preparations seem almost fun. They carried armloads of wood to the porch, then covered it with canvas to keep it dry. From what Maggie could see through the blowing snow, the men were having problems getting the horses inside. Dave and two other men she hadn't met yet were trying to herd the animals toward Simon, but they were going in every direction but the one they were supposed to. They trotted back and forth, becoming more agitated with every passing minute.

"Haven't they ever seen a blizzard before?" Maggie shouted to Bertha.

"It's their instinct, telling them to run to shelter," the older woman yelled back, "only they forget all about the barn."

Will was struggling with a big bay, pulling on his rope and trying to get his hand on the halter so he could lead the horse inside. The powerful stallion was rearing and sounding so frenzied he was keeping the other ones frightened, and they milled back and forth while Simon, Pete, and another man kept trying to herd them into the barn.

Maggie had seen frightened horses brought out of a burning barn one time, and they had all had blankets thrown over their heads. Without thinking of what she was doing, she tore the scarf off her head and ran near Will, shouting to him to take it. Her movements made the huge horse even more agitated, and he reared in a desperate attempt to get away. Will was knocked to the ground, and the horse took off into the swirling snow.

"Damn you! What in hell did you think you were doing?" Will shouted at her.

"I was trying to get his eyes covered so he wouldn't be so scared!" she shouted back at him.

"Maggie! What are you doing out here anyway? Get back in the cabin where you belong!" He shouted to Simon, "I'm going after him!"

Simon and the others were hard put to keep the rest of the herd from following the stallion, and they paid no attention to Will as he grabbed one of the horses nearest him and swung up on its back. Without thinking, Maggie followed suit and, thankful for the ease with which the outlandish outfit let her accomplish the feat, climbed onto another horse. She'd been riding since before she could walk, and she could ride bareback more easily than with a saddle.

She caught up with Will quickly, her horse seeming to

catch the excitement that coursed through her as they
flew across the frozen ground. Will was going slow,
watching the ground to see the direction the big stallion
had gone. He turned as she reached him and shouted,
"Get back to the ranch! This is no place for a woman!"

"I'm coming with you! It was my fault he left, and I'm
going to help find him!"

"You're going to get killed is what you're going to do!
Hell, you'll probably get us both killed! You don't know
the first thing about blizzards!"

"I don't know the way back to the ranch, either! Are
you going to take me?"

They sat glaring at each other through the swirling
snow, and finally he said, "Fine! But I'm not going to
slow down for you. You keep up or you'll get lost."

She nodded, bent her face to the wind, and followed
along close behind him. The tracks were filling fast, and
Will set a brisk pace, cantering along beside the trail the
stallion had left.

Will was fuming inside. The fool girl should have
known better than to make quick movements around a
horse, especially one that was already spooked. She'd
grown up around horses, according to Simon. What had
she been thinking? Now he not only had to risk his own
life to get the stallion back, but he had the burden of
keeping her safe, too. Maybe he should just turn around
and take her back while he still could.

The stallion wasn't like the wild horses that roamed
the ranges and knew how to defend themselves. Except
for the two years Will had spent chasing around the
country, the horse had spent all his life in barns and
paddocks. He'd be defenseless if a cougar or wolves
chased him down. Without his bloodlines, their new
mares would be useless, and who knew if they could
even find another stallion like him.

Will made a choice and prayed it was the right one. If
he had guessed correctly, the bay was headed up the
creek to the shelter of the pines around the summer
pasture. This was the trail they'd used the past four years
to take the cattle up there, and there was a good chance

the horse had instinctively gone that way. Pete and Bertha's old cabin was up there, too, and with luck he'd find the horse and be able to get him and Maggie to the cabin before the storm hit full force. There was no way they could make it back to the ranch in time. He cut across the trail and headed up the side of the mountain.

When they got to the shelter of the pine forest, the lack of wind almost made Maggie fall off her mount. She hadn't realized she'd been pushing so hard against it. Will stopped to give the horses a breather, but he didn't dismount. Maggie had come up behind him and stopped, too, unwrapping the wet scarf from her face.

He had expected her to look beaten or scared, but instead she was grinning, and her eyes were flashing sparks. Her cheeks were red from the cold, and her hair, as usual, was falling out from under the hat on her head. "Do you know which way he's heading?" she asked him.

Will couldn't take his eyes off her face as he answered, "I think so. We summer-pasture the cattle up here, and he's heading along the same trail. I'm just hoping we get to him before the wolves do."

"Wolves? Is that why you're so worried about him?"

"Oh, I don't know what I'm worried about! Wolves aren't really likely to attack him unless he gets hurt, but there are lots of other things that could happen to him. We have a couple of nice colts out of him, but they're not ready to go to stud yet. We need his bloodlines."

"He's a beautiful horse," she said as they started out again.

"There's only one other like him."

"Do you have that one, too?"

"I did. I bred and raised them both."

"What happened to the other one?"

"Someone took him from me." Jake Greeley took his horse. *The lady sure knew good horseflesh,* he'd said, and the whore told Will that Greeley had ridden out of town on it after he'd killed its owner. Will's wife.

Now he and Maggie spotted the big bay ahead in the trees, pawing the ground and neighing a greeting at their arrival.

"There you are, boy," Will crooned to him. The stallion was still skittish and danced around in the deep snow. Still talking gently, Will guided his horse up to the bay and slipped from the broad back. He was only a few feet away now, and the great head tossed nervously; then Will had the rope in his hand and was sliding it up to the halter. Once he had the halter in a firm grip, he tied the rope to a tree with the other hand. Only when it was secured did he relax and look at Maggie.

She had been watching, her heart racing. The snow was coming in thick now, the wind penetrating even the dense growth of pines, and if they lost the horse again, it might be for good. She had no idea how far they'd come but could tell from the sound of the wind that it would be a miracle if they made it back.

"Are you okay?" he asked her.

"Yes," she said, nodding, "I'm fine. Now what?"

"We need to find shelter, and soon. Pete and Bertha's old cabin is up here, and if we don't lose the way, we might be able to make it there. We'll have to go the long way, around the mountain in the trees, because if we try to cut across the flats, we'll be lost for sure. Otherwise, if we get on the other side of this hill and the wind's too fierce, we may have to dig in."

"All right," she answered calmly. "What do you need for me to do?"

He was amazed at her calm reaction. She'd not gone into hysterics and seemed capable of almost anything. The more he got to know her, the more convinced he became that she was meant for life out here. "We'll ride on either side of him, taking it slow. He's still not too sure about the storm, and he's not used to running free."

She walked her mount slowly up to his side while he untied the rope, and still holding it in his hand, he swung back up onto his horse.

"Why don't you loop it around your hand?" she asked in a quiet, soothing voice.

"Because if he took off again, he might take me with him. There's no way I could hold him with no saddle on this horse."

She nodded, and they started out, going as fast as they could in the ever deepening mantle of white.

It seemed like hours later that they spied the cabin. They had been walking the horses through the deep snow under the pines, which was hard going. The horses slid and shied sideways, but they kept going. Will knew he wouldn't get lost if he stayed right inside the tree line, but he also knew that if they missed the cabin in the curtain of snow, they'd be spending the night out in the open, and he wasn't willing to risk exposing either the horses or Maggie to that. His knees went weak with relief when he slid from the back of the sorrel mare he was riding and led the two horses up to the front of the cabin. He tied them to a sapling and forced open the door while Maggie tied her horse, then came to stand silently beside him.

The interior was in better shape than he'd feared, and the fireplace looked intact, but there was no wood, and he hadn't an axe. He'd figure out something later, but for now he had to get the horses inside the lean-to that had served as a storage shed. It would be tight, but the three horses would fit, and they'd be safe from hungry predators and the snow that sometimes smothered animals who weren't protected from it.

"Do you think you can come out and help me get them in that lean-to?" he asked her.

"Of course," she replied. She still hadn't complained, and he felt guilty for some reason.

The wind had come up even more, but they got the three skittish animals inside and barricaded the sagging door, which looked as if it would give with one kick. Once inside, the horses settled down. They were worn out, too, Will thought as he tried to figure out what they were going to do to keep from freezing to death during the night.

"Couldn't we break those limbs off by jumping on them?" Maggie was asking him.

"What?"

"For wood. Those trees over there look plenty dry. The wood should break pretty easily."

He looked where she had indicated, and saw a pile of

fallen trees that Pete had probably dragged to the site to cut up. The limbs looked quite sturdy to him, but it was the only solution apparent, so he waded through the knee-high snow to them.

"See, like this." Before he could stop her, she climbed up on one of the trunks and jammed her instep down on a branch, breaking it off. She almost lost her footing when it gave so easily, and he grabbed for her. She braced her hands on his shoulders and pushed herself back up.

"It works!" Then she laughed, and he thought if any woman could laugh in a situation like this, she could make it through anything.

Systematically they broke the limbs off, and he carried them back through the deep snow and dumped them on the cabin floor. After the pile had grown to what looked like enough to carry them through the night and possibly the next day, they quit, and she followed in his prints. The snow was coming faster now, and the pathway filled in as soon as they passed.

"Maybe the storm won't be as bad as you think," she said to him when they went inside and wedged the door shut.

"It'll probably be worse," he answered grimly. "Spring blizzards are never good." As if the storm sought to prove him right, the wind set up a howl that made her back crawl. It sounded like some tormented creature. "We're on the lee side of the mountain, so you don't notice the wind so much back here, but I've been through plenty of blizzards, and this is a bad one, for sure."

It seemed colder in the cabin than it had outside, and despite the clothing she was wearing, she was shivering because she had gotten wet. She could see nothing in the small room that promised creature comforts, and she was hungry. It must be late afternoon, and neither of them had eaten all day. But overshadowing the cold and her bone-weariness was the thought that had been in her mind since he had told her they were heading for the cabin. She would be spending the night alone with him.

She could feel the nearness of him inside her chest,

and her throat felt dry with nervousness. She moved as far away from him as she could get, took off her mittens, and wiped her damp hands on the long coat. Her heart was thumping, and it wasn't all from exertion. She tried not to watch him, but found herself drawn to him, fascinated with the way he moved. A mountain lion would move like that, and the thought sent goose bumps down her back.

Will had no matches, but he always had his flint and a knife with him, so he shaved the driest piece of wood he could find and after a time had a small fire going.

"Thank goodness the chimney draws," he said, and she laughed.

"If it didn't, I'm sure you'd find a way." The compliment pleased him immensely. He had been feeling like a fool for taking off in the storm without anything at all. He had planned to catch the horse and head straight back to the ranch, and hadn't even though as he'd jumped on the back of the nearest mount and headed off. Even though there was no way he could have known she was following him, Maggie's appearance had changed things completely and made him lash out at her in his helplessness due to his lack of preparation. She didn't have any idea of the fix they were in, but he did. He knelt before the flames, holding his hands out to the warmth.

"You'd better get over here and get warmed up," he told her. "It's gonna be a long night."

They sat as close to the fire as they could get without touching, one on each side, facing each other. He knew they'd be warmer if he held her, but he wasn't sure he could trust himself to do that. He wanted her too much. Just the nearness made his body ache with desire for her, and it seemed there was something between them so intense that he could feel her even as he sat two feet away. He looked at her face instead. "You really are quite remarkable, you know that?"

She blushed. "Why on earth would you say that?"

"Because any other woman would have had a fit of the vapors or at least complained about the mess I'd gotten you into."

"Will, you seem to forget that I got us into this mess in the first place."

"No, you didn't. I was upset, but that was no reason to take it out on you."

"Oh, Will, if I hadn't run at the poor animal like that, you'd probably have been able to get him quieted and in the barn, and you know it."

"Only probably?" He grinned at her, and the warm smile lit his face, bringing a rush of emotion to her that made her eyes water.

"You're a very nice man, Will," she said quietly.

His gaze skittered over her face, then returned to the fire. "Not as nice as you think." He stared into the flames, wishing he could take her into his arms and kiss her, and she watched the light dance in his eyes and over his face.

"I think you're a lot nicer than you give yourself credit for."

He sighed and turned back to her. "There's a lot about me you don't know."

"Why don't you tell me?"

"I can't."

"Okay. Then I won't ask again."

"Maggie, it isn't that I don't want to tell you. I wish I could. Maybe then I could leave my past behind. But until that past catches up with me and I deal with it, I can't go on." He looked at her earnestly. "Do you understand that?" *Please say you do. I need you, Maggie, but I can't have you just yet.*

"Perhaps. There are things in my past I need to deal with, too. Things about myself I need to come to terms with before I can give anything of myself." *Oh, God, please don't let it be anything bad. Please let there be a future for us.*

The logs fell in a shower of sparks and broke the spell between them. Will felt suddenly hot and rose to take off his coat. Maggie came up to her knees, peeled her heavy coat off and folded it to sit on, then pulled the big boots off and stretched her feet toward the fire to dry her socks.

Will had carried over some more wood and was

brought up short at the sight of her. She had on his clothes. His pants, his shirt, and probably his longjohns. Next to her skin. He swallowed and, carefully averting his eyes, moved past her to put the broken branches in the fire.

His heart was thumping painfully, and his body reacted in spite of his willing it not to. He'd seen some of the older ranch women like Bertha in pants before, but the younger ones wore split skirts or rode sidesaddle. He hadn't thought about the fact that she'd ridden bareback and astride. The long coat, one of Simon's by the looks of it, had hidden her clothing from him.

He squatted by the fire, poking the embers with a stick, while his thoughts raced.

"Will?"

He couldn't look at her. "What?"

"Is there any way we could get some snow and melt it? For water, I mean."

"Sure. Cowboys have been using their hats to drink out of for years." He stood up and turned away from her. "I'll go get some."

Opening the door would have cooled the warming room, so he pulled back one of the shutters, and scooped in enough snow to fill his hat. While he wiped his hands off on his thighs, he chanced another look at her and was sorry he did. Her hair was in a tumbled mass around her shoulders, and she was idly combing through it with her fingers. The firelight silhouetted her and turned the dark red strands to fiery copper as they fell. He got a tight feeling in his stomach. He knew he was going to do something he'd regret, but he didn't seem to be able to stop himself. Or maybe it was just that he didn't want to. It had been so long since he'd wanted a woman this bad. Maybe never. He didn't remember ever feeling so out of control.

He carried the hat to the fire and set it down, then without even thinking about what he was doing, he went to his knees behind her and began combing through the tangles with his own fingers. Slowly he lifted a handful of the thick, soft tresses and worked gently from the bottom up, then let the strands fall so he could see the light on them.

Maggie pulled her legs in, Indian style, and closed her eyes, hardly daring to breathe for fear he would see the effect his nearness had on her. Her heart thumped painfully, and she wondered wildly what would happen if he kissed her again when they were so alone. She wanted him to, but she was terrified that he might. She thought she should suggest they sleep on opposite sides of the room, for propriety's sake, but didn't trust her voice to say the words.

She was totally unaware of the effect on Will as the denim of his pants pulled tight around her slim legs when she moved. She had pulled the shirt out of the waistband and had opened the first few buttons of the shirt, revealing the longjohns underneath. He looked at the woolen undergarment buttoned up to her throat, and all he could think was that they were his.

Damn, he wanted her. And here they were in this tumbledown shack, without even so much as a blanket to cover the floor. They had no food, and, from the sound of the wind, one of the worst blizzards he'd ever seen was swirling around them and could keep on blowing for days. They might not even get out of this alive. And she was so beautiful, so warm, so totally desirable.

The storm seemed far away as he took her gently in his arms and kissed her. She melted into the curve of his chest, laying her head against his shoulder. He sat then and pulled her up tight against him, with one leg behind her and the other bent over her legs. He placed soft slow kisses all over her face, and she turned to him and met his mouth with fire of her own.

He closed his eyes and tried not to think of what they were doing. Simon kept trying to intrude on his thoughts, and Will wondered again if she was a virgin. Then Jake Greeley trespassed across his mind, and he pulled away from her.

"We can't do this, Maggie."

"I know." Her voice was small and tight.

"I'm sorry."

"It's all right. I understand."

"No, you don't." He pulled her tight against him again and rested his chin on her head. "And I can't explain. Not now." She didn't answer, and he thought his chest would explode with the pain.

He held her that way for a while, gently rocking her, then murmured against her hair, "You'd better button up your shirt." He was only so strong, and her willingness weakened him. He was all right with the flannel shirt, but the sight of his woolens next to her skin undid his resolve. "It's going to get plenty cold in here, even with the fire," he said, trying to explain without telling her the real reason he wanted her covered.

She bent her head and hastily began fastening the buttons.

"Why are you wearing my clothes?"

She looked up at him, startled at the question, and blushed. "Bertha got them for me. She said if I was going outside, I had to wear them. Otherwise, I had to stay inside and cook. I . . . guess I should have asked you first."

"No, it's okay. In fact, I like it very much. I just never saw a woman look quite like that in pants before."

"Oh! Bertha told me it was quite common." She was mortified now, and he could see it in her face.

"Well, on women like Bertha, clothes like that don't look . . . well, like they look on you." That seemed to embarrass her further, so he decided maybe he should change the subject. "Listen, it's going to be a long night, and we can't sit here like this. We're going to have to find some way to get more comfortable."

She quickly disentangled herself from his embrace and stood up in one graceful move. She bent over to pick up the long coat, and he hastily clambered to his feet to keep his eyes off her hips in his pants.

"The water's all gone from the hat. I'll get some more," she stated, then went over to the shuttered window as he had done before.

"Here, let me help you." He dashed ahead of her and pulled the heavy wooden covering aside. She gave him a quick smile, then quickly scooped the hat full of snow. The window had been open at the top when he'd gotten the first snow, but now it was completely covered. He didn't want to get her worried, so he didn't say anything, but she said, "It seems to be getting worse, doesn't it?"

"Maybe. It's hard to tell. If may blow itself out in an hour or two."

"Or last two days. You don't have to coddle me, Will." She grinned. "I won't get an attack of the vapors, I promise."

"Thank you for that, at least." He cocked his head to the side and smiled at her.

"What?"

"Nothing. It's just that you're so different from other women."

She turned her head away quickly to hide the swift rush of tears that formed in her eyes. Her emotions were very fragile, and she was furious with herself that she couldn't control them more. He took her shoulder and turned her to face him. "What's wrong?"

She shook her head, unable to speak, and he lifted her chin up so he could see her face. She had her eyes closed, but the tears were running down her face. He gently kissed her eyes, not knowing what he'd said to make her cry. "Tell me, Maggie."

She shook her head against him, then said in a voice muffled against his chest, "I can't be like other women. I've tried, but I can't."

"Why would you want to be?" He honestly couldn't see what she was getting at.

"Oh, Will"—she lifted her head then and looked him full in the face—"it's obvious, isn't it? Men don't like me. I'm tall, and plain, and too thin, my hair is an awful shade of red, I can't keep my opinions to myself, and I simply cannot bat my eyelashes at a man and giggle!"

Will couldn't help himself. He threw back his head and laughed.

"What is so funny?" she demanded, hands on her hips.

"You. Don't you realize women like that are a dime a dozen? A man can only take so much giggling and batting of eyelashes before he goes out and gets himself a mistress like you."

"My, you really know how to turn a lady's head, don't you?" Her eyes were throwing sparks now, all directed at him. "Well, I can tell you this, Will Sutten. I will never be any man's mistress!"

She was furious, and jerked away from him, but he grabbed her shoulders in a firm grip and held her there. "Now you're the one who can't see what's right in front of your eyes! That's what I've been trying to tell you, Maggie. I've never met a woman like you before, if I could, I'd marry you tomorrow!" he shouted at her.

"Why can't you?" she shouted back.

"Because I can't!" He pulled her tight against him again and said again, more softly, "God help me, I can't."

He rocked her back and forth for a long time while the snow melted in the hat and seeped out at their feet. Finally she said, "The water's all gone again," and he laughed. They scooped some more, this time watching until it melted and then drinking long and deeply of it.

"I'd better take some to the horses. If I remember right, that fallen-in hole back there goes out to the shed. Pete built this into the hillside on three sides, so it's warmer than most cabins around here. Bad thing is the wood rots sooner," he said as he pulled the soft wood away from the opening and squeezed through. Maggie peered into the darkness after him, wondering what she'd do if he didn't come back, but then he called, "This is it!"

He came back, banging something against the walls as he tried to maneuver through the small opening. "I found a bucket!" he said as though he'd found gold. Indeed, in their circumstances the bucket was the more valuable find. Together they filled it with snow, and after it had melted by the fire, they put more in. When the bucket was three-quarters full, he went back to the lean-to.

"They're mighty thirsty," he said, and they repeated the process twice more before the horses had had their fill. In the meantime, Maggie poked around the cabin to see if there were any more discards they could put to use. She had found a pile of burlap sacks, filthy but dry, and had shaken them out a window on the leeward side of the cabin until she thought they'd be all right to sit on. That window had been clear of snow up to the windowsill, but she couldn't see the trees through the swirling curtain of white.

She had thought that as soon as the storm was over, they could just get on the horses and ride out. But the cabin was quickly becoming buried. How much longer would it be before the snow stopped coming? And if it was this bad here in the shelter of the trees, how much worse was it on the flats they would have to cross to reach the safety of the ranch?

Fear struck her suddenly, and she wondered if they would get out of here alive. Would she die here, never knowing what it was like to be loved by a man? She didn't know what to make of Will. He seemed attracted to her, but something was making him hold back, and she didn't think it was honor alone. If they were trapped here for several days, what might happen? She still felt a desperate longing for him, but she couldn't make the first move. He must think she had loose morals as it was. But for some reason morality didn't seem as important as it always had before. If he wanted her, if he took her in his arms again, she wouldn't let him stop. She knew that as sure as she was standing here, and the thought terrified her.

Will came back in then and found her standing there, the sacks in her hands. Silently he took them from her and placed them on the floor, then covered them with his coat. He put wood on the fire and placed more nearby, then took her and lay down beside her, with her coat over the top of them and his arm as their pillow. Filled with their own thoughts, they stared into the flames until they fell asleep.

❧ 8 ❧

"Where do you think they are?" Bertha had been going to the window every few minutes, as though she could see them coming through the blinding snow.

"I don't know," Simon replied, "but Will has the sense to seek shelter. He'll keep Maggie safe." He said this as much to reassure himself as Bertha. This was a bad storm, for sure, and he only hoped they'd made it to the shelter of the trees before now.

"They ain't got anything with 'em. Them horses wasn't even saddled."

"Shut up, Pete," Simon ordered the old man, and motioned toward Bertha, who was fiddling with the stove, stirring the stew for the hundredth time.

"Surely they'll be back soon. That stallion couldn't have gotten that far."

But they didn't come back, and as darkness fell and the drifts piled up, Simon became more and more worried. He was responsible for his niece. If he'd seen her go, he'd have stopped her. But the two of them had been long gone before he found out about it, and by then it would have been suicide to go after them.

He wouldn't be able to face his brother and Elizabeth if anything happened to Maggie. He clung to the thought that Will knew what he was doing. He tried not to think that she might not even have found him and was out there alone. He stared into the black night and saw only his own reflection in the glass.

The three of them had been pacing the kitchen for

hours, sitting at the table periodically, gulping hot coffee. Finally Simon turned from the window. "We're not doing them any good waiting up. It's obvious they aren't coming tonight, so we might as well get some sleep. At first light we'll go out and find them."

Several times during the night, Simon awakened and listened to the wind howling around the cabin. Toward morning, he thought he detected a lessening in the wind's ferocity. By first light he was up and dressed. Bertha was at the table when he came out, sipping a cup of coffee. "You can't go out there yet."

"I think the wind has died down some."

"You're wishing. It's worse, if anything. You might as well go back to bed."

Simon knew she was right, but he was too restless to sleep. Men had died in storms like this just going from their cabins to the barns, and there wasn't anything he could do but begin pacing again. Pete came out, exchanged a knowing look with Simon, and sat down at the table.

There was a noise at the door, and the three of them jumped to open it, but it was only Dave.

"What are you doing out in this?" demanded Simon.

"We got a rope tied from the bunkhouse to the barn, and from the barn here, so nobody gets lost out there. They make it back yet?"

"No. We thought maybe you were them."

"Will's too smart to be moving when it's blowing like this. He's holed up somewhere, is my guess. Even if he thought about trying to make it back on his own, he's got Maggie with him. He won't risk her."

Simon nodded. More to have something to do besides pacing than because of the need, he suggested they go out and check on the horses. The cattle were on their own; no doubt there would be some dead ones, but there wasn't anything they could do about that, either. But Simon wasn't used to not being in control, and he didn't like it. If he only knew they were together he wouldn't worry so much. He trusted Will with his life, and with Maggie's, too.

*   *   *

Will was feeling much the same way. He was furious with himself for coming out unprepared and risking Maggie's life. Once before he had let a woman he loved die because he hadn't been prepared, because he hadn't taken proper precautions, and now here he was in the same predicament. There was no excuse for a man to be caught without any supplies. Not out here where death fell swiftly on the unprepared. His stomach was growling now, and he knew Maggie must be hungry, too. She was still sleeping, her head cradled by his wrist and hand. He turned toward her and thought how good it felt to have her, close and warm against him. He hadn't ever thought to find love again, but here it was. He watched her sleeping and thought about that. Could he let the past go and meet the future? Her presence had settled down around him like a comfortable shirt, and she fit.

He bent his head forward and kissed her ear, softly, then trailed his lips down her neck. He didn't think she'd affect him in the daylight as she had in the firelight the night before, but as she turned against him, opened her eyes, and smiled, he was lost again. They were lost in each other's eyes, and he slowly leaned toward her. She wanted him to kiss her, wanted him to touch her, but she was much more in control of herself this morning than she had been the night before.

She stretched and rolled over on her stomach. "The storm's not over."

"No." Maybe it could go on forever, and he'd not have to face the past.

"How much longer, do you think?"

He got up then and, shaking his numb hand to get the blood moving in it again, crossed the room to the wood pile. "Not much longer. The wind has died down some."

"I need to go outside."

"You can't go outside. Are you crazy?"

"Well, I can't go inside." She was humiliated to mention her need in front of him, but she had been holding it all night and couldn't much longer.

He looked at her and frowned, then realization came.

"Oh. Well, I guess I went out by the horses last night. I never thought you might need to go, too." He couldn't look at her, even though it was a perfectly natural thing to have to do. The outhouse behind the cabin had long since fallen in, and besides, she couldn't go outside, anyway. There were no chamber pots here, though, so the lean-to was the only place.

"I'll go with you to show you the way," he offered.

"I think not. I'll be perfectly all right alone." It was bad enough that he knew, without his coming along. "I'll check on the horses while I'm there."

She pulled the boots back on and headed for the small opening in the back of the cabin. Now that it was light outside, she could see a bit in the passage, and it didn't seem as bad as it had the night before. She slid in between the fallen timbers as she had seen Will do, and hunched low as she crept along toward the light. She could hear the horses and could tell from the odor that they hadn't been so shy.

If she'd had on her skirts, she could have lifted them and spread her pantaloons apart. But the man's outfit she was wearing made the whole thing rather difficult, to say the least. By the time she'd gotten the pants down and figured out the opening in the back of the longjohns, she didn't think she'd be able to hold it another second.

As she made her way back down the tunnel, she decided this was it. She could put up with no food and with drinking melted snow out of a dirty hat. She could put up with sleeping all night on a hard floor that remained cold despite Will's welcome warmth, and having no means of bathing or even combing her hair. But she absolutely could not do what she'd just done again. They were leaving, and soon.

When she crawled back through the opening, Will was facing the fire and had his coat on. He turned to her as she came up behind him. "Do you think you can ride?"

"Absolutely," she said without hesitation and took the coat he handed her. He helped her on with it.

"Wrap up tight. It's worse out there today than

yesterday. The snow is going to be a lot deeper, and the horses will have a hard time breaking through."

"Has it quit snowing?"

"Yeah, I think so. It looks like it's just blowing. If we stay in the trees again, we can get around to the back of the ranch and then follow the creek bed right up to the back door." He tried to sound more cheerful than he felt. They probably had a fifty-fifty chance of making it back, but he couldn't keep her here any longer. They had to go in the daylight, and it was going to take most of one day to get back. Another night here was completely out of the question.

He had untied the horses and watered them again by the time she came out. She was completely covered except for her eyes. She took her horse without comment and pulled herself on its back. He marveled at her grace and the ease with which she rode. If he ever got free, and she consented to marry him, he would never quit telling her how much he admired everything about her.

The storm had blown in from the northwest, blowing up the slopes and depositing heavy drifts on the back side of every obstacle in its way. Will hoped that if they could just get around the mountain, the other side wouldn't be so bad. The going was easier than he had feared—and much harder than Maggie had even imagined.

She tried to stay alert, but as the hours wore on, she found herself drifting into daydreams about Will. And about the night before. She'd have let him do anything he wanted, and the thought scared her. Where were her strict morals? Gone. Gone with his first touch. This must have been how Cathey the serving maid felt when she let Charles get her with child. What would it be like to have Will get her with child?

Maggie wasn't ignorant about coupling. She'd spent enough time in the stables to know not only what went on between animals, but also, thanks to the gossip of the stable hands and scullery maids, what went on between men and women.

She had never even tried to imagine it with Charles, perhaps because she hadn't loved him and found it hard even to think about making love with him. She almost laughed now as she remembered that she had admired his hands. His were pale and sickly next to Will's. His lovemaking would probably have been the same as his courtship—halfhearted and without emotion. Will left her in no doubt that his would be a fiery courtship. His lovemaking could be no less.

She sighed and tried to guess what kept him from her. Did he have a wife somewhere? That thought hadn't crossed her mind before. What if he did?

Whatever it was, she didn't care. He had told her he admired her and that as soon as he could he'd explain his problem to her, and that was all that mattered. She allowed herself to hope again that she would know love, marriage, and children.

She was so deep into her thoughts she didn't notice when Will stopped, and she almost ran her horse into his. Thank goodness, she thought, the horse had been paying attention.

They were standing in a clearing looking over the tops of the trees. The majestic mountains to the west blended in with the sky, and she had a hard time getting her direction, but down below she could glimpse dark shapes through the blowing snow that looked like buildings. "Is that it?" she asked excitedly.

"Yes, but once we're down there, we won't be able to see it like this." He turned to her, his voice dead serious. "If we lose our bearings, we could wander around for days."

"How are you planning to go?"

He pointed to a line of white that meandered toward the ranch buildings in the distance. "See that depression there? That's the creek." At that very moment the whole valley disappeared as a strong gust picked up the loose snow again. "The water should be frozen, but you can never be sure with all the hot springs around here, so we're going to have to feel our way one step at a time. We'll know if we get out of the stream bed because of the thickets of willow growing on both sides. The hard part will be knowing when we get to the ranch. I'm counting on the horses to tell us that. We won't be able to see it from down there."

His stomach was full of knots, but he knew it was their only chance. They couldn't have stayed in the cabin indefinitely with no provisions, and if wolves had smelled the horses, he'd have been defenseless. He'd come away without even a gun. It rankled him because he knew better. He could make excuses, but there wasn't one good enough for a man to be out without even so much as his gun. It would never happen again. That's how men died, and he had a very good reason to keep on living now. Could he release the hold Jake Greeley had on him? Maybe. Maybe his love for Maggie could make him forget the picture he carried in his mind of Greeley and his wife on a bed in a whorehouse.

"Are you sure you should go yet? It's still blowin' hard out there, and you don't even know what direction they went." Pete stood at the hitching rail and spoke to Simon, who was tying his bedroll on the back of his saddle. Dave and two other men were also getting saddled up to go.

"Pete, you said yourself they didn't have anything with them. How long do you think they'll last out there in this cold with no food? Will didn't even have his gun on. He has no saddle, not even a goddamn blanket. Now if you can't help, get out of the way."

The snow had quit in the early afternoon, but the wind was picking up what was on the ground and blowing it with enough force to block the barn from the view of the men in front of the cabin. Simon had waited as long as he was going to, however: nothing was going to stop him from going on this search. They had packed food, canteens of water, plenty of blankets, and even a tent. It offered scant shelter at best, but in a crisis anything was better than nothing, and Simon figured they could set up a base camp and search in circles around it.

He went back into the cabin and took the cup of hot coffee Bertha handed him.

"If we're not back in three days, send for help," he instructed the woman.

Her face showed the strain of worry and lack of sleep. "You'll be fine. Will can take care of them, you know that."

"If they're together. What if she never found him?" He set the cup down on the table. "Damn! If only I'd known she was going. I'd have stopped her!"

"Well, you didn't, and there's no use beating yourself over the head about it. I saw her go and I couldn't stop her. No one could have." Bertha had been feeling the same way, blaming herself for letting Maggie go.

Pete poked his head in the door and informed them the men were saddled and ready to go.

"Well, that's it, then," he said, wishing his insides would quit shaking.

"Be careful, Simon." She didn't mean to say it but couldn't help herself.

He smiled at her. "We will."

The others had mounted already when he got back out to the hitching rail. He wondered again if he was a fool for heading out before the wind died down, but knew he didn't have a choice. They had plenty of provisions and would be taking it slow, staying together. He swung into his own saddle, and Pete handed him the reins he'd been holding.

"Keep Bertha from worrying, Pete."

"Hell, nothin's gonna keep her from worryin', and you know it. You just take care."

Turning the horses in the direction Will and Maggie had taken, they set out, Simon in the lead and all the animals tied together with lengths of rope. Simon hesitated when he reached the back of the barn and the white wilderness stretched out ahead of him. It was like starting out into a place he'd never been before, because all the familiar landmarks were obliterated by the curtain of blowing snow. He checked the lead ropes, then turned back toward the buildings to get his bearings.

Suddenly one of the mares lifted her head and whinnied, then another one. The men looked at each other and strained their ears to hear the answering call from the stallion. Simon thought he heard it, then Dave nodded, and he knew it wasn't just his imagination. *Please,* he prayed, *let Maggie and Will be with him.*

He couldn't tell the direction the stallion's call was coming from, but the mares began pawing the ground, and the men were having trouble keeping them settled. Close. The stallion was close. Simon strained his eyes and turned his head, listening.

"There," Dave said, and Simon looked in the direction he was pointing. He thought he could make out some dark objects moving in the white. He called out, "Will! Maggie!" and started his horse toward them. Then they appeared, Maggie slipping from her horse and throwing her arms around Simon, laughing and crying at the same time, and Will on the big bay, trying to keep him away from the mares. Two of the men finally took the stallion into the barn, and he went as willingly as a docile lamb on a rope.

"Now he goes," Will said dryly.

"He must be hungrier for oats than mares," Maggie quipped, and Will replied, "That's what makes him a dumb animal." They shared a secret smile.

While Dave and the other hands attended to the horses, Maggie and Will were brought into the cabin and set down at the table, where Bertha placed enough food before them to feed an army.

"Good heavens, woman, there's only two of us! You have enough food here for a roundup crew!"

She shrugged. "When I get worried, I cook."

"It looks wonderful, Bertha," Maggie told the woman. "I feel as though I could eat all of it."

"Don't tell me you missed us, Bertha," Will said between bites.

"Of course I did, you darn fool. What did you think you were doing, taking off like that with not so much as even a saddle on the horse? And you, young lady"—she pointed her finger at Maggie—"the very idea of riding off after him like it was summer or something. Why, you could have been killed out there!"

"I found that out and I assure you all it will never happen again." Maggie was so thankful to be back alive.

And yet she wouldn't have given up the time spent with Will for anything on earth.

They talked the afternoon away around the table, sipping coffee long after the dishes were washed and put away. The winds died down toward evening, and the men went out to see how the animals had fared.

"You get some rest, Will. We can take care of things outside," Simon told him as he and Pete dressed to go out. Will followed them out onto the porch and came back a few minutes later.

"Maggie. Come outside with me. I want you to see something."

She grabbed the big coat and followed him out around the house to the front porch. "Oh, Will," she whispered as her eyes took in the sight of the snow-covered peaks of the Tetons bathed in the rosy hues of a winter sunset. The sun had slipped behind, stretching beams of light through to the valley floor, and the sky above was awash in pinks and purples, fading to deep blue above the clouds wreathing the peaks.

The sheer beauty of it, the solemn stillness of the land, brought tears to her eyes, and Will put his arm around her shoulder and pulled her up against his side. They stood that way for an hour, oblivious to the people in the cabin behind them, and watched until the last glow faded to darkness, and the sky filled with myriad sparkling stars.

"It seems like a dream," she said to him, her voice a whisper on the night air, and he nodded. "We're lucky to be alive." Was that why everything seemed so much more beautiful than before? Or was it because they were seeing it together?

They didn't hear Simon come around the porch until he said quietly, "Maggie, Bertha has hot water ready for you to take a bath. We'll be in later."

Will squeezed her in the cover of darkness before taking his arms from around her, and she slipped from his side and made her way around to the kitchen door. If she couldn't be in Will's arms, then a hot bath and comfortable bed were all she wanted in the world right now.

Simon waited until Maggie had closed the door, then

leaned against the cabin, one foot up against the logs, and lit a cigar. Will knew Simon well and knew he had something to say to him, so he stayed where he was and waited for whatever it was that was coming.

"I don't know how to put this, Will." Simon wasn't usually at a loss for words.

"I know what you're going to say, but nothing happened up there. You have my word on that."

"It doesn't matter, and you know that."

"What are you saying?"

"You've compromised her reputation, Will. I'm her guardian." He shrugged his shoulders.

"Wait. Let me get this straight. Are you telling me I have to marry her?"

"Isn't that the way you see it?"

"No, it isn't. If and when I decide to get married, I'll do the asking. No one is going to tell me who I'm going to marry."

"Will, you forget I walked in on you two the other night before we went out for dinner."

Will had the decency to color. "I didn't say I wasn't attracted to her."

"That was more than attraction. You're not talking to a stranger here, Will. I know you and I know you don't indulge in idle flirtations. As a matter of fact, in the four years I've known you, I've never even seen you so much as glance at a woman, and heaven knows you've had opportunities aplenty with all the mothers who've thrown their daughters at you."

"No, I don't indulge in idle flirtations, so you have to know my intentions are honorable."

"That's good to hear. I'll talk to Maggie."

"No, you won't talk to Maggie."

"Will, listen—"

"No, Simon, you listen. I'll handle this, in my own way, in my own time. You don't even know if she wants to marry me! What if she has other ideas altogether? I don't flatter myself into thinking that she's chomping at the bit to become my wife. After all, what do I have to offer her? A room in her uncle's house?"

"That's not true, and you know it. Half this ranch is yours, and if you weren't so damned stubborn, it would have been settled long ago."

"That's my choice. And the other will be, too." He swung around to face the older man. "You've been like a brother to me, Simon, and don't think I don't appreciate it. But this thing between Maggie and me is personal. It's something we have to work out ourselves."

"Just answer one question. Does this have anything to do with the man you're after?"

"That's personal, too, Simon," he said quietly, then turned and walked off the porch, leaving Simon in the cold darkness with his cigar.

❦ 9 ❦

Maggie hadn't allowed herself as much time as she would have liked in the bath, because she felt it was awful to keep the three men out of their own house. Bertha had told her they'd be in the bunkhouse swapping tales with the hands and really wouldn't mind, but she still felt guilty. Now she was sitting in her rocking chair, which she had pulled up in front of the window, while she combed her hair dry. The bedroom door was open enough to let heat in, but closed enough to give her privacy. She had donned her flannel nightgown and wrapper but was still chilled, so she had wrapped a quilt around her before sitting down.

The stars weren't quite as bright through her small window as they had seemed while on the porch with Will, but as she sat in the cool darkness watching them, she felt close to him still. Her mind wandered, drowsiness almost getting the best of her. She heard the door open, and then Simon's voice. Pete answered, and the sounds of their conversation seemed to drift into her consciousness from far away. Quiet laughter. A chair scraping on the wooden floors. The clang of the wood stove as someone opened it up, then the muffled clunk of wood being dropped in. The homey noises and the mingled scents of wood smoke, coffee, lye soap, and freshly baked bread made her feel as if she belonged here.

The door opened again, and then Maggie heard Bertha's voice. "Will! We were just wondering if we could get into town for church tomorrow. What do you think?"

Maggie didn't hear his answer, but she was suddenly wide awake. If tomorrow was Sunday, this had to be Saturday, and Dr. Wolcott was supposed to have come out to pick her up for the dance. It was long past five, but was he still coming? Could he come, or were the roads impassable? Guiltily she hoped he wouldn't be able to make it. It seemed like years ago that she had promised to go with him, and so many things had happened to her in that length of time that she wasn't even the same person who had determined to go and have a good time with the young doctor.

"Maggie?" The voice at the door was so sudden it made her jump. Uncle Simon tapped lightly on the wood. "May I come in?"

"Of course, Uncle Simon," she answered as she rose and crossed the room to open the door wider.

He smiled at her. "It's good to have you back unharmed. I didn't know what I was going to say to your parents if I let anything happen to you."

She put her arms around his waist and her head on his chest and gave him a hug. "Don't worry. First of all, nothing could have happened to me with Will there to take care of me. And second, my parents know me well enough to realize that any trouble I get into I do by myself."

"Are you sure you're all right? Nothing happened up there?"

She smiled at him. "Dear Uncle Simon, promising my parents you'd protect me as well as they would. Believe me, nothing happened. I can't say I didn't want it to, though."

He chuckled. "You're so much like your mother, Maggie."

"Did you love her very much?" He became very still, and she wondered if she'd offended him.

"Who told you I loved her?"

"No one. I saw the picture in your front room. I guessed the rest."

"It was a long time ago."

"And yet not so very long, if you still have feelings for her. Did you know her before she was married to my father?"

"I knew her—we both did—from the time we were little children. I always loved her." His eyes took on a faraway look, and he continued. "Everyone thought we'd get married. Lizzie and I were the same age, and Lawrence was five years older. We used to laugh at his pompousness. He always took life so seriously, and Lizzie and I wanted only to have fun."

He didn't say anything for a long time, and finally Maggie asked softly, "What happened, then?"

He met her eyes, and smiled. "Lizzie grew up and became Elizabeth, married the brother who was truly right for her, and had this wonderful daughter."

"And you?"

"I don't know. Sometimes I think I still haven't grown up. I've spent a lot of years trying to find out what I want to do with my life."

"But what about this ranch? You've worked hard to make it prosper."

"It's filled up some lonely hours. It's good for a man to have something to build, but if he has no one to leave it to, then what's the use?"

"What about Kate? Have you asked her to marry you yet?"

"Maggie, Maggie. I can see I'm going to have to be careful what I say around you."

"That didn't answer my question. I'm not being nosy, you know. I care about your happiness."

"Well, then, I'll tell you. I did ask her, and she turned me down flat."

"Why? Did she give you a reason?"

"No, and even if she did, I wouldn't tell you. Now what about you?"

She drew back. "What about me?"

"Do you still have feelings for Charles?"

She laughed. "Oh, Uncle Simon, I know now I never had 'feelings' for Charles. It just seemed the thing to do at the time."

"And Will?"

"Touché." She wandered over and dropped back down into the rocker. "How can I say what I feel for a man I hardly know and yet feel like I've known all my life?"

"Hmmm. This sounds serious."

"I don't know. It might be someday. I vowed after Charles that I would never get myself into a position like that again. I think a year or two of courtship before marriage wouldn't be out of line. Surely in that length of time you would get to know someone well enough to know if you wanted to spend the rest of your life with him." And, she thought, he'd have time to take care of whatever it was that kept him from her.

"It's hard to say. I thought I knew Lizzie better than any other person on earth. Kate, now, is very hard to get to know. She keeps so much hidden, even from me. I find that exciting, in a way. She'd never bore me, because I'm always finding out something new about her. I think that's the way a marriage should be, don't you?"

"I don't know. Wouldn't that be a bit scary? What if you found out something after you were married that upset you?"

"Maggie," he said with a laugh, "I guarantee marriage will get you upset more than once. If it doesn't, you're not really living. But if you truly love someone, you can work it out."

"I'm not sure if I'm strong enough for that."

"Of course you are. Meet life and love head-on, Maggie. Don't make the same mistake I did and live your life alone. It's no good to be alone. People were meant to have partners, and if you're lucky enough to find your partner, don't make excuses for not marrying him."

"Are you saying you think Will is my partner?"

"Maybe. I'm just saying give him a chance. He's had a lot of hardship in his life, and he may not be the easiest person to get along with, but he's a good man. He'd be good to you and give his life for you, if he had to."

"My, my. A man like that sounds almost too good to be true," she teased him.

"Just like your mother. I'd better get out of here while I can."

"Thank you, Uncle Simon. I know you're trying to look out for me, but I can take care of my own emotions, at least."

"I'm sure you can. Good night now."

"Good night. And Uncle Simon?"

"What?"

"Don't give up on Kate."

"No danger of that, young lady."

He left her alone then, and her thoughts returned to Will. He was on the other side of that door, and all she had to do was open it to see him, but she didn't. She'd said she could take care of her emotions. Well, she'd better start thinking more with her head than her heart. Only that was a very difficult thing to do when he was near her. Her brain just quit functioning, it seemed, and her body took over. She sighed and turned back the quilts to get into bed. The sheets felt icy cold, and as she fell asleep she didn't even think about the fact that Chase had never come to pick her up. Her last thoughts were of how warm she'd been sleeping in Will's arms.

As often happens, the days following the blizzard were full of sunshine so bright it was blinding, and Will explained snow blindness to Maggie "—and a person can't see anything but white. It's scary and dangerous, because it's easy to lose your way or fall in a hole, because you simply cannot see."

They were walking on snowshoes behind the barn, on the flats they'd raced across during the blizzard, following the stallion, who now seemed perfectly content to stay in the barn or corral. Maggie was wearing the same clothes she'd worn that day, feeling more comfortable in them than she had thought possible. She had gone to return them to him, freshly laundered and folded neatly, but he had told her if she was to join them in the running of the ranch, the pants would be a lot more practical than long skirts. She had agreed, and the outfit became her usual daytime wear.

Will had been trying for days to get the girl alone so he could talk to her, but with seven other people around, and travel out of the question, he hadn't been able to accomplish the task. Every time he'd think they were alone in the barn, one of the hands would show up. On the cabin porch, Pete or Simon seemed always in evidence. He had even slipped with her into the frigid front room, knowing full well no one went in there in the winter, but Bertha chose that day to clean the room for the coming spring.

The snowshoes had been a late-night inspiration. He had lain awake long after the others had fallen asleep, contemplating crossing the kitchen to her room, but he figured the way his luck had been running, someone would have been there already, keeping watch over the girl. They had ridden one day, but Simon had volunteered to go along, and rode in between Maggie and Will, the latter wondering how in tarnation the older man thought his niece could get courted when the two of them were never left alone.

Then he thought of the snowshoes. There were only two pairs, one belonging to Pete who was unable to stand the long walk to the trap lines in the winter, and the other Will's, which had been made so he could help the old man out in the first year or two, before the trapping was given up altogether. He grinned in the darkness and planned his next day, complete with picnic lunch.

The lunch was on his back in a pack he'd fashioned after the ones the fur trappers used, along with blankets and water and some jerky wrapped in parchment. He hadn't told either Maggie or the others what he planned, getting up before even Bertha to prepare the repast and secrete it in the bedroom in the barn. When he had returned to the cabin, the others were already up and dressed. After breakfast he and Maggie had gone outside as usual, and he explained the snowshoes to her, asking if she wanted to learn how to use them. She had readily accepted the challenge, and now they were half a mile from the ranch buildings, and no one could get to them without a great amount of trouble.

"You're right. I can't even see where the land dips and rises. What happens if you do fall into a hole?" Maggie asked him.

"Sometimes you get buried and can smother. If you should happen to fall, keep your hands and arms moving in front of your face to keep the snow away from your nose and mouth." He demonstrated by raising his arms to eye level and making vigorous circles with his open hands in front of his face. Maggie laughed at his antics, then tried it herself, feeling good inside.

Maggie didn't know where they were going and didn't care. The day was full of glorious sunshine, and the fresh air invigorated her. She had missed her walking tremendously, especially since she couldn't even get on a horse and canter across the open fields as she was wont to do at home. The snowshoes had been awkward at first, but now she was matching Will step for step, her legs nearly as long as his, and they were covering a lot of ground, leaving the confines of the ranch far behind.

"Do you want a drink?" Will asked. "I brought two canteens full."

"Never be caught without again, right?"

"Right. You have no idea what could have happened to us, Maggie."

"Of course I do. I told you I'm reasonably intelligent and well informed. I've read enough to know that we could survive several days on water alone, although we would probably have been too weak to walk back out. The horses would have needed some food, but I figured in a pinch we could have dug down under the snow and pulled up dead grasses for them. As long as they were nourished they could have carried us out. If hungry wolves or other predators had come after us, we'd have had to sacrifice a horse to them, but with three horses and only the two of us we would more likely than not have made it. Also, by the next evening, the winds had died down enough that the ground blizzards weren't a danger anymore, and the moon was full, so if we'd had to wait that long, we could have, too."

She had stopped walking when she began her speech,

shading her eyes as she looked at Will, and he thought again how strikingly beautiful she was, and how good to be with. He marveled that she knew things from reading that had taken him years of experience to find out. The snowshoeing had seemed to come easily to her, and he made plans to take her up to the National Park, Yellowstone. He had been there several times, hiking to the sights one couldn't see from the tourist coaches that made their daily runs through the interior of the park. There were lovely high meadow lakes all around them here, too, and he'd take her to see them as soon as the trails were passable.

They had climbed to the same spot from which they had seen the ranch on their trip back from the cabin, and she turned to look across the valley, the cruel storm still a vivid, though almost unbelievable memory. They had lost several head of cattle, and when Maggie had seen them, their pitiful faces encased in ice, she had shuddered in fresh fear for what might have happened to them.

"Are you hungry yet?" he asked her. It was near noon, and they'd been steadily hiking for several hours.

"Starved. Here, let me help you," she answered, holding the pack as he slipped the straps from his shoulders. "We can sit on this rock. I'll bet it's warm from the sun."

"I brought blankets to sit on."

"My, you thought of everything, didn't you?"

He laughed. "If I'd been this prepared before, we'd still be in that cabin, away from all the company down there."

"Hmmm, they are a bit intent on socializing, aren't they? I never thought I'd get to know the hands so well."

"I've known them for years, and I can tell you I've learned more than I ever wanted to know about any of them these past couple of days. It's irritating the fire out of me."

"They're quite transparent in their intentions, but it seems rather late to offer themselves as chaperon for the two of us," she mused.

"That's what I want to talk to you about, Maggie."

But he was silent as they settled onto the blankets to bask in the warm spring sunshine. She took off the heavy coat now that she was warm from her recent exertions, and added it to her pile of blankets. The rock wasn't quite as warm as she'd thought it might be.

Will took the packets of food out of the pack and placed them on the blankets near her, then took off his own coat and stretched out opposite her.

"What's what you want to talk to me about?"

He turned on his side and raised his head on his arm so he could look at her.

We started this whole thing half-assed backward. Out loud he said, "I think we need to start all over again, this time from the beginning. Ours were unusual circumstances, to say the least, and somehow we found ourselves in compromising situations without any contrivance on the part of either of us."

Maggie blushed and replied, "My parents would be horrified if they knew."

"Maggie, I never meant to sully your reputation. I respect you tremendously."

Maggie gave a halfhearted attempt at a smile, and the sad look he'd seen in her eyes once before returned. Her heart constricted. This was the part where he'd tell her that although he had great respect for her, he loved someone else.

Will's insides twisted. "I want to get to know you better, Maggie."

She lifted her face to the sun, away from him, closed her eyes, and took in a deep breath of the clear air. She wouldn't cry in front of him.

"Maggie." He hesitated, not knowing what was going on inside her heart and wishing he did. "Maggie, we don't know anything about each other. Normally a man and woman spend a lot of time talking before they start touching. We started out touching and haven't even gotten to the talking part yet." She still wouldn't look at him. He tried again. "I find you fascinating, Maggie Longyear, and I want to know more about you."

She looked at him then, uncertainty on her face. He wanted more than anything to take her in his arms and let her know exactly how he felt about her, but that would make his words a lie. "Do you think we could start over? Get to know each other and then see where it leads us?"

"We could try." But how could she keep him from knowing that she wanted to be in his arms? How could she keep herself from showing how much she loved and wanted him?

He smiled at her, took her hand, and placed a single kiss on it. "Let's eat, then, because we'll have to start back soon. I'm surprised they haven't sent out a search party." The plain food tasted enormously good to both of them, and they slipped unconsciously back into the light banter they'd shared while Maggie had been nursing Will's head injury. Both were reluctant to see the day end.

Will finished eating and stood up, stretching, while Maggie gathered the picnic things and put them back in his pack.

"Do you think you could make me one of these, too?" she asked him.

"A pack?" He turned to look at her. "Of course. Try that one on, and I can see how big to make it."

She tried to pull the pack on, and he went behind her to help. The closeness made his insides tumble again, and he stepped away quickly. "How does that feel?"

"Good." She turned around and grinned at him. "I thought it would be heavy, but it isn't. I wish I'd had one of these back home." She shrugged back out of it and dropped it to the blanket.

"What was your home like? What did you do there?" He leaned against a big rock outcropping and watched her movements.

"Surely Simon has told you about Longacres," she replied, but he shook his head, and she answered with a question of her own. "Where are you from?"

"Virginia." He hadn't ever told anyone out here where he was from.

"Then my home was probably a lot like yours." She

didn't know if he was rich or poor, and didn't want to seem boastful. "As for what I did, I'm ashamed to admit that I really didn't do much of anything. I read a lot, went for long walks and rides, worked some around the stables—not very productive, I'm afraid."

"Do you like this place?" he asked suddenly.

"The ranch? I love it," she replied.

"No, I mean this place, in this clearing."

She looked around. The clearing was flat, surrounded by trees on three sides. The rock where they sat covered the face of the hill, and they had an unobstructed view of the valley and the mountains. She tried to imagine what it would look like without all the snow, and decided that, yes, she did like it. "It would make a good place for a cabin. Do flowers grow up this high?"

He had been holding his breath, waiting for her reply, and let it out slowly. "Of course. This clearing looks like a carpet of blooms in the summer. There's a spring over there, and just over that rise is a lake. When the snow melts a bit more, I'll take you over there."

"Can't we go there now?"

"Not today anymore. It will take us until dark to get back as it is. I don't know about you, but I'm not ready to be stuck out here again anytime soon."

"Oh, I don't know," she teased. "We came through unscathed the last time." *Except for our emotions,* they both thought.

He looked at her, at her dark eyes full of desire, and murmured softly, "I don't think I could spend another night alone with you. I'm only a man, after all."

She smiled, not knowing what to say to him. He was a man, all right, and one who made her senses tremble. She didn't know what to make of his words which held so much promise, yet kept her at arm's length.

"We'd better get back. The sun will be behind the peaks soon." He moved to the blankets and picked up her coat, holding it so she could put it on, then donned his own. He couldn't quite meet her eyes. Did she know the effect her words had had on him? Was it an invitation, or was she an innocent? Whichever, he had to keep his distance. Maybe Simon was right to keep them chaperoned. Their relationship was fragile, and he didn't want to do anything to jeopardize it.

During the days that followed, Maggie and Will became friends, and both cherished the friendship because neither had ever known another like it. They talked about everything except their feelings for one another and the parts of their past that kept them apart.

Maggie was afraid to be alone with Will, while at the same time she wanted nothing more. In the mornings they both rose early to be together as long as possible, then spent breakfast trying not to look at each other. If his hand accidentally brushed hers while passing dishes, she blushed deeply, and he jumped back as if he'd been burned. They'd been scolded by Bertha more than once for dropping a dish in that manner, and both of them were embarrassed that they couldn't hide their feelings more successfully.

One bright, clear morning, Will announced that he would teach Maggie to shoot that day.

"I'll come along," Simon announced. "But don't expect her to learn in a day."

Maggie grinned. Simon knew perfectly well that she could already shoot, and she sensed a setup.

Will grinned. "I'm counting on her not to learn in a day."

"Are you sure this is something I need to know?" she asked innocently, and Will assured her it was.

They went behind the ranch house, away from the livestock, and Will set up tin cans on the fence in a row. He checked and loaded the revolver, then checked it again before handing it to her.

"Now," he explained, "this is the trigger, and when you pull it back, the gun fires, so don't pull it back until you're ready to shoot, and don't shoot until you've pointed it at your intended target."

She gave him a withering look. "I've seen guns before. My father has several revolvers and rifles."

Simon laughed. "Lawrence is quite a good shot, too. She may have inherited his eye."

"Okay, then have at it." Will crossed his arms and stood behind her, near Simon.

Maggie didn't know what to do. Should she play the young girl afraid of guns, or show him what she could do, had been able to do since she was a child? She had offended more than one young man by beating him at the traps, but somehow she didn't think Will was of that calibre. She appealed to Simon with pleading in her eyes, but he looked away, toward the mountains. She decided to be true to herself. Raising the gun in one smooth motion, she sent the first can flying.

"Damn!" Will exclaimed.

"I told you she might be good." Simon winked at his niece.

"Are you sure you never shot a gun before?" Will had the feeling he'd been duped.

"I never said I hadn't shot a gun before. You just assumed I hadn't. That was pretty good, though, wasn't it?"

"Yeah, it was good. Now let's see you do it again."

She missed the next can, then hit five in a row.

"Did you see that, Simon? She didn't even take aim!" Will exclaimed.

"Do you want to teach me to take aim?" she asked saucily.

"Never mind. You're doing fine."

She hit at least four out of every six shots, so Will moved her back farther. When she'd gotten the new bearings, she did just as well, but her arm was beginning to tire from the heavy gun and the repeated recoil.

"We'd better call it a day. Her arm is going to be sore tomorrow as it is," Simon finally said.

She was inordinately proud of herself, because she'd looked good for Will. She had the feeling he was proud of her, too, and knew it when they reached the barn later to put the tin cans in a bucket before feeding the horses. Guilt was nagging her, however, so she decided to confess.

"Will, I should tell you that I've been shooting since I was a little girl."

"You were holding out on me?"

She nodded. "I still remember the first time. I had followed my father and the other men out to the field to shoot, and I told my father I could do that, too. He told me I was too little, that I wouldn't even be able to hold the gun, and I said, 'Oh, but I can. I'm sure of it.' So he gave me a gun, and I shot it. Landed on my backside, and missed the target by a mile, but I didn't drop the gun. I've gone on the hunt since I was twelve."

"Well, you sure surprised the heck out of me. Not many men can shoot that good, much less a lady."

"I told you, I'm not a lady. And I'd rather be out shooting than baking bread, I assure you."

"Well, they both have their place, but I do like fresh, hot bread with butter."

"Bread-making is not really my forte." She was uncomfortable that she didn't know the first thing about cooking.

"I don't care if you never make me bread, Maggie." He was standing inches from her, and they could both feel the current drawing them together. He raised his hand and lifted a stray strand of hair from her cheek across her jaw as he moved it behind her shoulder. She felt a chill down her spine and closed her eyes, wanting to stay like that forever.

He looked down at her face, at her closed eyes, and wanted nothing more than to kiss her, to take her in his arms and make her his, but he couldn't, and he cursed the fact. He had to get off the ranch and get that nearly unthinkable deed done so he could come back to her and tell her what was in his heart. It was easy to let the days go by without action, because she was so good to be with, but he couldn't continue forever in this limbo. It wasn't fair to her, either.

"Maggie," he started, then stopped.

"What?" She opened her eyes and looked at his face above hers, full of longing, and of something else she couldn't read.

He almost told her how he felt, then remembered Simon's warning. *Don't take her heart and then go get yourself killed. I won't have her hurt.* He wouldn't hurt her, either, if it was in his power to stop, he thought, and answered, "We should go into the house now."

She nodded, confused and slightly hurt. What was it? she wondered. What kept him at a distance from her when it was obvious he wanted her? She wasn't blind. It didn't take any experience to see the desire, the smoldering passion, in his eyes. Even though she'd never even remotely experienced such heady feelings, she now recognized them for what they were. Was it her? Was she nothing but an amusement while he was stranded out on the ranch, to be forgotten as soon as he could get back into town? She wasn't sure enough about her own attraction to rule that out completely. She mutely followed him out the big door.

Chase Wolcott had ridden up the valley as soon as the roads permitted travel. He hadn't been able to get word to Maggie Longyear that he'd not be able to pick her up for the dance, and even though he knew Simon would explain it to her, he still felt the need to apologize. He hated to keep a pretty girl waiting. He rode up to the rail, dismounted, and looked around the yard. He spied Maggie and Will coming out of the barn and called to them. "Will! Miss Longyear!"

Maggie stopped dead in her tracks while Will stepped forward to shake hands with his friend. She was wearing Will's clothing and was horrified that the young doctor had caught her that way. She knew she must look a mess, with her hair windblown and her cheeks an unladylike red from the cold. She wished she could sink into a hole and disappear, but she was not to be so blessed, for Dr. Wolcott was coming toward her, a smile of greeting on his face.

"Miss Longyear, I apologize for standing you up for the dance and I came to ask if you would forgive me and give me another chance. There's to be another dance this

Saturday. Could I hope that you might allow me to escort you to it?"

She was spared from answering as Will stepped forward and declared, "Maggie's going to the dance with me."

Surprise showed on her face as she raised startled eyes to him. He was looking into her eyes with an intensity that made her shiver. They hadn't even discussed going to a dance together, but the idea pleased her very much. She turned back to the doctor and smiled graciously. "Thank you very much for asking, though. And of course I forgive you. The roads were impassable." What was she to think of Will? He pulled her heart and her emotions back and forth like a swing.

Simon came out of the cabin then and, after greeting Chase, invited him for supper. Western hospitality was new to Maggie. Meals, and the guests attending them, had been carefully planned far in advance where she grew up. She didn't think a guest had ever been asked to share a meal with her family on the spur of the moment.

Maggie hurried into the cabin and closed herself in her room where she changed out of the outlandish outfit of Will's, hoping Chase hadn't noticed what she was wearing because of the long coat. Her hair was tangled from being out in the wind, and she tore a brush through it, determined to wear it coiled around her head in a braid in the future. She dashed water on her face and hurriedly donned a gown of soft peach lawn before entering the main room again.

It was fascinating to listen to the young doctor talk, and she realized why visitors were so welcome in an area where travel was so limited because of the weather. As she set the table, moving in and out among the men, she learned a month's worth of news in the valley. Chase was filling them in on all the local gossip, and Maggie quietly moved behind the men seated around the long table and began helping Bertha dish up the crisp, golden fried chicken, mashed potatoes, biscuits, gravy, carrots, and green beans. Maggie herself had gone to the cellar to pull the carrots and beans from the sand in which they were stored for the winter. It amazed her that anyone could take such shriveled and dried vegetables and make them taste as good as Bertha did.

Chase watched her, sorry that he'd missed the chance to take her to a dance before Will, because she was lovely to look at. But he had never seen his friend so obviously taken with a woman before, and he was glad of it. Will had always seemed lonely to him. He'd tried to introduce him to several of the girls he knew, but Will had replied that if he wanted to get involved with a girl, he could take his pick from the ranchers' daughters who were obviously out to get a husband, settle down, and raise a passel of children.

It amused Chase to see the exchanged glances between the two of them, and he sighed for a lost chance, but knew there were plenty of other nice-looking girls around. He never lacked long for feminine companionship and wasn't yet ready to make a permanent match, either. Unlike Will, he just didn't have any qualms about light romances or a night at Kate's, if he felt the need.

After they had finished off the huge meal with apple pan dowdy topped with thick cream, Simon turned to Chase and asked, "How about a game of checkers?"

Chase leaned back in his chair and put his hands on his belly. "Oh, I wish I could, if for no other reason than to let this delicious meal settle before I have to ride back to town. But I'm afraid I can't tonight. I have two stops to make on my way back, and another patient I should see in town. I'll take that for an open invitation, though, and someday when I have time, I'll take you up on it."

They said good-bye to him then, and Will and Maggie walked him out to his horse. Will had his arm around Maggie's shoulder as the doctor rode around the curve of trees and out of sight, and he was reluctant to remove it. This was the way it should be, only they should have their own cabin, he thought. When the snow melted and the meadows were full of wildflowers, he'd take Maggie back to his special place where he planned to build their cabin and tell her.

"I love it here, Will," she said softly in the darkness. "I

didn't know I would. Everything is so different from what I've known all my life."

"It's a good life, Maggie." He pulled her closer to him. "A hard life, but the rewards are worth all the hardships."

"Are they?"

"Of course. Oh, Maggie, sometimes when I look at those mountains, I get a feeling inside . . . I don't know . . . it fills me with grandness. And the land, it's so full of wonderful things, the little lakes up high, the meadows full of flowers, waterfalls, and crystal-clear streams. I'll take you up on Signal Mountain one morning before dawn, so we can watch the sun come up. The valley floor is sometimes covered with a low-hanging mist, and it seems like something out of a dream world, paradise. The beavers are so abundant, they'll never be trapped out, and they have helped shape the valley with their dams. From up on the mountains, you can look down and see it all like some god from ancient times surveying his kingdom.

"Sunsets are different every day, and I always try to stop what I'm doing to savor them. The mountains themselves seem a presence, almost, there from time out of mind, and holding steadfast long after we mere mortals are gone from this earth. It's so cold up there that there are glaciers, great masses of ice that never melt. And on one of them, that one over there," he said as he pointed to a wide mountain, flatter at the top than the Tetons, "that one is Mount Moran, and there's a black streak running up the face of it that they say is the cooled lava from an ancient volcano. The rest of the mountain wore away from around it, it's been there so long. In this valley, I can easily envision the very fires of creation."

Maggie could, too, as she listened to the man she loved, his voice impassioned over the home he loved. Yes, she could learn to love it as much as he did, she was sure of it. They could have such a wonderful life together if only the invisible obstacle could be cleared from their past.

Saturday came quickly, and Maggie was in her room trying to decide what to wear to the dance. She changed into a dress every evening for supper, but she wanted to wear something special since this was her first real outing with Will in public. She had discarded several choices, wanting nothing that would remind either her or Will of the red dress she'd borrowed from Kate, and the disastrous evening that had followed. She couldn't decide between an apricot silk, which might be too fancy for a country dance, and a more modest yellow gown that she felt wasn't quite enough to impress him.

Bertha came in and looked at the pile of silks on the bed. "Land sakes! What must your mama and daddy be thinking, to buy you so many dresses!"

"Oh, these are only a few of what I have. I couldn't bring everything."

"Well, all I can say is that you'd better marry a rich man if you plan to spend so much on frivolities."

"Bertha, I've had 'frivolities' all my life. They were more important to my mother than to me, and, believe it or not, I prefer Will's old clothes to any of these to wear around here. But I cannot decide which to wear to the dance. Would you help me?"

Bertha hadn't done much fussing with fancy dresses in her life, but she had a good sense of style, and she didn't like either of the dresses Maggie held up. "What else do you have?"

Flustered, Maggie held each one from the bed up, and each time Bertha shook her head.

"Maybe I don't have anything suitable."

"Nonsense. Any of these would do, but you want to look special, don't you?"

Blushing, she replied, "Yes, of course."

"Are there any more in there?" Bertha indicated the closet, which was full of hanging gowns, and went over to have a look herself. She slowly looked at each gown, then stopped at one and looked over it up to Maggie's face. She nodded and brought the gown out. It was a deep turquoise silk, simply decorated, the neckline neither too low nor too modest. Maggie had passed over it because of its simplicity. Bertha chose it for the same reason.

"You want a man to look at you, not your dress. If you

were going with the doctor, now, that yellow dress would
be just fine, or any of the others. The other one you
showed me, that peachy one there, that's a mite high-
falutin for one of these dances." She fingered a dress on
the bed and smiled. "My, how I would have loved to
have a dress like this when I was your age. 'Course, back
then we were lucky to have two dresses, one for Sunday
meeting and one for work. There wasn't money for more
than that."

"Do you think we could alter one of these to fit you?"
Maggie asked excitedly.

"Oh, heavens no! I'm too old for any of these. I'll just
be wearing my black silk."

"Really, Bertha, I have a light blue that might work."
She rummaged along the line of dresses. "Here! What do
you think?"

Bertha's head had never been turned by a fancy dress,
but as she looked at the lovely ice blue gown Maggie was
holding before her, she thought maybe, just once, it
would be grand to go to a dance in a dress like that.

"It would never fit me. I'm a good foot shorter than
you." But as she said it she thought, yes, it could be
altered. The lines were simple, the skirt unfettered with
banding or ruffles that might make the job difficult.
"Besides, I don't want to ruin your pretty dress."

"Nonsense! You said yourself I have too many, and
that's one that never has suited me anyway. Try it on!"
Maggie urged.

Bertha blushed and took the lovely silk in her shaking
hands, not believing she was really going to do this, but
determined that she would.

Two hours later the men came in to get themselves
ready to go. The two women were through with their
baths and were in Maggie's room, where Maggie had
volunteered to fix Bertha's hair. The silvery strands were
thick and abundant, and Maggie had no problem fash-
ioning a very becoming upsweep secured with silver
combs and pins.

Bertha stared, and the woman who stared back from
the mirror looked so different she almost lost her nerve.

The pale blue dress set off her hair to perfection and brought out the blue of her eyes. Oh, she thought to herself, if only she'd had this dress when she was seventeen and still blond, before the harsh climate and years of hard work had taken their toll. She sighed and settled for this night, forty years later, when her Pete would be proud to show her off. She hugged Maggie, a quick hard squeeze, then left to go to her husband.

Pete was speechless when she slipped into their room a few minutes later as he was putting on his string tie. His hands stilled their motion, and, the tie forgotten, he moved slowly toward her. She looked like a grand queen, her hair in a shining coronet on her head, and her blue eyes sparkling. He stared at her for a few minutes, then smiled, seeing her as she'd been when he married her, so long ago. She was once again as beautiful as the first day he ever saw her, dancing in a sun-drenched meadow of wildflowers, surrounded by butterflies, her berry basket forgotten at her feet. He held out his hands to her now as he had then, and she came to him again, their feet remembering the dance, albeit at a slower pace, as they moved silently around the small room in each other's arms.

Will was alone in the kitchen when Maggie appeared. He looked her up and down slowly, his eyes caressing every inch of her. His attitude toward her had undergone a change. Before, she was just a very desirable woman. Now she was special, she was loved, and she was his friend. He sent her a silent toast, and she smiled and curtsied. The deep turquoise of her gown gave her a glow and made her hair take on an even richer hue. She was wearing it down, the sides pulled back with combs, and she looked as fresh and beautiful as the first flowers peeking from under the winter snow.

He felt slightly impatient as he looked at her, but much of the impatience was with himself. If he was going to marry her, and he was quite certain he would ask her, he should just do it and get it done with, so he wouldn't have to constantly keep a hold on his desires lest he forget himself with her. And yet he couldn't come to grips with what had happened with his wife, couldn't just put it in his past and forget it. He had to keep reminding himself that he and Maggie had only known each other for a matter of weeks, and it was too soon to propose marriage anyway. The two sides of his subconscious battled within him, leaving him drained at times.

Pete and Bertha came out of their room, and a moment later Simon appeared.

"My, but don't you two ladies look lovely tonight!"

His voice brought Will out of his musing. He turned to Bertha and agreed. "Bertha, I have never seen you look so fine!"

"Aw, go on now. It was Miss Maggie's doing and all." For the first time since they'd known Bertha, she seemed to have nothing to say, and they were all delighted.

"Are you trying to make old Pete jealous, Bertha? Shame on you!" Simon scolded.

"She's going to be the belle of the ball, for sure. And with Pete's bad legs, she's just going to have to dance with all the other men there," Will teased.

"Now, you boys keep yer jawin' to yerselves. My Bertha ain't a gonna dance with no other men 'cept me, and I'll thank ya to remember it." Pete admonished the two younger men while Bertha sent a look of gratitude toward Maggie.

Maggie looked at the couple, still in love after forty years, and wondered if she and Will would be the same. It was hard to imagine them at that age. She'd be sixty-three, and Will . . . she had no idea how old Will was. Something else to find out about him. She smiled up at him as he came to her to help her on with her cloak.

The night was balmy for spring, and the group, including Dave and the other three hands, set out with high spirits. Once they got to the main road, they met up with other revelers and traded good-natured ribbing and teasing back and forth. At one point one wagonload of young people started a song, and it was soon passed along the line. Maggie loved it, cuddling in close to Will, a smile on her face. She could have ridden that way forever, but the miles went quickly, and before she was ready, they arrived in town.

The dance was packed. Everyone was very tired of the long winter and had been looking forward to going to town for weeks. People who never came to the dances came to this one, and the musicians could hardly be heard above the roar of talk and laughter. The dance floor was too full for Will's taste, so he escorted Maggie over to the refreshment table, stopping to introduce her to friends and neighbors several times along the way.

Bertha was an instant hit and basked in the attention, something she had had very little of during her life. Pete took her out and turned her around the floor in a polka that belied the pain in his legs, and Maggie's eyes grew damp with tears as she watched them.

Simon had dropped the group off and had gone to get Kate. He didn't think she'd really go with him, but he wanted to try one more time. She seemed to have the belief that she'd not be welcome there, and although he realized there would be those who would scorn her presence, he wanted to believe that most of the people there would accept her as a member of the community.

When he got to her door, she greeted him in a dressing gown.

"You're not ready yet? I told you I'd be here at seven." He'd ridden in a couple of days earlier to see her and ask her to go to the dance with him.

"And I told you I wasn't going."

"Come on, Kate. I want to take you out somewhere other than the hotel for once. Do you realize we've never been anywhere but there in four years?"

"Simon, I can't go to the dance. I wouldn't be welcome."

"How do you know that? You've never tried, have you? You might be surprised. These are good country people. They're not going to shun you."

"I've been surprised one too many times by 'good country people,' Simon. Whatever you might think, those women don't want a woman who runs a saloon and brothel to be around their men. It's too much of a threat to them. Reminds them that they have to keep on their toes, or the man they think loves them will come to the Seven Squaw to get what he doesn't get at home."

"Kate, Kate, marry me, and then I'll take you away from all this. You won't have to hide away ever again."

"I'd never do that to you, Simon. You know as well as I do that wherever we might go, people would find out, and then your good friends would shun you, too. My life is mine, and I accept it, but I can't mess up yours, too."

"You can't mess up my life. Kate, I'm forty-two years old. I'm beyond caring what people think of me. All I care about is being happy, and I can't be happy if you won't marry me."

"What about your brother and his wife? Would you care if they wouldn't accept your wife?"

"They already know all about you and your life," he lied.

Kate sighed. "Why can't we just keep on the way we have been? I've not even looked at another man since I met you. I'm here for you any time you want me. Why isn't that enough?"

"I want children, Kate. I want to build a cattle-and-horse empire to leave to my sons."

She turned quickly away from him. "I can't have children, Simon."

"What do you mean, you can't have children?"

"Something happened when my son was born. I was told I could never bear another child." She hadn't told Simon all her past, but had selected parts of it to share with him. He knew she had had a son who'd died, but she hadn't told him it was an Indian child, nor that it was the tribe medicine man who had told her there would be no more children.

Simon was temporarily taken aback, as his future dreams revolved around the children he so wanted, but he recovered quickly. "I don't care about children, Kate. I want to marry you."

"Liar."

He dropped down into a chair, and with his elbows on his knees he lowered his forehead into his hands for a moment, then, clasping his fingers under his chin, he stared up at her. "I'm tired of being alone. It's no good to build something alone."

"Then go find yourself a nice woman who can give you what you want, Simon, because I can't." She had tears in her eyes and turned away from him so he wouldn't see.

"I don't want another woman, Kate. I want you."

"Well, you can't have me. Not on those terms." She looked at him again. "I think you should leave now."

"Do you deny that you love me as much as I love you?"

"What does it matter?" She pushed him toward the door and opened it.

"It matters to me."

She looked into his eyes for a long moment and then said, "I can't." She closed the door on him before she let loose a torrent of tears. She loved Simon enough to brave the onslaught of public outrage if she married him, but what if he wasn't that strong? She knew she couldn't let herself love again, only to have it snatched away like all the other good things in her life. And so she let him go, and cried herself to sleep alone.

❧ 10 ❧

Will and Maggie were dancing a waltz, lost in one another. They were acutely aware of each point of contact between them, and they had to struggle not to press closer. Maggie felt as if she were floating in a dream, with music coming from far away. Will was an excellent dancer, and she idly wondered where he'd learned to waltz. It didn't seem in keeping with the rough life she imagined he'd led. The music stopped, and a few seconds later, when they realized it, they stopped, too, and looked deeply into each other's eyes. Will tore his gaze away first, not willing to have her see what might be in his eyes. As he scanned the crowd aimlessly, he noticed Simon come in the door alone, a look of thunder on his face. Maggie saw his frown and followed his eyes until she, too, saw her uncle. She'd never seen him look so fierce, as though he could smash in the face of any person who dared to even look at him. They hurried over to him.

"Uncle Simon, what's wrong?" Maggie was the first to reach his side.

"Nothing's wrong." And to Will, "Where can a man get a drink around here?"

"Over here," Will answered and led the way to the refreshment table, where, along with the punch and sandwiches, there was a goodly supply of whiskey.

"How much for a bottle?" Simon asked the man behind the table, who told him and then accepted the coins placed in his hand. Will's frown was deepening because he'd never seen Simon act this way before.

"Simon, do you want to go home? We could go now, take the horses, and the hands could come in the wagon later."

"No, I don't want to go home. I want to have a good time." He took a deep swig on the bottle, and Maggie and Will exchanged a look of concern. Whatever the problem was, it had upset Simon terribly to make him act so completely out of character.

"Uncle Simon, tell me what happened." Maggie was scared by the look in his eyes.

"Nothing happened. Can't a fellow just have a good time without having to explain it to everyone?" he said crossly. Then he moved across the crowded floor toward the group standing against the far wall. Pete and Bertha had seen him by this time and they had come over to the younger couple, concern on their faces.

"What happened to Simon? Kate turn him down?" Bertha asked, and suddenly it became clear.

"Of course! Oh, Bertha, that must be it. He went to pick her up, and she wouldn't come with him."

"She knows her place, then." Bertha sniffed. Her disapproval of the woman had been the one thing she'd had against Simon. Other than that, he was a good and decent man, and why he'd associate with a prostitute was more than she could understand.

"What do you mean by that?" Maggie asked indignantly.

"The woman runs a whorehouse, Maggie," Will told her.

She turned on him angrily. "Uncle Simon said she's not one of them, and I believe him."

"Maybe she is, and maybe she isn't, but the fact remains that she is in the business."

"These are fine folk hereabout who are willing to forget a past transgression if a person shows repentance for it," Bertha said, "but how can they forgive her when she flaunts it in front of their eyes every day? If she was truly sorry for her sins and wanted forgiveness, she'd quit what she's doing."

"But Uncle Simon told me—" Maggie began.

"He told you what he'd like you to believe, maybe what he himself wants to believe, but he's wrong."

Maggie looked at her beloved uncle and felt great pity for him. Why couldn't he find happiness? Was he doomed to a life of loneliness?

By this time he was dancing with a tall blond girl who was laughing up into his face as he swung her around the floor. The dance ended, and he grabbed another eager partner from the ranks of females. Simon Longyear was a good catch, and he seldom came to these affairs. The men at the dance far outnumbered the women, however, and finally he found himself without a partner. He went over to the chairs and sat down, taking yet another long drink from the bottle in his hand.

The others from the ranch had decided to maintain a hands-off policy, just watching him in case he became intoxicated. When he went for his second bottle, Will tried to stop him.

"You've had enough."

"Like hell, I have. Now get outta my way." His words were slurred, and he waved on his feet as he made his way through the crowd to the dance floor.

"We have to get him out of here," Will told Maggie, "and fast."

"How do we do that?"

But they were spared trying to find a way because Simon had picked a fight with a young giant of a man and had been knocked flat on the floor. Maggie hurried to his side while Will and Pete kept the crowd from a free-for-all. Simon was out cold, with a silly grin on his face, and Maggie was mortified for him. Her uncle was handsome and proud. He'd be humiliated if he knew what he looked like.

The ranch hands had come forward and carried their boss out to the wagon. They had never seen him drink more than one drink, maybe two, and wondered what had caused him to act this way.

"Maggie and I will take him back to the house. There's no reason for the rest of you to leave the fun," said Will.

"You'd be better to take him out to the ranch. He won't be needing to be anywhere close to that woman when he wakes up. Pete and I can catch a ride with the Dungans. They go right by our place, and I know they have room in their wagon." Bertha didn't want to leave the dance, especially to nurse Simon after he'd made a fool of himself over a prostitute.

"You're probably right. We'll see you at home later, then."

Maggie had settled into the back of the wagon, cradling her uncle's head in her lap and wrapping herself and him in blankets. She thought about what Will and Bertha had said about Kate. Was it true? Was that what had caused Simon's behavior tonight?

"I'm sorry we had to leave so early," Will said over his shoulder.

"Oh, that's all right," she answered. "Besides, it was even more crowded there than it is at the ranch."

"Well, there won't be anyone there tonight."

"Uncle Simon will be."

"Only his body. Who knows where his mind is, but it won't be on us. We can sit in front of the fire and talk until the others get home. There'll be no one to disturb us."

"It would be nice to talk to you for once when I wasn't freezing cold." They always seemed to have to go outside somewhere to be alone.

"Oh, Maggie, I'm sorry! I never knew you thought of it that way."

"I'm just teasing you, Will. It's never cold when you're around."

"Is that so?"

"Yes, that's so. Why don't you hurry those nags up a little so we can get there faster?"

When they had gotten Simon into his bed, Will undressed him and covered him up. Maggie put some logs on the fire in the front room and had settled into the deep cushions of the settee when Will came in to join her.

"Alone at last," he teased her, and she grinned at him, then shivered.

"Are you cold?" he asked, taking the woven throw off the cushions behind her and wrapping it around her shoulders. He slipped in beside her, his feet on the low table in front of them.

"Did you have fun?" he asked her.

"Oh, yes. I'd never seen most of those dances before, though. The waltz was the only one I was familiar with."

"I noticed you danced with Chase."

"Yes, he was good enough to ask me, and I couldn't turn him down for one dance when I'd turned him down for the evening."

"You could have."

"Are you jealous?"

"Maybe. Do I have a reason to be?"

"Never," she said, and the conviction in her voice gave him a degree of comfort he hadn't thought possible when he'd watched her dance not only with the doctor, but also with several other men who were also years younger than he was. He was twelve years older than Maggie, but when he was with her he felt younger than he had in years.

He had tried all evening not to think about how desirable she looked in the dress she was wearing, and now that she was in his arms, it was even more difficult. She smelled warm and flowery, and his head filled with the scent. One kiss, he told himself. What harm could one little kiss do?

The fire was warm, and Maggie leaned her head into his shoulder, closing her eyes. How good it felt to be here, she thought, as if she belonged to this man. She allowed her mind to drift into one of her frequent daydreams of him, so that when he lifted her chin and placed his warm lips on hers, it was part of the dream.

She kissed him deeply, wanting nothing else than to be there, in the cozy cabin in front of the fire and in his arms. She knew without thinking about it that if he wanted her, all of her, she would give herself to him without protest and risk having a child. She would risk anything just to be near him, to have him want her.

Will was fast losing himself. Each time he'd kissed her, it had become harder to hold himself back, and this time was proving no different. His body reacted fiercely, and he knew he had to stop before he did something they'd both regret.

"This isn't the right time, Maggie." He disentangled himself from her arms, then held her hands tightly.

She knew, she knew, but when would it be the right time? She closed her eyes and dropped her head back against the cushion, giving him a very fetching view of her slender neck and the lovely skin bared by the low gown.

He let out a hard breath of air and said, "If we were married, we'd have a dozen children. I can't keep my hands off you when we're alone." She blushed at his words and attempted to hide her embarrassment as she tried to pull her dress up.

He wrapped the coverlet around her with shaking hands and covered the temptation.

She felt the need to lighten the atmosphere. "You're good at that. Do you get a lot of practice?"

"I haven't done this for years, but I guess there are some things a man doesn't forget."

"What happened that made you stop?" she teased.

"My wife died."

"Oh. I'm sorry. I didn't know, Will." Was this why he kept his distance from her?

He shrugged. "It was a long time ago." *And yet so recent it still burns in my soul and keeps me from you.*

She was suddenly curious and full of questions, but she sensed that she couldn't ask him about it.

He fell silent then, lost in his thoughts, and didn't notice when Maggie slipped from the settee and went silently to her room. She undressed, shaken by what he'd told her and by her own wanton behavior. She had acted the way a prostitute would act, she was sure of it. Was she any different from Kate and her girls? Was it just because she had never been in a position where her virginity was compromised that she was still pure? His wife had probably been a true lady, proper and of strong moral character. Not at all like herself, throwing caution to the wind when Will was near. But she knew that until now she had felt only an inkling of the tremendous power Will had over her. Just being near him set her heart racing and gave her a shaky feeling. She could know nothing of the storms of passion that would overtake her, but she felt a slight foreboding that made her uneasy. It took hours to fall into a troubled sleep.

They all slept late the next morning, but by the time Maggie came out to the kitchen, everyone except for Simon had already finished breakfast. Will was nowhere to be seen, but Pete sat at the table savoring a cup of hot coffee, and Bertha fussed around the stove.

"Did you sleep well?" Bertha asked her, peering closely at her face. The girl had been sleeping when they'd come in last night, and Will had come in from outside right behind them, but she still wondered what had gone on the night before. There was a throw crumpled up on the floor in the front room, and the cushions had been disturbed.

"I slept wonderfully. How's Uncle Simon?"

"He ain't up yet," Pete said gleefully, "and he's gonna wish he wouldn't wake up for a few days, at least."

"Serves him right, too. The very idea of drinking a whole bottle of whiskey. It's a wonder it didn't kill him." Bertha showed her disapproval in her whole posture, looking as if she was just waiting for the man to come in so she could chastise him for his behavior the night before.

But Simon, when he did finally make an appearance, looked so utterly miserable that none of them had the heart to tease him. He had one eye tightly closed, and the other was open only far enough to see where he was going. His shirt was open, his suspenders hanging down to his knees, and he was in his stocking feet. That was so out of character that Maggie was alarmed. He was never less than neatly groomed.

"What're you gawking at?" he growled at the three of them.

Pete picked up a week-old newspaper he'd acquired at the dance the night before and buried his head in it, and Bertha began washing dishes with as much clattering as possible.

"Damn it, woman! Can't you do that without so much noise?"

Bertha dropped a pan on the floor, and it rolled across the room, ending with a resounding clunk against the iron stove. She went over, picked it up, and sent a burning glare toward Simon, but he was holding his throbbing head in his hands and missed it.

Maggie sat across from him and solemnly watched him until he could stand the scrutiny no more.

"Go ahead and say it."

"I wasn't going to say anything."

"Of course you were. No woman can resist the temptation to make a man feel even more miserable than he already does, especially if the cause is drink."

"Uncle Simon, I'm concerned about you."

"Don't spare any concern for me, Maggie. I'm fine. I did something stupid"—he paused as Bertha snorted— "but as soon as I get rid of this headache, I'll be fine."

"Why don't you come into the front room with me? It's cooler in there and not nearly so noisy." Maggie wanted to get him alone so she could ask him what had happened last night.

"Good idea. Would you bring a cup of coffee for me? I don't think I could carry it in there without spilling some."

She followed him into the other room and set his cup down on the table where Will's feet had been the night before. He stretched out with one leg up on the cushions and one arm across his eyes. He let out a painful groan as his body settled into place.

Maggie put her elbow up on the arm of the chair and nonchalantly covered her mouth with her hand to hide her twitching lips. She'd never seen a man with a hangover before and was amused that anyone would do something so terrible to himself.

"I tried not to give up on her, but she makes it hard. She won't give, I won't give."

"What did you say to her?"

"I went to pick her up, and she wasn't even dressed. She told me she never had any intention of going."

"Did she tell you that when you asked her?"

"Yes, but I thought I could persuade her."

"Why wouldn't she go?"

"She thinks she wouldn't be welcome."

Maggie thought of the comments she'd heard the night before and had to agree. "Won't she give up her business to marry you?"

He sighed. "I don't know. I don't know anything anymore. I thought if I kept at her, she'd change her mind. She's a stubborn woman, but she says she loves me. She's content to keep on the way we're going until we die, I guess."

"And you're not?"

"Maggie, I've been alone for twenty-four years. Before that I thought I had a future with Lizzie, and when I lost that I just drifted. The years are gone—they just tumble past—and I finally realize I have to stop and take control over my life, or the rest of it will be the same. Just drifting through, not really living.

"I'm afraid of that, too," she admitted.

"Of what?"

"Being alone. Of having the years get away from me, and one day I'll wake up too old to marry and have a family."

"You won't be alone, Maggie. Will for one seems quite taken with you," he said carefully.

"I don't know about him, Uncle Simon. At times it seems as if he is taken with me, and I think perhaps he'll ask me to marry him. Then a look comes into his eyes, and he's off away somewhere, as though he's just waiting for the right moment to leave here and see what's over the mountains."

"He has something he needs to deal with, Maggie. Give him time. He'll come around."

"What things? What is it that keeps him at a distance?"

Simon shook his head. "It isn't good to dig into a man's past. You might find out something you don't want to know." Maggie thought about that for a while, then lifted her head to her uncle.

"Maybe Kate has some things to deal with, too."

"Maybe. I never thought of that."

"Can you ask her? Or is that digging in the past?"

"If she wants me to know, she'll tell me."

"Maybe there's something in her past that she's afraid of your finding out. Maybe she thinks if you do you won't love her anymore, and she's afraid to risk breaking her heart."

"You've very wise, Maggie. Like your mother." He looked at Maggie, so like her mother in many ways. "She made the right choice, you know. I could never have been happy back there, following in my father's and grandfather's footsteps. I wanted to make my own mark in this world."

"Will said something like that. That's probably why the two of you are friends. You don't expect more than the other can give."

"That's a good thing to remember. I may be asking more of Kate than she can give."

"Let me talk to her. You just stay away from her for a while. She'll get to missing you the way she did when you came back east, and she'll realize she doesn't want to lose you."

"It didn't work the last time."

"But you couldn't come to her because you were too far away. If you're right here, and simply choose not to see her, it would put a different light on things."

"Maybe you're right." He smiled at her. "Thank you, Maggie. You're a good girl."

"Not so very good, Uncle Simon."

She left him alone then and wandered back out to the kitchen. She felt restless and wondered where Will was. She contemplated changing clothes and going out to find him, but that would be as bad as allowing him too many liberties, so she didn't. There were a few books in the cabin, but none of them seemed interesting, and the paper was full of things she already knew from the gossip at the dance.

"What's the matter with you, girl? You're wandering around here like a lost sheep." Bertha was up to her elbows in bread dough. "Why don't you help me with the baking?"

Maggie plopped into a chair and sighed, deciding it was time to confess. "I can't cook, Bertha."

"Why can't you?"

"I don't know how."

"What do you mean you don't know how? Surely you can cook something."

"No, nothing. The closest I ever came to cooking was dishing up a bowl of soup for Will."

Berthan turned and stared at the girl, unable to believe what she was hearing.

"Are you telling me your mama didn't teach you anything at all about cooking?"

"I know it's awful, but I never thought I'd need it, you see."

"Now why would you ever think a thing like that? Even if you never had a family to cook for, you'd need to know how to feed yourself, wouldn't you?"

"Not really." She shrugged. "There were always cooks around to do it."

"Oh." Bertha understood now. "You really were a spoiled miss, weren't you?"

Maggie reddened and tried to explain. "I was never any good at any of the things girls were supposed to do. Cook threatened to quit if my mother let me in the kitchen again."

Bertha had never heard of such a thing. "Well, what can you do?"

"I know a lot about horses. My father allowed me to spend as much time as I wanted with him, and I learned from him. I liked being outdoors much better than being in some stuffy drawing room."

Bertha couldn't help herself. The laugh started deep inside her and built until it was shaking her tiny frame. She was almost choking with the hilarity of it when Will walked in the door.

"What on earth is wrong with her?" he asked Maggie, who was definitely not laughing.

"I can't imagine," she said quickly. "Do you need help outside?"

"No. I just came in for a cup of coffee. That is, if there is some."

"Of course. Why don't you go back outside and I'll bring it to you?"

"I want to warm up, Maggie." He looked at Bertha, who was trying to get herself under control, and at Maggie, who was obviously trying to get rid of him. "What's going on here?"

"Nothing is going on," she answered firmly. "Bertha is just having some kind of fit."

"The girl," Bertha got out between gasps, "the girl doesn't know how . . . to cook! She . . . didn't think . . . she'd ever need to 'cause her daddy . . . would pay someone to do it for her!"

"What?" he asked, confused.

"She thought there'd . . . always be servants . . . around to do . . . it for her." Bertha finished and let loose with fresh bursts of hilarity, wiping her eyes with the hem of her apron.

"You can't cook?" he asked the now blushing Maggie.

"No, I can't cook. Now that we have that settled, can we forget it?"

"But, Maggie," Will said to her seriously, "you have to know how to cook something."

"Well, I don't."

"No wonder I had to suffer through Simon's cooking when I was laid up." He rubbed his chin thoughtfully and added, "Of course, that was probably the better of two evils."

She glared at him. "There was no need for me to learn how to cook."

"You've got to learn, Maggie. You need to learn how to cook. Every person on this ranch can cook at least enough to survive. If you're going to live out here, you've got to."

Maggie let out a long-suffering sigh and closed her eyes. "All right. I guess I can learn something." She looked at Will and then at Bertha, saying "but—and this is fair warning—you will eat everything I cook. If I have to learn to do something I hate, you will all suffer from the results."

❧ 11 ❧

"You cannot be serious." Maggie was sitting at the kitchen table reading the recipe for headcheese off a slip of paper Bertha had handed her.

"What do you mean?" Bertha asked innocently.

"I can't do this. If I even tried to do this I would throw up. I know I would. Even reading about it makes me queasy."

Will looked up from the accounts he was working on. "What makes you queasy?"

"This recipe. Here, let me read it to you." She spread the recipe out between her hands on the table and tried not to think about what had caused the odd stains on the paper. "Having thoroughly cleaned a hog's head or pig's head, split it in two with a sharp knife, take out the eyes, take out the brains, cut off the ears, and pour scalding water over them and the head, and scrape them clean." She looked up at Will, her face a funny color, and said, "Shall I continue?"

"Oh, my all means," Bertha interjected.

Maggie looked at them, unable to believe they honestly weren't sickened by the directions. She knew that she, for one, would never touch headcheese again. She took a deep breath and continued. "Cut off any part of the nose which may be discolored so as not to be scraped clean . . . Oh, I can't go on." She jumped up from the table and ran outside, taking great gulping breaths of clean, fresh air.

Will came after her and put his arm around her shaking

shoulders. He chuckled. "Bertha was just having fun with you. She doesn't expect you to do that stuff."

"But, Will, if I was married to a rancher out here, I'd have to learn how to do that stuff, wouldn't I? I'm afraid I wouldn't be much use to a man."

"Oh, Maggie, you don't have to cut up a whole hog to put a meal on the table. You can fry meat, make biscuits, boil some vegetables—it really isn't that hard."

During the next few weeks, Maggie's culinary attempts went from absolutely awful to passably good. The people who had to suffer through the lessons never complained, but they often rummaged through the icebox or pie safe late at night. She was so proud of her offerings that they didn't have the heart to hurt her feelings, so they gamely tried everything, learning early on to take very small helpings so they could clean their plates.

But the day came that she produced a whole meal that was surprisingly good, and they all praised her effusively, knowing full well the hard work and determination she'd put in to get to that point. After that she shared the cooking chores with Bertha, though she still preferred to be outside, much to the relief of the older woman, who'd never seen a person make such a mess just whipping up a batch of biscuits.

The days passed quickly, and the breezes carried the smell of spring on them. The hands who had left for the winter began returning to the ranch, getting ready for the roundup of new calves from off the range. Maggie had never seen a roundup and was looking forward to it. Pete had outfitted his chuck wagon and was packing in supplies. The ranch, which had seemed a quiet, restful place in the winter, bustled with activity. Maggie wanted to be everywhere at once, and her cooking lessons went by the wayside.

One day Maggie was heading out to the corral where they were breaking horses when she heard a horse and turned to see Chase Wolcott riding up. Will came out of the barn and spied the doctor at the same time.

"Chase! What're you doing out here?" Will asked as he stepped forward.

"Hullo, Will, Miss Longyear. Man got thrown from a horse up at McLean's. Del Summers. You know him."

"Sure do. How is he?"

"Broke a leg and cracked a few ribs. He'll be fine in a few weeks." He dismounted and tied his horse to the rail. "Is Simon around?"

"Yeah. He's in the corral, back of the barn. Maggie, why don't you go in and tell Bertha to expect a guest for supper? We'll be along."

"All right. I promise to let her do the cooking."

Will laughed and watched Maggie go inside, then stopped as he noticed the serious look on his friend's face. "What's wrong?"

"You and Simon both need to hear this."

Chase followed Will as he crossed the distance to the barn in three strides, then went through the gate to the corral, where Simon was watching one of the hands break a horse. Simon watched the rider intently, not acknowledging the men's presence for a moment, until, satisfied with what he saw, he turned to them.

"Doc! Good to see you." He shook the doctor's hand. "What brings you out this way?"

"I've just come from McLean's. I thought I should stop and tell you the news."

"What news is that?"

"You remember those two innocent settlers the Wyoming Stock Growers Association hanged for rustlers a couple of years ago and that the WSGA boys have been accused of hiring guns to kill any other suspected rustlers?"

"Yes, but no one's been able to prove it or to lay those two ambushings last year at their door, either." Simon looked at Will, who nodded his agreement.

"Well, it's apparently true. Word has it that the association has hired a bunch of guns from Texas to come up here and wipe out the so-called rustlers. They're paying every man jack of them fifty dollars for every rustler shot, no matter who actually does the kill. They apparently aren't too picky about how guilty anyone actually is. Someone got a list—they're calling it the 'dead list'—of people up in the northern part of the state that the association wants out of the way. Simon, there are seventy names on that list, all of them just honest, small ranchers. Not a rustler among them, or anyway that's what they're saying. McLean says it's time the settlers banded together and fought back. The maverick law has already wiped out some of the smaller ranchers, and it can only get worse. I hear some of the ranchers in Johnson County are trying to start their own association, and McLean thinks we ought to band the valley ranchers together and join them."

Just then the supper bell sounded, and the three men hesitated, all thinking the same thing. Finally Simon decided for them. "Bertha's lived here all her life and knows what's going on, and Maggie needs to know, too. Being prepared is their best defense."

They went into the cabin then, and when Bertha saw their expressions, she knew Maggie hadn't exaggerated. Something was wrong.

"All right. You men just set yourselves down here and eat first. We can talk after," she commanded, and they obeyed her. Conversation around the table was desultory during the meal and dwindled into nothing as the two women cleared the table, then set big mugs of coffee in front of the four men.

"Now," the older woman said, "let's have it."

Simon started. "Bertha, you know about this, but Maggie doesn't." He turned to his niece. "A group of men, some of them ranchers, some just hired managers of big spreads, banded together a few years back, thinking they were going to control all cattle production in the state. Wyoming was a territory then, and laws were put into being by money and political influence mostly, instead of by common sense and decency. Anyway, as more and more settlers came into the state looking to start their own spreads, these men started the Wyoming Stock Growers Association. Now, what you have to realize is that most of these men didn't know a whole heck of a lot about ranching. Mostly they liked their own illusions of grandeur, and they spent their time in a fancy club in Cheyenne, trying to out-impress each other.

"They spent so much time in Cheyenne, as a matter of fact, that the cattle they were supposed to be raising were near like to being untended most of the time, and word got out. Rustlers did work their way through the state, accounting for some losses, but mostly cattle were dying because the fools didn't know better than to overstock the range, and weren't around to move the herds to high ground to keep them from drowning in flash floods during sudden rain storms.

"Anyway, most of these so-called cattle barons had to answer to investors and owners and couldn't admit to being fools, so they blamed rustlers for all their losses. To most people back East, even intelligent, well-informed people, Wyoming is still wild and untamed. They believed the stories they were being told, and so the lie had to continue, making the place seem as bad as possible."

"So the WSGA is trying to control the whole state as far as grazing land," Maggie said, frowning, "while trying to hide their laziness and incompetence from their financial backers."

"That's right," Simon answered her.

"And the small ranchers, who are settling land legally, are threatening their grand way of life, so they're passing laws that are unfair to them?" she asked.

Simon nodded. "They've passed laws that, on the outside, appeared to protect the ranchers from rustlers. The worst of these, as far as I'm concerned, is the maverick law. It stipulates—by the law of the state, mind you—that any unbranded stray calf on open range belongs to the WSGA and is auctioned off to the highest bidder. Almost all ranchers, big and small alike, graze their cattle on open range. Most of the small ranchers can't pay the exorbitant prices that calves bring at the auctions, so they lose their own calves. Also, it's been rumored that the proceeds from these sales are being used to hire what they call range detectives."

"Hired guns, more like it," Pete interjected.

"That's right. A couple of years ago, two innocent

people were hanged for rustling," Simon continued. "One of them we all knew. His name was Jim Averell, and he didn't even have any cattle. He wasn't interested in raising livestock. He just wanted to run his general store in peace. We stopped by there several times. He was a good man, but he made the mistake of choosing land that, although owned by no one, had been used for grazing by one of the association members. The other one they hanged was a woman who lived alone out there. No reason for it."

Simon stopped and rubbed his eyes, deep concern showing in his very posture. Chase continued with the news he'd heard that day, which he had already told Simon and Will, earlier, finishing with, "and, as a concerned citizen, I'm all for joining in with the new association. What do you men think?"

"It's not our fight," Simon said slowly, "but it could be at some point. They've never quite gotten over the fact that I wouldn't join the WSGA, and those men don't like being crossed."

"Nope," Pete interjected, "I remember the ones what come here that last time. Said if you wasn't with 'em, you must be against 'em. This payin' no-good hired guns to shoot people don't sound too good."

"No, it doesn't," Simon agreed. "Bertha, maybe you should take Maggie and move into town. There won't be many hands around here when we start the roundup. I'd feel better if you two were away from the ranch and in town where there are plenty of people around."

"I never took to town life, Simon, and I don't mean to start now. I can shoot as well as most of these men, and I can take care of myself."

"Maybe so, Bertha, but I have to answer to my brother for Maggie's safety. And she can't stay in the house in town all alone, either." He hesitated. "Maybe she could stay at Kate's."

That had the desired effect.

"Simon Longyear! Your niece will not stay in a saloon! My word, what must you be thinking?"

"I don't mind staying at Kate's. She's been very good

to me." Maggie wasn't too sure about being left in Bertha's tender care for several weeks.

"You don't have to do that. It won't kill me to spend a few weeks in town, I guess." Bertha settled the issue. "Just give me time to put things in order first."

"It'll be a few days yet before we're ready to pull out. In the meantime, I'll alert the men and have them take watches. There's nothing that indicates we're in any danger here, but then, I don't suppose they broadcast their intentions to everyone."

"Those ranchers up in Johnson County did," Chase told them. "They openly stated that they intended to hold their own spring roundup, and the WSGA had better not stick its nose in."

"How many do you think McLean will get rounded up to go over there?" Simon asked Chase.

"Hard telling. It's roundup time here, too, but I'd say as many as can be spared will probably go."

Will hadn't spoken yet. He'd been doing some hard thinking about his future. About his and Maggie's future. He knew that if the state wasn't safe for small ranchers, he might as well pack up and head back to Kansas. But he couldn't do that. He wouldn't do that. His home was here in Jackson Hole, and no one, especially not some arrogant bastards who spent their time lounging around in some fancy club in Cheyenne, would take it away from him. He hadn't let on when Chase had told the story, but when he heard the hired killers were from Texas, he knew where to find Jake Greeley.

"I'll be going," he stated softly, and Maggie felt fear grip her heart.

In the end, both Will and Dave left to help in the fight. Dave, surprising all of them, announced that he planned to marry before the year was out and start his own spread. He felt, as did Will, that if they let the WSGA overrun the small ranchers in Johnson County, the association wouldn't stop until they had the whole state under their control, and no one but members would be able to use the open grazing lands.

There were altogether about twenty men who left from the valley. Their sense of urgency was heightened when Josiah McLean tried to send a wire to Buffalo, the Johnson County seat, and it didn't get through. It was a grim force that set off, and the ones they left behind stood silently on the cold spring day and watched them ride out of sight.

Maggie had kept her tears in check, not wanting Will to know she wasn't as strong as the others. Brenna McLean, Josiah's wife, and Judith Morcroft, whose husband had also gone, were left virtually alone with small children to take care of. Maggie couldn't understand how their husbands could leave, even with the assurances that the neighbors would watch out for them while their men were gone. Neither woman shed a tear, simply accepting what had to be. One of Brenna's little girls, a dimpled black-eyed beauty of around two, started sobbing when she couldn't see her papa anymore and noticed the silence around her. Brenna bent down and picked her up, hugging her tight, then gathered her three other little ones into her wagon and left.

Judith's father asked her if she wanted to bring the children and live with him while her Adam was away, but she said, "No, Papa, thank you. I will ask you for help if I need it, but the ranch is all we have. I need to be there."

He nodded and helped them into their wagon, then mounted and rode toward his own ranch. The rest of the watchers slowly dispersed and went their separate ways, still mostly silent. Maggie felt her throat tighten and eyes burn, but she would not cry. She had never before realized how easy and uncomplicated her life had been up until now. If she needed anything, her father provided it. Their home was secure, their lives a simple routine, days running into weeks, weeks into years. If she had married Charles, her life would have been the same. All the obstacles had long ago been surmounted, the struggles ended long before she was even born.

These people out here, though—they were the brave ones. The ones who had left their own secure worlds to venture out in search of a dream. They had found that dream here in this valley, as thousands before them had found their own dreams, and they were willing to fight to keep it. Would she be that brave? Maggie wondered. Would she stand with her children and watch her husband ride off, knowing full well he might never come back? Would the dream be worth his death?

No, she thought, it wouldn't. For without Will, what dream was there? What was the use of going on if he wasn't there to share her life with her? And if she had children . . . No, if she had children, that would be the reason the men would go, wouldn't it? Yes, that was why the men rode off and the women stood dry-eyed and watched them. It was for the children's future.

She thought of her own great-grandfather who had left his father's horse farm in Kentucky and had settled in the South Carolina of his mother's birth, struggling to found his own dynasty for his son and his two grandsons. And for his only great-grandchild, Maggie, and for the children she might one day have. For the first time in her life, she was filled with something she never had felt before: pride in her ancestors and in herself. The men had followed their dreams, the women their men. Did the women share in the dream, too, or did they simply love, and, loving, know no other way than to follow their husbands' dreams, offering support and encouragement where they could?

Maggie had always wanted to travel, to see the world, but she had no vision, no dream to be her guiding star. She doubted she had ever wanted anything in her life she'd have fought for except Will. But Will did, and she loved him, so therefore she waited. She looked around her at the valley, at the people she had met today, and wondered if this would be her home or if she would leave in the fall when her parents came.

Two days later she and Bertha packed up to go to town. They had a wagonload of supplies and their clothes, which Simon had insisted they add to, as there was no telling how long they might have to stay; with Will and Dave gone, he couldn't spare any more men from the roundup to run and fetch for them. They were to take as much as they thought they needed for a month or more. Bertha grumped over that, insisting it was all a lot of foolishness. In a few days their men would be back, and life would return to normal. Maggie wasn't so sure. She didn't know the men well, but the look on Will's face had told her he took the situation seriously. Simon, too, had seemed preoccupied, and even the hands had had an uneasy manner about them.

Some of the men had already gone to join in the roundup, and the few who remained would leave as soon as the women did. Pete had taken his chuck wagon up the day before, and Simon and one of the hands would ride out to join the others after escorting the women into town. On this ride Maggie drank in every aspect of the scenery around her, fearing that this might be her last time to see it. She couldn't seem to shake her uneasy feeling that something bad was going to happen.

Two hours after arriving in town they were unpacked, the men had left, and the two women were sorting through and storing their belongings and supplies. Bertha used Simon's room, as she didn't want to climb the stairs, and she was in there putting her clothing in the dresser when Maggie, who was in the kitchen, heard a light knock on the door. It opened almost as soon as the knock ended, and Kate poked her head through the opening.

"Hello, Maggie! What are you doing here?" she asked brightly as she came in and took off her cloak, laying it across the back of a chair.

"Uncle Simon thought we'd best come here until the trouble with the WSGA was settled," Maggie replied.

"Oh, that. Why? Did he think you were in danger?"

"I'm not sure. Mostly I think he was being careful. How have you been?"

"I've been fine." She looked toward the door to Simon's room. "Is Simon here, too?" she asked, as though it meant nothing in the world to her.

"No. Just Bertha. The men are all needed on the roundup." Kate's face fell, and Maggie thought for a moment she might start crying, but then she took a deep breath, smiled at the girl, and said, "Well, then, you're going to need somewhere to get away to. You're welcome at my place anytime. I heard Will went along with the others, so you're probably feeling pretty lonely."

"Thanks, Kate," she said, then added wistfully, "I had no idea loving someone would be so hard. If only I knew for sure what his intentions were, it would make it easier."

"Didn't he propose yet?"

"No. I'm not sure he intends to. Sometimes I think he might, and then other times he gets this look in his eyes. He's seeing something far off somewhere, and it scares me. I get the feeling he's waiting for something to happen, and I don't know what it is, or what it will mean when it does." It felt good to talk about Will with someone again. Despite the negative opinions of Bertha and Will about Kate's reputation, Maggie stubbornly clung to the relationship with the older woman. She liked Kate and knew she alone of all the people in this place understood what she was going through.

"What happened when you went to the dance with the handsome young doctor? Didn't he get jealous?"

"Oh, Kate, they called that dance off because of the blizzard, and when the next one came along, Will took me."

Kate grinned. "Was it fun?"

"Yes. We left early though."

"And why was that?"

"Because Uncle Simon got falling-down drunk, that's why."

"No one told me that." Kate frowned.

"I don't imagine they thought you'd care. You hurt him, Kate."

Kate crossed the room, her back to Maggie. "It was his own fault. He knew I couldn't go. He's known for years. I don't know why he thought this time would be any different."

"Maybe he's changing, Kate. Maybe seeing you once in a while isn't good enough for him any more."

"Well, it has to be. I told him when we first met how

it had to be, and he accepted it. It's too late to change the rules."

"Who made the rules, Kate?"

They were interrupted by Bertha coming into the room. When she saw Kate, she sniffed and, not saying a word, went to the stove and added wood to the fire that Simon had started before he left. Kate and Maggie exchanged a look of conspiracy as Kate nodded toward her place, then said very politely, "Well, I just stopped by to see if you needed anything. I really must be going."

When the door had closed behind her, Maggie turned to the older woman and asked, "Why don't you like Kate? What has she ever done to you?"

Bertha sniffed again. "She offends the sensibilities of the ladies of this valley, and if you know what's good for you, you won't be spending any time with her. She's not for the likes of a young girl like you."

"Does that give you the right to be rude to her?" Maggie couldn't believe she was defending a prostitute. What would her mother think? But then, her mother would also have been aghast at the way Bertha, a hired servant, acted.

"And just what was I supposed to do, missy? Invite her to supper? You have that woman in here, and you won't be welcome in any of the homes in this town, or in the whole valley, for that matter. No wonder your uncle thought you needed looking after."

"I do not believe that all the women here are of the same intolerant opinion as you, Bertha. From what I've seen, they're capable of judging a person on that person's own merit, not by what appearances may or may not indicate."

"You mark my words, young lady. I guess I can't tell you what to do, only give you the benefit of my experience, but I'm telling you, you will rue the day you ever met that woman."

"You seem to forget you're talking about the woman who will most likely become Uncle Simon's wife."

"You just remember that men get forgiven for things a woman would get hanged for socially. You go consorting with the devil, and pretty soon people start to think you're hell-bound, too."

Maggie stared at the woman and shook her head. "I don't think there's any further need to discuss this."

The next day dawned bright and clear. Maggie left the house in the late morning and set out toward Kate's. She had told Bertha she was going to the general store to get some supplies, but she knew the older woman could see through her ruse. There was precious little they needed that they hadn't brought with them.

Bertha watched her go, knowing full well she'd end up at the saloon but knowing she was powerless to put a stop to it. Maggie was Simon's niece, and he saw nothing out of the ordinary in her socializing with that woman. How could he, when he himself was ensnared by her practiced charm? She sighed and returned to her work. She had tried to tell Simon it wasn't a good idea to come to town. Now there would be the piper to pay.

Maggie crossed the street to the general store, greeting several people she'd met at the dance, and entered the double wooden doors of the building. She had always loved the general store back home, and this one gave her that same childish feeling of wonderment. Goods for every imaginable need were stacked on rows of shelves that reached to the high ceiling, from which baskets, lanterns, buckets, and any number of other items were hanging. Breathing deeply of the smell of dyes, leather, the coal stove, spices, and sawdust, she smiled to herself.

"May I help you?" The man who spoke had wire-rimmed glasses on the end of his nose, twinkling blue eyes behind them, a bald head ringed with curly white hair, and suspenders holding his gray pants up over a portly belly.

She grinned in delight. "You certainly may. Here's a list, and I'd like to look at the yard goods, if I might."

"By all means. They're right over here." He became the salesman. "I've some new spring colors in and a nice selection of silks."

She followed him to where bolts of cloth lay in rows,

and he turned and asked over his shoulder, "Aren't you Simon Longyear's kin?"

"Yes, I'm his brother's daughter. Do you know him well?"

"That I do. Think the world of him, too. There's a man who stands by his convictions."

Maggie wanted to ask what he meant by that remark, but she didn't. She wondered if it had anything to do with Kate but was reluctant to broach the subject since she didn't know what kind of reaction she might get. It might be better just to let the conversation continue, and see what she might discover.

"It runs in the family. My father is the same way. Once he truly believes in something, it's almost impossible to sway his thinking. Believe me, my mother has tried."

The man laughed. "I'm Archie McCaver."

"Maggie Longyear. Pleased to meet you, Mr. Mc-Caver."

"My wife is around here somewhere." He looked toward the back of the store. "Zollie! Come out here and help this young lady with the yard goods." He lowered his voice to a whisper and said, "She'll try to pick your brain for any gossip she can get out of you, but don't pay that any mind. She's a good woman." He said the last with obvious pride, and Maggie felt a pang, wondering if a man would ever talk about her like that—if Will would ever tell a young girl that she was a good woman, after they'd been married for forty years. She smiled. A gossip, but a good woman.

A large woman with hair so black it couldn't be natural came bustling around the corner of one of the yard goods tables, smoothed her hair, brought herself up straight, and offered her hand to Maggie. "Good day to you. I'm Zollie McCaver. Who might you be?"

"Maggie Longyear. Simon Longyear's niece. It's a pleasure to make your acquaintance." She felt an unlikely urge to curtsy before the regal presence of the woman.

"Maggie? That's not your real name, is it?"

"Uh, no. It's Margaret."

"Good. I can't abide naming a child by a nickname. A person needs a good strong name to get by in this world. Now, tell me about your father, who must be Simon's brother, and your mother. I assume they are both still living?"

"Well, yes, they are," she began, but was interrupted by the woman asking, "And why are you here? It seems rather strange for a young girl like you to be so far from her parents and staying with her unmarried uncle. Why, he's not even got a wife to chaperon you. He does what he pleases, that man. What were your parents thinking when they sent you out here?"

"Bertha," Maggie managed to get in between the chatter. "Bertha is there to chaperon me."

"Bertha? Yes, her husband is your uncle's hired man, isn't he? But is she qualified to act as a chaperon? I'm not sure she knows the ways of society, don't you know. But, still, it's better than nothing. Are you staying in town or at the ranch? Why these men would want to live out there when they have a house in town, I can't imagine. Oh"—she stopped and peered at Maggie with narrowed eyes—"didn't I hear something about the foreman getting hurt and you nursing him? Was this Bertha in the house at that time, too? You know, dear, your mother would no doubt be pleased that you offered your tender care to the man, but I'm sure she'd be the first to tell you that it isn't seemly for a young, unmarried girl to be in a sickroom with a man. Your uncle, now, he wouldn't know, nor care a whit, about what people might say, so you just heed my advice, dear, and I'll keep you on the straight and narrow."

An exhausting hour later, Maggie left the store, vowing never again to get caught by Zollie McCaver. What a self-righteous busybody! It was with an air of defiance that she headed unerringly in the direction of the Seven Squaw Saloon, knowing the obnoxious woman was watching, and entered the front doors without hesitation.

Behind her store window, Zollie McCaver almost died

of shock, then hurried out the door to spread this latest bit of news to her friends.

When Maggie's eyes had adjusted to the darkness which was such a contrast to the bright sunlight outside, she was surprised to find the saloon deserted, save for the man behind a long bar, polishing glasses and hanging them up. He hardly looked up from his task, so Maggie made her way to the door that led to the hallway she'd gone through with Simon the first night they'd come here. She'd not been through the saloon again, preferring to use the back door when she'd come to visit Kate before, so it was with surprise that Kate opened the door and found here there.

"Maggie! Did you come through the saloon?"

"Yes," she admitted, then told her the story of Mrs. McCaver. "I know it wasn't right but I just couldn't help myself."

Kate laughed. "Yes, I've run into the good woman myself, so I know your temptation, but, Maggie, you really shouldn't have, you know. I feel bad enough as it is, without ruining your reputation, too."

"Oh, Kate, why don't you just marry Uncle Simon? He could take you away from all this."

"I can't marry him or anyone. Now, would you care for some lunch? I think Della is just about ready to put it on the table."

Maggie knew enough to put her feelings aside for the duration of the meal, but as soon as the two of them were alone again, she pressed further.

"Kate, I don't know what you think you've done that makes you unable to marry Uncle Simon, but don't you think he's strong enough to handle whatever it is? If he's willing to overlook the fact that you run a saloon, I should certainly think you could."

"Oh, Maggie, if only it were that simple. But it isn't. He thinks he knows all about me, but there are things I'm afraid to tell anyone, least of all him. I'm too afraid of losing him."

"Don't you realize that if you don't marry him, and cannot give him a satisfactory reason why, you're going to lose him anyway? He loves you, Kate, but he won't wait forever."

"Has he told you that?" Kate asked softly.

"Not in so many words, but I do know he's got this feeling that time is running out for him, and he wants a wife and family before it's too late."

"I can't give him a family."

"What do you mean?"

"I can't have children, Maggie."

"Is that why you can't marry him? Because if it is, that's a stupid reason. He'd understand, I'm sure he would. Why won't you give him a chance?"

Kate sighed and looked at Maggie for a long moment before coming to a decision. "Come here and sit down. I want to tell you a story." She patted the cushion beside her and, when Maggie was seated, she took her hand and clung to it, closing her eyes tightly. "This isn't easy. I've never told anyone all of it before." Maggie kept silent, only holding Kate's hand between hers and waiting.

"I don't know who my parents were," she began finally. "I grew up in an orphanage in New York City, and when I was too old to stay there anymore, they sent me out to work as a scullery maid in one of the big houses belonging to a very wealthy family. It was probably a good thing I had lived in the orphanage, because it was rough there, and I had to learn to be strong or die.

"At first things went very well. I worked hard, and the other servants were kind to me. I'd been there almost a year when they hired Ben, and the first time we saw each other, we fell in love. He was nineteen, and the youngest of five boys, so he knew he had to make his own way in the world. There were just too many mouths to feed and not enough land to go around, so he came to New York and found a job in the stables of the house where I worked. We planned to be married, and for the first time in my life I thought that I had a chance at happiness.

"Then the family's grown son came home from a tour of the Continent. One night the family was out, and I was in the mistress's room, turning down her bed and readying the room for her return, like I did every night when her maid had off. The son came back early, or maybe he never even left, I don't know, but he came upon me there. I bobbed a curtsy, and made to leave, but he stopped me and asked me my name.

"I told him, as coldly as I could, then said I must ready his mother's bath, so would he please excuse me. He said the bath could wait, because his mother would be out very late, and besides, he wanted to get to know me better. He grabbed me and forced a kiss—I tried to turn away, to get away, but he was stronger than any man I'd ever known. He began to tear my dress off. I fought him like wildcat, my only thought to save myself for my Ben."

Kate stopped then and, pulling away from Maggie, put her hand over her mouth. She closed her eyes for a moment before going on. "I swear by all that is holy that I didn't mean to kill him. He let go of me with one hand to open his trousers, and I reacted blindly. I twisted around and shoved him with all my might. There was a small footstool behind him, and he fell over it and hit his head on the edge of the fireplace. He just lay there, not moving. I stood and stared at him, unable to move, and then Elise, another of the girls he'd been after, came running to see what the noise was. She could see right away what had happened, and before I even knew what she was doing, she'd snatched his purse from him and, taking out a few coins for herself, shoved the rest at me, and said to hide it well, change clothes, and get back to help her carry water for the lady's bath.

"I was shaking so hard I didn't think I could make it down the stairs, much less do as she'd said, but I did, and met her in the kitchen, where we each took two buckets of water and headed up the stairs again like we'd done many times in the past. She was chattering away as if nothing had happened, and then when we got to the room, she screamed. She screamed so loud she scared the wits out of me, and I dropped my buckets, and water was everywhere, and I was trying to mop it up with my apron when the other servants came, and then the master and his lady were summoned and they came home, and the doctor, and there was so much confusion, no one even noticed me. Elise babbled on and on about the two of us coming into the room with our buckets of water, and there he was, and about how he must have fallen and hit his head. The doctor agreed with her and added that the man had been drinking, so very likely he'd stumbled and fallen over the step.

"There was a terrible commotion, what with the funeral and all, and no one even thought to look for his purse. When everything had quieted down, I told Ben. Told him all of it. I hadn't even had the nerve to look at the money, so I had no idea how much was there, but Ben counted it—there was over five hundred dollars."

Kate stopped and sighed, her eyes seeing something far away. "It was a fortune, and we took it and ran. We left the city as quickly as we could and bought passage to St. Louis. We were married there and had a few weeks together while we prepared for the journey. Ben thought it best that no one know we had any money, so we stuck with our original plan to work on the wagon train. We were only four weeks out when we were attacked by Indians. Ben was one of the first ones shot, and he died in my arms. Part of me died there with him.

"It was all over so fast. Seven women were taken prisoner, to be slaves. The work was hard, but we were left alone for the most part. The man who got me was good to me in his own fashion. He didn't beat me, and I became rather fond of him. I had a baby. A son. He died. After that I really didn't care if I lived or died, or ever got away. My son was so little, and when he got sick, there wasn't anything I could do to save him. The tribe's medicine man waved feathers over him and mumbled some chants, but there were no doctors, you see, and so he died. I buried him with Della's help, and I think she's the only person in the world who understood, because she'd lost all of her children, and her husband, too, in the attack. But I just didn't care anymore after that.

"Then one day a scout came tearing into the camp with the news that the soldiers were coming. I saw our chance.

I found the others, all six of them, and we gathered our things and simply walked out of it all. We headed in the direction from which the scout had ridden, thinking he must have come from the fort. We walked all the rest of that day, me hoping we weren't lost, and trying to make the others think I knew the way. Right before dusk we heard horses and hid until we saw they were soldiers, and then we came out and just stood there, waiting for them.

"They of course thought we were 'ladies of the evening,' so to speak. That was humiliating enough, although as it turned out three actually were. But you can't imagine the change that came over those men when they found out we'd been captives for four years. It was as though we had smallpox. They shuffled us out of there as fast as they could," she continued bitterly. "It was the same wherever we went.

"So there we were, seven women, alone and shunned by the world we'd struggled so hard to get back to alive. The three girls who'd been prostitutes before said they were used to being ignored by society, but it was hard on all of us. Then one of them suggested that we just start a whorehouse somewhere. It shocked me at first. No matter what I'd been through, I wasn't ready to become a whore, and neither was Della, but we talked about it. We considered our options and realized we had none. I had no home to return to, and no matter where I went it would only be a matter of time before my past caught up with me, and it would start all over again. It was the same for all of us. So we made a pact. We'd looked out for each other for four years, and we'd continue to do so for the rest of our lives. I offered my money to buy a place, and we agreed to get on the next stage that came through, get out at the seventh stop, and that would be the place.

"So that's how we ended up here. We called the place the Seven Squaw out of defiance, but so far no one has questioned it, and that's why we stay here. Della cooks and keeps the place clean for us. I do the books, which I'm surprisingly good at, by the way. I seem to have inherited some business sense from those unknown parents of mine. The others keep the place running, but it's the saloon and gaming tables that really bring in the money, believe it or not. The girls mostly work for themselves."

Finished with her story, Kate lifted her hands, then dropped them to her lap. She held her breath, waiting for the reaction from this girl before her—waiting to see the rejection of a murderess and an Indian's squaw. When she finally grew brave enough to look at the face in front of her, she was shocked at the compassion she saw there.

"No wonder Uncle Simon admires you so," Maggie said.

🏵 12 🏵

The small force led by Josiah McLean reached Buffalo, the Johnson County seat, just before a heavy snowstorm hit the east side of the Bighorn Mountains. As they rode into town, they noted an uneasy atmosphere, with several men eyeing them closely, hands on guns. A curtain would fall back into place here and a door silently close there across the street. Will felt the back of his neck prickle and knew from the silence of his comrades that they felt the same.

Will had the feeling he'd been in this place before. Tattered remnants of wind swirled down the street and sent shivers up his spine. He remembered the feeling. It was like Kansas when he'd gone to get Charity. They rode slowly up to the sheriff's office, dismounted and tied their horses, looking around carefully, trying to get a fix on the source of their uneasiness. The jailhouse door opened with a creak, and a man stepped out on the porch. He had a gun cradled in his arms and stood with his feet apart, looking down at them.

"What can I do for you fellas?" he drawled as his gaze flitted from one to the other of them.

Josiah stepped up on the steps but found his way blocked to the porch. He took off his hat, holding it in both hands, and declared, "We've come from Jackson Hole to help you with your roundup. We heard you was fixin' to run your own, without the so-called help of the WSGA."

"That so," the man said with no indication of his feelings.

"Yes, sir. We tried to wire you that we were coming, but the telegraph operator said he couldn't get through. We hustled right on over here, thinking you might be having a spot of trouble."

The man spat downward, then fixed his stare on Josiah. "How do you know I'm not the WSGA?"

McLean took a step backward, unsure of what to do. The other men seemed ready to bolt, so Will decided it was time for him to step in.

"Sheriff, we know you're not from the association because we know they're on their way here right now. We talked to a man from down around Casper late yesterday who told us they were headed up here to Buffalo to put a stop to your roundup. We're small ranchers ourselves and we just decided to take a stand with you people. We've been riding hard for two days and could use a rest, so if you'd kindly point out the way to a hotel, we'll be going there."

The sheriff spat again. "How'd you know I was the sheriff?"

"Sheriff in Jackson told us what you looked like. Not likely to confuse you with someone else," Josiah stated, emboldened by Will's words.

Letting himself relax, the sheriff grinned, knowing that his bright red hair and long handlebar mustache had proclaimed to the men that he was indeed Red Angus. "You men are right welcome. I already sent some of my men out to get reinforcements, and here you show up. I'm gettin' a posse together and plan to ride out within the hour. If you're coming with me you don't have time to rest, but you could get a hot meal. I'll send one of my men along with you to see you're treated right." He turned his head toward the door. "Silas! Get out here!"

A skinny little man came out and, nervously shifting from one foot to the other, looked at his boss. "Whatcha need, Sheriff?"

"I need you to take these fellas over to the hotel and

tell Clara to fix them up with some hot vittles, and quick. They come to help."

"Right, Sheriff. Come on, boys, and I'll get you fixed right up."

The others turned and, leading their horses, followed the deputy, but Will put one foot on the porch and leaned on his knee. "Do you know what you're riding into, Sheriff? The man we talked to said they had a whole army of gunfighters and were planning a slaughter. We rode all night after that."

"I do know, mister. A couple of men came riding in here, hell-bent for leather, saying they'd been chased by some men who were part of a large force who'd descended on the K.C. Ranch, south of here, and were using the house for target practice. They say there were at least two dead men, maybe three. I'm going to need all the help I can get, so I'm grateful to you men for coming the way you did."

"What are you planning? Do you have enough men and ammunition to win this one?"

"Don't you worry about what I'm planning." He was still a bit wary of the newcomers. "I'll tell you what you need to know, when you need to know it."

Will grinned. "We really have come to help." He extended his hand to the sheriff. "My name's Will Sutten. My partner, Simon Longyear, and I have a cattle-and-horse ranch in Jackson Hole."

"Simon Longyear! You're his partner?" A man with a deputy's star on his chest came out of the door behind the sheriff and strode toward Will, extending his hand. "I've known Simon for years. Since he first came out west. We had some good times together. Name's Bill Hutchinson. You say you're Will Sutten?"

"That's right. We've been partners for about four years."

"Seems I do remember Simon mentioning he had a partner. How's he doing? Haven't heard from him for a couple of years now."

"He's doing just fine. Out rounding up our cattle right

now, as a matter of fact." He grinned, remembering. "Simon's told me about some of your escapades."

The deputy grinned in response. "Yeah. It's just as well those days are over. We're both too old to go gallivantin' around the country, but we did have some good times, for sure."

"Bill," Sheriff Angus said, "Why don't you take him over to the hotel and pick up the stuff I ordered. They should have it ready by now. Tell 'em to put in extra. Looks like snow's moving in."

Bill looked toward the north as the first flakes began swirling in the chilling wind. "Yeah. Maybe we should wait this one out. I don't like the looks of it, comin' from that direction."

"We don't have time to wait out a snowstorm," Red said with determination. "Those men are headed this way, and we'd best be meeting them out of town. We don't need any innocent bystanders killed by stray bullets."

"But, Sheriff, we don't even know who in town is with them. Someone cut those telegraph lines. How do we know they haven't planned the whole thing to lead us into an ambush? Get us out of town so they can take over?"

"We don't. All I know is that some citizens of my county have been murdered in cold blood, by the telling of it, and it's my sworn duty, as well as yours, to get the ones that did it. We can't just hole up here like a bunch of frightened old ladies and wait for them to make a move on us. We got to go out and take a stand. Besides, I got the town covered. I wasn't born yesterday, you know."

The deputy grinned at Will. "He's always reminding me how old he is, like it isn't obvious he was born a whole heck of a lot of yesterdays ago."

"Get out of here, Hutchinson, before I send you up to the Ladies Aid Society meeting. They did tell me it was my duty to see that they were sufficiently protected. I could spare you real easy."

"You wouldn't know what to do if I wasn't there at your right hand, and you know it."

"You want to find out?"

"Nope, I'm on my way." He winked at Will, who tried to keep his mouth from twitching, and they headed toward the hotel.

"How come you folks headed over this way?" Bill inquired. "How'd you hear about the trouble?"

"Man came riding through the valley and told about the roundup you were having. We didn't find out about the trouble until yesterday. I don't know how much you know, but from what we heard, if it hadn't been for some heavy snow, you might not be here now. Seems they got held up for a couple of days right out of Casper. This guy seemed to think they planned to come in secret-like and kill off the sheriff and deputies and take over the town. He talked to a man who saw a list of names, maybe seventy or so, that were marked for death. Small ranchers, most of them, and some cowboys that have been on the blacklist."

"Yeah," Bill said grimly, "that's the same we heard. Sheriff Angus is right, though. They don't know we heard anything yet, and we still might get the best of them if we can surprise them. We stand a better chance if we don't wait for them to surround us."

"That's my thinking, too. How many men do you have?"

"About fifty so far. Some men have ridden out to get reinforcements. They are to meet us at a rendezvous south of here. We hope to come at them from all directions."

Less than an hour later, Will and the men who'd come with him were deputized, and they set off with the force gathered by Sheriff Angus. They rode far into the night, charged up for the battle that might await them. The snow got deeper as they rode south, giving evidence of the heavy snowfall the night before, but now they encountered nothing more than flurries.

By the time the sheriff called a halt, Will was exhausted and knew the others who'd had no sleep for two days must be feeling the same. They set up camp quickly, and Josiah joined Will by a crackling fire, handing him a cup of coffee.

"You think we'll surprise them?" he asked Will.

"I don't know. Doesn't seem to me that this is much of a covert operation. Hell, you could hear us coming for miles."

"Yeah, that's what I thought, too."

Suddenly a gun went off, and the sheriff crossed to the man who did it in two strides, then knocked him to the ground with one blow to his jaw. Every man fell silent at the fury on Red Angus' face as he ground out his words. "Every man jack of you better listen to this and listen good, 'cause I'm not gonna repeat it. This is no Sunday-school picnic. These are hired guns who'd as soon shoot any one of you as look at your ugly faces. We're messing with big money when we're dealing with the WSGA, and money talks. Look at what they got passed through the stage legislature. Now, we got to be smarter than they are. You all know Frank Canton." Murmurs went through the crowd. Bill whispered to Josiah and Will that Canton was the former sheriff of Johnson County, now chief detective of the association.

"He isn't a fool, and even if the men he works for are, it's his mind we have to deal with," Angus went on. "You men want to see your families again, you better get a different attitude, and quick. Now, if they didn't hear that shot, which isn't likely, we might be able to surprise them, but it's my guess they got outriders just like we do, and they know we're here.

"And just in case any of you got ideas about glory, you better wipe 'em out of your mind right now. We're going to do this by the law, and, by God, I'll shoot the first one of you doesn't remember it. Now get some rest, if you can. We're going to need it."

The sheriff's fears of detection were soon proved to be well-founded as one of his men came riding in, reporting that the force ahead of them had regrouped and were drilling, military style, under the direction of what looked to be a trained soldier. There were a lot more men than had originally been suspected, and they obviously weren't green recruits. "They looked like any platoon of fighting men I ever saw," he added.

"Shit!" the sheriff exploded. "Bill, you are going to have to take over here. I'm riding back to town to see if I can get a telegraph through to the state militia and alert the citizens. This may be more than we bargained for. When the recruits get here, send some of them to town 'cause I got the feeling we might need 'em there. Hell and damnation!" He rubbed his hand over his face in exasperation, then mounted his horse, spinning around to say, "I'll be back as soon as I can." Then he galloped off the way they'd come.

"Where are they?" Will asked the outrider quietly.

"They were down the road a few miles, but they cut through a fence and look to be heading for the TA ranch. That's bad, 'cause that ranch has a fort built around it, and there's nothing but open land between us and them."

"How open? Flat or hilly? Any trees?" Will questioned.

"Rollin' like, some dry washes." He shrugged. "No trees to speak of. Crazy Woman Creek runs around the back of them."

Will turned to Deputy Hutchinson. "I think we should get there before first light and try to get dug in. You know the area—is it hilly enough that we could hide like the Indians do? Maybe dig some rifle pits, come in along this creek?"

Bill and Hank, the other deputy, looked at each other, both thinking of the terrain around the ranch in question. Hank spoke first. "Could be done. We don't have much time, though."

"Then I suggest we don't waste any of it," Bill declared and gathered the men around them, explaining what they had in mind.

When dawn arrived, thankfully late because of the heavy cloud cover, some fifty men had dug in around the force holed up at the ranch. Their informant hadn't exaggerated, and the deputized force felt the full weight of fear settle in their bellies. During the pre-dawn hours,

Sheriff Angus had brought a force of about forty more men to join in and he informed the group that the whole town had turned out to defend their way of life, a merchant giving away blankets, guns, ammunition, and anything else needed. He added, "Even the Ladies Aid Society is helping. They decided what they knew best was to cook, so they've been at it all night. A wagonload of the finest cooking in Wyoming is following close behind us, and they say they'll keep going as long as we need it."

"Maybe I should have taken you up on the offer to guard them," Bill joked. "That would sure beat sittin' here waitin' to be targets."

"Well, you did good so far. More men are coming in all the time, and we should have a good sized force before noon." He studied the ranch. "You sure they're all in there?"

"Pretty sure. Haven't seen anyone on the outside, and we got men stationed all around. They've been busy, too. It's not going to be easy to get at 'em."

"No, but we got time on our side. They got no way to get more food or ammunition."

"Maybe we should see that they don't even try to get any," one man said. "We could pick off their horses pretty easy from here."

"Yeah. Maybe that's not such a bad idea," Angus agreed. "See what you can do. You seem to have things pretty well under control, and all you need to do is hold them until the militia gets here."

"Did you get through?"

"Hell, no! We got a man on it, but we got to realize the WSGA might be trying to send for reinforcements, too, so maybe we'd best sit tight until the man I sent gets through to the governor."

The sheriff was right, and by noon over three hundred men had amassed on the hills surrounding the ranch. They shot the horses, until the remaining ones were quickly whisked into the barn; then they started on the cattle. A man who someone said was named Arapahoe Brown came and without any fanfare took over the forces, laying plans to work up to the ranch by cover fire, then set fire to the log fort and what buildings they could reach. It seemed a workable plan, and the men, eager for action after hours of waiting, readily accepted the challenge. Whenever a group of men made a dash forward, those remaining in the trenches rained bullets on doorways and windows, preventing anyone from shooting with any accuracy from within the compound.

The spotty shooting continued into the night, without either force gaining or losing ground. Sometime while Will and some others had finally succumbed to exhausted sleep, the sheriff came into the base camp and notified the group that word had gotten through to the governor about the armed force that had come to the county, shot innocent citizens, and resisted arrest. The ranchers' request for military aid from Fort McKinney had also gotten through.

But another day and night passed before the help arrived. In the meantime, the sheriff's men had found the supply wagons loaded with dynamite brought by the association, and they had built a Trojan horse of sorts out of one of them with hay bales and timbers. The plan was to set it afire at the last minute and send it roaring into the wooden fort. Firing began in earnest when the men inside the ranch house saw what was coming at them. They must have realized the dynamite had been left behind in their mad scramble to safety, and they were desperately trying to stop the approach.

Will had volunteered to head the force going with the wagon, and he was at the forefront, watching the path of its movement. Most of the bullets raining on them whizzed past or hit the bales of hay, but one bullet grazed the hay bale within an inch of his head, and he ducked lower, peering out from under the ponderous load.

"Do you think we can make it?" cried one of the men behind him, and he answered, "I have no doubt but that we will." His calm voice seemed to give them new courage and they surged forward with a mighty shove just as the first bugle notes came across the clear air.

"The military! They're here!" someone shouted, and

then they were all cheering the approaching force of soldiers, whose flags could be seen flying in the dawn light.

Sheriff Angus met with the officers while both sides of the foray waited in silence. Then the sheriff rode with officers and flag bearers up to the ranch gates and were met with a white rag tied on a stick. The force inside surrendered, but only to the military. Sheriff Angus was furious but impotent to oppose orders from, of all people, the President of the United States. He would have wanted the bastards in his own jail where they could be given a speedy trial and hanged for their misdeeds, but this thing was far bigger than any of them had realized. When the full knowledge of the WSGA's plans came to light, they were all more shaken than they cared to admit.

The Members of the Association had hired what amounted to killers to stop any further encroachment by small ranchers into what they considered their domain. They had already controlled the territory for many years, but with the steady influx of settlers their grip on the area was loosening, and they didn't want to lose their power. They thought if they killed the ringleaders who had planned the roundup in Johnson County, most small ranchers would leave the state. It would be weeks before the whole of their plan was revealed, but the men there heard enough to be jubilant that they had prevailed— with or without military intervention.

Josiah McLean approached Will and Adam Morcroft, who were watching the men being led from the house, and said, "What do you say, boys? Shall we head home? I think our work here is done."

"Home? I was hoping for a hot bath, a hot meal, and a clean bed where I could sleep for about two days before we headed out," Adam grumbled, and Will grinned and agreed. His work wasn't done by a long shot, and he wasn't ready to head back to Jackson Hole.

"Just let me get my horse. It's over by the creek. I'll meet you back here," he said to the two men, then stretched and headed around the ranch buildings toward the small copse of trees where he'd left his big bay tied.

He stopped dead in his tracks when he passed the corral, for his horse was inside. "Why, those dirty bastards! How'd they get my horse? Weren't we supposed to have men guarding them back there?" he asked one of the men near him.

The man shrugged his shoulders and replied, "I don't know, mister. They just brought that horse out of the barn. He's been shot, though."

"Shot!" Will took two long strides and inspected the side of the big horse, which had a bullet graze down the flank. "Damn them!"

"Well, sir, it was our bullets that done it."

Will sighed and gave a half smile to the young man. "I know. I didn't mean to get angry at you."

Just then Bill Hutchinson called from behind, "Will! I got your horse for you. You ready to go?"

Will spun around and saw that the deputy did indeed have his horse by the reins and was leading him up to the two men. Will's heart stopped for a long instant, and he had trouble taking a breath.

"You all right, Will?" the deputy asked, his voice full of concern. "You look like you seen a ghost."

"I just did," he replied, his voice shaking.

"Why, mister," the young man said, "this wasn't your horse at all, then. I can see how you made the mistake, though. They sure do look alike."

"Yeah, they sure do." Will turned to the deputy who handed the reins of Will's horse to him. "Thanks, Hutchinson," he managed to say.

The deputy rode away, and Will's mind was swirling. Greeley was here, had to be. That horse was Will's own, raised from a foal, and he couldn't mistake it anywhere. He managed to get both horses back to the meeting place and tied them up, then sought out McLean and told him to ride on ahead, and he'd catch up with them.

As nonchalantly as possible, though his heart was still pounding, he slowly approached the men who'd been taken prisoner and were ready to be transported to the fort. Greeley wouldn't know him, so he was safe from discovery. He'd never told anyone, not even Simon, whom he was after, and he'd never asked questions that might draw attention. But would he know Greeley if he saw him? All he had to go by were a whore's words six years before—he was big, she'd said, and he had one brown eye and one blue eye. Would that be enough to identify the man who had haunted his dreams for all these cursed years?

He walked the ranks of men slowly, back and forth, peering intently at their faces. He had never been this close before, not once. He'd always been two days, four days behind. His chest hurt, and his hands shook, but he knew when the time came he'd be able to hold his gun as steadily as though he were shooting targets on a Sunday afternoon.

He panicked when the order came to move the prisoners to the fort, and he stood in a group with some others, searching each face as the men passed by him. He had about given up hope when an altercation broke out near the end of the line, and a scuffle ensued between a soldier and one of the prisoners. Will leapt forward to the aid of the young soldier, taking the prisoner by the shoulders and managing to hold him until two other men in uniform made their way through the crowd and latched onto him. The man turned with a growl and threw Will a look of pure hatred. And he looked out of one brown eye and one blue eye.

❧ 13 ❧

"It isn't any good, Maggie. Even if he understood, even if Simon could find it in his heart to forgive me, what if someone, somewhere, recognized me? How could I do that to him? He's a wealthy and respected man. He should have a wife who could command the same respect and admiration, not one with a past so tainted she herself can hardly bear to think about it."

Maggie was curled up on Kate's settee several days after Kate had unburdened her soul, and she was still trying to convince her to give Simon a chance. "Hogwash! Kate, nothing that happened to you was your own doing. How can you hold that young girl responsible for any of it?"

"It doesn't matter. Don't you see that? It just doesn't matter. I am who I am, and I've done what I had to do, but that was only my own life. I can't mess with another life, one I have no right to."

Maggie sighed. They'd been over this so many times and were no closer to coming to any sort of agreement than they had been from the start.

"I'm sorry I even told you. I thought you'd understand, not hound me to death about it."

Maggie laughed. "Liar. You're not sorry you told me, because you want me to tell Uncle Simon for you. But I'm not going to. You're going to tell him yourself."

"I'm not!"

"Oh, yes, you are. According to Bertha's calculations, you have approximately ten days before he comes to fetch us back to the ranch. That's ten days for you to figure out how you're going to do it. You're going to have to be more convincing with him than with me, because he loves you. He isn't going to believe you've turned him down for things you couldn't even help. Now, if you were a real outlaw, a train robber for example, he might think twice about marrying you. You'd just never know when the posse might catch up with you, and it could be in the middle of a dinner party. That might be awkward in front of his business associates. But no one is after you, Kate. No one even knows what happened. The only thing chasing you is your own ghosts. Lay them to rest, Kate, and get on with your life. You owe yourself some happiness."

"You almost make me believe it could happen."

"Of course it could. It will."

Kate's eyes filled again. She felt weepy all the time now. "If I didn't know better, I'd think I was pregnant. I've not cried this much in my whole life before."

"You said you had a son. Why can't you have more children?"

Kate blew her nose delicately into her handkerchief. "I don't know. There just weren't anymore after the first one. The tribe's medicine man said I was barren."

"But how could you be barren if you had a child already?"

"He didn't say, actually." She giggled. "He waved a spear over my stomach, then hung a bag full of some foul-smelling concoction over me, and apparently from the way it turned he could tell. It's funny, really. I never questioned him. I just took his word for it, because there were no more children."

"Kate, what did Ben look like?"

She smiled, remembering. "He was slender and had deep brown eyes with the longest lashes. He had dark, almost black hair that kept getting into his eyes. I always told him I'd cut it for him, but he wouldn't let me." Her eyes filled with tears again. "See, there I go, crying like an idiot."

"It's not idiotic. You've revived a lot of painful memories. Kate, could that baby have been Ben's?"

Kate looked at Maggie, shock showing in her face. "I . . . I don't know."

"How long do you guess it was after you were captured that you were made the wife of this Indian?"

She shook her head, her mind racing back to that time. "I was so scared and so full of sorrow over Ben's death that I didn't even try to keep track of time. I figured I'd be dead, anyway. Besides, I didn't even know I was pregnant. Della told me. You don't learn anything about pregnancy in an orphanage. Babies arrive at the door in a basket, and how they got there was anyone's guess."

Maggie was excited now. "But don't you see? If Ben had dark coloring, he could have been your baby's father! Maybe it was your Indian brave who was barren."

Kate paced the floor, shaking her head, unable to think clearly. "It could have been. I just don't know. I can't remember."

"Would Della know, do you think?"

"Yes! Yes, Della would! I'll get her." She hurried off in the direction of the kitchen, Maggie close on her heels. When they'd blurted out the questions, Della took Kate gently by the shoulders and said, "Honey, I thought you knew it was your Ben's baby. There was no way you were with that savage long enough for it to have been his baby. The shaman knew it, too."

"Ben's baby. And I never knew. He wanted babies, sons, so much, and he never even knew I was pregnant!" Kate dropped down in a chair and sobbed, and Della knelt on the floor beside her, holding her and rocking her, murmuring soothing words over and over. Tears ran down Della's cheeks, too, and Maggie remembered Kate telling her that the woman's five children had been killed in the fight also. Her own eyes filled with tears for the waste of it all. If only Kate and Della had refused to go into the wilderness, Maggie thought, they would still have their families. It was all so confusing. If you loved a man, did you stay behind and wait alone, or go with him even though the way was dangerous?

Maggie wandered back out to the drawing room, then got her cloak and let herself out the door and down the hallway to the door in the back. As she passed the general store, Zollie McCaver took note and mentioned to her customer of the moment that Simon Longyear's niece spent far too much time in the company of fallen women, and "it's just pure speculation, mind you, but something tells me she was in trouble back home, and that's why her parents sent her out here."

"We got a telegram delivered here," Bertha announced as she entered the door, "and it's for Simon. I'm riding out there to give it to him. You'd best come along."

"A telegram? Who is it from?"

"I don't know, and I don't mean to open it to find out. We'll know soon enough."

Maggie's stomach was tied in knots all the way out to the ranch. Telegrams weren't usually sent if the news was good, and she'd had a funny feeling about Will. She prayed he was all right.

Smoke hung over the clearing from the branding and cooking fires, and Bertha commented that bad weather must be on the way if the smoke wasn't rising. It looked like total chaos to Maggie as they rode in. Cows and calves bawled as they were separated, the calves on their way into a log corral to be branded. Several riders were trying to round them up, but the cows kept interfering, trying to defend their offspring. Dogs ran and nipped at the heels of the cattle, and this spooked the calves even more. Men were yelling, trying to be heard above the cacophony, and overlooking it all, a satisfied look on his face, was Simon, sitting astride his horse on a small knoll.

"What brings you ladies out today?" his booming voice carried to them.

"A telegram!" Bertha shouted, and his expression changed immediately as he reached out for the envelope she passed to him. He tore the flap open and pulled out the single page within.

"Well, what does it say?" Bertha demanded, but Maggie was scared to know. She held her breath as he answered, "It's from Will. He's not coming back right away, but Dave should be here shortly."

"But why?" Maggie asked, able to speak again. "Does it say why he's not coming back now?"

"He had some business to take care of."

Maggie saw Bertha and Simon exchange looks, and she blurted out, " There's something more! What is it?"

"Nothing, Maggie. Will's a grown man. He can take care of himself, and you don't need to worry about him. He'll be back when he can." Simon turned to Bertha. "What have you heard? A man came from one of the other ranches yesterday and said the fighting is over and the association members are in jail."

"Well, the paper doesn't say jail. They were taken to Fort McKinney, and now they're being moved to Cheyenne. Talk is that they're going to get away with it."

"They murdered two people, from what I heard."

"Yes, but they actually were rustlers, to hear tell. They got the governor in their pocket, anyway, so it doesn't matter," she added bitterly.

"No, it doesn't, and we have work to do. I think Pete has dinner ready if you two want to get a bite before you leave."

Whatever it was that was keeping Will, it must be terrible for her uncle to keep it from her, and Bertha was silent despite Maggie's appeals all the way back to town.

Maggie's only hope was that Kate knew the whole story, and she fairly flew through the growing dusk to the Seven Squaw, not taking the time to go around to the back door. She raised more than a few eyebrows as she rushed through the main room of the saloon and disappeared through the door at the back. She'd been seen there before but then she had been in the company of her uncle, and everyone knew about his relationship with Kate.

"That a new girl?" one young cowboy asked the men at the table with him.

"Nope," replied one man, "that's Simon Longyear's niece. You know him. Raises horses up the valley."

"Yeah, I know him. So what's his niece doing in a whorehouse?"

"She's probably visitin' Kate, seeing as how that's gonna be her new aunt."

"She really Longyear's niece?"

"So they say. Must be true, anyway, 'cause Will Sutten is courtin' the girl."

"Bet he don't know how much time his lady friend spends here. He don't never step foot in this place, hisself," inserted another man at the table. His wife was good friends with Zollie McCaver, so he felt he had an inside on the girl.

"Where is Sutten? Didn't he go over to Johnson County with that bunch?"

"Yep. They should be comin' back afore long."

"Maybe he shouldn't have left her. She's probably gettin' pretty lonely about now, wouldn't you say?"

The young cowboy grinned. He'd had a few shots and was feeling pretty good. "Maybe I just better go ask her."

"Yeah, Tom, why don't you just do that? She'll be comin' out the back door later. She don't often come through here."

"How will I know when she's leaving?"

"Kate comes in here at the same time every night. The girl leaves then."

"All right. I'll just do that. Show her what a real man is like."

The others laughed, and one slapped young Tom on the back. Soon their talk drifted on to other subjects, and they started a game of poker. One motioned to the bartender, and he set them up with another round of drinks.

A man sitting at the table behind them had also seen the girl coming through and had found her very interesting. He had come in about an hour earlier, after a long bath at the hotel. The past two days, which he'd spent riding in circles before finally coming over the pass to Jackson, had been hard on him, and he wanted to relax.

This was his old stomping ground, but no one had recognized him as yet. He'd had a scare at the hotel when he'd recognized a woman he'd known years before, but he managed to keep from being seen by her. It was funny, he thought, but when you were away, you thought the place you'd left was the same, and then when you came back, new buildings had gone up, new faces sat at the tables. Maybe it was just as well: he wasn't that keen on anyone remembering who he was. He had taken a little extra precautions, like the patch he was wearing on his left eye. He had changed his whole image while he'd been in Texas, and it wouldn't have surprised him if his own mother hadn't recognized him, if she'd still been alive.

He was wearing a black suit and snowy white shirt, a gentleman's outfit. His black hair, once long and straggly, was neatly cut and combed, with the silver streaks at his temples giving him a distinguished look. A wealthy look, he thought. His hands were clean, the nails neatly trimmed, and he limited himself to one drink now. He used to drink half the county under the table in the old days, then got into fights and wound up thrown in jail more often than not. The sheriff was different now, too. He'd checked that out on his way over to the Seven Squaw.

Even this saloon was new. He wondered if the Kate the men referred to was the owner. And he'd have to go meet the Longyear fellow to find a suitable replacement for the horse he'd left behind when he'd been taken prisoner by the military, and perhaps gain an introduction to the man's niece. Two days into the trek from Fort McKinney to the railroad station at Douglas, he'd simply slipped away. The guards had orders to keep the prisoners from getting killed, not from escaping. So it had been easy enough to accomplish, though his first try when they'd just been arrested, had been stopped by one of the damned ranchers. Maybe that was just as well. He might have gotten shot there, with feelings running as hot as they'd been that day.

The WSGA job had seemed a simple enough task at first, and the pay sure was good. Fifty dollars to every man for each rustler killed. He'd known—they'd all known—there weren't any real rustlers, so going against simple ranchers had seemed as easy as shooting at bottles. But he was smart enough to know when it was time to get out. Except for a few nights in his younger days when he'd been drinking, he'd never been in jail and he didn't want to try it again. Jackson had always been his place to lay low after trouble, although it bothered him that people from here had been in Johnson County. What if someone recognized him? Maybe he should go up to his cabin. It should be stocked by now, if Millie had done what he'd told her. But he had gotten used to a better way of life, and better women, too, and the cabin and Millie had lost their appeal. Since he knew he'd made some promises to her that he had no intention of keeping, it wouldn't do to meet up with her. She had lost her looks, gone seedy on him, and he didn't want to start that relationship up again. He'd have to be careful if he stuck around.

He thought of the long-legged Longyear beauty and decided to stay in town for a bit. He'd just play it safe, keeping his wits about him, and staying one step ahead of the law. He'd made it that way for a long time. He sat back and sipped his whiskey, biding his time until this Kate made her appearance, and watch to see if the young cowboy did go after the girl. If he did, she might be in need of assistance. And he was just the one to provide it.

"Maggie! What are you doing here?" Kate asked as she opened her door and quickly pulled the girl inside. "You shouldn't be here alone at night, and you definitely shouldn't be coming through the saloon! What are you thinking?"

"Oh, Kate, Uncle Simon got a telegram from Will, and he won't tell me what's in it, but he says Will won't be coming back for a while. I think he's found his wife, and you have to tell me the truth. Is he married?"

"I don't know anything about Will. I really don't know him very well. He's never come in here as far as I know, and Simon usually doesn't discuss other people's business. I'm afraid I can't help you. What makes you think he's found his wife?"

"Why else wouldn't he be able to marry me? He told me he couldn't marry me now because there was something in his past he had to deal with. What else could there be that would prevent him from marrying someone?"

"Perhaps he's running from the law?"

"I thought of that, but it doesn't make sense. For one thing, he's hardly made a secret of his life here, and for another, he wouldn't very well go riding into a place where he was wanted."

"Maybe he would, if he thought he could clear himself of whatever charges were against him."

"Then why didn't he do it before? Why wait until now?"

"He didn't have any reason to before. I should know. My past didn't really matter to me until I met Simon. Then it was too late to change anything, but maybe Will thinks he can."

"But why wouldn't Uncle Simon tell me that? And I think Bertha knows what it is, too. I saw the look she exchanged with Uncle Simon when he told her what was in the telegram, and I could tell there's something they're hiding from me. I asked her right out to tell me, and she wouldn't."

"Perhaps he made them promise not to."

"Kate, Will knows me well enough to realize I wouldn't hold something in his past against him. I'd do anything in my power to help him. I don't want to start out with secrets between us."

Kate sighed and with her eyes closed, lay her head back against the cushions. "We're a lot alike, you and I. We're both dealing with the same situation, only on different sides."

"Well, from my side I'd advise you to tell Uncle Simon everything, so he doesn't imagine the worst, like I am. Let him decide. You have nothing to lose, after all."

"I have a great deal more to lose now than I did this morning."

"What do you mean?"

She smiled, her face glowing. "I went to the doctor."

"You're pregnant!"

"Yes. I can't believe it, but I am."

"Oh, Kate, I knew it! That's the most wonderful news in the world! Uncle Simon is going to be so thrilled! Oh, I wish I'd known when I went up there today. He needs to know as soon as possible so he can make plans for the wedding."

Kate frowned, the joy going out of her face like a lamp blown out. "Maggie, nothing has changed there. I still can't marry him."

"What do you mean, you can't marry him? You have to. You can't have a baby without being married. It's bad enough that it won't be nine months."

"A woman like me doesn't have to worry about the usual conventions of society. As a matter of face, most women like me get rid of their babies. But I want this baby more than anything in the world."

"Kate, Uncle Simon isn't going to let you have his baby without being married to you. It's his baby. He's the father. He wants this baby, too. You can't take it from him. He won't let you."

"He won't know."

"Oh, Kate, you can't do that! You can't do that to him when he loves you and wants you to have his children."

"Of course I can. I plan to go away for a few months."

"You try that, and I'll tell him myself. I just may ride up there and do that anyway. Tonight."

"Why would you hurt him like that?"

"What, you don't think he'll know the child is his? What are you going to do, tell him you adopted it?"

Kate blushed. "As a matter of fact, I was thinking of that."

"That's stupid. He'll never believe you, and besides, what are you going to do with a child in a whorehouse? Do you want your daughter raised in a whorehouse, Kate? You don't think I should be here, but you'll have this child here all the time. Think about it, Kate."

"Then what would you have me do? Get rid of it?"

"No, of course not! Kate, why are you so stubborn? Don't you see that this solves everything?"

"I can't discuss this any further. I have to go to work now," Kate said abruptly, then got up and brushed past Maggie. "You can let yourself out. You know the way."

"Kate, running away from this isn't going to help anything. You have to give Uncle Simon a chance."

Kate turned back to Maggie, her face reflecting her anguish. "Maggie," she whispered. Then she started crying. "All my life I've been at the mercy of others. They all let me down. My parents, whoever they were, left me alone. The orphanage was utter hell, my life directed by the whims of a madman who'd just as soon beat as feed me. Then there was that rich bastard who thought I belonged to him, and thought nothing of taking what he considered his. And I was, I was his. He could have raped me, killed me even, and no one would have said a word. After that, it was Ben who decided I was going to move out west, and then he left me, too. Don't you understand? For the first time, I am in charge of my life. I decide what I will do, where I will go. No one has control over me, and I don't need to depend on anyone to provide my living. If I don't like a person, I can tell him to get out of my place. My place, you hear that? This is my place, and I won't give it up. I can't. Not even for Simon. I love him, God knows I love him, but what if I grow to depend on him and he lets me down, too? I couldn't bear it again, Maggie. I think I'd just die."

"Shhh, Kate, it's all right. I really do understand." She hugged the older woman, smiled at her, and said, "See you tomorrow."

As Maggie let herself out, she wondered what kind of friend Kate would think she was when she found out she'd told Uncle Simon about the baby. She suspected that Kate would not be pleased with her. She decided to seek out Della and talk to her about everything. Maybe she could shed some light on the matter.

Della had been reading when Maggie knocked on her door, and she took off a pair of wire-rimmed spectacles as she ushered Maggie in. "Land sakes, child! You got no business being in here this late. What would Kate say?"

"I've just come from there, and she said the same thing. I need to talk to you, Della. About Kate and the baby, and my uncle."

"Oh, so she told you about it, did she?"

"Yes. Della, I just don't think it's right that she doesn't want to tell him."

"I don't always agree with what Kate says or does, but she has to do what she thinks is right."

"I can't let Uncle Simon live his life without knowing he has a child. He wants one so much."

"I'd think twice before I went messing in someone else's life, if I were you. What makes you think you have the right to tell him?"

"He's my uncle, I love him dearly, and she won't tell him. She said so."

"Why don't you just keep quiet for a while, honey? When that baby starts moving around inside her, she won't be able to keep from telling him. I know, I had five of them. It's just something you have to share. It's an awful sad thing to go it alone."

"But she said she was going away. She said she was going to tell him she adopted the baby."

"He isn't going to believe that. And between you and me, I don't think she'll be able to go away. Being a mother does something to you. Nesting instinct, I guess."

"Are you sure?"

Della laughed. "As sure as the sun rises. You just wait and see. She'll come around."

"Thank you, Della. You've made me feel much better about the whole thing."

"Glad to help out. I think of her as my daughter, even though she thinks she's the one taking care of me. I won't let her ruin her life. If I have to hog-tie her and drag her to the altar, I won't let her throw this chance away."

Maggie laughed. "I believe you really mean it!"

"Believe it, honey, believe it."

Maggie was still laughing as she left Della's room and made her way down the hallway to the back door. She really had been foolish to come through the saloon, and she wouldn't repeat the mistake. She turned the corner, fastening the frogs on her cloak, and didn't see the person standing in front of the door until she ran into him.

"Oh! I'm so sorry! I'm afraid I wasn't looking where I was going," she apologized to the young man who was peering at her with a leering grin on his face. "They'll come looking for me if I'm late for dinner, so I really must be hurrying along," she lied, then tried to pass him.

But he caught her arm. "Not so fast, Miss Longyear, is it?" His breath smelled like whiskey, and she was suddenly afraid. She jerked her arm away, but he caught it again and pulled her close to him.

"Miss Longyear is such a mouthful. What's your first name?"

"I don't know how you know my name, but if you know who I am, you must know my uncle. He will be out looking for me now, and I wouldn't advise you to be caught holding me against my will." She had started to shake and prayed he wouldn't notice.

"Your uncle is on roundup. He ain't gonna come looking for nobody. Now why don't you and I get to know each other a little better? I'll treat you real good." He pressed his face close to hers.

She knew Della was only doors away, and there were people in the saloon. She took a deep breath to scream.

He clamped his hand over her mouth. "You don't want to do that, now. I ain't gonna hurt you. I just want to talk a little." He leaned against her, trapping her against the wall, one hand over her mouth, the other sliding up her waist to cup her breast.

She didn't think, she reacted. She brought one knee up, between his legs, then slammed her sharp heel on his foot, twisting sideways as she did it.

"You little bitch!" he growled, then spun her around and jerked her arm up behind her back. "I thought we could have a little talk, but I see you want to play rough. Well, I can play rough, lady, don't you doubt it."

"I don't think the lady is interested in what you have in mind," said a deep voice behind them, and Tom swung around to meet the steely gaze of a big man with a patch over one eye.

"Why don't you just mind your own business, mister? This don't concern you."

"Oh, but it does. I happen to be a close personal friend of Miss Longyear's and I don't take kindly to the way you're treating her. Now, let her go and get out. We can settle this without any bloodshed."

Tom was uneasy now. The whiskey had made him bolder than he usually was, but the man had a sobering effect, for sure. Still, he wanted this girl, and the men inside had told him she came here all the time. In one smooth action, he released Maggie and swung his fist around to take the big man. But his hand never found its mark. He felt as if his head had exploded; then everything went dark.

Maggie fell to the floor when he took the pressure off her, and she knelt there, cradling her arm, which surely must be broken, from the feel of it. The big man in black had hit the drunken cowboy one blow to the jaw and knocked him out cold. He tipped his hat to her.

"You're lucky I came along when I did. That young cowboy seemed intent upon making your acquaintance." He reached down to help her up to her feet. "Jacob Grainger, at your service." He made a mock bow, sweeping the hat from his head. "And you don't know me. It seemed the most expedient way to deal with the chap."

"Well, it worked, and I'm very grateful to you. How did you know my name, though?"

"I overheard one of the men in the saloon say your uncle raised horses, and as I'm in the market for one, it caught my interest."

"Yes, he does raise horses. There are some fine ones out at the ranch, and I'm sure when he gets back from the roundup he'll be glad to show them to you."

"I must be going. It was a pleasure to make your acquaintance."

"Thank you again, Mr. Grainger. I don't know what would have happened if you hadn't come along."

He bowed again and disappeared into the saloon. Maggie didn't want Della or Kate to know what had happened, for fear they would forbid her to come again, and since she was none the worse for her experience, except for a sore arm, she slipped out the back and ran the distance to the house.

Maggie lay in bed later and thought about the messes people made of their lives. She wondered if her mother had cried over Simon. Had she loved him more, but just couldn't marry him? She couldn't imagine her mother loving anyone but her father, but one time she had been young and, according to Simon, in love with him. Maggie cried for her mother, and then for her father and uncle, and even Kate, who couldn't allow her own heart to be broken again, and so was denying the love that awaited her.

Will lay in bed that night, too, thinking of Maggie. He hadn't thought he'd miss her so much. He missed her laughter and her quick wit. He missed being close to her, smelling her hair, touching her skin.

There had been times since Maggie had come into his life that he thought he could give up the quest—simply let it go. But when he looked right into the eyes that had haunted him for six years, he knew with certainty he'd been fooling himself. He hadn't seen the man again—no one was allowed in to see any of the prisoners—but as long as he was locked in there, Will was staying put. He wouldn't lose Greeley again.

He hated keeping Maggie in suspense when all he wanted to do was ride straight to her and put an end to the waiting, but he couldn't. He could only trust that she was waiting for him and would understand when he told her what he'd had to do, that he'd had to kill a man before he could be free to marry her. He didn't allow himself to think he might be dead, or that he might go to prison for murder. He had planned the deed carefully during the time he'd spent waiting for Greeley to get out of jail, and figured he'd have to make it look like self-defense, by taunting the man enough that he called him out. And when they faced each other on the street, he'd have to be quicker. That was all there was to it.

So many years of his life had been lost because of the hatred he felt for Greeley that he didn't want to waste any more. His thoughts and dreams had become so full of Maggie Longyear, he'd be set adrift without her. She had to be waiting when he got back.

❧ 14 ❧

As Maggie and Bertha were sitting down to breakfast the next morning, there was a knock on the door, and Maggie opened it to find Chase Wolcott there. She hadn't seen him in so long, it was like greeting an old friend.

"Come in, Chase! It's so good to see you. What brings you out so early today?" she asked as she took his coat.

"Set yourself down here and have some breakfast. We've got plenty," Bertha invited.

Chase grinned. "I could smell your cooking from my place, Bertha, and just had to come over to see if I could get some."

"Well, as long as we're in town, you have an open invitation to stop in any time. I've always got a pot of something on the stove." She bustled over to fix him a plate, and he held Maggie's chair for her, then did the same for Bertha when she returned with the plate heaped high with ham, eggs, fried potatoes, and thick slices of crusty, warm bread, the butter already melting into it.

"If I ate like this every day, I fear I'd get as round as Archie McCaver," he joked. "Actually, I was called out before light this morning, over to Holloway's. I have to go out to old Mrs. Adams' ranch today, and I wondered if you'd like to ride along, Maggie."

"Oh, I'd love to! I've been cooped up inside for too long, and I dearly miss being outside in the fresh air and sunshine."

"Dr. Wolcott! You know very good and well you can't

take her out riding in your carriage alone!" Bertha exclaimed.

"Oh, I have that covered. You remember little Bessie Fields has been staying at her aunt's place in town here for the winter, because she was sick so much, and her parents wanted her to be close to the doctor?" Bertha nodded, and he continued. "Well, I'm taking her out to her folks today and bringing Mrs. Adams back in with me. Her rheumatism has gotten worse again, and if she can get down here, her sister-in-law will see that she gets to the hot springs. So you see, I couldn't have better chaperons."

"Well," Bertha said with a sniff, "I guess that sounds all right. Although Bessie Fields is hardly old enough to act as a chaperon."

"She's eight in years but much older in experience. She'll do just fine." He winked at Maggie.

After Maggie had changed into warmer clothes, Bertha handed her a basket filled with lunch fixings. Chase thanked her effusively, and they left to go pick up the little girl. She came running out, her aunt behind her, as they stopped in front of the house.

"Dr. Chase, Dr. Chase, you came!"

"Well, of course I came," he replied as he jumped down to lift her up beside Maggie. "You didn't think I'd forget my best girl, did you?"

Bessie beamed, looking around her as if she were setting out on some great adventure. Maggie looked at the child, her blond ringlets framing a round, pink little face and her blue eyes shining with anticipation, and felt a pang of regret for her own lost innocence. It seemed a lifetime ago that she last felt so totally carefree, but she realized that it actually was less than six months since Charles Eversley had shattered her serene life by asking for her hand in marriage.

"What's your name? Mine is Bessie." The little girl looked eagerly up at Maggie.

"Maggie. I'm glad to meet you, Bessie."

"Are you going to marry Dr. Chase?" she asked innocently.

"Bessie," her aunt reprimanded, "you watch your manners! It isn't polite to ask questions like that."

Chase colored, but Maggie wasn't embarrassed. She was used to the children she had taught in Sunday school, and she knew the outrageous questions they popped out without thinking. Besides, she felt nothing except friendship for the young doctor, so she met his eyes with a genuine grin of amusement, which he returned.

After Chase lifted Bessie's small bag into the back of the carriage, they set off. As they climbed up out of the protective depression in which the town sat, the wind picked up, and Maggie was glad Chase had told her to dress warmly. Bessie snuggled up next to her, and Chase reached behind him to pull out a couple of warm, wool blankets, which Maggie wrapped around them. Bessie was excited and asked questions faster than they could possibly be answered, but after a while the fresh air and steady clip-clop of the horse's hooves lulled her to sleep, and Maggie held her close against her side.

"She's quite a handful," Chase commented.

"Yes, she is," Maggie replied, "but she's adorable. What fun it must be to have a child who's curious about life and full of adventure."

"Were you like that as a child?" he asked.

Maggie laughed. "Probably. I never thought about it before. I was always tagging along behind my father, in the stables where I no doubt shouldn't have been. My poor mother finally gave up trying to keep me in the house. I'm afraid I'm not very interested in cooking and needlepoint."

"I know what you mean. My mother wanted me to learn how to run the farm, but I liked nothing better than to hang around old Doc Schultz's place in case he needed help during an operation. My mother thought it was a gruesome inclination, but curiously enough, my father seemed to encourage it. He gave all he could spare, and then some, to put me through medical school."

"And what do they think of you now?"

"My father died about six months before I graduated.

My mother hasn't changed. She hasn't forgiven me for leaving the farm."

"I'm sorry." Maggie didn't know what to say to ease the doctor's obvious sorrow.

"Don't be. Life has a way of working itself out, quite apart from our own wishes. Sometimes when we think we've lost everything, the experience turns out to be a blessing in disguise."

She nodded, and they rode along in comfortable silence for awhile. She thought of Charles and of coming to Wyoming and finding Will.

"Do you know Will very well?" she asked him.

"I'd say as well as anybody does. Will kind of keeps to himself."

"Do you know about his wife?"

"You mean the one who died?"

"There are others?" she asked, aghast.

He laughed. "No, no. Not that I know of, anyway. What does she have to do with you?"

"I think she's still alive, and I think he found her when he went over to Buffalo."

Chase whistled. "What makes you think so?"

"Chase, he told me he loved me, and he'd marry me if he could, but that there was something in his past he had to deal with before he was free to do so. What else could it be? If it were something else, like being wanted by the law, he could tell me."

"Maybe he doesn't think you'd understand."

"He knows me better than that. I'm not some shallow, frivolous, little thing that would be shocked and faint into his arms."

"Will Sutten's a fool."

"Why do you say that?"

"He's a fool for letting a woman like you slip through his fingers. I wouldn't be that stupid."

Now it was Maggie's turn to blush. "You've very kind, Doctor."

"Oh, ho! So it's 'doctor' now. A moment ago it was Chase. I liked that better."

She laughed. "All right, then, Chase. You got me flustered."

"You're very honest, Maggie. I like that. In fact, I like a lot of things about you." If Will was fool enough to let her go, Chase wasn't.

She blushed again. "I'm going to have to go back to calling you 'doctor' if you keep that up. Dr. Wolcott, as a matter of fact."

"No you won't. Let's be friends, Maggie. I've never met a woman I could talk to like I can to you. It's a refreshing change, and I don't want to spoil it." A very heady experience, too, he thought. Here was a woman he could imagine working beside him in his practice. Not to mention how nice she was to look at. He'd have to take it slowly, though, and court her without her knowing. She still thought she was in love with Sutten.

Maggie was confused, but she really did enjoy talking to Chase. He was interesting and talked to her as if she had some brains. Men, in her limited experience, tended to talk to women with the assumption that a female wouldn't have anything more in her brain than thoughts of gowns and catching a husband. Will had been different, too. Was that why she'd fallen in love with him? she wondered. They had become friends after all, and she missed him terribly. Would he come back, or would he stay with the wife who'd left him? She thought of the unknown wife, and wondered what she was like. Had she left him, or had something happened? There were so many questions she wanted to ask, but she had no one to provide the answers.

"Maggie?" Chase asked, looking at her with a smile. "I didn't mean to upset you."

"Oh, Chase, you didn't upset me. I was just thinking about Will."

Maybe this was going to be harder than he thought. "At least you've gone back to 'Chase.' I think we could both use a friend, don't you?"

She smiled and nodded. "I could surely use one."

"Good. Now, Bessie's ranch is right up this little valley here, and we'll drop her off, then I'll take you to a place I like, and we can have our lunch before picking up Mrs. Adams."

"Dr. Wolcott! What would Bertha say!"

"I really don't care. I must assure you, though, that I will behave in a most gentlemanly way. You have no need to fear for your reputation while you're with me." Doubly so, he thought, because a doctor's wife, like the minister's wife, had to be above reproach.

When Maggie woke her up, the little girl squeezed her eyes against the light to peer at her surroundings. "Oh," she exclaimed, "I'm almost home!"

"Yes, you are, darling. I'll bet you're anxious to see your family again." Maggie hugged Bessie.

As they pulled into the ranch yard, a young woman, blond and blue-eyed like Bessie, came running out of the cabin.

"Seth! She's here!" she called and then was at the carriage, catching Bessie as the child threw herself into her arms. A man came out and enclosed the two in a big hug. Then he looked up at the doctor, his face filled with gratitude.

"You made her well again, Doctor. Thank you." His voice was husky with emotion. He dug in his pocket and pulled up a few coins which he held out to Chase. "It's not much, but if you need more, I'll get it to you, I promise."

Maggie's eyes filled at the obvious joy in the reunion. Chase, too, had been affected by the homecoming. "Keep your money, Seth, and use it to buy good food and warm clothes for Bessie. She's growing fast."

The man's eyes were shiny with tears as he nodded, then turned again to his family. When Chase and Maggie left the ranch, the mother, father, and daughter were going inside, still holding each other.

Maggie and Chase were both silent for a long time. Chase drove the carriage up a road beside a fast-running stream swelled with the waters from melting snow. Breaking the silence, he told her, "Later in the year, that whole rocky area down there is full of water as the snow begins to melt in the high country."

"You won't get rich that way, you know," Maggie commented, returning the subject to his charity.

"Who said I wanted to get rich?" He smiled at her, and she smiled back. "As long as I have enough and I can live here in this valley . . ." He shrugged and let the sentence hang.

He brought out Bertha's basket, and they ate lunch, exchanging light banter. Then Maggie put the basket away as Chase maneuvered the buggy back down the road. "Maybe we can come here this summer," he suggested. "We could sit on a blanket instead of huddling under one on a buggy seat."

"I'd like that," she said, and his heart lightened.

Their next stop was at the ranch of one of the first men to make his home in the Wyoming Territory. He had been a big man once, but was now bent and grizzled, his face wrinkled and brown like a leaf. His arms and legs seemed too long for his body, and his hands were huge. He poured them each a large tin cup of coffee, then lowered himself to a chair and pulled aside his split pants leg to let the doctor look at his wound. While the doctor poked and probed, Charley talked.

Maggie was enthralled by his tales of the early days, when the wildlife was so abundant "you only had to step out on the porch to shoot yer supper." He described the elk migration and told her no-where else in the country could you see something as awesome as the huge herds making their way between summer and winter feeding grounds. Maggie had seen the huge herds but hadn't imagined they all set out at once for high country.

"Yep, in the summer you don't hardly see any at all, 'cause they all go up there." He indicated the mountains behind his cabin. "Lots of deer, too, and antelope and moose. I seen my share of bears here, I can tell you."

He winced as Chase pulled the soiled bandages off a large gash in his leg. Maggie thought she'd be sickened by the sight, but to her surprise she wasn't. She was keenly interested as the doctor cut away the remaining bits of cloth and bathed the wound.

"It doesn't look too bad, Charley, considering you doctored it yourself."

"I been doctorin' myself since long before you was a gleam in yer pappy's eye, young man, and I doctored lots of others, too. I reckon I know a thing or two might surprise you."

Chase laughed. "I'm sure you do, Charley, and some of those things might just be better than what we were taught in medical school. I've seen some home remedies work when everything I have to offer fails."

"Well, I put arnica liniment on this here after two or three days of changing the poultice. I always keep some made up."

"It worked. The edges have grown together well, but you're going to have a scar that wouldn't have been so bad if you'd let me stitch it up."

"Hell, boy—oh, pardon my language, miss—but what do I care about the looks of a scar? Ain't nobody gonna see it but me."

"You're right, but sometimes if the edges grow together raggedly, there is some pain associated with the wound for the rest of a person's life."

"I already had pain all my life. I broke more bones than you'll ever see, been shot with arrows and bullets, had more 'an one go 'round with bears and such, and I lived to tell about it. A little scar ain't gonna do me in."

"You'll probably outlive me, Charley. I don't have the gumption you do," Chase told the old man, who grinned, pleased at the words.

"You'll do, boy, you'll do. It just takes some growin'." He looked at Maggie and winked. "And a good woman to help you on the way."

Maggie blushed then, as she hadn't when Bessie had said much the same thing. She couldn't quite meet Chase's eyes, but then they were leaving, Charley thanking them effusively, and Chase protesting that he hadn't done anything. Maggie couldn't help herself. She hugged the old man and told him she was very glad to have met him. He swiped his hand under his nose and told her she had to come back and see him.

"Don't wait for this good-for-nothin doctor to bring you, neither. Yer uncle's place ain't so far from here."

"I'll do that. Thank you for the invitation. I plan to go riding every day when the weather permits."

They said their good-byes and left, Chase holding her hand for perhaps a moment longer than necessary when he helped her up into the buggy. Or was that her imagination? *Please don't let it be,* she prayed, *because I certainly don't need any more complications in my life right now.* She thought of the doctor and how his patients seemed to think the world of him. She couldn't think of it now, until her relationship with Will was decided, but Chase was certainly a very nice man. It wouldn't be hard to be with him, as he was totally undemanding. But then the image of Will came to her, his mouth devouring hers in a hungry kiss, his hands seeking to possess her body, and she closed her eyes, wondering if the doctor could ever evoke those same feelings within her.

"A penny for your thoughts," Chase said softly, watching her closed eyes and an expression on her face he couldn't quite fathom. She looked utterly desirable with her face pink from the outside air, her hair falling loose around her face, and he thought it just as well they'd soon be at the Adams' place. Usually women fell at his feet, so to speak, and it was a new experience to have one indifferent to him.

"I was just thinking about how your patients think you're so wonderful. It must be nice to be so adored."

He smiled, resisting the impulse to say he wanted only her adoration, and said, "Wait until you meet Mrs. Adams. You'll change your opinion in a hurry."

Mrs. Adams was certainly not the undemanding passenger Bessie had been. As Chase helped her out to the buggy and introduced her to Maggie, the first thing she said was, "Well! I can see why you took so long coming to get me, but don't you go getting any ideas. I'll have the front seat, and you can sit in the back, girl." And to Chase, "Why you don't have a closed carriage is beyond me. It'll probably be the death of me to ride out in the open like this, and it'll be your fault, young man. Why, old Doc Hemple would never have made me ride like this. He paid attention to my delicate constitution, unlike you young doctors with your newfangled notions."

As Mrs. Adams was a very large woman, it was difficult to imagine that she had a delicate constitution. It looked, rather, as though she enjoyed a hearty appetite, to say the least. Chase had to squeeze to fit beside her on the seat where there had been room for Bessie between him and Maggie. She had a long nose topped with a deep crevice from having frowned all her life, and her eyes were quick and darting, not missing anything. The strings from her bonnet were lost somewhere in the folds of her chin, and she had steel-gray hair, not a strand of it out of place.

Maggie couldn't meet Chase's eyes for fear she'd burst out laughing, so she busied herself with getting settled in the back. After Mrs. Adams fussed about the way he tucked her mounds of blankets around her, she fussed about how he should load her luggage, which was considerable. By the time it was all in, Maggie was snug and warm in the midst of all the bags and packages. When they finally had everything to the old woman's satisfaction, they started out, and she didn't leave off her criticisms or gossip until they reached town. Maggie decided to allow the woman to think Chase had just given her a ride. He had to live and practice here, and since it was obvious what kind of woman she was as she slandered everyone within the valley and some beyond, Maggie didn't want to give her any fuel for her vicious tongue.

She jumped out as soon as they came rolling to a stop, and called as she ran up the steps, "Thank you for the ride, Dr. Wolcott. Uncle Simon will be grateful to you, I'm sure." Then she disappeared into the house before he had a chance to get down.

When he had taken Mrs. Adams to her brother's house, he drove back to talk to Maggie. He was driving down her street when he saw a man in a black suit ride up, dismount, and go up to knock on the door. Chase waited until the door was opened, then drove his buggy up and hurried up the walk. He was just in time to hear Bertha say, "I'm not in a position to give you permission to call on Miss Longyear. Her uncle will be here tomorrow, and you can ask him."

"Perhaps we could ask the lady herself," the stranger said smoothly, as Chase came up behind him and said, "I'm here to get Maggie, Bertha, if you'll tell her." He turned to the man, and offered his hand. "I'm Chase Wolcott, doctor in these parts."

The man looked at the hand offered him and hesitated, then quickly shook it, and said in a cultured voice, "Pleased to make your acquaintance, Doctor." Chase noticed that he didn't offer his name.

"It seems I've come at a bad time," the stranger said. "Perhaps another day." He tipped his hat and, leaving Chase and Bertha at the door, remounted and rode off down the street.

When Chase was inside, he asked Bertha, "Who was that man?"

"I don't know, and I don't want to know. He's no good, though. I could see that when I first looked at him. He's got no business coming around here asking after Maggie, either."

"But did he say how he knew her?"

"No, he didn't. There's something familiar about him, though. I know him from somewhere. Oh, I know this is on account of her going to that saloon. I told her no good would come of it."

Maggie came in, having changed her clothes and tidied her hair. She smiled as she saw Chase. "You got away from her, then?"

"Finally! It's funny, but the ride home seemed much longer than the ride up there."

"That's for sure," she agreed.

"Who're you talking about, old lady Adams?" Bertha asked. "She's the worst gossip in the valley." She shot a quick look at the two of them. "I hope you didn't give her any reason to turn her vicious tongue toward the two of you."

"No," Maggie replied. "As a matter of fact, I made it

a point to ignore Chase. I caught on fast that she would take any incident, however slight, and turn it around in her mind."

"So that's why you got so cold all of a sudden," Chase said. "I did wonder what I'd done to offend you." He held up his hand to Bertha. "I swear that my behavior was beyond exemplary."

"I don't know what that means, but it had better mean you kept your hands to yourself," she warned.

Chase and Maggie laughed. "Bertha, he was a perfect gentleman. We're only friends, after all."

Chase wasn't thrilled to hear her say that, but he knew he'd have to bide his time.

"I brought your basket back. The food was delicious as always," he said to Bertha, who took the bait.

"Why don't you just stay for supper? I have plenty."

"Oh, no, I've already eaten two meals off you today. I shouldn't impose," he protested.

"Of course you should. I can't be happy if I'm not cooking for someone. And just the two of us don't eat enough to warrant the bother. Now, you just sit down and don't fret a bit about eating here. I'm sure Simon would agree."

"Maggie, there was a man here," Chase commented when they'd gathered at the table, "asking permission to court you, according to Bertha. Who is he?"

Maggie frowned. "What did he look like?"

"Older, some gray in his hair, big man, wore a patch over one eye."

"Oh, him. His name is Grainger. I wonder why he came here."

"He wanted permission to come calling," Bertha explained. "I told him he'd have to take that up with your uncle."

"Well, I certainly don't welcome his attentions."

"Where did you meet this Grainger?" Chase pressed.

Maggie blushed. "I got into a bit of a fix with a drunken cowboy, and he came to my rescue. He said he was in the market for a good horse, and I told him to talk to Uncle Simon."

"A drunken cowboy!" exclaimed Bertha. "That's what comes of you going into that place. I told you you'd be best to keep away from there."

None of them felt quite easy about the man, Grainger, coming to the house. They decided it would be a good thing to let everyone think she was under the protection of the doctor.

Chase made a habit of dropping in nightly thereafter, joking with the two women equally, trying to become a fixture in Maggie's life. The stranger didn't come around again, and soon they had all but forgotten him.

But he hadn't forgotten them. He watched the doctor go to the house night after night, and the more he couldn't see the girl, the more he wanted her. He was a patient man, though. Sooner or later she'd come back to the saloon when he was there, and then he'd deal with her. Yes, he could wait. He'd get what he wanted.

Will had been waiting at Fort Russell for ten weeks. Many times during the long days and nights he'd given serious thought to giving it up, but then the man would come to him in a dream, now with a face to match the eyes that had been the only features he'd been able to imagine before, and he knew he couldn't be free of the ghosts that haunted him until the man was dead. It never occurred to him that perhaps the old ghosts would be replaced by new ones.

He left his lodgings and made his way to the fort, as he did every morning, and heard the excited murmur going through the crowds of people standing there—the prisoners would be released today! His heart pounded in his chest as he realized the end of his quest would come soon, and he pushed his way through the throng of waiting relatives, friends, and sensation-seekers to get next to the door. He wouldn't lose that man again.

He hadn't been waiting long when the door opened, and a cheer went up from the ones outside. The wait was over. The men came out and rushed to waiting wives or others, and Will searched each face that passed. He hardly noticed the crying and hugging going on among the Cheyenne group. He was waiting for the Texans.

It was obvious when the WSGA members were out and the Texans started. While the former group looked much the worse for their experience, the hired guns strutted like the celebrities they were. They filed past and headed toward the street; no loved ones waited for them. The long line of men was getting shorter, and Will panicked. Where was the man? He couldn't have missed him. His face had been indelibly etched into his brain, and there was no way Jake Greeley was going to get by him. But he did. Will frantically searched through the crowd, turning men around by their shoulders, gazing into each face as though willing Greeley to be there. He asked the men if they knew him, but no one had heard the name. Finally one man asked Will, "Did he have funny eyes? Like two different colors maybe?"

"Yes, man! Where did he go?"

"He took off one night when we all were headed down here from Fort McKinney. He wasn't here at all."

Will took the man by the arms and shook him. "He has to be here. He was inside with you. I saw him!"

But the man shook his head and asked his companion, "Didn't Jake get away up north?" and the other man agreed that, yes, he hadn't been inside. He added, "They took one of them fancy photographs of us all while we were in there. Maybe you can look at that and see if your man is there."

Will moved in a daze of shock and disappointment toward the building. He knew in his heart Greeley wouldn't be in the picture—the two men had no reason to lie to him—but he had to see for himself. When he searched the faces in the photograph, his heart sank. Jake Greeley wasn't there.

If he had ever in his life felt like crying, it was now. The sorrow he had felt when he found Charity gone was nothing compared to the burning pain inside him now. Wasted. Almost eleven weeks wasted. And Maggie was back in Jackson Hole, waiting, wondering what was keeping him.

If he lost her because of this, he would never forgive himself. What a fool he had been to fill his life with emptiness, for that was what he'd done. He had made that choice, had chosen to believe that Greeley had taken Charity from him and had to be punished for it. He had known for a long time, from the beginning really, that it was really Charity who had stolen his dreams, Charity who had left him, and Charity whom he had been trying to punish. But he couldn't, because she was dead, and so he had blamed Greeley. Guilt had driven him, but it wouldn't any longer. He was no killer, and all he wanted in the world was to settle down with Maggie and build a new, full life. He would never know what his wife had been seeking when she'd gone to town that day, but there was nothing he could do about it now except bury it along with his memories of her.

He turned abruptly and ran into a woman, grabbing her by the shoulders to keep her from falling. She lifted her head, and his heart almost stopped when he saw her face. *It was Charity.*

❧ 15 ❧

Maggie was standing in the corner of the dance hall waiting for Chase to bring her a glass of punch. They had attended every one of the weekly socials, and she had become quite good at the country dances. Her foot tapped in rhythm to the music, and with a smile she greeted several people she'd come to know; then she spied Mr. Grainger coming toward her, and her smile was replaced by a frown. She thought she'd seen the last of him when Chase began coming over every night, but one day after they'd moved back out to the ranch, he came riding up to the cabin to see Simon about a horse. He had asked permission to court her, and Simon had told him she was taken, but he seemed to be everywhere she went. She had even taken to going to Kate's early in the morning unless Simon was with her, because that was the only time he didn't seem to be around.

She moved away from the corner and went to stand by Pete and Bertha, murmuring to the couple that he was after her again. Bertha still thought she knew the man. It bothered her that she couldn't remember where, but it bothered her even more than the man seemed unable to take no for an answer. It was obvious the girl didn't want to have anything to do with him.

Maggie was sorry she had ever been nice to Mr. Grainger. He had seemed such a gentleman the night he'd come to her rescue that it was hard to believe his actions since that time. Something about him made her uneasy, but she couldn't really pinpoint what it was because he always acted with the utmost good manners.

Just as his eyes found her again, Chase was at her side.

"Would you please take me home, Chase?" she asked him, and after one look at her face he said, "Of course."

He escorted her out the door and to his waiting buggy. The vehicle had become as familiar as the ranch to Maggie, as she'd spent many hours in it during the past weeks. She often went with the doctor on his rounds, always with a chaperon at least part of the way, and she was growing more fond of the young doctor—so much so, in fact, that sometimes she truly regretted that she couldn't bring herself to love him instead of Will, because it would have been so much easier. But the feeling just wasn't there.

One day they had been having the promised picnic in a meadow carpeted with wildflowers, and he had leaned toward her as though he were about to kiss her. She had jumped up and asked what the flowers were called, and he had never made a move toward her since then. She felt guilty but realized he was enjoying their outings as much as she, so she didn't stop going with him.

"Why don't you just take me to Kate's, Chase, since Uncle Simon is there," she said now, when they had left Pete and Bertha. Kate hadn't told Simon about the baby yet, but she hadn't left, either. Sooner or later, something was going to have to happen.

"Maggie, can we talk?" Chase asked her.

"Chase," she hesitated, afraid of what he was going to say.

"I know. Don't ruin it," he said ruefully. "But do you really feel nothing for me?"

"Of course I feel something for you. I've never known a friend like you. If things were different in my life, perhaps there might be something between us, but for now there can't be."

"Because of Will?"

"Yes, because of him, and because of me."

"Will you promise me one thing, Maggie? If he doesn't come back, or if you can't marry him for some reason, will you at least think of me?"

"Chase, if it weren't for Will, I would be head over heels in love with you." She smiled at him. "You're a good man, Chase."

"Hmmm. Maybe I should be bad. Being good doesn't seem to have gotten me anywhere."

"It wouldn't matter, Chase. Even if you weren't such a gentleman, and say, kissed me, if it wasn't right, it just wouldn't be right."

"May I at least try? You know, so I'll know, instead of wondering for the rest of my life?"

They had pulled into the alleyway beside the Seven Squaw, and no one seemed to be around. She hesitated but thought she at least owed him that much. He'd been a good friend these past weeks. But what if it wasn't nothing? What if his kisses did to her what Will's did? She had to know as much as he did. In a way, she knew him better than she knew Will, and this would be a good test. Shaking, she whispered, "One kiss, Chase, and that's all."

He knew he had to give it his best shot, because he only had this one chance to show her how much he loved her. He'd grown up without much love and had used many women over the years to satisfy his desires, but he had never fallen in love before. He'd had to use an iron will not to touch her, but he knew the entire friendship would have been ruined if he had. This might be the end, too, but he had to know.

He put one arm around her back, pulling her close to him, and lifted her chin with his other hand. Her skin felt so warm in the night air. He lowered his lips to hers, then lost himself in the kiss, letting weeks of wanting her come through.

Maggie didn't expect to feel anything and was shocked when she did. She jerked away from him, looking at him with startled eyes.

"Maggie?" he asked her. "What's wrong?"

"Oh, God . . . Chase." She covered her lips with her hands and stared at him helplessly, unable to stop the tears from filling her eyes.

"Maggie, I didn't mean to hurt you. I'm sorry!" He

was totally bewildered and felt a crushing pain in his chest.

"You didn't hurt me, Chase." She dropped her head against his chest, and he closed his arms around her.

After a bit he asked softly, "It was there, wasn't it?"

"Yes . . . no . . . I don't know. Oh, Chase . . ." She was scared, not knowing what all this meant.

The pain left him, and he felt he could fly if she asked him to. But he also knew it was time to back off, to give her a chance to come to grips with her feelings.

"I think you need time to sort this out, Maggie. Maybe I should take you back to the house."

"Yes. I really don't feel up to seeing Kate or Uncle Simon right now."

He turned the horses around and headed back down the street, then turned to go up to her house. He jumped down to help her, but she was already on the path up to the door.

"Maggie?"

She turned to him and said in the darkness, "I'm sorry, Chase. I . . . we never should have done that." She disappeared into the house.

He waited until he saw she had lit a lantern and bolted the door, then he walked slowly back to his rig. *Damn you, Sutten,* he thought, *you're one lucky son of a bitch.*

Will was feeling anything but lucky. He had seen his close friend in a lover's embrace with the woman he loved, and his heart was wrenched out of his body. "Maggie," he whispered to the air, "why couldn't you have waited for me?"

He hadn't believed the talk around the hotel earlier, as he'd overheard Zollie McCaver tell old Mrs. Adams that Simon Longyear's niece was working at Kate's. He knew about Maggie's relationship with Kate, and he also knew both of the old women's penchant for dirty gossip. But when the shopkeeper's wife had told about the older man who was seeing Maggie, he hadn't known what to think. Maybe it was all innocence, and Zollie was up to her usual tricks. But then Mrs. Adams had told of Maggie spending so much time with the doctor, and how they had eyes for only each other, and that's when he'd gone outside to lean against the hotel and have a smoke. That's when he'd seen Chase's buggy pull up at the saloon with Maggie in it and had witnessed the loving embrace the two had shared.

Damn her, he thought, damn her for a cheating hussy. And if the story about Chase was true, what about this other man? The one she met at the saloon? Were all women the way Charity had been? Did they all run to another man's arms the minute you turned your back on them? He was exhausted from days and nights in the saddle, switching from one horse to the other to get back to Maggie, and after seeing what he'd seen, he was filled with such anger he knew if he confronted her tonight he'd likely kill her himself. He didn't care what any of them thought, he would stay in the hotel tonight. He couldn't even bear the thought of looking at her, of hearing the lies she was bound to tell him. The image kept going through his mind of her naked in the bath, and Chase's lips, not his, lowering down to kiss her cheating lips. She was no better than Charity.

He had been shaken to the core of his being when he'd seen his wife. He'd thought all these years that she was dead, that he had buried her on the knoll behind their home, but she had laughed when she'd told him he'd buried a young cowboy Greeley had killed in a fight over her. "You were always such a fool, Will. Didn't it occur to you to open the casket to see if it was really me?" she'd asked him. She had changed, gotten hard and bitchy from following Jake Greeley all across the country. She was no longer the delicate, sweet innocent he'd married. Since that day long ago he'd left to go on the roundup, he had carried a picture of her in his mind—her pale blond hair loose and blowing in the endless Kansas wind, making her look like a child, her huge blue eyes full of tears, and her thin, white arms clutching the porch railing. She looked twenty years older now, her brassy, dyed hair up on top of her head, her face painted like the whore she was. Innocence was not a word one could use to describe anything about her.

He didn't want to think of the confrontation they had just had, when she told him she was there waiting for Jake Greeley to get out. He'd asked her why, and she'd laughed and told him Greeley was twice the man he was, both in bed and out. He'd almost killed her before someone pulled him off her, and he'd spent the night cooling off in the town jail. She had come to see him before she left the next morning, and she told him she'd divorced him soon after she left him back in Kansas.

He looked at her, at her hard face made up like a two-bit whore's, at her cheap, tawdry clothing, and discovered that he felt nothing but pity.

"You won't mind, then, if I go through the divorce process just to make sure it's legal?" he'd asked her.

"Honey, you can bet your bottom dollar it's legal. I didn't want you to have any control over me or my money." Her smile was triumphant as she faced him there through the bars.

"What money? And what about Greeley? Doesn't he have control over you?" He scoffed at her attempt to put him down, but the part about the money rankled. He'd chastised himself a thousand times for having too much pride to ask his father for a loan to tide him over until he could make his own fortune. He hadn't wanted something handed to him, though, so he hadn't asked. The poverty he'd made Charity live in had, he thought, been the reason she'd left.

"My inheritance. And I'm too smart to make the same mistake twice. He doesn't even know about it."

He frowned. "Then why did you leave? They told me in town that you'd gone after him for his money."

She laughed. "You never knew, did you? I didn't marry you so I could go live on some godforsaken dirt farm in Kansas. I married you because I couldn't get control of my money until I married. Even so, my parents would still have controlled me if we'd stayed in Virginia. You got me away from them, and there wasn't anything they could do about it. My grandparents left me their fortune, and I planned to spend it the way I wanted to. Only I never took you for a fool, to turn your back on your own family's money. Jake, now, he's a man who appreciates the finer things in life."

Will couldn't resist. "Then what's he doing with you?"

Her face had taken on an ugly look, and he knew she'd have slapped him if there hadn't been a deputy watching.

She had left without saying a word, and an hour later, when he was released from the jail, he heard she'd left on the stage. He had ridden for days to get back to Maggie, to put an end to the waiting. He cursed himself for a fool, figured Greeley and Charity deserved each other, and planned to marry Maggie as soon as decently possible. And now he'd come back to find that she was making a cuckold of him as soon as he turned his back. He'd not have believed it if he hadn't seen it with his own eyes, and no amount of denying it could take that away. He turned and went back into the hotel, got a room and a bottle, and stared into the darkness while he drowned his dreams in rotgut whiskey.

There was another man watching the couple, too. He'd followed them from the dance, keeping some distance back, but he saw them kiss. And he didn't like it. He'd patiently courted the girl for weeks now, and she wouldn't give him the time of day, and yet she let the doctor do anything he liked. *Well, Miss Longyear,* he thought, *we'll just see how you like your men.* He guessed that if Wolcott had wanted to take her back to his rooms, she'd have gone. Just as she would go with him back up into the mountains to the cabin he had there. He'd make her pay for treating him like some smelly saddle tramp. Yes, Miss Maggie Longyear was going to pay.

The dance had been on a Friday night, and Maggie spent most of Saturday furiously cleaning the house. Simon had ridden out early in the afternoon to see Kate, and after she was finished and had cleaned up, Maggie followed him on foot, as they were to have supper together. She met Della in the kitchen as she came through and asked, "Has she told him yet?"

"I don't think so, honey."

"How long are we going to wait before we do something, Della? We can't let this go on. What if she leaves?"

"She isn't going to leave. She's starting to show, and although she can hide it under her dresses, she isn't going to fool a lover."

Maggie blushed. It was hard to picture her uncle as Kate's lover.

"Della, did you ever love anyone but your husband?"

"No, we were childhood sweethearts. But I know plenty of women who said they loved two men. Now me, I don't believe it. I don't think you can love a man with all your heart and betray his trust with someone else. I just don't believe it."

"I didn't used to think so, either."

"Now, what's all this about, honey? You have a problem you want to talk about?"

"I don't know, Della. Chase, Dr. Wolcott, kissed me last night."

"And?"

"And . . . I wanted him to. It felt right to be there, in his arms, but then I felt guilty because of Will, and now I don't know what to do. I don't want to be unfaithful to Will, but what if he doesn't come back? I can't keep Chase hanging while I try to decide between them. I've always despised women who keep two or three men on a string. I'm just not like that, Della!"

"Has Will asked you to marry him?" Della asked gently.

"He said he'd marry me if he could, but he couldn't."

"He give you a reason?"

"No, and that's the problem. Della, I don't know anything about men. Maybe he was lying to me, stringing me along. Why can't life just be simple, black and white? I was always honest with him about my feelings, and about everything else. Maybe I was too honest."

"You can't be too honest. But it doesn't sound like you

made a commitment to Will." Della sat beside Maggie and put her arm around the girl's shoulder. "Now, what about your doctor?"

"Oh, Della." Maggie sighed. "It would be so easy to love Chase. He's intelligent and makes me use my mind, too. I'm fascinated with the work he does, how he can poke here and there and tell someone what's wrong and how to fix it. I've even helped him with some surgeries, and he told me I was an excellent assistant. I thought it would make me sick, but instead I watch every move he makes and try to anticipate which instrument he'll be needing next so he doesn't have to ask.

"His patients adore him, and he's so good with little children," she went on. "He even got old Mrs. Adams to laugh one day, and I'd guess it's been years since she'd done that!"

"Ummm, that's all very nice and shows why the people here like him so much. But how do *you* feel about him?"

"Being with him makes me less homesick because he's like a good friend."

"And Will doesn't make you feel like that?"

"Will . . . I don't know how to describe what Will makes me feel like." She closed her eyes and let out a long sigh. "He's like a summer storm that dropped into my life and turned it upside down, and then blew out again. I'm still reeling from the effects."

"Some women can take living with constant turmoil in their lives, and some can't. You have to decide what's right for you."

Maggie sighed. "I just wish he'd come back so I'd know one way or the other."

"I know, honey, I know. And he will. You just wait and see."

Just wait and see, Maggie thought. It seemed she'd been doing a lot of that lately, and it didn't seem to be getting her anywhere.

"Oh, I thought I heard voices in here!" exclaimed Kate as she came into the kitchen. "I heard you left the dance early last night. Did your doctor get a call?"

"He's not *my* doctor, and no, he didn't. That Mr. Grainger was there again."

"Oh." Kate frowned. "I thought Simon told him you weren't interested in his suit."

"He did. Several times. He just doesn't seem to hear it."

"Who doesn't hear what?" Simon asked as he followed Kate through the door.

"That Grainger fellow. He was at the dance, bothering Maggie again," Kate explained.

"Well, we'll be going back out to the ranch tomorrow. At least it will be harder for him to get to you there. I can't believe he was bothering you here, and none of you told me about it."

"You were on the roundup, and besides, he hasn't done anything wrong," Kate told him.

"I won't need to be gone from the ranch anymore now. And the talk today was that the WSGA prisoners got out of Fort Russell two days ago and are having a big party to celebrate their release. Will should be coming soon."

"Uncle Simon," Maggie asked him, "what do those men have to do with Will being gone?"

"I can't tell you, Maggie. He'll have to tell you himself when he comes back."

"Do you know for sure he's coming back?"

"He said he was. I can't tell you any more than that."

Maggie sighed, but felt better than she had for a while. If Simon was right, maybe Will would be back any day now, and he'd tell her the whole story. And maybe he'd taken care of whatever he had to do so he'd be free to marry her. Her heart seemed to lose the weight that had held it for so long, and after supper, when she walked home with her uncle, she almost skipped.

Maggie awakened early the next morning, dressed, and left the house before Simon woke up. She didn't go to Kate's every morning, but she and Simon were going back to the ranch today, and she wanted to talk to her friend about what Will's return might mean. When she reached Kate's kitchen, Della was there mixing up bread for the week's baking, but Kate hadn't awakened yet, so after a short chat with the older woman, Maggie let herself out the back door of the saloon and headed around the building toward the street.

Jacob Grainger was waiting for her. Her first thought was to turn around and go back inside, but she knew how little protection the hallway offered, so she pushed on, nodding to him as she passed.

When his hand reached out to stop her, she jumped but was determined not to show her fear. "I don't have time to chat, Mr. Grainger. I really must be going."

"Oh," he said, his voice low and threatening. "I think you can stay. You've been ignoring me these past weeks, you know, and that isn't very nice."

"Mr. Grainger," she said in what she thought was a haughty voice, "take your hand off me. I have made it quite clear that I do not accept your attentions, and it is most unseemly of you not to comply with my wishes."

"You will accept my attentions, lady—" he began but was stopped short when a male voice said, "I believe the lady asked you to take your hands off her," and Maggie looked up to see Chase, a look of thunder on his face.

Grainger stepped back from Maggie and bowed. Maggie shuddered as he left the two of them and disappeared around the corner. Chase opened his arms, and she rushed into them, badly frightened. "Where's Simon, and what are you doing out here alone?" he demanded.

"He's home. I didn't want to disturb him and I thought I'd be safe this early in the morning. It's Sunday, for goodness sake!"

"Sunday, or any other day, don't be going anywhere alone." He escorted her back to the house and told her he'd be back later to talk to Simon. Something was going to have to be done about Grainger.

Will had seen Maggie come around the back of the whorehouse with a tall man in a black suit, then watched her once again fly into Chase's arms before they left together. Did the woman know no shame that she went from one lover's arms to another? Did Chase know of her duplicity, or did she cuckold him, too, with her promise of love?

Will was so filled with pain and fury he knew he couldn't stay and watch anymore. He'd been awake all night. He had tried to give her the benefit of the doubt, but he'd seen her twice now, and that was enough. She'd obviously spent the night in the whorehouse with the man in the black suit. And Chase? Had she slept with him, too? He thought of the way she'd looked in the red dress of Kate's. Had she worn another dress like that when she seduced Chase? Had she dressed like that for the other man? Other men? Who knew how many there might be?

As Will rode toward the ranch, he laughed wryly at himself when he thought of all the times he could have had her and stopped because he didn't want to sully her reputation. Now that he thought of it, she never had even tried to stop him. He was always the one to call a halt before things got out of control.

"Damn her cheating heart," he said out loud. "Damn the sly, treacherous bitch."

By the time Simon and Maggie got back to the ranch, Will had downed another half bottle of whiskey and was waiting on the porch, his chair tipped back, his feet on the rail.

When Maggie saw him, her heart thumped with joy, and she cried, "Will!" and jumped down before the buggy stopped to run to him. She knew something was wrong before she reached him. He didn't get up; he didn't even look at her.

"Will?" she asked, tentatively, her steps slowing.

"Miss Longyear," he said, still not looking at her.

Simon came up behind her, and she looked at him beseechingly, a look of bewilderment on her face. "Will?" Simon asked. "Is everything all right?"

Will still sat staring at the mountains, and Simon motioned for Maggie to go inside the cabin.

Something bad was wrong. Maybe his wife was here. It seemed hours before she willed her hand to turn the latch and go inside. When she finally did, her heart was still pounding hard. She looked around the kitchen, trembling, and into the front room, then the bedrooms. At the door to Will's room, she stopped, then made herself look inside. Empty. She collapsed against the wall, shaking with relief.

But, she thought, if he hadn't brought back his wife, what was wrong? What could make him not even look at her? She went and lay in the center of her bed, curled up in a ball, and waited for Simon to come in.

Will didn't look up as Simon stepped up onto the porch. He was in no mood to discuss the matter with the man who had allowed it to go on right under his nose, because he was so caught up in another whore's wiles.

"What happened, Will?"

"Nothing. He got away."

"Got away? How?"

"Apparently he escaped before they even got to Fort Russell. He was never even there."

Simon nodded. "What now?"

"Nothing's changed."

"I see." Silence. Will picked up the bottle beside him and took another deep draft. Simon watched him. "How is this going to affect Maggie?"

Will shrugged. "I never made any promises to her."

"You made a promise to me."

"Hell, Simon, no one knows and no one cares. Compared to what she's been up to while I've been gone, it's nothing anyway."

"What's that supposed to mean?"

"You figure it out." Will took another long drink and slumped back in the chair. Simon looked at him in disgust and left him sitting there, thinking it would serve him right to drown in the stuff. At least then Maggie would be free of him. He was beginning to be very sorry he'd even brought his niece into this.

Simon found Maggie on her bed and sat beside her, his back against the headboard, one long leg stretched out in front of him and the other on the floor. How was he going to explain to her without betraying Will's secret? The thought came to him that Will didn't deserve the courtesy, but he just couldn't bring himself to tell her. Honor was a terrible thing sometimes.

"Uncle Simon?" her voice came to him, childlike, and he felt his throat tighten.

"Yes?"

"What's wrong with him?"

"I don't know, Maggie. Sometimes people do things they themselves don't even understand."

"What happened while he was gone?"

"I can't tell you that. He asked me not to."

"Don't you think it's okay to tell something, even if someone asked you not to, if it might help?"

"No, I don't. A man's word is his reputation. It's hard to accept sometimes, but that's the way it is."

Maggie thought about that. "I think you should go to town and make Kate tell you."

"Make Kate tell me what?"

"I can't tell you. She made me promise not to."

"Maggie, what is it? Is something wrong with her? What?"

"I'm sorry, I gave my word."

"Is this a scheme, to get me to tell you about Will?"

"No, it isn't. I wouldn't do that."

"I know you wouldn't. Just tell me this. Is she all right?"

"Yes," she said and smiled at him, "she's just fine. I got to thinking about what you said about people doing things they don't understand themselves. I don't want to see the two of you ruin your lives, that's all. I think she needs you now."

He looked deep into Maggie's eyes and saw only truth there. He gave her a quick hug and said, "Give him time. He has some things he has to sort out."

"I know. I'm not even sure how I feel about anything right now."

"Pete and Bertha are right across the way, and the men are here, too, if you need help."

She smiled at him. "I won't need any help. I'm going to bed. And I'll lock my door," she added when she saw the look on his face. "You just go. At least one of us can be happy."

All the way back into town, he tried to figure out what might be wrong with Kate that she'd need him right now. She had seemed in excellent health, her eyes glowing, and her skin, when he'd caressed it the last time, smooth and supple. She'd been in good spirits, not letting on that anything was wrong. And yet there was something that had nagged at him until he'd pushed it out of his mind during the night. What was it? He'd been rubbing his hand over her belly and had stopped . . . Yes! That was it! Her belly, usually so flat and smooth, had seemed rounded, and he'd been about to mention that she seemed to be putting on weight, but then he thought she might take offense. Then an idea hit him like a swift kick to the head. But it couldn't be. She couldn't have children, she'd said. Could she have been wrong?

He kicked his horse into a full gallop, and when she opened the door to him she knew by his expression that he knew, and her face split into a wide grin. He slammed the door shut behind him, and, picking her up, carried her to the bedroom and let her know how thrilled he was at becoming a father. It was some time during the night that the last of her fears fled, leaving her with a sense of peace and rightness that she should spend her life with this man, whatever the future might bring.

Will saw Simon ride off, and it took a while for his sodden brain to realize Maggie was in the cabin, alone. He probably wasn't as drunk as he should have been, because a short time later when she came out to help the hands with the chores in his clothes, his senses reeled at the sight. She looked even better than he remembered, and he got angry again that she had acted the part of a virgin with him.

He sat and watched her moving among the hired hands, and his muddled thoughts saw her leading all of them on, as she'd led him on. He picked up the bottle and threw it out into the brush as hard as he could. Then, with his feet on the porch railing, he rocked back and forth, still watching her.

Two hours later, when she came up onto the porch, he was sobered up a bit but was still too drunk to talk to her. And too drunk for the effect her body had on him. She sat on the railing with one foot up on it, and wrapped her arms around her knee. Her face and that glorious hair of hers took on the golden glow of the sunset, and he shifted in his chair.

"Will," she said after a bit, "what is it? What is it that keeps you so apart, so detached? What is it you're waiting for, Will, before you can take part in life again?"

He stared at her a long time, then turned his face toward the mountains. He dropped his feet from the railing, stood up, and came close beside her. She held her breath, terrified of what he was going to say.

He took her chin in his hand and gazed deeply into her eyes, then let his arm drop and looked back toward the now deep purple peaks. Finally he turned to her and said, so softly she almost didn't hear it, "I'm just waitin' for sundown, ma'am." He turned on his heel and disappeared into the house.

Maggie stayed where she was for a long time, letting the breeze, gentle as a whisper, cool her flushed cheeks. Fragments of thoughts floated through her mind, but she wouldn't let herself dwell on Will. She didn't know what it was that had hardened his heart against her, but she loved him and she'd wait. She'd wait as long as it took for him to deal with whatever it was that haunted him. Only she wished he'd tell her, share his pain so she could help him through it.

She sighed and followed him into the house after darkness had fallen. He was besotted with drink tonight, but there would be other nights, and she had time. She hadn't had supper and wondered what the men would do if she showed up at the bunkhouse door to share their meal. She smiled. They'd take it in stride, as they had taken everything else outlandish she'd done, including the wearing of Will's clothes.

Nothing really seemed good to eat, so she wandered

into her room. Will was sleeping by now, no doubt, in the room across the kitchen, and the two of them were in the house alone. She thought of the last time they were here alone and was filled with sadness. They had had such good times. Remembering her promise to Simon, she carefully latched the door. She didn't bother to light the lamp. The moon was full and gave her plenty of light to see by.

She stood at the window as she undressed, and she felt Will's presence. What would he do if she went into his room? she wondered. Would he think her wanton? Or would he welcome her to his bed? She'd never find out, though, because she had no intention of crossing that kitchen. When she was completely naked, she stood for a while in front of the window, letting the moonlight bathe her skin. She made a wish on the first star, then let the curtain fall back in place. Turning, she crossed to her bed to pick up her nightgown, which was folded across the footboard.

"You looked lovely, standing there like that." His voice came from her bed.

She stopped and stood utterly still, not knowing whether to run or stay. He had been sitting there, waiting for her. Would she ever understand this man? He'd told her he loved her, and she was to wait for him. But when he returned, he was cold and indifferent. Now he was waiting for her in her own bed, and she had been standing there, her whole body exposed to his gaze. Her heart pounded so hard she thought it might break her ribs.

Will hadn't known what he planned to do when he went to her room. He certainly hadn't expected her to be unaware of his presence or to undress herself right in front of him! He'd figured that when she lit the lamp she'd see him. By the time she started taking off her clothes—his own, as he now remembered—he couldn't bring himself to stop her. For, in spite of all he knew about her, he still wanted her. Even if she'd been with someone else. He had wondered before if she'd been a virgin when she came to Jackson Hole, and he figured now that she in all likelihood hadn't been. She surely wasn't now. And yet he still wanted her.

In the next instant all his frustration came falling down around his shoulders, and he got her mixed up with the other one, his wife, who'd done the same thing, and he reached for her, pulling her down onto the bed with him. Their lips found each other, and they met with a gnawing hunger bred from weeks of frustration. His hands covered her breasts, and then he slipped one hand down across her smooth stomach and slid his fingers between her legs. She gasped and opened for him, and his sodden brain recognized her for the whore he thought she was.

Will didn't think about what he was doing. He was punishing Charity for what she'd done to him, and punishing Maggie for being like Charity. He raised above her, then plunged deep inside her, and as soon as he felt the resistance, he knew he'd made a mistake. As soon as he felt the tearing flesh, and heard her quick intake of air at the prick of pain, he knew he should stop. Sobriety came to him suddenly, almost making him pass out. But he could no more stop than a volcano could cool its fires and settle back down into the earth without erupting, and so he continued, deeper and harder, and the years of anger and fear and frustration culminated in a mighty flame of passion that burned the very darkness surrounding them.

❧ 16 ❧

Maggie lay flat on her back, her hands resting on her stomach beneath her breasts, and stared wide-eyed at the ceiling above her. She knew she should get up. There was that faint change in the night that indicated dawn was very close, but she couldn't seem to make herself move. She'd been that way for hours, waiting for sunrise.

Will. The name came to her, unbeckoned, and then his face and the feel of his hard, hot body against hers. She closed her eyes and willed him back again, but he was gone.

She had finally found the answer to the longing inside her, had finally had the fires quenched. She felt as though they had been moving toward each other all their lives, and when they met, each had found that part of themselves that had been missing.

She'd thought about the shame she might face if anyone found out, and hadn't cared. She knew she belonged with Will Sutten, and if that was the only way she could have him, that was the way it would be. But no one had told her about the pain. The pain filled her chest so she could hardly breathe, and was so tight across her throat she thought she'd surely be strangled by it. She lay there and tried to put it all together, tried to make sense of it all so she could figure out what to do. And she wondered where he'd gone.

Will rode hard into the night, hating himself for what he'd done. He'd taken something from her he couldn't give back, and when he thought of it, he whipped the horse more. It took some time for it to sink in that he was going to kill his horse, but when it did, he stopped, dismounted, and walked the foaming beast to cool him down.

The horse would be all right. Maggie wouldn't. Why hadn't he trusted her? He knew she was different from Charity, different from other women, who used a man to get something. All Maggie asked for was to be loved, and he had taken that love and thrown it back in her face. There wouldn't be another first time for her, and there was nothing he could do about it.

But what was it he had seen between her and Chase? And what of the man in the black suit, the one she'd come out of Kate's with? He knew he couldn't rest until he found the answers, and when he did he'd have to figure out what to do.

When the horse wasn't blowing anymore, he remounted and let the animal set the pace. He didn't know what he was going to do, but he found himself at Chase's door just as dawn broke over the mountains and bathed the Tetons in a rosy glow.

Chase opened the door to his knock, and when he saw who was there, said, "Will! Come in, come in!" He closed the door and added, "You ought to be horse-whipped. Does Maggie know you're back?"

Chase didn't miss the tortured look in his friend's eyes as Will replied, "Yes." Then, "Oh, God, Chase, I may have done something horrible to her."

"And what is that?" Chase asked carefully. His own emotions were tangled up with the woman, and the answer mattered very much to him.

"Chase, I saw the two of you in your buggy by the saloon last night."

Chase colored, but he met Will's eyes evenly. "And you thought we had betrayed you?"

Will nodded, knowing what was coming, and feeling lower than a snake's belly already. "Well, what was I supposed to think? And this morning she comes out of the whorehouse with one man and flies into your arms again."

"You damn fool. You don't deserve that woman!"

Will stared out the window. "I know I don't. And I've probably already lost her, but I thought she was doing the same thing Charity did."

"Tell me about Charity, Will," Chase asked. "Is she dead? Maggie seemed to think you'd found her."

Will dropped his head into his hands and shook it slowly back and forth. The whiskey he'd consumed was beginning to make him sick, and his head hurt abominably.

"No, she's not dead. I thought she was. I buried her, Chase. With my own hands I dug the grave and buried her, only now I find out it wasn't her at all, and here I've been chasing the man I thought killed her. I've been after him for six years, Chase, six years! He was there, right there, and I let him get away again." He looked up, his face full of anguish, appealing to the doctor to understand. "He's dogged my days and haunted my nights. Everywhere I look I see his eyes, one brown and one blue. It's as though he's the devil incarnate. He's kept me from telling Maggie how I feel. And now I find out Charity wasn't dead at all. She left me for him—she's been living with him for all these years. She even told me she divorced me. All these years I've been living a half life because of her."

"I'm sorry, Will. But you can trust Maggie. She's not like that. I'd give a lot to have her love me, but I knew all along it was you."

"And what I saw . . . ?" He knew the answer but had to ask.

"You were gone, she didn't know where you were, when, or even if, you were coming back. She told me she loved you, but I talked her into letting me kiss her, thinking maybe she didn't know her own heart. I was wrong," he said simply.

"God, I've been a fool, Chase. You don't know how much so." He shook his head, and his face showed his remorse.

Chase didn't know what Will had done, was afraid to know. "Damn you, Will. If you hurt her, I'll kill you."

"I hurt her, but I'll make it up to her if it takes the rest of my life. No more looking back for me. I have some things I have to take care of, get my affairs in order, and then I'm going to fall at her feet and beg her forgiveness. I pray she'll understand and consent to marry me."

Chase looked at Will, his own face full of regret for what might have been, then he offered his hand to his friend. "Good luck to you, Will."

"Thanks. I'll need it." Will got up to leave, then turned and asked, "I don't suppose you'd put in a good word for me?"

"Get out of here, Sutten, before I change my mind and go carry her off to Europe or somewhere."

"Thanks, Chase. A man couldn't ask for a better friend."

Will set out from the doctor's with a new purpose in his stride. He would go to the house first and get cleaned up, then go find Simon. He had a lot of explaining to do and needed to get his financial affairs straightened out. Then he had to face Maggie.

Chase closed the door behind Will and knew he would indeed go out to the ranch and talk to Maggie. He felt somewhat guilty for having tried to seduce her away from his friend, anyway; and besides, he hadn't talked to her since their kiss in the buggy. Rescuing her from the scoundrel at the Seven Squaw didn't count.

As he rode out of town later, he wondered what Will had said to hurt her, and if she would forgive him. If she wouldn't, friend or not, Chase would take her for himself.

Maggie had gotten up before the sun lightened the sky and dressed hurriedly in Will's clothes, then slipped out to the corral, hoping to get away before any of the hands, or, more specifically, Bertha, saw her. Her face was a mess, and she'd done nothing more than pull her hair back in a ribbon. What did her appearance matter now?

She led the horse away from the buildings out of

earshot before she mounted, then she set out cross-country to town. He must have gone to the house there. She didn't let any thoughts form about what she was going to do when she confronted him, or what she'd do if he wasn't there. She didn't think at all, just letting the rhythm of the horse calm her troubled mind. She was doing the only thing she could think of to retain her sanity.

Maggie Longyear had become an obsession with Jacob Grainger. The more his attempts to seduce her were thwarted, the more determined he became that he would have her. He had figured out her schedule and knew where he could meet her so that no one was likely to come along.

He had gotten up early that morning, deciding this was the day. The snooty little bitch had repulsed his advances for the last time, and even if he had to kill her, he would have her. Sometimes it was even better that way. He dressed carefully and left his room, sauntering down the boardwalk to the hotel for breakfast, where he could have a view of the whole square, and of who came and went. Yes, it was a mighty fine day, he thought, as he saw the doctor ride out of town. Even that bastard would be out of his way.

Chase rode into the ranch yard, not quite sure what he'd say to Maggie when he saw her. He hoped he could help her sort through her thoughts about Will, but he knew it would be hard. He was almost afraid to see her face.

He rapped on the door, then walked in as he usually did. The kitchen was deserted, and no fire even burned on the hearth. He crossed the room to the door of Maggie's bedroom and saw Bertha standing there, staring in horror at the sheets. Chase followed her gaze and saw the flecks of blood before Bertha realized he was there and hastily pulled the quilt up over the undeniable proof that Maggie had lost her virginity the night before.

He stared at Bertha, as horrified as she was. Damn Sutten! He'd kill him!

"Where is she?" he demanded.

"Lord help us," she said, shaking her head back and forth. "I didn't know. I thought Simon was here with them. I should have been here. He'd been drinking, you see, and he was in an ugly mood. Wouldn't even look at her, or at any of us. Just sat on that porch, downing a whole bottle. Simon never should have left without telling me. I heard Will ride out, late, and in a big hurry. I figured he was riding out his anger."

"It's all right, Bertha," he soothed her, "just tell me where she is now."

"I don't know. She rode out early. Why was he like that, Doctor? Did he kill the man who killed his wife? Was that why?"

"You know about that man?"

"Only that he found him. He couldn't be free, you see, until the man was dead. I didn't think he could kill a man, when it came right down to it. Maybe he couldn't."

"Who is the man? Did he tell you?"

"No, he never told anybody, far as I could see. Maybe Simon knows."

"All he told me was that the man had one brown eye and one blue. Not much to go on for six years, is it?"

"Jake Greeley," Bertha said suddenly.

"What? Who's Jake Greeley?"

"That's who he is, the Mr. Grainger that won't leave Maggie alone! I knew I remembered him from somewhere, and it was his eyes. He has one covered with a patch, but I know it's him."

"It's who, Bertha? What are you talking about?"

"Jake Greeley. Jacob Grainger. They're the same man. He has one blue eye and one brown eye. He's the man that killed Will's wife. That's why Will came here, to the valley. He knew that Greeley was from around here a long time ago. I worked as a cook in the hotel, so I knew the goings-on around town. He was no good, a bad one from the start. Everyone in town breathed a sigh of relief when he left. He's been gone a long time, ten years maybe."

"Bertha, are you sure?"

"He looks different now, but I'm sure. Doctor, you got to go find Maggie. If he gets his hands on her, there'll be the devil's own to pay."

"Bertha, Will is in town. I'm assuming Simon is at Kate's. I've got to get Simon, and we have to stop Will from running into this Greeley unaware, or there's going to be some blood shed, and it might be Will's. His wife isn't dead, Bertha. I can't explain it all now."

"But what about Maggie?"

"Where do you think she went?"

"My guess is that she headed out cross-country to town. She does that sometimes because it's faster than taking the road. She must have been going to her uncle."

He tried to think what to do. "Bertha, you get some of the men and send them into town. I'll ride the way she might have gone, and if I catch up with her, I'll take her to my house. Greeley may be looking for her at Simon's place, and I don't want her to be alone. Tell the men about Greeley and Will, so they know to expect trouble, and from where."

He rode out as Bertha rang the bell to call the men in. He was no tracker, but the prints where she'd led her horse, then mounted and rode out across the meadow were obvious, even to him. He traveled at an easy canter, following the trail she'd left, knowing she was headed to town. She had at least an hour's lead on him, but she didn't seem to be in any great hurry, so he might catch her before she rode into a dangerous situation. He wished there was some way to get word to Simon and Will, neither of whom had any idea of who Grainger really was. And Maggie. He tried not to think about what would happen if the man got to her alone.

Will had cleaned up and set out to find Simon. He had made such a hellish mess of everything. Why hadn't he trusted Maggie? He knew enough to know that all women weren't like Charity. He'd been so angry, though, so full of impotent anger that he'd wanted to kill someone, and that someone was the wife whose supposed death he'd spent six years trying to avenge. For the first time he forced himself to take a long, hard look at the woman he'd thought he loved. He'd known what she was really like. He just hadn't wanted to face it.

He faced it now, remembering the sly, seductive looks she had exchanged with different men—and he knew. It was no fault of his that she'd left. If he hadn't gone on the roundup, she'd have found some other way to get to town. The guilt that had been riding him for six years broke away from him in pieces, flying away on the warm summer breeze.

It was midmorning when Maggie reached the edge of Jackson. She had gone more and more slowly the closer she got; she had even ridden to a spot on the banks of one of the creeks where she had once discovered that otters played. The otters hadn't been there, and after a time she'd walked her horse along the swift-flowing water, all the time trying to think what she'd say to Will when she did find him. What if he still wouldn't talk to her? Her whole future rested on the forthcoming confrontation, and it terrified her. She would either find happiness or be doomed to a life alone.

When she got to the house, it had a deserted look that told her Will wasn't there, but she checked anyway, going from room to room looking for him. She came back to the kitchen, not sure what to do. She'd been so sure he'd be here. Maybe Uncle Simon would know, she thought, and headed toward Kate's. Things must have gone reasonably well the night before for them at least, since he wasn't at the house and hadn't come back to the ranch.

She wasn't sure what she was going to do. She couldn't tell Simon and Kate what had happened. Simon would be likely to kill Will. But Maggie wasn't a sixteen-year-old innocent who needed her uncle's protection. She was a full-grown woman, and she had to make her own decisions about her life, as Kate did. Della had said she had to decide whether she could take constant turmoil in her life or whether she wanted serenity. She knew, despite the anger that had driven Will to do what he'd done, that she wouldn't be complete without him. It was as though she'd waited all her life for him. When she'd kissed Chase, not expecting to feel anything, her reaction had stunned her. But she knew now that that kiss was nothing compared to the storm of passion that overtook her when Will touched her.

As she crossed the square, Jake watched her the way a bird of prey might watch a tiny field mouse, and he marked her passage with satisfaction. When she had disappeared behind the saloon, he casually got up, stretched, and sauntered in that general direction, careful not to make it obvious where he was headed. No one would suspect him, but it didn't hurt to be careful about what people might remember afterward.

Chase missed Maggie. When he got to the house in town, neither she nor Will was there. He felt a moment of panic, then tried to calm himself into believing the two of them were together somewhere. But where? He decided to go to Simon without any more delay. He didn't know when the hands would reach town, but he couldn't wait for them.

He got to the square in time to see the man Bertha swore was Jake Greeley leave the hotel and move in a slow, but deliberate line toward Kate's place. His first thought was that Maggie must be there. There was something about the way the man moved that reminded him of a wild animal, slinking through tall grass toward its intended victim. He cut back around through the alley. He didn't know what Greeley had in mind, but he was going to find out.

At the Seven Squaw, Will was told by the bartender that Simon had left with Kate early that morning. He headed back to the house and as he rounded the corner, he saw several of the ranch horses there and figured Simon had found out about the night before and had come to find him. He deserved any punishment Simon meted out to him, but they had to let him talk to Maggie first. He searched the horses for her mare and felt a rush of relief when he saw it tied with the others.

Dave and Pete came out of the house, and someone called from the stable, "She isn't in here, either!"

The two men were joined by Bertha, who spotted Will. "There's Will," she cried and ran down to him. "Where's Maggie?" The men were right behind her, and he thought, *They don't know.*

"I don't know where she is. I'm looking for her myself."

"We can deal with what you did to her later," Bertha said, dashing his hopes of no one finding out before he could talk to Maggie herself, "but right now there's something you need to know. I don't know if you heard yet, but there's a man been bothering her, coming around even after Simon told him she wasn't interested. I knew the man from somewhere but couldn't place him. Then Chase told me something about the man you're after, and it all fell in place." Will's stomach knotted in fear of what she would say next. "Will, it's Jake Greeley. I know him from way back. He's got one eye covered with a patch, and he's got himself all fancied up, calls himself Jacob Grainger, but I know it's him. And Maggie came riding in here alone after you left her. Chase was going to see if he could get to her before Greeley found her. Have you seen Chase?"

"Not for a while," he answered. "Maybe they're together."

"Let's all pray they are."

"Dave, you come with me," Will said, "and Pete, you take the others and spread yourselves around town. See if you can spot any of them. If you get to Maggie or Chase, let them know we're here, and if you spot Greeley, at least two of you follow him, and someone come and let me know. Dave and I will go around through the back alleys to Kate's. If she isn't there, we'll come out the front of the saloon, and then you'll know to search the town. One of us has to come across one of them if they're here."

Will and Dave went in opposite directions, Will going

by way of the doctor's house, which was deserted, then going around the back of the stores surrounding the square. Dave signaled to Will with a low whistle, and Will noted his position. They were two buildings away from the Seven Squaw's back door and hadn't seen anyone yet. Will slipped into Kate's stable, and a few moments later Dave met him there.

"Do you think Simon could have taken her back to the ranch?" Will asked. "The bartender said they'd gone for a buggy ride."

"I don't see how we'd have missed them," Dave answered. "We came right along the road, and they couldn't have gotten past us."

"I don't like this. Something's not right."

Dave nodded, and by unspoken agreement they left the stable and moved quickly across the alley to the doorway, flanking both sides of it. Will wished he knew where Greeley was. It was very likely Maggie had come here to talk to Kate, but where were the horses and buggy?

He reached across and slowly opened the door, then moved in front of it, his gun pointed at the interior. Chase was in a crumpled heap on the floor, and Will quickly dropped to his side to feel for a pulse. There was one. He was bleeding from a wound on the head, but otherwise seemed unharmed.

"Chase." Will shook his shoulder, and the doctor slowly opened his eyes, and, seeing Will, tried to get up. Will pushed him back down, and said, "Take it easy, Doc, head blows are nothing to mess with."

Chase grinned, then remembered. "Will, the man who's been after Maggie, he's here."

"He do this to you?"

"Yeah. Guess I don't know much about following someone. He was waiting in the doorway for me."

"Chase, where's Maggie? Is she here, too?"

"I don't know. I saw him cross the square like he was on her trail. That's why I followed him. I didn't see anything before he hit me."

"We gotta get you out of here, Chase."

"I can get myself out. You go find Maggie."

"There are men from the ranch all over town. Find one of them, and tell him what's going on."

Chase nodded and made his way back out into the alley.

Will waited until Chase went around the corner of the building before turning to Dave. "Where to? I don't know my way around this place."

"Kate's rooms are down there. I think Della is right around the corner, and the back stairs are by her door."

"We'd better check Kate's first. That's the most likely place she'd have gone. You sure there's no way Simon could have gotten past you?"

"None. We came right along the road. The only way is if he left while we were at the house."

"Maybe we're making too much out of this."

"Yeah, she's probably at Kate's, and Simon's there with them."

Neither of them believed that, and they made their way cautiously to the end of the hallway. Will pressed himself on one side of the door, and Dave did the same on the other side. Will nodded, then reached for the doorknob and threw the door open. No sound came from within. They looked at one another, then threw themselves inside, their guns drawn. Nothing. They slowly moved around the perimeter of the room, checking behind furniture and in closets, then checked the other rooms the same way. The apartment was empty.

"Where to now?" They were in the kitchen, and Will's heart was pounding in fear. He kept trying to convince himself that Maggie was safe, was with Simon. The ghosts of his past would be nothing to the demons that would pursue him if anything happened to Maggie after what he'd done to her.

"Della's room. It's right outside this door." Dave went to the door, slowly turned the knob, and inched it open. "The hallway's clear," he said softly.

Della's door was ajar, and he threw Will a quick look. They flanked it as they had the last one, and listened. Will heard what he thought was a moan, and Dave's face confirmed that he had heard it, too. Will inched the door open with his gun, and his heart almost stopped at the mess the room was in. Furniture had been overturned, there was a broken lamp on the floor, and a woman's form was partly visible behind the settee. Another moan threw them into action, and Dave moved to the woman's side while Will checked the bedroom beyond.

"Della! What happened?" Dave asked urgently. Will closed his eyes in relief that it wasn't Maggie.

"He got Maggie . . . he took her . . . I tried to stop him."

"Who took Maggie?" Will dropped to his knees beside the woman.

"That Grainger fellow. The one who's been pestering her."

"Where's Simon? Did he go after them?"

"No," she said, struggling to get up. "He and Kate went to Rock Springs to get married. They left at first light."

Maggie had gone in the back door of Kate's, and, finding no one in her apartments, had sought out Della. The woman's face broke into a huge grin when she saw who was at her door.

"They went and got married!" she informed Maggie.

"Married! But where . . . and when? Why didn't they tell anyone? I wanted to be there!" Maggie wailed.

Della couldn't keep the grin off her face. "I told you it would work out, honey. Kate, she wanted to wait and have you and Will stand up for them, but Simon, he said he didn't want to risk her changing her mind, so they were going to do it right away. They left for Rock Springs before it was hardly light out, he was in so much of a hurry to get that ring on her finger."

"But why couldn't they get married here? Why go all the way to Rock Springs?"

"Kate just felt better about going away from here, where no one knew her, to keep the talk down. I think Simon wanted her all to himself for a few days, too. He was that happy about the baby." She put her arm around

Maggie's shoulder. "You'll have plenty of time with them when they get back."

Della suddenly realized what Maggie was wearing. "Maggie, what's wrong? Why are you dressed like that, and why are you in town? Simon said you were out at the ranch, and Bertha would look after you."

"There's nothing bothering me that can't wait until they get back." She smiled at Della. "Believe it or not, I dress like this all the time out at the ranch. These clothes are more sensible than long skirts."

"What would your mother say, girl? Does Simon know you wear that?" Della was horrified.

Maggie laughed. "Of course he knows. You should know by now that Simon doesn't follow the rules."

Della shook her head. "Well, whether your uncle approves or not, I'd advise you to get changed before Zollie McCaver sees you running around town like that. She doesn't need any more fuel for her nasty tongue."

"I think I'll head back out to the ranch now, anyway." She reached for the door handle and turned to smile at the older woman. "Thank you for worrying about me."

"Do you have a hat, maybe, to hide your hair?" Della frowned as she looked at Maggie. With that man Grainger always on her tail, she didn't need to go asking for trouble.

"No," Maggie said with a laugh. "But I promise to take the back way so no one will see me. Does that make you feel better?"

"Some. I have a derringer here that you can take. It's so small you can hide it, but it gets the job done. I haven't needed it for years." She went to a small desk and opened a drawer. The gun lay on her palm as she brought it over to Maggie. "Try it for size."

Maggie picked the gun up and held it, getting the feel of it. "Are you sure you don't mind? I'm sure I'll be just fine."

"Of course I don't mind. Now you just tuck that away, in your waistband or somewhere. If you had skirts on, you could hang it underneath." Della was studying the outfit, trying to see where best to put the weapon.

"Maybe I should just stick it in my boot for now," Maggie suggested.

"That's about the only place it isn't going to show," Della agreed.

Maggie pulled up the long pants leg and slipped the gun down in the tall boot. There was plenty of room, as she'd come away without the usual two pairs of socks. Maggie hugged Della.

"Thank you, Della, for being a good friend."

"Well, you just take care and keep your wits about you. If you see that Grainger fellow, you get yourself right back here, you understand?"

"I'll be all right, Della. I'll go straight to the ranch."

She hugged the woman again, and opened the door to leave. Grainger was in the hallway, leaning against the opposite wall.

"You'd better get the sheriff," Bertha told Will. "Jake Greeley is no one to mess with."

Bertha stood clutching the hitching rail in front of the house, watching Will pack his provisions on his horse. Dave and one of the hands stood nearby, and two others had gone after Simon.

"I stand a better chance alone. If he sees a posse coming after him, there's no telling what he'll do to Maggie." Will wasn't about to have an audience when he met his nemesis. He didn't know the man's ways, couldn't read him, and he wasn't willing to take a chance with Maggie's life. "If I'm not back by morning, Dave will get the sheriff, and they can bring all the men they want. If I haven't caught up to them by then, I'll more than likely need help." His face was grim as he tightened the cinch and checked the ropes on the pack. He had two rifles and his pistols.

They had brought Della back to the house with them. Pete had attended to the doctor's wounds, stitching up the gash on his head almost as well as Chase himself could have done, but the young man was in no shape to take care of anyone else. Bertha was left to care for Della,

who had suffered a broken leg and wrenched her back so
that she could hardly move.

Maggie had tried to shut the door before Grainger got
inside, Della told them, but he was too quick for her and
slammed the door open, throwing the girl to the floor. Della
had picked up a lamp, thinking to hit him with it—Maggie
had her gun for protection, and Della grabbed the first thing
she saw—but he threw the settee against her, then jumped
over it and hit her over the head with his own gun. She
didn't know any more than that. Obviously Maggie hadn't
been able to get to the gun in time.

Will just prayed she was still alive. If she was alive,
he'd get to her. He had to, to make right what he'd done,
and nothing on this earth was going to stop him. He
swung up into his saddle and brought the horse around.

Several people recalled seeing Greeley leaving town
in a buggy, but reported he had been alone. Will wasn't
fooled—Maggie must have been in the buggy and
Greeley was headed up the valley. Bertha remembered
he'd had a cabin up by Jenny Lake years ago. Millie, at
the hotel, had confirmed it and told him the exact
location. Taking a chance with her, he had told her that
Grainger was really Jake Greeley, that he'd been living
with another woman for years, and that he had now taken
Maggie up there. She was so upset, she told him
everything she knew. Will set his horse at an easy canter
and headed up onto the flats, then cut around to the west
to follow the base of the mountain up to Jenny Lake.

Millie was a simple woman, but she was loyal, and
after she'd cried a bit she began to think that the only
reason Jake had come back was to get her, like he'd
always promised, and that the Longyear girl had thrown
herself at him. After all, hadn't he told her to stock the
cabin and he'd come for her? Then she began to feel
guilty. What if Will found him and killed him because of
the information she'd given him? She'd waited a long
time for Jake to come back to get her, and she wasn't
going to let the chance get away from her. It was
probably all a big misunderstanding, she told herself as
she saddled up a horse and went after them.

❧ 17 ❧

Maggie's hands were numb from the rough ropes that bound them, and she could hardly breathe through the filthy rag she'd been gagged with, but at least she could see now. Greeley had wrapped her in a blanket and dumped her on the floor of a buggy. She hadn't been able to see the direction they were headed, and they had ridden across country for miles before he allowed her to sit up; then she could see from the location of the mountains that they'd been heading north out of Jackson. Grainger slowed the horses to a walk as they topped a slight rise, and Maggie saw a sight she would never forget. A huge herd of buffalo grazed in the lush basin. There must have been thousands of them, great shaggy beasts moving slowly along.

Grainger turned to her and said quietly, "We're going to ride through that herd. I would suggest you stay as quiet as you can, and don't make any sudden movements. If they stampede, we'll be trampled to death, buggy and all." A cold smile crossed his face. "It would be a pity if you died before we got to know each other better."

She threw him a look of pure hatred, which she hoped hid the fear pawing at her insides. No one knew where she was, or even that she was missing. Della was dead, Simon was gone, and there was no one else who could help her. Chase wouldn't know, and Will was gone. If only she'd been able to reach the derringer before Grainger had gotten to her, before he'd killed Della. Her eyes filled with tears again. Poor, dear Della, who'd tried her best to save Maggie's life. Now she was dead, and Maggie was probably going to be, too. The only thing that kept her going was that she still had the gun in her boot. At some point Grainger would let his guard down, and then she'd kill him.

They moved slowly down into the herd. The buffalo were much bigger than she'd thought, and she willed her body to utter stillness. She could hear their snorts and the sound of chewing. Some of them lifted their heads as the horses and buggy moved among them, and several moved a little restlessly, but they held. Maggie wondered why they'd ridden right through them when they could have gone around. It must be that they were headed to a place directly beyond the herd. Her eyes scanned the landscape. From what she could discern, they were north of Simon's ranch, which would mean they were near old Charley's place. If she could get free, that's where she'd head. It was closer than town, and she wouldn't have to cross open country.

The buffalo herd was spread out over several square miles, on both sides of the Snake River. As the buggy neared the water, Grainger changed directions and headed for a clump of thick willows. Maggie was relieved when a small log structure came into view. They weren't so far that she couldn't walk to help if she couldn't manage to take a horse with her. She noted the surrounding terrain carefully, planning the best way to escape.

Grainger didn't talk to her. He turned the buggy and backed it into a small lean-to on the side of what appeared to be a barn, then left her in it as he unhitched the horses and led them around the front of the building out of her sight.

Maggie's heartbeat quickened as her mind searched frantically for the means of escape. Her eyes scanned the hillside behind the cabin for a pathway to the top while she struggled with the ropes binding her feet. She could use her bound hands to claw her way to the top if she had to, but she couldn't get ten feet without her feet free. She couldn't hear what Grainger was doing, but she assumed he was hiding the horses and feeding them to keep them quiet if they'd been followed, and that meant she didn't have much time. He had tied her knees as well as her ankles, and she was concentrating on the knots at her knees, thinking she could slip her feet out of the oversized boots. A quick rush of tears had to be blinked away as the bindings came free and she managed to push one boot off. She could slip the ropes off and then the put the boot back on. This accomplished, she took a deep breath and tried to hear some sound that would indicate Grainger's whereabouts.

Maggie scooted along the buggy floor, thankful for Will's clothing—it made her whole escape easier. Her own long skirts would have hampered her progress through the willow thickets. She slid out of the buggy and stood, then had to sit again until a rush of dizziness passed. Come on, she told herself, *this is no time to go weak.*

She was still struggling with the wrist bonds as she backed around the buggy. Keeping her eyes on the place where he had disappeared, she silently slipped out the other side of the lean-to. She was terrified, but she made herself focus on escape. If she could only get her hands free, she thought, she'd get the gun. Then she wouldn't fear the blackguard anymore. She hadn't dared risk his finding out she had it before, when she couldn't use it.

Frustrated and knowing she was running out of time, she managed to take the bank, wrapping her bound hands around the trunks of saplings and bushes to pull herself up. Her heart was pounding, and her chest burning with the need for more air than she could get through the gag. The boots hampered her progress because they were so big she couldn't dig her toes in, and she weighed the risks of abandoning them in favor of her bare feet, trying to stuff the gun in her waistband, but surely if he caught her, he'd find it, and then she'd have no protection.

The top of the bank was only inches above her head now. As she topped the rise she thanked God for keeping Greeley busy so that he hadn't come to check on her, and with one last great effort, she pulled herself up with shaking arms and rolled several feet down the other side, coming to rest against a boulder. She couldn't see anything but sky from her position deep in the thicket.

Her first priority was to free her hands. A sharp edge of rock caught her attention, and she scrambled over to it and began sawing the rope on it. After what seemed like several minutes, she saw that she'd done no more than make the rope dirty, so she knew she'd have to get moving with her hands bound. She crouched behind the boulder and worked at the gag while she tried to get her bearings. It wouldn't do her any good to run in the wrong direction.

She took a chance and slowly stood up. Then the skin on her back crawled as a mocking voice said, "I see you're ready to ride, Miss Longyear."

Jake Greeley hadn't kept one step ahead of the law all his life by being stupid. He trusted no one, least of all a woman, and knew she'd try to escape as soon as he left her to saddle the horses. He also knew she wouldn't get very far.

He'd come through the buffalo herd to hide their progress and now rode up the river for the same reason. Someone, sooner or later, would be coming after the girl, and he didn't intend to make his job easy. When they came up out of the water, he again chose to ride through the herd of bison; when they got to the edge of the little lake at the base of the mountain, he took out a whip and used it on one of the shaggy beasts. It wasn't enough to start a full-fledged stampede, but they'd move enough to cover the prints from two shod horses. He sat and watched until he was satisfied that the beasts had run across their path and crossed the river before he jerked on the reins of the horse holding the girl and started up the mountain.

Maggie wasn't feeling quite so brave anymore. She knew what Grainger had in mind now, knew the need that drove him. But she also knew that she'd kill him, or herself if necessary, before she let him touch her. It couldn't come to that. She had to escape before he got that far. She studied the lay of the land. They were crossing a meadow now, a small lake to their right at the foot of the mountains, a field of the huge boulders they'd climbed through before on the left. They were climbing higher into the mountains.

The sun slipped away, and a cold blanket of air floated down from the glaciers above them and settled around her. As darkness began to creep down on the mountain, panic began to gnaw at her. No one would find her in the darkness. Not even Will.

Will knew he was racing against the coming darkness, and he cursed himself again for acting like a fool. His actions—no one else's—had gotten Maggie into this and if he allowed anything to happen to her, his soul would be lost forever.

He had to take the chance that they were headed for the cabin. Millie had told him how to get there, and he set off at a canter as he came out of the river on the western side. His mind was furiously scanning his options. It would be dark long before he found his way to Greeley's place if he went the way the woman had told him, but there was another way to get to the cabin. It was almost straight up the face of the mountain, and he'd have to leave his horse, but even afoot he'd be way ahead of Greeley and Maggie. He'd have to make it before darkness closed in, though, because it would be suicide to attempt the climb in the dark.

He rode to the hidden falls, then led his horse up around the back and into a small open space where the animal could get water and grass. He hobbled the horse, then took his pack and loaded it with the guns, ammunition, ropes, and a blanket. He hefted the pack on his back, thinking of the last time when Maggie had lifted it for him. The shadows were already deep. He tied the pack around his waist and started climbing.

They were surrounded by total darkness, and Maggie was terrified. Grainger's very silence was disconcerting. He'd never looked back at her even once, had not said a word. Her hands were numb with cold and the loss of circulation from the rope bindings, but she clung to the saddle with every bit of strength she had. The night was overcast, and there weren't even any stars to light the way. She could hear the horse's hooves slipping on the rock surfaces, could hear small stones fall down, down, down, echoing and fading into silence far below. She didn't want to think how far.

Where was he taking her? Were they crossing the mountains? The gun against her booted foot had rubbed her ankle raw, and her back ached from the awkward position in which she was riding. Maybe she should just fall off the horse and go the way of the rocks. The tumble would surely kill her, and then she wouldn't have to bear this any longer. She was afraid that if they didn't stop soon, she'd start sobbing hysterically; she was losing control of her emotions. *Will,* she thought. She had to keep thinking of Will, had to believe that he loved her and was coming after her. But did he love her?

She thought of what she'd done to Chase, leading him on and playing with his affections, and felt hot tears splash onto her cold cheeks. She hadn't meant to encourage him, hadn't meant to hurt him. She'd been honest with him from the start—he knew she loved Will. How had it all turned so wrong? Now both men probably hated her. How had she come to this? she wondered. Had every minute in her life led her to this place, on this mountain in the darkness, with a crazy man taking her God knew where?

They had stopped. It had taken a while for her numbed senses to realize it, and she had no idea how long they'd been there. Why had they stopped? Was he going to take her here, in the blackness where she couldn't see to get away? But if it was too dark to see the trail, he wouldn't see her get her gun, either.

"Get off the horse." His voice startled her. He wasn't close, but she couldn't tell where he was.

"I can't see." Her voice sounded weak and thin. She cleared her throat.

"Get off the damn horse and be quick about it." The voice was quiet, but brooked no disagreement.

She slid down and fell to the ground, startling the horse. He shied away, nervous in the darkness. She strained her eyes, listening for Grainger's footsteps so she knew where he was. Both horses were nervous, sidestepping and tossing their heads. Was there a wolf close, or a bear? Was Grainger going to leave her here? She had never been in such total darkness before. It closed in around her like a presence, and it terrified her. How could she save herself if she couldn't see him coming for her?

"There's a hundred-foot drop off the trail here. I suggest you stay put until I get back."

Relief flooded through her. He wasn't going to try anything just yet. She had time. He led the horses away and tied them up a distance from her. Then she heard him creep stealthily away from her. She had no idea of where he might have gone, or why he had left the horses, but she wasn't going to waste the time given her. She had to get her hands loose. She had already loosened the knots back at the river, and he hadn't checked them again. She drew her knees up and rested her hands on them, then used her teeth to pull at the ropes. It had looked easy in the light; she had no idea if she was loosening them or making them tighter now. All she knew was that once she got them free and she could feel again, she'd be able to move, on her hands and knees if necessary. She would not be waiting for him when he came back.

Millie had lost her way in the dark. She'd never done this at night, and the trail wasn't exactly how she'd remembered it. Her horse had stopped and wouldn't go any farther, and she didn't know what to do. Horses were smart. Maybe the trail had fallen away right ahead of them. Maybe she should get down, try to turn him, and go back down until morning. She looked up at the sky. The moon had been full the night before, but tonight there were clouds. She could see a couple of stars, though. Maybe the clouds would clear and she'd be able to see. One thing was for sure, and that was that she couldn't sit here on the horse all night. Still, she thought, she couldn't be too far from the meadow where the cabin was. She slid off the horse and moved slowly ahead of him, sliding forward with one foot to feel for the trail. Her heart thumped hard in her chest.

Suddenly something dropped in front of her, and she tried to scream, but nothing came out. Just then the moon broke through a hole in the clouds, and she saw Jake Greeley clearly.

"Jake! It really is you!" she gushed, fear making her chatter even more than she usually did. "I didn't believe it when he told me, and I had to see for myself. I knew you'd come after me like you always said you would. I got all the supplies to the cabin like you told me to, and I waited, Jake, because I knew you'd come."

"Perhaps you should lower your voice, Millie. You don't know who might be wandering around in the dark." Something in his tone sounded strange to her, should have warned her, but she couldn't stop herself from asking.

"Why didn't you come for me, Jake? Why did you disguise yourself as that Grainger fellow? Are you running from the law or something? Is that why they're after you?"

He had taken her arm and held it a touch too tightly, almost painfully. "Who's after me, Millie?"

"Why, Will is, and the others in the morning. I felt bad for telling them . . ." The warning bells sounded too late, and she knew she'd made a terrible mistake.

"What did you tell them, Millie? Did you tell them who I was?" His grip had tightened, and fright made it hard for her to swallow.

"No," she squeaked out, "they already knew that."

"Millie, I really need to know what you told them. I might have to hurt you if you don't tell me, and I don't want to do that."

"I t-told W-Will . . . where your . . ." She stopped, tears streaming silently down her cheeks.

"Where my what, Millie?"

She was shaking violently now and couldn't stop her teeth from chattering. She clung to him like a drowning person, but he just stood there, clenching her arm and waiting.

"I-I came to warn you, Jake, so's you'd k-know and get away." She appealed to his face, pleading with him. "I'm s-sorry, Jake, b-but he t-told me you t-took that Longy-year girl, and I b-been waitin' for you all this t-time."

"A pity, Millie, that you couldn't keep your mouth shut. I really had planned to come and get you and take you away like I always promised."

She felt a shred of hope. Here he was saying he'd been planning to come for her after all.

"D-do you mean it, Jake?"

"Of course." He smiled at her right before he pushed her off the side of the mountain. This time her scream not only sounded but reverberated from peak to peak until her life was cut off on the rocks below.

The scream sent goose bumps skittering across Maggie's body and started a gulping sob from deep within her that she couldn't control. *Stop it!* her mind screamed to her body, *because if you don't, he'll hear you and you won't be able to hide.* She had managed to free her hands and was rubbing them together to get the circulation going. Moonlight bathed the area now, and she felt confident she'd be able to stay on the trail. She quickly decided to abandon the boots; they were too big and clumsy and would mark her progress in the silent night. She slipped the gun into her waistband, then crept toward the horses. The animals had heard the scream, too, and were already tossing against the reins holding them. She figured it must have been a panther—Will had told her about their screams—and that would explain the horses' uneasiness. Grainger must have gone back to kill it, and she had to be gone when he got back. It had sounded so human, though, the scream, and Maggie knew she'd sound just like that if he touched her.

She freed the horses and slapped them on the rumps to

get them going. She couldn't use a horse because the noise it made would give her away, and she didn't want Grainger to have one, either.

In Will's dark clothing she melted into the shadows of the trees and rocks. The terrain was rough, and her feet were being punished for her impulsive discarding of the boots, but she knew this was the better way. The horses had taken off up a trail, and she followed their ascent, not knowing where she was heading. Several times she had to cross the trail because a huge rock or fallen tree blocked her progress. She kept listening for him behind her, but felt infinitely better now that she could get to the derringer. Suddenly the trees opened up, and a clearing was visible ahead. In the clearing was a cabin with a lantern lit inside, sending a glowing warmth through the night.

Her first instinct was to run to the cabin for protection, but her senses urged caution. This might be the place Grainger had been taking her, and she didn't want to stumble right back into a mess. Her instincts proved good as the horses trotted up to a shed behind the cabin and went inside. This was their home, then, she thought, and Grainger's. That bothered her. She had thought he was a stranger to the area, but obviously he was not. No wonder he had seemed to have everything planned so well.

The cabin door opened, and a woman stood silhouetted there, a rifle at the ready in her hands. She moved outside and searched the clearing in the bright moonlight, then disappeared into the shed. When she came out, the rifle was hanging at her side. Whatever she'd been afraid of, she wasn't anymore.

"Are you there?" Her voice carried clearly to Maggie across the darkness.

Maggie saw a man come from around the back of the shed and realized that the woman must have heard him, because she turned.

"Will!" the woman exclaimed, and Maggie's heart stopped.

"Well, Charity, we meet again." His familiar voice

brought tears to Maggie's eyes once more. She brushed them away quickly, but couldn't swallow the painful lump in her throat, couldn't tear her eyes away from the man she loved.

"Yes, we meet again. I didn't expect you to find me here."

"I didn't either." His voice held no emotion that Maggie could detect. There was a long silence, the two of them facing each other, and Maggie counting the seconds with her fiercely pounding heartbeats.

"Why don't you come inside?" she said to him in a silky voice as she moved close to him and put her hand on his chest. "We have a lot to talk about."

No, Will, don't! Maggie wanted to scream, but she didn't, and then it was too late because Will had followed his wife into the cabin. Maggie couldn't help herself. She took off at a low run toward the cabin, and, creeping up to a window, she peered into the cozy interior just in time to see Will take his wife into his arms and kiss her. His wife, small, blond, and helpless-looking.

Tears blinded Maggie as she stumbled around to the back of the cabin and collapsed against a rock, letting the sobs come, crying because the only man she'd ever loved was lost to her. It didn't matter now. Let Jacob Grainger find her, and she'd kill him, and then she'd throw herself off the side of the mountain.

Will had heard the woman scream, and the pain he'd felt when he thought Charity was dead was nothing compared to the convulsions of pain that tore through him now. Too late . . . too late again. And now she was gone. He'd had no right to the love Maggie had given him. It had been a wonderful gift dropped into his lonely and empty life, and he'd been worse than a fool not to have recognized it for what it was and cherish it with all his heart. Raw pain filled his throat and nearly choked him before he let it come out in a strangled cry as he beat the earth with his fists.

When he moved again, it was with deadly purpose. Twice Jake Greeley had taken away his life, his dreams, and he would pay for it. This time Will wouldn't stop until the man was dead.

Millie had given him good directions. The cabin was exactly where she'd said, and a light within told him Greeley had reached it before him.

He was starting to creep up to the back of the cabin when he heard horses coming. Squatting down behind a boulder, he watched the clearing as two riderless horses trotted across the clearing and went into a small shed. They had been saddled. Greeley must have spotted him, he thought, and sent the animals ahead to flush him out. That meant he wasn't in the cabin after all. But maybe he had a partner. Will waited, scanning the trees for movement.

He heard a slight creak, then saw a patch of light spread out across the open space. Someone was in the cabin and was coming out with a lantern. It was a woman. And the woman was Charity.

What was she doing here, if Greeley had been bringing Maggie to this same place? Then it hit him. Greeley didn't know she was there, hadn't known she was at the fort waiting for him. Had he seen her and then decided to kill Maggie since he could neither let her go nor bring her here? Or had Maggie put up a fight and been killed accidentally, so that Greeley was walking into this one unaware?

Charity came back out of the shed, relaxed and no longer watchful.

"Are you there?" she called into the darkness, and Will decided it was time to show himself. Greeley might still be in the trees, watching, but it was time to get it over with. Will didn't care if he lived or died now. He had only one purpose to his life, and he knew this night would see it fulfilled. He followed his wife.

Once inside the cabin, Charity leaned against the door and smiled seductively.

"I thought we parted on rather unfriendly terms, Will. I had no idea you'd come looking for me."

He decided not to enlighten her. He assessed the room while he went to sit on the edge of a table, a solid wall to his back, and in full view of the two windows that flanked the door.

"It was quite a shock to find out you were alive, Charity. You forget that I thought I buried you."

"Poor Will," she said as she moved slowly across the room toward him. "I never meant to hurt you." She slid in between his legs and leaned against him, lifting her face to his. "Forgive and forget?"

She kissed him, and he unemotionally let her, wondering at her game. He thought he saw someone at the window, thought he heard a noise. So she was setting him up. He pushed her away from him and stood looking down at her.

"Tell me why, Charity." He moved across the room so he wasn't visible from either of the windows or the door. "What did I ever do to you?"

"Oh, Will, it wasn't you. It wasn't me. It was just that we could never have got on together." She was restless now, standing at one of the windows with her arms crossed under her breasts. Was that the signal? Will wondered. He moved back to the table.

"I thought we shared a dream," he said to her. "I thought you could see what we were building as clearly as I did."

She stared out at the night for a moment, then answered softly, "There was nothing out there. Not for a thousand miles was there one thing that was beautiful." She swung around to face him. "The damn flowers couldn't even survive there, Will. Why would you think I could?"

"Why didn't you tell me about the money?"

She smiled wryly. "Because I knew it wouldn't make any difference. You'd have put it all into your dream, and then when it was all gone, nothing would have changed."

"Did it buy you happiness, Charity?"

She darted a look at him, then glanced quickly away.

"It's all gone, isn't it?" Suddenly he knew why she was here, why she was with the likes of Jake Greeley.

"There wasn't all that much. Not as much as it seemed when I was on that dirt farm, anyway. Jake—you'd have to know him—he's got a restlessness about him that I recognized the first time I laid eyes on him. It's the same way I feel inside." She smiled softly, and he could see that she was somewhere else in her mind, with music playing; she moved unconsciously to its rhythm. "Oh, we had a grand old time. We went to San Francisco and New Orleans, and just about everywhere in between. I saw things I never even imagined." She frowned suddenly and stopped moving. "And then, when the money ran out, we landed in Texas. It was pretty bad for a while, but then he heard about this job up here, paying so much for nothing, really. Killing people—that's second nature to him. And at fifty dollars a head, well, he couldn't pass it up."

"Doesn't it worry you, being with a man who can kill so easily? Weren't you scared when he killed that boy in Dry Springs?"

"Scared?" She laughed. "Hell, no! It was exciting!" Her eyes filled with a wild light, and there came a strange look on her face. "He's jealous of me. Real jealous."

"Charity, he was bringing another woman up here. A woman he's been after for weeks now."

He saw a flash of something in her eyes—maybe hurt, he thought—then she looked at him defiantly. "Jake's always bringing home strays. It doesn't mean anything. He always comes back to me in the end. Always."

"How did you know he'd come here?"

"This is where he comes when he's in trouble. We came here right after we left Kansas, after he killed that cowboy. And another time when he killed a U.S. marshal down on the Arizona Strip." She shrugged. "He'll be here sooner or later."

Neither of them heard the door open, but suddenly Jake Greeley was standing there with a gun pointed at Will. "Telling my secrets, Charity?" he asked.

Time seemed to stand still as the two men assessed one another, Will knowing the showdown had finally come. He was much calmer than he thought he'd be, and he realized it was because Maggie was dead; whether he lived or died didn't matter so much anymore. All that mattered was that Greeley would pay with his own life.

Charity slid nervously toward Greeley, keeping one eye on Will as she did so.

"You don't have to worry about him, Jake," she said, putting her arm around him. "He's not the law."

Greeley ignored her. His gaze never wavered from Will, who got a cold feeling in the pit of his stomach. He would have known, even if Charity hadn't told him, that he was facing a cold-blooded killer.

"Seems we meet again," he said to Will.

Charity looked quickly at Will, then back to Greeley, and she frowned.

"But you've never met him, Jake." She realized something was going on between the men, something she knew nothing about, and she tried to bring their attention back to her. "He's my husband." She put on a show of remorse, stroking Greeley's arm and demurely avoiding his eyes.

She must have experienced this same scenario many times, Will thought, as she lured unsuspecting men with her innocent face and lying eyes into the trap that awaited them. Was that how it was with the young cowboy he'd buried in Kansas? She'd said Greeley was real jealous of her, and that it excited her. How many men had she watched die? What kind of woman was she, he wondered, that she could watch a man being murdered and feel no remorse?

"You move fast. When did you meet him?" Nothing in the man's voice or facial expression gave a clue as to what he thought of this information.

"No, Jake, I was married to him before I met you. He's come after me, to take me back." Her eyes glittered with excitement, and her mouth twisted in triumph as she faced Will. He was sickened, watching her. All the years he'd wasted, the life with Maggie he'd lost, because once long ago he thought he loved this woman—and now here she was, plotting his death.

"You're a fool, Charity," Will said suddenly. "He was bringing Maggie Longyear up here tonight, and he killed her. You think he won't do the same to you if you push him too far?"

"I don't believe him, Jake. I know I'm the only one you love." Her voice had a touch of panic in it, and she clutched him with both hands. Greeley's eyes narrowed, then he smiled as he pushed Charity away from him with no more regard than if she were a pesky fly.

"That was Millie." He waited to see the effect this had on Will. Then, satisfied as he saw the younger man come to the realization that Maggie was still out there somewhere, he continued. "She had a change of heart, it seems, and came to warn me. I had to . . . deal with her. You see, I don't like double-dealing."

"I wouldn't betray you, Jake, you know that," Charity said, pleading. "I didn't know he was coming, either. He followed me here from Fort McKinney. I was there, Jake, waiting for you to get out, and he found me. I left him, back in Kansas. I didn't love him then, Jake. I left him for you."

"Shut up." The words silenced her immediately, and she backed against the log wall of the cabin, her hands flat behind her.

Will didn't spare her a glance. His thoughts were centered on Maggie now. If what Greeley had said was true, Maggie was still out there somewhere, alive. His heart sang with joy because he'd been given another chance, but he had to deal with this man first and then get to Maggie.

Will's hand had never left his gun. He wasn't an experienced gunfighter, though, and he knew he'd give himself away if he tried to move it. Also, Greeley's gun was already pointed at his chest. His mind searched frantically for a way out of this. What he needed was a diversion, and it came suddenly and without warning. It pulled Greeley's attention away for the split second Will needed to dive for the floor, roll, and come up shooting.

Maggie didn't know how long it took for her subconscious mind to tell her someone was moving in the trees from the direction of the trail. She had stopped crying and was staring up at the sky, letting the caress of the dark night breeze cool her cheeks. Her mind was numb, drained of thought. At first it was just a feeling, one that told her she was no longer alone in the darkness. Then tiny sounds began filtering into her brain, slowly waking her to a feeling of danger. Hardly risking a breath, she inched her head around the side of the rock and strained her eyes to see what it was that had intruded upon her solitude. A stab of fear jolted her back to full awareness when she saw Jacob Grainger steal around the corner of the shed where the horses were and slide silently across the space to the cabin.

Will! Her first thought was to shout, to warn him that the man was coming, but instinct stopped her from uttering the sounds. Her feet were slashed and bloody, but she hardly noticed the pain as she moved silently to the side of the cabin and chanced a look around the corner just as Grainger slipped inside. She covered the distance to the window in two steps, then watched at an angle, not daring to move across the opening.

She could see Grainger clearly now, and what she saw terrified her. This man, the man with death in his eyes, was what she had sensed behind his false manners; she had been right to be uneasy around him. She couldn't see Will, but the woman—Will's wife, she reminded herself—suddenly ran to Grainger and took his arm. They were talking to someone who remained hidden to Maggie, but who had to be Will. The woman said something, then looked across the room with an odd look on her face. What did that look mean for Will? How did his wife feel about him? Maggie had to see Will, had to know he was all right, and the only way she could do that was to get to the still-open door so he'd be visible to her.

Crouching low, with the derringer held ready to fire, she crawled across the remaining space and positioned herself to see through the opening. She could see part of him. He was sitting on the edge of a table, and the hand visible to her was resting against his gun. As she watched, he shifted, then tightened his hand. Without thinking about what she was doing, she slammed the door open and dropped her knees to the ground, then ducked behind the edge of the doorway when two shots rang out simultaneously. When she came back up, it was just in time to see Will's wife take up Grainger's gun and swing around to fire at Will.

Gut instinct pulled Maggie's arm up to fire the small pistol into the woman's chest. When she did, she realized immediately that in saving Will she had lost him forever.

The posse, led by Dave, arrived seconds after the shooting, just in time to see Maggie collapse against the side of the cabin. She had passed out, and they took her down the mountain in a travois at first light.

When she came to, three days later, her mother and father were there. They had missed her so much they came out early and arrived to such "goings-on," as Bertha described the events, that they declared they were taking Margaret home immediately. Maggie was filled with sorrow, not only because of what she had lost, but because of the things that had happened because of her. Much of what grieved Maggie had been erased, however, when Della had appeared in her room. She was moving slowly but at least she was alive.

Maggie didn't think she could bear to leave the people she'd come to love, but as soon as her parents were sure she was in shape to travel, they packed her onto the stage, then boarded the train, and before she knew what was happening she was gone. On the long trip home, she kept telling herself it was for the best. She couldn't have stayed there with Will hating her the way he did. And that he hated her, she was sure. He hadn't even tried to come to see her, to ask how she was doing.

After four frustrating days in Cheyenne, where he hadn't exactly been under arrest, but had been called upon to answer some questions by the authorities about the three deaths, Will returned to Jackson to find that Maggie was gone and had left no messages for him. He had tried to get in to see her right away, before he left, but was told she couldn't see anyone. He didn't know if it was that she couldn't or that she wouldn't, but he didn't have a chance to find out before the sheriff took him into custody. He had wanted to fall at her feet and beg her forgiveness, pledging his undying love for her. Even after what he'd done to her, she had risked her life to save his, and there weren't enough words to tell her what she meant to him. He deserved her hatred and scorn, and he could understand if she never wanted to see him again. But he would always regret that he hadn't had a chance to explain, and tell her how much he loved her.

❄ 18 ❄

Maggie had been home at Longacres for six long weeks, most of it spent in her bed. Her feet had been badly slashed on the sharp rocks on the mountain, and she was supposed to give them time to heal, but the wounds in her heart were giving her the most trouble. Day after day she lay there, willing herself to forget the man who had burned himself into her soul, but instead she daydreamed about him and about the life they should have had together.

If only she'd been able to talk to him, to beg his forgiveness for killing his wife. That death weighed heavily on her conscience, and she awakened sometimes at night, her body wet with sweat and horror, seeing the blood running down the woman's white bodice as she fell—down, down to a crumpled heap on the floor. She didn't remember anything after that until several days later, when her mother's voice brought her back from the place she'd been. She sometimes wished they'd let her stay there. The pain was almost too much to bear, loving Will the way she did and knowing he hated her. She didn't blame him—she'd been a wanton in his bed, and then she'd killed his wife—but if only she could have his forgiveness, she could go on with her own life.

The doctor was coming to see her again this afternoon, and she sighed, knowing what he was going to say. There was no reason for her to be abed any longer, she needed to get out and get some fresh air and sunshine, ride her horse along the beach, take part in some social gatherings. She didn't want to do any of those things.

A light tap on her door broke her reverie, and she turned to see the doctor come in with her maid, Brenna.

"Here she is, Doctor, right as rain!" Brenna exclaimed, a bright smile on her face.

"And still in bed, I see. Well, we're going to remedy that this very day!"

Maggie closed her eyes and sighed again. "I told you I don't feel like getting up."

"Nonsense! You have this whole household turned upside down worrying about you, and if it doesn't stop soon, I'm afraid I'm going to have your mother as a patient, too!"

Maggie opened her eyes in surprise. "Mother? Is she really so worried? I told her I was perfectly well." She didn't want to worry anyone, and she'd told them all she was fine.

"Well, she's still worrying," he said, looking over his spectacles at her. "They all are. It's very selfish of you to stay in your bed like an invalid when there's nothing whatsoever wrong with you." He reached out his hand to her and commanded, "Now take my hand, and I'll help you sit up. That's it, not too quickly."

Maggie moved over and allowed him to pull her to a sitting position, with her legs over the edge of the bed and her feet dangling from the high mattresses on the four-poster. She felt ashamed that she had caused worry and suddenly realized she'd been very self-centered the past few weeks. She slid forward and stood, then felt a wave of dizziness that made her clutch the doctor's shoulder for support.

"Sit down again!" she heard just as she fainted.

The doctor came downstairs half an hour later, a trouble frown on his face. When Maggie had come to, he had quizzed her, and then, following his instincts, he had done an exam. The news he had to give her parents was not good, but he must do it.

"Dr. Cavanaugh!" Lawrence said as the doctor entered

the downstairs drawing room where he had been waiting with Elizabeth, Kate, and Simon. They had been anxiously awaiting his verdict. "Did you get her out of her bed?"

"Yes, I did, and then she fainted," he said, reaching out to grab Elizabeth's arm as she tried to rush to her daughter. "I gave her something to make her sleep, but I'm afraid I have some news that won't be very welcome to you."

"What? Is she all right? Will she heal?" Elizabeth looked ready to cry.

Lawrence went to her side and commanded the doctor. "Out with it! What's wrong with my daughter?"

The doctor cleared his throat and closed his eyes a moment, then met Lawrence's eyes straight on and said simply, "She's going to have a child. In about seven months, I'd say."

Maggie was not sleeping. She had been stunned at the news the doctor had told her, and she was also thrilled.

Will's baby.

She closed her eyes to shut out any distractions, and pressing the palms of her hands against her belly, she tried to feel the life within her. She loved the baby already. If she couldn't have Will, she could be content with having his child.

But what was she going to do now? Her mother, although she loved her dearly, would be mortified to have an unwed and pregnant daughter. It would be necessary for Maggie to leave until long after the baby was born. But where could she go? She had plenty of money and could go anywhere she pleased. She could pretend to be widowed, and with that protection she would be able to move about the country freely, without censure, and without a chaperon. All that was left was deciding where she would start.

She was very sleepy now, but in the morning she would break it to them all.

Maggie surprised everyone the next morning by arriving in the breakfast room, fully dressed and in a cheerful, expansive mood. She greeted them and apologized for her behavior since she'd been home. She was shaking inside, wondering how to tell them she was leaving, but for now this was enough.

"Margaret, I'm glad to see you in such a happy frame of mind this morning, for I have good news for you," her mother said. "You remember your father's cousin, Henry Sexton, don't you?"

"Of course I do," Maggie replied as she took another of Cook's special sticky buns.

"We have arranged for you to be married to Henry in one week."

Maggie dropped the sticky bun she had been lifting to her mouth and stared at her mother in horror.

"Margaret," Lawrence began, "we thought it best . . ."

"*You* thought it best?" she cut him off. "You planned my wedding to an old man I hardly know without even consulting me? And when did all this come about?"

"Maggie," Simon cut in, "you're lucky he agreed to a wedding under the circumstances. You should be thanking your parents instead of—"

"You stay out of this!" she shouted at him. "I am going to tell you all this, and I'm only going to tell you once. This is my baby, and I—do you hear me—*I* will decide what to do about it! I have made plans already, and you needn't worry about being embarrassed about having a pregnant and unwed daughter around. I'll leave first thing in the morning." She threw down her napkin and ran from the room.

Elizabeth rushed up the stairs after her and caught her door just as she was about to slam it.

"Margaret, darling, please understand. We know it's not your fault. That man took you and had his way with you, but that doesn't mean we don't still love you. He's dead now, and no one need ever know about it. Don't you understand?"

"Dead?" Maggie turned to her mother, her face anguished. "He's dead?" She dropped to her bed, stunned.

"Why, of course he is, Margaret. You knew that. Don't you remember that Mr. Sutten shot him?"

"Mr. Sutten?" It suddenly dawned on Maggie what her mother and the others thought.

"Yes. Mr. Sutten, Will, or whatever his name is, killed the outlaw, and the sheriff and his men brought you down off the mountain, remember? I'm just so sorry the sheriff didn't get to him before he took you. But, Margaret, you mustn't allow this incident to color the rest of your life. You can still have a loving relationship with a man. Marriage can be very wonderful, not at all like what must have happened to you." She sat on the bed and took Maggie in her arms.

Maggie didn't know whether to laugh or cry, and the sound that came out sounded like hysteria. Her mother held her tighter and rocked her. What a mess she was in, Maggie thought. They all thought Jacob Grainger had raped her, and they assumed that she would be horrified and not want the baby. She couldn't tell them that Will was the father and that she wanted the baby more than anything in the world. She couldn't defile Will's memory by marrying a man old enough to be her grandfather. She couldn't bear the thought of his touching her after she'd known the caresses of a man she loved. What on earth was she to do now?

"Margaret, I don't know what you thought, but we will stand by you. You're our daughter, and Henry truly loves you and wants to marry you. He told me himself he had been about to ask for your hand when you became engaged to Charles. We've put much thought into this, and your father and Simon went to see Henry last night. He said he had great sympathy for you and would be honored to take you for his wife. He's quite pleased about the child, actually, as he never had any of his own, and he's agreed to take you on an extended tour of the Continent, returning after the child is old enough that six weeks won't be discernible. Don't you see that it's the perfect solution?"

"I don't love him," Maggie wanted to cry.

"Love will come, Margaret, with time."

"I can go away, Mother, and tell people I'm a widow. No one would ever need to know."

"What, and have your child among strangers? Margaret, we are a family."

"You're worried about me having my baby among strangers, but not that I should marry one?"

"Henry is not a stranger. You've known him all your life."

"And you've known him all your life, and Grandmother probably did, too."

Elizabeth closed her eyes and sighed. "We're getting nowhere with this discussion. The plans have been made, Margaret. When you are able to think this through, I know you will agree that this is the only practical solution. Now why don't you get some rest, and we'll talk again later."

Rest, Maggie thought when her mother had closed the door behind her, was not what she needed. She had been resting for almost seven weeks, and now what she needed was to get outside and exercise. She changed into a split skirt and cool summer blouse, wishing for Will's pants, which had been left behind. She had to get outside and clear her head.

She didn't want anyone to know where she was going, so she slipped out the back of the house as she'd done since childhood, and she made her way to the stables. No one needed to saddle a horse for her, and she accomplished the task quickly, mounted, and trotted around the outbuildings until she was out of sight of the house, then let the stallion have his head. They flew along the sandy drive to the beach road.

The sky was slightly overcast, just enough to take the glare out of the sun, and she sat on the sand staring out across the ocean. A slight breeze lifted her hair and brought the fine spray showering over her. The waves lapped just short of her boots, and she idly watched them flow forward and recede, reminding her of her own life. What was she going to do?

Could she marry Henry Sexton? He was nice enough, for an old man, but could she actually marry him? Maybe he only wanted a companion and didn't intend to share her bed. That was a possibility she hadn't considered before. If that were the case, it perhaps wouldn't be so bad. But she really didn't want Will's baby to bear some other man's name.

Was her mother right that marrying Henry was the only solution?

It couldn't be. There had to be another way, if only she could find it.

"Margaret!" Her father's voice cut into her musings, and she turned to see him picking his way across the swampy ground leading to the isolated beach. "Someone's here to see you!" He motioned for her to come with him. "Someone from Wyoming!"

Will! He'd come after her!

"Where is he?" she asked excitedly as she got to her feet.

"He's up at the house, waiting for you. It's that young doctor, Dr. Wolcott."

The waves retreated again, and her heart dropped back in its place.

"Chase? Chase is here at Longacres?"

"Yes! I told you he's come to see you. You need to hurry along and get changed. Your mother figured you came out here, and that you wouldn't be dressed for company. You won't want him to see you in that outfit."

She laughed. "He's seen me in a lot worse than this. He won't mind."

When they reached Longacres, Maggie hurried around the side of the big house and felt tears leap to her eyes when she saw Chase. How good he looked, she thought. Solid and steadfast, like nothing else in her life at the moment.

"Chase! What on earth are you doing here?" she called to him, and he turned to her, a smile of greeting on his face.

"Why, I've come to see you, of course! What else do you think would prompt me to travel all the way across the country?" He grinned and held out his arms to her.

She ran to him and hugged him, unable to stop the tears from spilling out onto her cheeks.

"Ah, Maggie," he crooned, "what's this? Tears? I thought you'd be happy to see me."

"I am, Chase, I am. You just look so good to me."

He closed his eyes and held her closely. "I couldn't stay away any longer, Maggie. I couldn't get you out of my mind, so I had to come and see how you were."

She pushed away from him and wiped her eyes with her hands. "I'm fine, I'm wonderful, in fact. And especially so now that you're here," she said as she led him to a garden bench where they sat down. "Tell me about everyone. How's Della, and Bertha? What's Pete up to? Did Dave get married?" She didn't ask about the only one she truly cared about.

He laughed. "Well, let's see. Della is fine. She had headaches for a while that kind of worried me, but she's all over that now. Dave hasn't gotten married yet but plans to in November, I think."

They talked about the happenings in Jackson Hole since she'd left, then Chase grew serious.

"Maggie," he said as he took both her hands in his, "I've come to ask you to marry me." Then he added quickly, "You don't have to give me an answer right now, Maggie. Just think about it." His heart was heavy with dread, and he wasn't sure he wanted to hear her answer.

Her eyes glistened with tears as she looked up at him and said, "If circumstances were only different, Chase, I'd marry you today." She looked down at her lap and added, "But I can't."

"But why not, Maggie? I mean, I realize you may not be head over heels in love with me, but I'd be good to you. I'd take care of you and love you so much you couldn't help but love me back."

"Chase," she began, unable to meet his eyes, "I'm not what you think."

"You mean about Will and you . . ." He paused and lifted her chin so he could see her face. "I know all about that, and it doesn't mean anything to me. I swear it doesn't."

"It means everything to me," she answered softly.

"No, Maggie, I didn't say that right. I just wanted you to know that it wouldn't be between us. I understand that it wasn't your fault. It's in the past, and it won't matter in our marriage."

"But what about the child I'm carrying as a result? Won't *it* matter?" She looked straight into his eyes as she said it and saw the shock, the shutting down.

"You . . . you're with child?"

She nodded.

"From only one time with him?"

"Yes," she said simply. The look on his face hurt almost as much as anything else she'd had to bear.

He turned away from her and gripped the edge of the bench. His shoulders were hunched, his head down, and she was terrified that he might be crying. Her own eyes filled with tears again, and she hastily wiped them away as he turned back to her.

"You don't have to have the baby, Maggie. There are ways—" he started, but she cut him off.

"No! This is Will's baby, and nothing, *nothing*, is going to stop me from having it!"

He grabbed her arm as she started to run from him, and pulled her close. "I'm sorry, Maggie. I didn't mean to—"

"Of course you did. You might be willing to marry me if no one knew I'd been bedded by another man, but with a child it would just be too awkward, wouldn't it?"

"Maggie, I'm a doctor. I can't just do whatever I like if I'm to live in Jackson and make a living."

She smiled wryly at him. "There are other towns, other states."

He hesitated a second, but it was long enough.

"Oh, Chase. It doesn't matter anyway. I'm betrothed to another man, and we're to be wed this Saturday."

"Well, you don't waste any time, do you? And does he know about the baby?"

"Of course he does. The wedding has been arranged so quickly for that purpose."

"What about Will? Doesn't he have any say in what happens to his child?"

"I'm sure he doesn't care. And why this sudden concern for Will's feelings? You were all ready to kill his child a moment ago."

"I wouldn't have. You just caught me off guard. It was the last thing I'd expected."

"Me, too," she said in a small voice, her throat tight with emotion.

"Oh, Maggie, I'm sorry. I . . ." He hesitated, hating himself for not being able to hide his shock about the baby. "Do you love this man you're going to marry?"

"I hardly know him. He's a distant cousin of my father's. He's a widower with no children, so the baby was all right."

"How old is this man?" He was horrified at the coldness in her voice.

"I don't know, fifty, sixty. I didn't ask."

"God, Maggie, you can't do this." He took her by the shoulders. "You'd be better off married to me," he teased, while his heart was breaking for her.

"I could never marry you, Chase, even if you really wanted me. You're too entwined with my memories of Will, and I'd look at you every day of my life and see him. This man, Mr. Sexton, will evoke no memories whatsoever. That's the only way I'll get through this."

He held her to him, wondering why, if she loved Will so much, she'd left Wyoming without a word to him. She'd been awfully sick for several days there, but when she'd come out of it, she could easily have gotten a message to him if she'd wanted to. Was there something else he didn't know, that Will hadn't told him about their relationship? Had there been some misunderstanding?

Chase loved Maggie enough to want her to be happy, and Will was his closest friend. He wouldn't have come at all if Will hadn't told him it was all over between them. But Will had given him the impression the break had come from Maggie.

"Maggie, did you talk to Will before you left Wyoming?"

"No."

"Why not?"

She looked up at him, surprised that he would ask. "I killed his wife, Chase. He would hardly have wanted to talk to me." So it wasn't the loss of her virginity that she held against him.

"He was long over his wife, Maggie. She was a little insane, I think, from what he told me. He wouldn't have blamed you for her death."

Then there was nothing to keep him from her. He could have come all this time, and he chose not to.

She stood up and took a deep breath. "Well, I hope he's able to get on with his life now, as I must get on with mine. I understand you're to join us for dinner, so I'll show you to the house, and then I must change. My father tells me Mr. Sexton, Henry, will join us also, so you'll be able to meet him."

❧ 19 ❧

By the end of the meal, Maggie was almost in tears, and Chase was more convinced than ever that she shouldn't marry the man her parents had chosen for her. He had watched in disgust as Henry had taken every chance to touch her, from holding her hand to placing his own on her thigh. Chase watched her growing more and more upset, and he knew he had to do something. He didn't know her parents well, but it was obvious to him that they placed more importance on appearances than their daughter's happiness. If she went through with this marriage she would wither up and die, and that wonderful spirit would be silent forever. He knew that he would never forgive himself if he didn't do all he could to prevent the wedding from taking place.

When he could be with her again, he would work on her to try to talk her out of it. Even if she never married, she would have to be better off than with Henry Sexton. The man had to be closer to sixty than fifty, but either way, he was more than twice her age, and she was too good to waste on him. He had been a tall man, but was starting to stoop, probably from looking down women's gowns, Chase thought to himself. His hair was long in the back and mostly gray. He was clean and well-groomed, but there was something about his face that reminded Chase of Jacob Grainger. His eyebrows were bushy and white, his eyes squinted, his nose was long, and his lips were full and wet. Chase could only imagine what Maggie must be thinking.

When Simon and Kate left the room early, Chase hoped it was because they couldn't bear the thought of this marriage taking place any more than he could, and he took the opportunity to make his leave also. He almost appealed to Simon, but he wasn't sure how his friend would react. Simon had told him he and Kate didn't approve of the marriage, but because of what had happened, they felt horrible guilt for leaving Maggie while they went to get married, and now they had no right to interfere. Chase felt no such restriction and decided to take the matter in his own hands. A scheme was beginning to form in his mind, and he only hoped he could pull it off. Even if things didn't go exactly the way he was planning, he would at least know he'd done all he could to save Maggie. He swung up onto his horse and set off at a canter into town, while his thoughts covered every option. He only had six days, and he knew it would take all of that.

Maggie fled to her room as soon as Henry left, and she threw herself across her bed, sobbing. How could she bear to be married to that man when he'd have the right to handle her all he wanted? It was patently obvious to her that he wanted much more than just a companion, and she didn't believe she could go through with it.

Her door opened, and her mother came in.

"Margaret, we have to talk." She sat on the bed and stroked her daughter's hair. "What did you and the young doctor talk about today?"

Maggie could talk about Chase. She turned over and stared out the window. "He came to see if I'd changed my mind about my feelings for him," she admitted.

Elizabeth sighed. "Did he ask you to marry him?"

"Yes."

"And you turned him down?"

Maggie swallowed and looked up at the ceiling, working her mouth to keep from crying. "He changed his mind when I told him about the baby."

"Oh, Margaret. Why did you tell him?"

"Mother, he's a doctor. Don't you think he'd have

guessed, for heaven's sake? Besides, what kind of marriage would we have if I'd deceived him from the very start? I think too much of him to even consider it."

"Darling, I just want for you to be happy. When he showed up at the door, I thought . . ." She hesitated. "I know Henry isn't your idea of a perfect husband, but you might grow quite fond of him. He has some admirable qualities."

"Forgive me, but none were apparent today."

"I know. He was rather forward, but in less than a week he'll have that right as your husband. All I'm asking is that you give him a chance. He's asked to court you properly, and your father gave his permission. Maybe you'll be able to see a different side of him and make this whole thing easier."

"Mother," Maggie said as she looked up with tears in her eyes, "why must I marry anyone? Why can't I just have my baby somewhere away from here?"

Elizabeth's eyes were wet, too, as she took her daughter in her arms. "Where would you go? To a convent? That could be arranged, but then you'd have to give the baby up afterward. You couldn't bring it back here, or you'd be shunned by everyone. You'd have no life outside of this house, and even if you chose that way for yourself, would you subject this child to being a bastard?"

She lifted Maggie's chin and gave her a kiss on her forehead. "Right now it seems terrible, but give yourself a chance to get to know Henry. We wouldn't allow you to marry a horrible person, you know."

Maggie nodded and closed her eyes.

"Well, I'll just leave you to rest a while. The wedding will be announced tonight at supper, and all the family will be here. I've already told my parents, and they're very happy for you." Maggie still didn't answer, and Elizabeth felt a heavy weight on her heart as she left the room.

Maggie felt like such a fake. Henry had brought her an engagement ring, and all the guests were oohing and aahing over it. She pasted a smile on her face, feeling nothing. Henry had his arm around her, and his hand was kneading her shoulder as he offered a toast to his betrothed. When he was done and they had been wished well for what seemed like the hundredth time, she shrugged out from under his caress and went to the window, where she stared out into the garden.

Will came to her there and took her hand, lifting it to his lips and caressing her with his eyes. "You're the most beautiful woman I've ever seen," he said to her, and she smiled prettily at him.

"May I have this dance?" he asked, and she answered him, "But of course. I'd never dance with anyone but you."

"Who are you talking to?" said a voice behind her, a real voice this time, and she shook the image of Will away and turned around. Henry stood there with an odd look on his face.

"I'm sorry. What did you say?"

"I asked who you were talking to. Is there someone outside?" He was frowning at her, and the look in his eyes almost frightened her.

"There's no one. I wasn't talking to anyone." She moved away from the window, and he pushed the casement open and peered into the growing dusk of the garden. Seeing no movement, he turned back to her.

"Would you care to go out into the garden? It's a lovely evening, and I could use a breath of fresh air." His eyes raked across her, and she had to use iron control not to shudder.

"It would surely be rude to leave our guests," she answered, inching her way back to the others.

He took her arm a bit too tightly and said, "You must learn to do what I ask, Margaret. They will understand our desire to be alone together."

Her face had a look of sheer panic on it as the old man pulled her out the long doors. Chase saw it, and he slammed his drink down. He moved quickly across the room, getting outside just as Henry pulled Maggie to him roughly and smeared a kiss on her.

Chase cleared his throat loudly and strode toward them purposefully. They jumped apart, and he said smoothly, "Oh, sorry to disturb you, but I really couldn't take another minute inside. How do you people bear the heat and humidity down here?"

Half an hour later, it was obvious that neither man would give, so Henry, as graciously as possible, suggested they go back inside and join the others. He could wait a few more days, he thought, and then he would have her all to himself.

Early the next morning, Maggie went to Chase's door and asked him if he wanted to go for a walk with her. He readily accepted her invitation and met her outside. They started off without speaking. She was so glad to be in motion that the doctor was just barely able to keep up with her.

"Whew!" he said when they stopped. "Do you always walk that fast?"

She laughed. "I'm sorry. I guess I just have long legs."

He looked down at her admiringly, then met her eyes. "That you do, and quite lovely ones, if I remember right."

"Dr. Wolcott!" she said, laughing.

"I'm only a man, after all, Maggie. And I admitted long ago that I'd fallen under your spell." He looked into her eyes, regret on his face. "I wish things could have been different."

"So do I." Tears threatened again, but she would not allow that today. She only had a few days of freedom left, and she wasn't going to waste one of them. She spun away from him, swinging her arms, and said, "But I don't want to talk about any of that today. Now come along, and I'll try to remember that you're out of shape."

He following her on an enchanting tour of the Low Country, from thick jungle-like undergrowth to the sandy beaches, where she told him to take off his shoes and stockings as she did. While they wandered along picking up shells and bits of flotsam, she told him how she used to dream up stories of the exotic ports from which each bit came, and she told him how she'd kept them all in her room so she could pull the treasures out on rainy days and pretend she had brought them back from those places herself. They stopped at last under a huge tree, and Chase dropped gratefully at its base, while Maggie plopped down in the sand.

He sat back and marveled at her, falling in love all over again. Not once did she mention gowns or balls or any of the frivolities that had consumed his sisters' lives. She was totally unconcerned with her effect on him, not bothering to tidy her windswept hair or to wipe the sand off her skirts. He knew now what had caused the charming array of freckles across her cheeks and the graceful way she moved.

The week passed quickly, and Maggie felt a greater and greater sense of impending doom as Saturday drew near. Several times after spending an hour thwarting Henry's gropings she had almost begged Chase to take her away, but she stopped herself, knowing it wouldn't be fair to him. His decency would have made him feel responsible for her, and she refused to become a burden to someone for whom she cared so much.

Elizabeth had wanted to have another gown made for the wedding, but Maggie had insisted on wearing the one she'd had for her marriage to Charles. They told her it was bad luck, but what did she care? Her marriage would be utter hell no matter what dress she wore.

She tried not to think about her wedding night and all the thousands of nights that would follow. If she hadn't been carrying her precious cargo, she'd have killed herself rather than submit to him. But then, she reasoned, if she hadn't been pregnant, this wedding would not be taking place. She lay awake night after night trying to find a way out, but it was useless.

Friday night came, and there was a rehearsal dinner. She felt alone in the midst of all the festivities, detached from the whole business.

She tried to slip away, to Will, but she couldn't find him. Hours later, alone in her room for the last time, she lay awake, too disconsolate to sleep. When the first faint streaks touched the sky, she dressed and left the house, going to her special beach. There, finally, he came to her.

"*Maggie.*"

"*Oh, Will, you came. I was afraid you wouldn't anymore. I couldn't bear it if you stayed away, and I'll need you more than ever now.*"

"*I won't leave you. I'll always be there when you need me.*"

She sat there, feeling his presence and telling him about the child within her, until long after she should have been home. The sun topped the horizon and spread like wine across the still water, touching her with its glow and giving her a sense of peace. Her life had been planned, and she had to make the best of it. Reluctantly she left and returned to the house, just as her parents were sending someone out to look for her.

As she was whisked up to her bedroom, she felt a sense of déjà vu while the hairdresser worked alongside the dressmaker, who had let the gown out. Maggie felt no eager anticipation this time. There wouldn't be many guests—just family and very close friends—and she was just thankful she wouldn't have to face all those people again.

They had planned an early afternoon wedding so that the couple could leave on their trip abroad that same evening. Maggie hadn't even listened as Henry had described the places they'd go and the ship they'd be on. She didn't care. They could have gone straight to his house and stayed there for the rest of their lives, for all she cared about the whole thing.

She was finally alone in her room and she appealed to Will.

"*Oh, Will, why couldn't you have been free to marry me? Why did I fall in love with you? Why couldn't it have been Chase, or someone else?*"

"*I didn't mean to make you love me. I didn't mean to love you. I'm no good for you.*"

"*You're the best thing that ever happened to me.*"

"*And the worst.*"

And the worst. Before she met Will she'd been settled, peaceful in her existence. Because she'd known him, been loved by him, she would never be the same. The years ahead would bring great loneliness, but she would always have her memories. And she would have the child.

Maybe her mother was right, and she would grow fond of Henry. Perhaps he would be kind enough to her that love would come with the passage of time. But it would never be the same kind of love she'd known with Will. She remembered thinking when she'd been about to marry Charles that she had felt something was missing, and she had finally found that something with Will. She would never know it with another man.

A light tap sounded on her door, and she turned to see her father waiting there, as he'd done once before, and she couldn't help tears from forming. He looked at her and felt his heart break at the sadness in her eyes. He prayed they were doing the right thing. Henry was a good man, a settled man, and he would give Margaret the stability she needed to cope with the child. If only she would give him a chance, her father knew they could have a satisfactory marriage.

This time as they walked down the hallway, Maggie steeled herself to keep from breaking down and sobbing. She felt as though she would bolt through the door at any moment, and she wasn't sure she could actually keep herself from doing so.

Chase was sitting near the front of the room, directly behind Simon and Kate. Kate's eyes showed she'd been crying, and she dabbed at them now. Simon, sitting stiffly between his wife and sister-in-law, thoroughly disapproved of the proceedings, but he knew it wasn't his place to say anything. Elizabeth sat serenely, and Chase knew she'd made up her mind that this farce of a wedding was the right thing for her daughter.

When Maggie and Lawrence came down the stairs, nothing in her face showed that she felt any emotion at all. She looked straight ahead, at neither the guests nor her waiting bridegroom. Chase couldn't tell what she felt. Had she accepted the marriage enough to resent his intrusion, or was she terrified inside and in need of someone to intercede on her behalf? He settled back in his seat, knowing what he had done and hoping it would be the right thing.

Lawrence led his daughter up to Henry, kissed her on the cheek, and placed her hand in that of his cousin. He went to sit down next to his wife, and only the minister saw him close his eyes as he prayed for Margaret's happiness.

Maggie heard every word the minister said as if he were speaking in slow motion. The room was hot and seemed to spin slowly around her as the voice droned on and on. She felt slightly dizzy as she stood there, wondering if she had the nerve to bolt.

"Is there any man present who knows why this man and this woman should not be joined together in holy matrimony? If so, let him speak now or forever hold his peace."

Maggie held her breath, then couldn't stop a sob from breaking forth.

"I know a reason they can't be wed."

Every head in the room save one jerked around to see who the speaker was. He was coming forward around the seated guests, his eyes never leaving Maggie's back.

"Who are you, and what do you mean by disrupting this ceremony?" Henry demanded indignantly.

"I'm the father of her child, and she won't be marrying anyone but me," Will said.

❧ EPILOGUE ❧

Will Sutten shoveled the dirt with a steady rhythm that matched the song he was humming. He didn't know the song, but it was one Maggie hummed to their son when she rocked him to sleep at night. The tune was part of her, as was the scent of her hair and the softness of her skin. He was as lost in the essence of her now as he had been a year ago when they'd wed.

It was late in the year to be starting the building of their new home, but he wanted to have a start on it before the snows came. Simon and Kate were staying at the house in town and had told Will to take his time, but he knew they wanted their own son to spend his first Christmas on the ranch that would one day be his. Will wanted the same for his son. His priorities had shifted. He had come so close to losing Maggie that he never took anything for granted anymore, never put off doing something until a later date. He knew only too well that it could be too late if he waited, as it almost had been. If it hadn't been for Chase sending the telegram that made him rush to her side, he would never have known the happiness that filled his life.

It had been a year of new beginnings for him, of receiving gifts he had long ago given up hoping for. The wedding had been the first.

He smiled now as he remembered it. Maggie had started to fall, and he had leapt forward and caught her up in his arms. She had looked at him with utter joy in her eyes, and he had grinned at her, asking, "Am I too late for the wedding?"

She had cried then and wrapped her arms around him as though drowning, and he had persuaded the minister to marry them there, just like that, while everyone in the room was milling around, trying to find out the story of the stranger who'd come in, and discussing the news about the baby. Everyone was so concerned with the gossip and the fight that seemed imminent that no one paid any attention to them as they said "I do," lost in each other's eyes. Henry and Lawrence were almost to blows because Henry had been humiliated in front of his relatives and friends, and he felt Lawrence was to blame. Simon was trying to calm them down, while Kate and Elizabeth watched them and sobbed. No one even noticed as Will asked Maggie to show him the way to her room, and, once there, he made up for the first time by showing her just how beautiful loving could be.

Simon and Kate told them later that no one had noticed they were gone for the longest time, until the minister had come up to Lawrence and Henry who were arguing. He told them he'd finished with the ceremony uniting Miss Margaret and Mr. Sutten and thought he'd take his leave.

Henry had almost died of apoplexy, and a great fuss was made over him. Then he was taken home, and the guests had made rather reluctant departures, their curiosity not having been satisfied. Lawrence and Elizabeth were shocked to find Maggie gone, and, still furious from the confrontation with Henry, Lawrence was ready to go find and kill the man who'd been the cause of the whole thing. It took Simon, Chase, and Kate to get him calmed down enough that they could explain about Will and Maggie. When Elizabeth understood that Will was the father of the child and that Maggie loved him, she added her entreaties to those of the others, and finally Lawrence was convinced to let matters go. What choice did he have, his wife pointed out, when the whole county knew by now that their daughter was pregnant, and that she was now married to the father?

The next day had been awkward, but then Will had made his peace with Maggie's parents.

He sought out Chase and told him that he'd never known such friendship existed and that he owed his life to the doctor. Seven months later, when they'd delivered the child from the woman they both loved, they had rejoiced together, and Maggie and Will had thanked Chase by naming their son after him.

Will hadn't imagined fatherhood could be so astounding. He looked at his tiny son and felt emotion swell up inside him, knowing how close he'd come to losing him forever. When he held Maggie as she nursed the baby, he felt utter completion inside.

Maggie was a remarkable wife. She was joy and surprises, laughter and sunshine. He never knew quite what to expect from her, but everything she gave to him was good. She provided a haven for him to return to in the evening, and he didn't know how he had existed before she came into his life. He did know that he didn't deserve one small part of the love she gave him. He also knew he would never again doubt her love for even an instant.

"It's ready!" Maggie's voice came to him across the flower-strewn clearing, and he leaned the shovel against the pile of lumber and crossed over to her. She had brought a picnic lunch to him, and it was spread out on a blanket. Her cooking had become wonderful, and it was hard to remember she'd not been able to make coffee a little over a year before.

The baby fussed, and Will lifted him out of his basket. He held his son in his lap while he ate, and he and Maggie voiced their dreams for the future.

Later, when Chase had fallen back asleep and Maggie had gently put him in his snug bed, Will pulled her to him on the blanket and made love to her there in the field of wildflowers.

Then he picked her a bouquet of them to remember it by.

Wildflower Romance

A breathtaking new line of spectacular novels set in the untamed frontier of the American West. Every month, Diamond Wildflower brings you new adventures where passionate men and women dare to embrace their boldest dreams. Finally, romances that capture the very spirit and passion of the wild frontier.

__**LIGHTNING STRIKES** by Jean Wilson
   0-7865-0024-7/$4.99
__**TENDER OUTLAW** by Deborah James
   0-7865-0043-3/$4.99
__**MY DESPERADO** by Lois Greiman
   0-7865-0048-4/$4.99
__**NIGHT TRAIN** by Maryann O'Brien
   0-7865-0058-1/$4.99
__**WILD HEARTS** by Linda Francis Lee
   0-7865-0062-X/$4.99
__**DRIFTER'S MOON** by Lisa Hendrix
   0-7865-0070-0/$4.99
__**GOLDEN GLORY** by Jean Wilson
   0-7865-0074-3/$4.99
__**SUMMER SURRENDER** by Lynda Kay Carpenter
   0-7865-0082-4/$4.99
__**GENTLE THUNDER** by Rebecca Craig
   0-515-11586-X/$4.99
__**RECKLESS HEARTS** by Bonnie K. Winn
   0-515-11609-2/$4.99 (May)

Payable in U.S. funds. No cash orders accepted. Postage & handling: $1.75 for one book, 75¢ for each additional. Maximum postage $5.50. Prices, postage and handling charges may change without notice. Visa, Amex, MasterCard call 1-800-788-6262, ext. 1, refer to ad # 406

Or, check above books and send this order form to:	Bill my: ☐ Visa ☐ MasterCard ☐ Amex	(expires)
The Berkley Publishing Group 390 Murray Hill Pkwy., Dept. B East Rutherford, NJ 07073	Card#_____	($15 minimum)
Please allow 6 weeks for delivery.	Signature_____	
	Or enclosed is my: ☐ check ☐ money order	
Name_____	Book Total	$_____
Address_____	Postage & Handling	$_____
City_____	Applicable Sales Tax (NY, NJ, PA, CA, GST Can.)	$_____
State/ZIP_____	Total Amount Due	$_____